Irish Myths and Legends

Irish Myths and Legends

Michael Scott

WARNER BOOKS

for Clare Binchy, a book of her own

A *Warner* Book

First published in Great Britain in 1992
by Warner Books Ltd
Reprinted 1994, 1995

A CIP catalogue record for this book is
available from The British Library.

ISBN 0 7515 1242 7

Typeset by Leaper & Gard Ltd, Bristol
Printed in England by Clays Ltd, St Ives plc

Warner Books
A Division of
Little, Brown and Company (UK)
Brettenham House
Lancaster Place
London WC2E 7EN

Contents

♣

CHAPTER ONE

The Son of Adam and the Daughters of Cain

I am Seth, the son of Adam and Eve.

I knew this world when it was young. I walked its fresh formed lands, swam in the newly created seas, disported with the beasts that the Lord God had placed on this earth.

And in my travels across the world beyond the Garden laid out by the Lord, but which He had forever closed off from us, I came to the island that would one day be known as Erin. And though I sailed around the tiny island, I never walked its emerald shores.

Before me there had been Adam, my father, the first man to walk this world. Then there had come Lilith, the first woman, made from the mud beneath my father's feet. But her likeness was imperfect and the Lord cast her into the darkness beyond the Gates of Paradise. Then the Lord fashioned the perfect woman from the flesh of Man, and this was Eve, my mother.

And the Lord fashioned a perfect Garden out of the wilderness He had created, and allowed my parents to wander the groves of this special place. They were as children in the Garden, innocent and curious and, with the minds of children, were tempted and seduced by the Fallen

One into breaking the Taboo. Their inquisitive and curious natures so angered the Lord that He cast them out of the Garden and set seraphim to stand guard before the gates.

This much my parents told me, and though I never doubted their words, I roamed this earth until I found the Garden, and I crouched in a cave in the hills above the magical valley, and watched the angels of the Lord, like blazing pillars of fire, stand before the four gates that led to Paradise.

Though the Lord God had cast my mother and father out into the World Beyond to wander lost and confused, He was merciful and allowed them clothes and shelter, else they would have surely perished. I know my parents took this as a sign that the Lord regretted His action and that they would be once more allowed to walk in the Garden, though that was never to come to pass.

And in time Cain and Abel were born unto them.

For a long time the world belonged to these four.

Perhaps it was the Fallen One who tempted Cain to slay Abel, in the same way that he tempted our mother, though my father said that Cain did not need the Fallen One's poisoned words to make him envious and jealous. He was imperfect since the day he was born. Cain's terrible crime cried out to the Lord and His vengeance was swift, but not completely pitiless, for though He could have taken Cain's life as His due, instead He chose to let him live, though He put a mark upon his forehead, cheeks, hands and legs in the form of bloody pustules. Then He cast him forth to wander the world, shunned by all who set eyes upon him.

In recompense for the death of Abel, Eve conceived another child and I was born unto them. I am Seth, the third son of Adam and Eve. There were others after me, and we in turn knew one another in the way of a man and woman and though now men shun such close unions, when the world was young, the Lord Himself deemed it correct. And our children had children in their own turn, and so the peoples of this world spread.

But Cain also had children. I heard tell that he bred with Lilith, our father's first wife, and though they were both monsters after a fashion, their children were beautiful, especially their daughters.

And when Adam learned that there was a new race abroad in the world, a race not blessed by God, a race bred of a cursed man and an outcast woman, he commanded that none of his seed should ever meet or breed with any of Cain's seed.

But the daughters of Cain were beautiful, and possessed a strange mesmeric power over the simpler sons and daughters of Adam.

And all who met them fell prey to their beauty, and from these unions – the sons of Adam and the daughters of Cain – new creatures, neither man nor beast, but something between, were born into this world.

Once I walked the Inland Sea and came across three of the daughters of Cain. They were tall and lithe, identical save for the colour of their hair – golden-haired, silver-haired, bronze-haired – naked save for the shells they had woven into their animate hair. They were disporting in the waves and, looking at them, I found it impossible to believe that the Lord would put anything so beautiful in the world for an evil purpose.

We lay together through the long afternoon and on into the night, and each was more beautiful than the last. When the sun rose in the morning, bringing the beach alive with light and sound, we awoke to discover that a length of matted wood and reeds had been washed up by the sea. We lashed the wood together with vines and creepers and pushed ourselves out to sea to bask in the brilliant sunshine, with the waves rippling the planks like a living thing. We drifted heedlessly on the waves, laughing, talking and loving as the day moved towards the noon.

And then the storm came up.

The Lord God had turned His face towards me, and seen my sin. In all His majesty and power He rolled in from the east in a mass of grey and black clouds. His anger rumbled deep in the core of the clouds, His temper flared white and terrible. The waves were lashed to a froth in an instant, our flimsy craft was tossed high. The vines snapped, poles breaking off, floating away. The Lord's anger pushed us across the Inland Sea at a terrifying speed. It threw us out between two tall cliffs of stone and into the limitless ocean. The daughters of Cain clung to me in terror, though I was no less terrified than they. Like me they were long-lived, for Man had not yet become weakened. In those early days of the world, it took a long time for the sons and daughters of Adam to die. Like me, the daughters of Cain feared that they would be tossed into the ocean. They would not die easily. It might take days. Days trapped beneath the water, alive but unmoving, conscious and aware while the countless creatures that swam and swarmed in the waters preyed upon their cooling flesh.

I lost count of the days we lay on the raft as it was tossed and thrown about. The storm turned and turned and turned again so that just as it seemed we were finally losing it, it would sweep back around again.

The Lord is slow to move to anger, but His anger, like His mercy, is limitless.

The storm pushed us north. Many times we were in sight of the coast, but the waves were too high and the wind too strong to allow us to approach land. The very character of the sea changed. The waters of the Inland Sea are warm and gentle, but these northern waters are cold and bitter.

The blue of the sea was replaced by the chill grey of the ocean. Day and night flowed together. Our only food was the fish that were tossed us on to the raft, our water the rain that spilled from the heavens.

Eventually, the storm died and the Lord turned His face away from us. Mayhap, he went to visit His anger on some of our other brothers and sisters in the further reaches of the world. We awoke to a morning of brilliant sunshine and a gentle breeze carrying the soft smells of earth and growth off a tiny island that had appeared during the night. I knelt and prayed then – even the daughters of Cain whispered their thanks to whatever deity they worshipped – thanking the Lord for having delivered us safely.

The tide carried us closer to the island. It was rich with growth and life, a thin golden curve of beach sheltered by trees the like of which I had never seen before. Strange birds crowded the branches, unusual beasts peered through the undergrowth.

Sand scraped against the bottom of the battered raft. The three daughters of Cain jumped into the water and waded ashore. And though we had endured many days of hardship and privation, they were still as lovely as the day I had first encountered them and against the shimmering green of the land, their hair – gold, silver and bronze – burned with a vivid brilliance. I would have gone ashore with them, but something held me back. I watched the three women disappear into the undergrowth and I heard their voices echoing flatly in the still air. I stood on the raft and breathed deeply, glad to have the stink of the salt and sea out of my nostrils.

I was about to step off the raft when a wave took it, lifting it high, jerking me off balance. I fell heavily, striking my head and as I lay there dazed, I could see the clouds moving by overhead, I could smell the odours of earth and life being gradually replaced by the familiar salt.

When I fully regained my senses, the island was a long way off. I thought I could see three spots of metallic colour against the softer green of the isle, but that might have been the blow to my head. I thought I heard voices, but I fancy that was only in my imagination.

I know it took me fifteen days and fifteen nights to reach land again. This was not the warm, gentle land of my birth, but rather a cold, harsher land, devoid of people but not of savage beasts. When the Cold Months came, they were harsh and bitter, and the Warm Months were unpleasantly hot and wet. I lost count of the number of times the seasons changed before I finally reached my homeland. Many times I would have perished had the Lord not turned His hand to me. But I was a young man when I left the Inland Sea. I was grey-haired when I returned. When I told my tale to my father, Adam, he nodded and simply said, 'It is the Lord's will.'

And so it is; the ways of the Lord are mysterious indeed.

Often I found myself wandering the banks of the Inland Sea, close to where I had met the daughters of Cain. I wondered what would happen to them, alone on that tiny island, without the solace of their brothers and sisters – and far away from the evil influence of their mother and father. Surely they would change? I couldn't help wondering why the Lord had set Banba, Fodla and Eriu on the tiny isle that would one day be known as Erin.

Perhaps He had prepared a special destiny for that place.

CHAPTER TWO

The Voice of the Land

'Land ho! ... Land ho!'

The lookout's shout brought everyone to the foredeck on the port side, straining to make out the shape of the magical land that they had heard so much about. This was the island they had quit their homeland to come in search of. But the early morning mist coiled and twisted across the waves, completely blanketing the land ahead.

Eber Donn, the eldest of the sons of Mil, made his way to the prow of the boat and squinted through the mist. The short, swarthy man shook his head in annoyance and shouted up to the lookout, who was strapped to the main mast, 'Report!'

Erannan, his youngest brother, shaded his pale eyes with his hands and stared across the sea, over the top of the shifting mist. 'I see a green land, golden-beached and forested. I can smell the scents of earth and wood from it.'

Eber Donn threw his head back and breathed deeply: all he could smell was the salt of the sea and too many humans crowded together in too small a space. 'Are you sure it's not a cloud?' he demanded.

A tall white-haired man stepped in front of the chieftain. Eber Donn was forced to look up into the older man's pale grey eyes. 'This is no dream, not this time,' the white-haired man said softly. 'You have finally reached your destination.'

'You're sure ...?' he wondered aloud.

'I'm sure,' Amergin the mage said quietly.

Eber Donn still looked doubtful, even though Amergin was one of the reasons they had sailed this course. The holy man had promised them that a special land, a magical land, lay in this direction. A land where one of their ancestors, the warrior-chieftain Nemed, had once ruled. His people, the Nemedians, had defeated the terrible Fomorians, but had been defeated in turn by the Firbolg. Many of the defeated warriors had fled to the land to the east of the isle of Erin, or even further south into the great land surrounding the Middle Sea. There they had prospered and grown strong again, but they never forgot the legend of the land of Erin. And now they were coming back. They were coming home.

Amergin looked up into the clouds, seeking out the pale orange disc of the sun. 'This mist will burn off soon.' He pointed off to the port side. 'Set your course there. We'll be less than four ships lengths off the beach when the mist goes; we'll beach her at low tide and make our way ashore then.'

Eber Donn looked uncomfortable. He ran his hand across his perfectly bald head. 'I don't like coming in so close to shore without having some idea where we're going. There could be reefs or rocks hidden below.'

Amergin went to lean over the starboard side and squinted down into the water, his almost colourless eyes taking the grey-blue of the sea. He crossed the deck to look at the port side, shading his eyes against the glare from the waves. 'If you hold this course,' he said finally, 'you will encounter no obstacles. There are rocks there, there ... and there,' he pointed. 'But if you keep to this course, they won't bother you.'

The captain was about to ask how the older man could speak with such authority, but contented himself with barking the orders to the crew. Amergin had been one of his father's closest friends and most trusted adviser. There were even rumours that they were related in some way, possibly brothers, though no one knew for certain. What was more certain was that if Mil had followed Amergin's advice he'd be alive today.

Amergin leaned against the prow of the wooden ship and stared into the mist, his head tilted to one side, listening, sorting through the sounds of the sea and wind, gradually blanketing them from his consciousness, concentrating on the sounds of the Otherworld, the realm of spirit and faerie. He was old now, far older than Eber Donn, the eldest son of Mil. He knew that he was suspected of being the dead king's illegitimate brother, but Amergin had been an old man when Mil himself had been newborn. He had advised Mil's own father and then Mil in turn and now he was advising Mil's own sons. Some called him a druid, or a wizard, a mage, a holy man, but in truth, he was none of these. Though his father had been human, his mother had been one of the non-human creatures that haunted the wild woods. From his mother the boy had received the gift of longevity, and her appreciation of the non-human world. Amergin never called himself a mage or magician – though he was both of these and more – but he preferred to think of himself as being in tune with the spirits and elements. Everything had an essence, a soul ... and if one listened to that voice, then one would acquire their knowledge, and knowledge was the ultimate power.

He listened now to the myriad sounds of the land ahead of him. It was rich in magic and power; the voices were strong, vibrant, clamorous, eager to whisper to him. He recognized wind and sea, earth and air, growth and spirit in the voices. The old man's lips moved as he distinguished the magical song of the land. See me, they whispered, hear me, they murmured, listen to me ...

'I am the wind off the sea ...'
'I am the waves that roll off the mighty ocean ...'
'I am the voice of the sea ...'
'I am the bull of seven battles ...'
'I am the carrion bird that dwells on the cliff face ...'
'I am the merest drop of dew ...'
'I am the most beautiful of all flowers ...'
'I am the strongest of boars ...'
'I am the wisest of all salmon ...'
'I am the deepest of lakes in this land ...'
'I am the spirit that drives man ...'
'I am the source of man's skill ...'
'I am the power of death ...'
'I am the spirit man calls God ...'

When Amergin looked back at Eber Donn, the old man's colourless eyes were silver with moisture.

'Well?' Eber Donn whispered, startled at the look that had come over the old man's face.

Amergin's smile was triumphant. 'This is the place!'

As Amergin had predicted, they were less than four ship lengths off the beach when the morning sun finally burned away the mist. The land opened up in a panorama of golden beach backed by a dark, sombre-looking forest. Now the scents of life and growth were clear and distinct on the air.

Eber Donn breathed deeply, savouring the rich earthy dampness after the dry, sharp saltiness of the voyage. Suddenly, his eyes filled with tears: his father should have been here to see this.

Amergin's calloused hand fell on to the captain's bare shoulder. 'He is here with you,' the old man said softly.

'While you and your brothers live, then he lives within you all. And the name of the sons of Mil will live long in this island's history. Why, in a hundred generations, this land will still belong to your people.'

Eber Donn nodded towards the land. 'And what about the Tuatha De Danann ...? They rule this island now.'

'Every race has its time, a world to live in. The Tuatha De Danann have already lived beyond their time; the world is changing, leaving them and their ancient magic behind. They drew their magical power from the earth and the sea, using it frivolously, thinking it unending, but it was not an inexhaustible supply. They have used a lot of the magic in this world. Within a hundred years, much of the magic will have gone from this world. Within a thousand, only the merest hint will remain. What you and I accept as normal, everyday parts of life, our children's children's children will wonder at.'

'I don't see the point, old man,' Eber Donn interrupted him.

'The point is that the Tuatha De Danann are weak; they can be defeated ... and then the land of Erin is yours.'

Eber Donn ran his hands along his bald head and stared at the land. Finally, he nodded. 'My ancestors once ruled this land; it is fitting that we should return here.' He looked sharply at the old man. 'Will there be war?'

Amergin shrugged. 'I do not know ... but I don't think the Tuatha De Danann will give up the land without a fight.'

Eber Donn nodded again. 'That too is good. If they were to give up the land then I would think that the land itself was not worth holding on to.'

'This land is,' Amergin said fiercely. 'This land is powerful. I have heard its voice, listened to its song.'

'I fear these Tuatha De Danann,' Eber Donn said suddenly, surprisingly, 'because they are close to gods. But

I think I fear you more, Amergin, because I think you may be a demon.'

The old man squeezed the warrior's shoulder, making him wince with the strength in the grip. 'I am neither ... I am simply a man, though I am both more and less than human.'

Mil's eldest son turned to watch the tall white-haired man make his way down the length of the boat. Whatever Amergin was – god or demon, wizard, shade or fetch – he was not a man. He was turning away to follow the old man when he spotted movement on the beach. The warrior ground his teeth in frustration. He had been hoping to make landfall before being spotted, but he should have known that these cursed De Danann would have spies everywhere. They had probably encircled the land with some sort of magical charm, which warned them when strangers approached. He knew his case was hopeless now. Landing a war party on the beach would be suicide in these circumstances. 'How many do you see?' he shouted up to Erannan.

'Three, brother.'

'Three what?' Eber Donn snapped. 'Three legions, three cohorts, three troops? How many?'

Erannan leaned forward to look down on to his brother's shining bald head. 'Just three, brother – no more. Three figures in long gowns of gold, silver and bronze. They look like women,' he added.

'Women?' Eber Donn swore. 'Witches then, sent to enchant us.'

'Worse,' Amergin said, coming up quietly behind him. 'These are the spirits of the land.'

Eber Donn rowed Amergin ashore in a small wood and leather coracle. Neither man spoke during the short journey from the boat to the beach; they were both concentrating on the three dark-cloaked and hooded figures standing high up on the beach, in the shade of the trees that bordered the sand. The figures looked vaguely female – though with the hooded cloaks thrown over robes of gold, silver and bronze, it was impossible to distinguish their features.

Sand rasped beneath the coracle. Steadying himself with one hand, Amergin hopped into the chill water, and then pushed the boat away, back into the waves.

'Let me come with you,' Eber Donn said.

The old man shook his head. 'Only I can do this. If I succeed, we will take this land. If I fail then the land itself will conspire to defeat us.'

'How will I know if you have succeeded?' the warrior called as the waves sucked the flimsy boat back out to sea.

'I will still be alive!' Amergin said grimly.

The old man could feel the power radiating from the three figures as he moved slowly up the beach. Their power was so potent that the sands beneath his feet were slowly curling and twisting into arcane patterns, and the air tasted metallic with power. Amergin felt the hairs on the back of his neck, along his arms and on his skull begin to shift and move of their own accord, and when he brushed his hand against his robe, a blue spark snapped from his fingertips to the cloth. Unwilling to approach too close to the figures, he stopped and bowed to each in turn. 'You honour me with your presence.'

'We bid you welcome.' The three figures spoke as one, their voices so perfectly matched that he found it impossible to tell one from the other. 'You heard our song?'

Amergin looked at the central figure, the woman dressed in gold. 'I am the wind off the sea, I am the waves that roll off the mighty ocean, the voice of the sea ...'

The three women nodded. 'You heard our call. Then, there are people of power amongst you?'

'We have been raised in the old ways.'

'Do you honour the earth?' This time the woman to the right, who was robed in bronze, asked.

'And do you respect the waters?' the woman in silver, to the left, asked.

Amergin bowed again. 'We honour the land which supports us; we respect the waters which give us life. Our rituals are the old rituals; our gods and spirits are those of earth and air, fire and water. We take no more than we need from the earth and what we take, we replace.'

The two outer figures looked towards the central, gold-clad figure, and Amergin guessed that the women were conferring silently together. He realized now that his every word was crucial; he had spoken to both spirits and demons before, but he had never experienced power such as this.

The woman in gold stepped forward, while her two companions moved away slightly. The old man actually felt the woman approaching as the air between them crackled with energy. He kept his eyes lowered: to look upon the face of one of these creatures was to invite blindness, madness or death.

'We are the Three that is One, and the One that is this land. We are the spirit of this place, the essence of the earth and water, the forests, the lakes, the cliffs and the bogs. We are the land.' Though Amergin was standing directly in front of the creature, her voice sounded lost and distant. 'Would your people settle in this place?'

'These are not my people, these are the followers of Mil, a proud and brave warrior who dreamed of this land. Now he is no more and his sons have sworn an oath to carry out his dying wish: that his people should one day return to this land. His sons lead them and yes, they would like to settle on this pleasant land.'

'There have been others before you, some rough and

crude, others gentle. The Tuatha De Danann have this land now. Do you think you can defeat them?'

'We can but try. They are a strong, arrogant race ... but perhaps that same arrogance might prove to be their undoing.'

'They do not honour the land.'

'The Tuatha De Dannan, the People of the Goddess, destroyed their last homeland,' Amergin said softly. 'I fear they would do the same again.'

The gold-clad figure nodded. 'We share that fear. I am Banba,' she said suddenly.

Amergin bowed, but said nothing.

'You will know that the gods depend upon the worship of men for sustenance. The more people who worship us, the stronger we become.'

The old man nodded again. All the gods of men vied for the faith of their worshippers. The faith of humans lent the gods substance and power.

'We are the Three that is One and the One is the Land,' Banba said softly. 'We are equal ... and yet we would wish that it was otherwise. The natural order is for one to lead, the others to follow. Swear to me now, old man, that your followers will name this land in my honour, and I will move against the Tuatha De Danann and you will be victorious.'

Amergin looked to the left and right at the two remaining figures in silver and bronze robes. 'They must not know.'

Banba nodded. 'They must not know for the moment, lest there be strife between us, and our battle tear the land itself apart. Name this land in my honour and every time my name is mentioned, I will draw strength from that.'

'I would be honoured to instruct my people to call this land Banba.'

The gold-clad figure hissed with pleasure and then, without another word, turned and moved silently back up the beach. Amergin was aware of a weight moving off his chest.

The silver-clad woman standing to Amergin's left came next. Her magical power was stronger, sharper, the air was acrid with energy. Whereas Banba's energy had been a solid pressure against Amergin's body, this was a harsher feeling, one almost of pain.

'I am Fodla,' the woman said without preamble.

'I am honoured,' Amergin said, keeping his eyes down, watching the ground, not daring to meet her gaze.

'Your people need me,' the creature said firmly. 'Instruct them to worship me ... and I will raise up the land in their favour. Agree to this, and you can leave here confident that this land is already yours.'

'We will name this land in your honour,' Amergin said. 'But what of the other two ...' he wondered aloud. 'What of your sisters?'

'They must not know,' Fodla said immediately, and Amergin noticed that even her voice was sharper, harsher than Banba's. The woman stepped back, and the human felt the wave of release as she moved away.

Amergin felt the presence of the third bronze-clad woman like the wash of warm water over his body. It was soft, all-embracing, and pleasant.

'I do not know what my sisters wanted,' the creature murmured, 'though I would imagine their request parallels mine. I am Eriu, and my request is the same ... my offer identical. Worship me and this land will be yours.'

The old man bowed. 'It is a proud name. I will do that. This land will be called Eriu.'

'My sisters must not know.'

'They will not. Grant us this land, and in the days and nights that follow, you will hear the followers of the sons of Mil speak of this land with your name.'

Eriu nodded. 'That will make me strong,' she said, drifting back.

Amergin waited until the three figures had resumed their original positions, with Banba in the centre, silver Fodla to his left, and bronze Eriu to his right. 'I am Amergin,' he said aloud. 'I have given you my name, and therefore delivered myself into your hands. I have sworn each of you an oath and in return each of you have made me a promise. I will keep to that promise ... will you keep to yours?'

'We will,' the women answered as one.

'Then so be it,' Amergin bowed. 'The days of the Tuatha De Danann are numbered, the rule of the sons of Mil is about to begin.' Turning his back on the three figures, he strode down the beach into the shallows. When he glanced back over his shoulder, they were gone. A smile twisted the old man's lips: he wondered what was going to happen when they discovered that he had tricked them. He wondered what they would think when they discovered that he was going to instruct each of the sons of Mil to call the land by either Banba, Fodla or Eriu. They would gain power, but remain equal.

He thought they might think it fitting.

Cuchulain,
the Hound of Ulster

♣

CHAPTER THREE

The Wedding

'He was the greatest of the heroes of Erin.

'Born of mortal woman and a god, his life on this world was brief and glorious. There have been those who have attempted to make him even greater than he was, those bards and scribes who have added feats and adventures to his saga. But there is no need for this: his legend is glorious and tragic enough.

'Now all the principals are gone and I alone remain. I knew the boy Setanta who became the warrior Cuchulain. I was amongst those who instructed and trained him; I alone have the right to tell the tale of Cuchulain, the Hound of Ulster.

'I am Amergin the Bard ...'

Dechtire felt the crawling tickle of an insect at the back of her throat and immediately turned her head to spit the mead into the fire. The flames hissed and spat, the thick syrupy liquid bubbling and boiling. The young woman swallowed again, and realized that it was too late: she had swallowed the tiny creature. Dechtire swore under her breath. It was just the perfect end to a perfect day.

The raven-haired, green-eyed young women checked the goblet for insects before taking another swallow of the

21

drink. Finding none, she finished off the last of the thick honey-flavoured drink in one long swallow. Maybe if she drank enough she'd be able to get through the rest of the night.

Dechtire glanced sidelong at the man she'd married that day. A man she'd never met before. He was Sualtim, a powerful chieftain in his own right, but not the king she'd always thought she'd marry. Nor was he handsome. Perhaps he had been handsome in his youth, but his youth was long passed now. The young woman drank another goblet of the sickly drink and glared down the table to where her brother was sitting, but he was so far in his cups that he was unaware of her bubbling rage. She had spoken to him earlier before the wedding, but he chose to do nothing about the situation. He claimed he could do nothing. He was Conor, King of Ulster, and she was merely a princess ... and, as such, a piece of meat to be sold to the highest bidder, given to whomever her beloved brother wished to appease or make a treaty with. He hadn't said as much openly, but she had inferred it.

Dechtire stood up so suddenly that the room swayed and shifted around her. She gripped the table and closed her eyes, squeezing them shut, opening them again, only to find that the room was still whirling slowly past. She remained standing until the room stopped moving.

A rough hand touched her bare arm. 'Wife, are you ill?'

Dechtire looked down into Sualtim's bloodshot eyes and resisted the temptation to spit into his face. The man was old enough to be her father. 'I am well, husband,' she said, speaking deliberately slowly, trying not to slur her words, but conscious that Sualtim was far more drunk than she was and probably wouldn't even notice. 'The heat,' she said vaguely, 'the excitement of the day ...'

'Of course. I understand.' The grey-haired warrior-chieftain

stared blearily at his wife. He supposed it was only natural
that she should be tired by the events of the day and she
was probably nervous and excited with the promise of
what was yet to come. He attempted a sympathetic smile,
but it came out as a leer. 'Why don't you retire to our
bedchamber, and I will join you shortly.'

'Why don't I do that?' Dechtire said, swallowing hard,
feeling her gorge rising. Though she was still a virgin, she
knew of the act between men and women, had even
watched the young men and women coupling in the fields at
the time of Harvest and Sowing. The thought of this foul-
smelling, drunken sot fumbling at her was almost too much
to even consider.

'A kiss for your husband,' he said, smiling, showing
broken, ragged teeth.

Dechtire patted his balding head. 'Later, husband, why
don't we save all that for later?'

Sualtim threw back his head and roared with laughter,
pounding the table with his fist. The girl had spirit! He
attempted to grab her as she shifted past him, but she
wasn't so drunk that she couldn't evade his grasp, and deftly
slipped by.

Dechtire made her way through the crowded chamber.
Most of the nobles of Erin had been invited to the
ceremony; even Fergus, the deposed king, whom her
mother had tricked into giving up the throne to Conor, was
there. The duped warrior was slumped across the table,
lying with his head resting on his folded arms. There was a
puddle of wine on the scrubbed boards, the dark liquid
soaking into the sleeve of his linen jerkin. Even from across
the room, amid all the tumult, she could hear his rasping
snores.

A hatchet-faced, grey-haired woman was sitting beside
Fergus. Her plate of food was almost untouched and she

had yet to finish her first glass of wine of the evening. The woman looked up suddenly and, catching Dechtire's eye, called her forward with an imperious finger.

Dechtire stepped across two hunting dogs who were gnawing at a chunk of meat, and approached the table. Keeping the table between them, she bowed slightly, 'Mother ...'

There was little love lost between Dechtire and Ness, her mother. When Dechtire looked at the older woman, she realized that here was what she would look like when she was fifty – if she lived that long. They shared the same sharp-boned features, the same grass-green eyes, the same luxurious hair. However, whereas Dechtire was pretty, her strong cheekbones giving her long face character, the skin had pulled tight across Ness's face, lending it a vaguely skull-like appearance.

'This should be a happy day for you, daughter.' Ness's voice was low and Dechtire had to step forward to hear her clearly. 'Yet you look far from happy.'

'Is the heifer happy when she is sold in the market?' Dechtire demanded icily.

'Sualtim is an important chieftain, a proud warrior ...' Ness began.

'And an old man,' Dechtire finished.

'It is a good match,' Ness said firmly. She glanced sidelong at Fergus. 'And a marriage is what you make of it. I married a king, but my price was to make him give up his kingdom for a year and a day so that my son could rule. Now my son rules permanently, and you are a princess because of it.'

'Your son rules because you used the year while he ruled to buy the loyalty of the other chieftains,' Dechtire reminded her.

Ness nodded. 'Men are weak, easily ruled, easily

controlled. Let me advise you, daughter. Allow men their petty vanities, allow them to think they are ruling, allow them to think that they are in control and they are as clay – to be moulded and twisted to your whim.' She sat back in the chair and lifted her goblet. 'That is my wedding gift to you. Conor is king because he is a man; you are a princess and will never rule this land, but you can wield far more power than your brother ever does because you are a woman.'

Dechtire bowed, biting the inside of her cheek to prevent herself from making a comment that she would later regret. Her mother had been manipulating people for so long now that it had become second nature to her.

She paused in the doorway of Emain Macha's huge central hall and looked back. This was the main hall, the Craobh Ruadh – the Red Branch, which gave its name to the knights of the Red Branch. On either side of the hall were the two lesser hallways of Craobh Dearg, where the king's treasury was kept, and on the opposite side was the Teite Brecc, the armoury. Dechtire supposed she should take it as a privilege that her wedding feast had been held in the great hall. Looking over the long room, it was interesting to see how many of the women were still awake and alert, and how many of the men had fallen into a drunken stupor. There was an argument taking place in one corner which, even as she watched, dissolved into a fight. No weapons were allowed into the hall, but both men still possessed their eating knives. However, they were too drunk to do any real damage to one another. In another corner a trio of men argued over a fidchell board. There were dogs everywhere, sleeping in front of the roaring fires or scavenging beneath the tables for food. Children of all ages wandered through the crowd. The straw which had been laid down fresh that morning, scenting the room with the soft odour of the fields, was now soiled and scattered, and the room smelt of sweat and vomit, food and urine.

Shaking her head, Dechtire turned away in disgust. This was not how she imagined her wedding day would be.

'My lady ...?' Moriath, Dechtire's Gaulish serving woman, came to her feet as her mistress stormed out into the corridor.

'I will retire, Moriath.'

'Of course, my lady.' The grey-haired woman bowed and fell into step beside the princess.

'You've been married, Moriath,' Dechtire said slowly. 'What is it like?'

The older woman took a few moments before replying. 'That's not a question I can easily answer, my lady. I was twenty years a wife and I've been ten a widow. There are good times and bad times. You will know happiness and much sorrow. You will know the pain of childbirth and the joy of children; the ecstasy of lovemaking and the sadness of death.'

'My mother said that marriage is what you make of it.'

The grey-haired woman nodded. 'There is much truth in that. A good woman will *make* a man more than what he is. A good man can never make a woman better than she is.'

'I'm too tired for philosophy, Moriath.'

'No philosophy, my lady. Just the truth.'

'But where's the love, Moriath? Where is the love?' she demanded.

The old woman wheezed her gentle coughing laugh. 'If you're looking for love, my lady, then find yourself a lover. A husband is security and respectability; a lover can be passion and irresponsibility.'

'Can a woman have both?'

'Not in the one man,' Moriath hissed. 'And I don't think one should be talking about taking a lover – at least not on one's wedding day!'

They continued on down the corridors in silence and walked out into the chill night air. The noises of ribaldry sounded faint and distant, muffled by Emain Macha's thick stone walls.

Sualtim had made his camp in the empty fields around the king's fort. The two dozen wood and hide tents that comprised his retinue were deserted now, and the scores of fires that had blazed through most of the day had died down to glowing cinders. A single guard leaned on his spear, dozing before the chief's tent, and Dechtire and Moriath slipped into the tent's musty stale interior without his noticing.

'You could have stayed at the fort,' Moriath said softly.

'I might as well get used to it,' Dechtire said bitterly. She coughed, the dust tickling at the back of her throat – she could still feel where she'd swallowed the fly that had fallen into the mead, could still imagine it was wriggling at the back of her throat. She turned over a thick woven blanket with her toe: moths had eaten their way through one corner and it smelled of damp and mould. It was only with a huge effort that she managed to control her temper. Her brother had been made a king; she had been made an object, traded off to some petty chieftain in return for his support, or to pay some debt.

'Moriath ...', Dechtire began softly, 'Moriath, about the way of a man and a woman ...'

The old woman hissed again and patted Dechtire's arm reassuringly. 'Sualtim will be too drunk tonight to bother you. In the morning he will feel too ill to do anything about it. He will spend the afternoon drinking and playing fidchell, and he will spend tomorrow night feasting with your brother. I have seen brides wait three or four or more days for their husbands to come to their beds and complete the marriage ceremony.'

Dechtire suppressed a smile. Up until the moment the druid had handfasted them, she hadn't truly believed that she was to be wed to a chieftain she had never even heard of before, never mind met. It happened to other women – but it wasn't going to happen to her. But now that she was married, perhaps she should do what her mother had suggested: she would make the best of it. 'Bring me a drink, Moriath,' she said suddenly, 'some of that foreign wine, or even water, but none of that sweet mead. My teeth ache with the taste of it.'

'Of course, my lady.'

By the time Moriath returned with the amphora of wine from one of the hot lands close to the Middle Sea, Dechtire was lying beneath the furs, her head resting on her hand, snoring gently.

The old woman tucked the fur higher around the young woman's shoulders and then bent to kiss her cheek. She whispered an ancient spell into the young woman's ear to bring her pleasant thoughts. 'Sweet dreams, princess.'

And Dechtire dreamed.

She was back in the hall, raising the glass to her lips, swallowing the drink, feeling the fly tickling at the back of her throat. She was spitting the fly to the floor ... but suddenly it wasn't a fly anymore: the tiny insect was changing, lengthening, growing, the iridescent wings wrapping themselves around the creature, clothing it in a shimmering robe, a close-fitting tunic. When the insect had completed its metamorphosis, a golden-haired, golden-eyed young man was standing in its place. The young man spread the shimmering cloak that clothed him and Dechtire smelt the sudden odour of herbs and spices, of freshly cut grass and the rich loam of the earth. Flower petals spun out of the interior of the youth's cloak and, for one brief moment, the interior of the cloak showed glimpses of a sun-wrapped land.

In her dream the young-looking man – though when she looked into his eyes, which were old and wise, Dechtire realized that this was no youth – came and knelt at her feet. Clutching one of her hands with his long fingers, he pressed it to his lips. Dechtire touched his hair; it felt like spun thread.

'I am Lugh,' the youth said simply.

'Lugh is a god,' she heard herself respond.

'Then I am a god.'

'What do you want, god?' Dechtire was *aware* that she was dreaming, but she was unable to do anything about it. Part of her conscious mind knew that she was asleep in Sualtim's tent outside Emain Macha. But the dream – this dream – seemed so real! She turned her head. She could clearly see the hall, the occupants frozen in various attitudes, some comical, others ridiculous.

'Is this a dream?' she asked.

The god shook his head. 'No. Your world is the dream. The gods and the spirit-folk live in the Otherworld, the real world.'

'What do you want with me?'

Lugh smiled and Dechtire had to squeeze her eyes shut from its brilliance. 'I loved you from the moment I saw you. But I could feel your sorrow, taste it on the air around you. I took the form of a fly to enter your world and place my mark on you so that I would be able to bring you back into my world. There is no sorrow in my world, no pain, no anguish.' The god rose to his feet, his huge golden eyes spinning. 'The choice is yours: will you come to Brugh na Boinne with me?'

'For how long?'

'As long as you wish. A night, a day, a year, an eternity.'

If it was a dream, then Dechtire was determined to enjoy it. When she woke up, she would be back in the stale, stuffy tent, lying beneath mouldering furs, probably beside a foul-smelling drunken old man. 'A day and a night,' she said, raising her arms to wrap them around the god's neck, pulling him closer, her lips brushing his.

Lugh nodded. 'And lest you be lonely, then you shall have some companions.' He waved a hand in the direction of the hall. Dechtire turned to look. One by one the women in the hall were disappearing, their figures melting, shrinking, their skins blossoming feathers, turning them into white doves, their fingers lengthening into wings. Bundles of clothes remained scattered on the ground to mark where the women had stood. Dozens of the white doves rose up into the air and wheeled around the room, obviously confused, until an ancient-looking black crow joined them, marshalling them together. Even without being told, Dechtire realized that the crow was Moriath. The birds circled around the room once more and then, led by the black crow, sped through the uncovered window, heading into the west.

Lugh leaned forward and kissed Dechtire. 'We will meet again in Brugh na Boinne,' he murmured. She closed her eyes as she felt the change come over her, and she knew she was assuming the shape of a bird. The dream was so vivid she could actually feel her body warp and twist, could hear the feathers rustle as they pushed their way through her pale skin. When she opened her eyes, the world had changed, distorted, grown to terrifying dimensions, and was without colour.

Too much mead ... too much wine. This was a dream, nothing more than a dream, just a dream.

But Dechtire knew that this was no dream.

CHAPTER FOUR
In Brugh na Boinne

♣

This was no dream.

Dechtire's grass-green eyes snapped open, her heart beginning to pound with the realization.

The very air felt different. It was warm and dry, redolent with herbs and spices, unlike the cooler, damper atmosphere of Erin. She was in a tent ... but not the tent she had fallen asleep in. Now the sunlight was filtered through shifting strips of thin gauzy cloths, spattering the bed she was lying upon with fragments and spots of colour. Her head was resting on a linen bag stuffed with aromatic herbs and she was lying beneath blankets that had been woven of a material that was flesh-soft to the touch. Raising herself up on her elbows, she looked around the tent.

The tent was a large circular construction. Long golden rods had been twisted and shaped to form the frame, while layer upon layer of multicoloured diaphanous cloths had been laid over the frame. The gentle breeze that riffled through the tent, rippling the cloth, allowed her glimpses of a lush green countryside that she knew was not part of Erin.

She knew she should be terrified, but she realized that she wasn't even frightened.

There was a flickering shape outside the tent and she saw a large black crow strut across the ground towards the opening. The warm, scented wind hissed through the cloths, blowing back a flap, allowing the brilliant sunlight to shaft into the tent's hazy interior. She saw the bird approaching the opening. The flap of cloth blew back and Dechtire blinked, shading her eyes from the light. When she opened her eyes again, Moriath was standing before her.

'You slept well, my lady?'

'Moriath, where are we?'

'Where do you think?'

'I dreamt about Lugh,' Dechtire said not answering the question.

The old woman nodded. 'And where do you think this place is?'

Dechtire looked at her for a moment, before asking, 'It is not Erin. It is Brugh na Boinne?'

Moriath nodded. 'This is Brugh na Boinne, the home of Lugh.'

'Are we still in Erin?'

Moriath considered for a moment before answering. 'The land of Erin exists in the world of the senses and the spirit; the first is a world we can see and touch, smell and feel, but the second is the more powerful, for it is the world of the imagination and the soul. We can do little with the physical world, but the world of the spirit is what we make it.'

Dechtire shook her head, not quite understanding what the old woman was saying. She knew that Moriath was regarded as a wise woman, and possessed some second sight. The old woman smiled at Dechtire's confusion. 'This is the Otherworld.'

'Did I really meet Lugh?'

'Did you see him in your dreams?'

'I saw him.'

Moriath nodded. 'Then he saw you; he fell in love with you, he brought you here.' She shrugged. 'Lugh is an impulsive god.'

Dechtire sat up, the cloths hissing away from her bare flesh. 'And now?' she asked. 'What happens now?'

Moriath smiled. 'That is up to you. You are a guest in this place, not a prisoner. You can return to your human husband any time you wish.'

The very thought of it made Dechtire shudder.

'But a word of warning, lady, you must not spend too long in this Sidhe world. Time runs differently here, it moves at a far slower rate than it does in the world of men. Just remember that. Surely you know the tales of the maidens who lingered a single night with the Sidhe folk, but who returned to their own people in the human world to discover that a hundred years and more had passed.'

'How long then should I stay here?'

'A day and a night,' Moriath smiled. 'That should be long enough.'

'Long enough for what?'

'To create a legend,' the old woman said enigmatically.

CHAPTER FIVE
The Golden Birds

'I went with my mistress into the Otherworld. I warned her that time flows differently there. A single day in the Sidhe world might be a year in the world of men ... or it might just as easily be ten years.

'When a maid is in love, time also loses all meaning. Time spent in the company of a loved one moves swiftly, but while that loved one is away, time drags its heels like a spent hound.

'Dechtire loved Lugh. And although he was a god, I think he loved her also. Time lost all meaning for the lovers.

'I have a little of the Sight, and that knowledge enabled me to keep a reckoning of the days that were slipping by in the World of Men. All my mistress knew was that she had spent a blissful day and night in the Otherworld. But she was gone from the world of men for longer than that ...'

A single day passed.

Later, Dechtire's memories of that time were hazy, indistinct. Images that had been vivid soon grew indistinct and faded like a barely remembered dream. The sounds of the Otherworld faded to a barely remembered noise. Moriath, the serving woman, explained to her that no human could properly understand the land of the Sidhe, that the sights and sounds, the very colours, had to be muted lest they blast the human senses with their strength and power.

What fragments of memory Dechtire retained, she cherished.

She remembered walking with Lugh through the fields that surrounded Brugh na Boinne. At times it looked just like the real world – though she was already beginning to question just what was the real world, her own, or this? But just when she was coming to accept it as being identical to her own, something would happen, a creature – a bird, a beast, or an insect that had no right to exist, something from the mythology of her own race would appear – and she would be forced to accept that she had gone beyond the human world into the realm of faerie.

She remembered returning to Brugh na Boinne with Lugh around noon – she assumed it was noon, because there were no shadows on the ground, though there was no sun in this Otherworld. Mindful of Moriath's warning to neither eat nor drink any of the Sidhe food, Dechtire received Lugh into her bed and throughout the long day that followed they made love so often that she lost count.

And as the dusky twilight rolled across the Otherworld, Dechtire knew without any doubt that she had conceived a child.

A year passed in the world of men.

Sualtim stood before Conor. The old warrior's face was flushed with anger as he listened to the young king. Finally, he spat on the ground. 'That for your promises!'

A murmur ran around the court and Conor's men began to edge away from Sualtim's warriors. No weapons were allowed in Emain Macha's halls, but hands went to eating knives or clutched amulets. Even the dogs that roamed the draughty halls began to growl, sensing the rising tension.

Conor started to come to his feet when his mother's fingers closed tightly over his arms. Ness's eyes were cold, her mouth a thin white line. She hadn't schemed to put her son on the throne over the rightful king only to have him usurped in turn by this ragged warrior. 'Listen to him,' she hissed, 'agree to what he says. He has a case which you must answer. Show that you are capable of justice.'

Conor glared at his mother before slowly subsiding on to his stone throne. 'What would you have me do?' he asked wearily.

Sualtim grinned triumphantly ... until he saw the expression of Ness's face. The warrior feared the woman far more than he feared the boy. A woman who could overthrow a king and place her son in his place could easily unmake a petty chieftain.

'I want justice,' he said simply. 'I married a maid a year past. She vanished on my wedding night along with her servant and maids. Fifty of our women were taken with her, their clothing left behind in this very hall as an insult to us.'

'We know all this, Sualtim,' Conor snapped. 'Our druids have ascertained that they were taken by magic, the ancient Sidhe magic. But beyond that, we know nothing. No human magician can work the Old High Magic.'

Sualtim's smile was triumphant. 'No human magician, lord, but it is not beyond the powers of one of the non-humans.'

Ness leaned over her son's shoulder to glare at the warrior. Her fingers bit painfully into Conor's flesh. 'There are none of the Sidhe or half-Sidhe in Erin now,' she snapped.

From the back of the hall, a white-haired, white-bearded man pushed through the crowd. 'There are still a few, lady, though they choose not to reveal themselves to the human-kind.'

Sualtim turned back to the king. 'This is Amergin, greatest of the druids.'

'Amergin is dead,' Ness said quickly.

The old man brushed past Sualtim and reached out to touch Ness's hand. She winced at the touch of his warm, dry flesh. Now that she was close to the old man, she could see that his extraordinary eyes were completely black, without white or pupil. 'I have not yet chosen to die, lady,' the ancient druid said very softly.

'Do you know where my sister is?' Conor asked.

'I know who took her.'

Ness's fingers tightened on Conor's shoulder, the long nails drawing blood. 'Where is she, old man?'

A ghost of a smile flickered across the old man's face. 'She is in Brugh na Boinne, with Lugh.'

Ness nodded, secretly pleased. Her one great fear had been that her daughter had been taken by a chieftain – such an event would have brought shame on the girl and her family. But there was no shame in a union between a god and a mortal. 'How do we get her back?' she demanded.

The ancient druid smiled. 'She may not want to come back. After the Otherworld, this mortal world of ours looks drab in comparison.'

'You speak as if from personal knowledge,' Ness muttered.

'I do,' Amergin said very softly.

'So now we know,' Sualtim said suddenly. 'I pledged you my loyalty and support in return for your sister's hand in marriage. But our marriage is in name only; it has never been consummated ... therefore, by the ancient law of this land, there is no marriage.' He looked at the druid as he spoke.

Amergin nodded in agreement. 'That is the law.'

Conor leaned back in his chair and looked at his mother.

The old woman's eyes were shrewd, calculating. 'Agree,' she muttered, her lips barely moving. 'Then suggest that you will ride in search of your sister.'

Conor sat forward. 'You are of course correct, lord,' he said easily. 'But surely Sualtim can attach no blame to me because Lugh stole my sister ...?' He attempted a smile, which failed. 'Who can predict the gods?' he joked. He looked across the faces of the assembled lords, but their faces were grim and unsmiling. Finally, he sighed. 'Could you take us to Brugh na Boinne?' he asked Amergin.

The ancient druid shook his head. 'I cannot bring you into the Otherworld, but I can show you one of the places where this world and the next meet. Perhaps there you will find what you are looking for.'

Conor rose to his feet. 'Warriors,' he shouted, 'today we ride in search of my sister, Sualtim's bride, and the maidens who were taken along with her. Who will ride with us?'

A dozen men growled assent.

'Gold for the men who ride with me,' he added.

This time the shout was louder, more sustained.

They had ridden south and west for most of the day in their wood and leather chariots. Conor and Fergus, his step-father, rode together in the lead chariot, while Sualtim and Amergin kept pace with them in the second chariot. A dozen chariots followed.

'They're up to something,' Conor said, risking a quick glance at the chariot behind them.

Fergus shook his head. 'I'm not so sure. Sualtim is a man of his word, rough and uncouth certainly, but he lives by the code of the warrior. Amergin's reputation is above reproach, but remember, he is no longer wholly human,' he added with a smile. 'And a non-human may honour something entirely different to a human.'

They made camp just before sunset on the top of a small rounded knoll. A chill wind was blowing in from the north, and the sparks from the huge fire they built went spiralling upwards into the heavens. Off in the distance wolves howled, and the guards posted around the camp paced nervously. Wolves – especially the larger packs – were a dangerous enough threat, but there were also bandits, petty chieftains and non-human beasts to contend with. Few of them would contemplate a frontal attack on the troop of heavily armed warriors, but they might be tempted to mount an attack under cover of darkness. However, while the troop's position on the hilltop was exposed, this also meant that it was more easily defended.

As the sun dipped below the horizon, it briefly illuminated a series of glittering golden stars high in the heavens. As Conor and his warriors watched, the points of light twisted and turned before establishing themselves into a long triangular formation heading off to the south.

'They look like birds,' Bricriu, one of Conor's advisers, murmured. The small dark man touched the king's arm. 'But what birds shine like that?' he asked. Amongst the nobles of Erin, Bricriu was known as Poison-tongue. 'Only one metal shines that bright, lord. Gold. Perhaps they are golden birds, lord?' he suggested.

'There are no golden birds,' Conor said softly, staring up at the glittering spots of light.

'We are entering the realm of legend. Perhaps the creatures of legend live here also. There are birds of gold in our mythology . . . birds that lay golden eggs,' he added insidiously.

Conor nodded, watching the points of light.

'Golden birds like that should belong to a king,' Bricriu murmured.

The birds dipped down suddenly, the spots of light winking out one by one.

'They have landed close by.'

Conor nodded slowly. What Bricriu said was true: a king who possessed golden birds like that would be powerful indeed.

'Yoke up my chariot, Bricriu. We will go in search of these golden birds.'

The small man suddenly looked nervous. 'And warriors, my lord. Should we not bring warriors?'

'No need, Bricriu. We have the chariot, we can run if need be, and swords and spears to fight if necessary. And besides,' he added, 'there's no need to let all Erin know about the golden birds, eh?'

'As you wish, my lord.'

When the chariot was ready, Conor strode up to the enormous bonfire and announced loudly, 'I am going in search of proper lodgings for my men. Bricriu has advised me that there may be a fort around here where we might spend the night.'

Fergus grabbed the younger man's arm. 'But this is madness, sire. Stay here; we've a good position here and enough men to fight off an army.'

Conor shook off Fergus's arm. 'No,' he said loud enough for all to hear, 'my men's comfort means more to me than my own safety.'

The warriors rattled their spears against their shields in approval. Fergus turned away, shaking his head in disgust. He knew what his wife had done, he knew how he had been tricked out of the kingship, but curiously, that didn't concern him as much as it should. He had found no pleasure in ruling, and he had discovered that he had neither the temperament nor the desire to hold together the various warring tribes and factions. Fergus enjoyed his food and drink, fighting and hunting: what more did a man want? There were occasions however – occasions like now

– when he regretted that he hadn't held on to his throne, at least long enough for a real warrior to take it from him, and not this arrogant, ignorant fool. The old warrior turned away and found Amergin staring at him. The druid's solid black eyes were like holes in his face. He raised his white eyebrows in a silent question.

'Is there a fort around here?' Fergus said shortly.

Amergin's lips twitched. 'There is – but not the sort that Conor is looking for, I fear.'

Fergus turned back to Conor. 'Wait, lord. It is not seemly that a king should endanger himself in this way. This is a wild and dangerous land; I will accompany Bricriu in your stead.'

The warriors stamped their approval and, realizing that he had been backed into a corner, Conor nodded graciously. 'You are a brave and honourable warrior, Fergus. I am proud to call you stepfather.'

When Fergus and Bricriu had climbed into the chariot, the king touched Bricriu's sleeve. 'Ensure he sees nothing ... and if he does, then ensure that he'll not be reporting it to anyone.' Aloud he said, 'May the gods grant you a safe journey.' And the king's smile was chilling.

CHAPTER SIX

The Palace

'That day I rode out with Bricriu Poison-tongue, I thought I was looking for shelter for the men of Ulster. It was only later that I learned that Conor and Bricriu's real mission had been to discover the whereabouts of the golden birds we had seen earlier.

'Little did we realize that we were merely following a destiny that had been laid down by the unseen gods to lead us to our destiny ... and the destiny of our land.

'So Bricriu and I set out with a different mission. I, at least, was successful: I found shelter for my men.

'I also discovered a legend ...'

The two men rode in absolute silence. There was no love lost between them; indeed, Bricriu had few friends. His malicious and spiteful nature was infamous throughout Ireland, and only an enormous measure of good luck, or perhaps a special interest by one of the gods – and six hired mercenaries who acted as his bodyguards – had ensured that his head remained on his shoulders for so long. His evil nature had corrupted and twisted him and his shoulders were perpetually hunched, almost as if he expected a blow, and made him seem smaller than he was. He had anticipated riding out with Conor, and perhaps finding the birds and claiming one or more for himself. Riding with Fergus was not part of his plan. But, always willing to turn any situation to his advantage, Bricriu thought that perhaps he might be able to use these circumstances to his own profit. Fergus was both honourable and stupid; Bricriu was neither.

The narrow road twisted and turned through barren scrubland. Recent rain had turned the ground to mud and the chariot lurched from side to side, the horses straining to pull the heavy wooden wheels through the cloying earth.

They finally crested the brow of a low hill and Bricriu reined in the horses. The animals steamed in the chill night air, creating ghostly shadows which wreathed the men and beasts. The sharp-featured man pointed down and to the left. 'There, I think.'

Fergus stared into the gloom and shook his head. 'There's nothing down there,' he said shortly.

'There is,' Bricriu insisted. 'At least, I'm sure there is,' he added hastily. 'I ... I rode through this part of the country a few seasons past. I'm sure there is a fort down there.'

Fergus turned away to hide the smile of understanding that curled his lips: he too had seen the golden points of light in the heavens, he had watched them come to earth. He had thought they might be shooting stars – the gods making war upon one another – but obviously Bricriu, and Conor too, had put a different interpretation on it. Obviously they knew something he didn't. He was a little insulted though that they should have thought he'd be fooled so easily.

'I'll be guided by you,' Fergus shrugged. 'But be prepared to fight,' he added, indicating the road with his spear, 'our path wends through deep shadow. If there'll be an ambush, it will be there.'

The hunched man suddenly looked nervous as he stared

into the gloom; he knew that in the event of an ambush the first man to die was usually the charioteer. With the horses running out of control, the warrior in the chariot would be unable to fight.

'Perhaps we should turn back,' he suggested, not looking at the older man.

But Fergus clapped him on the shoulder. 'No, we have the comfort of our troop to think of. We should press on.'

Bricriu glared at him for a moment before urging the horses to walk on.

The road dipped and turned through a dark, silent valley. The trees that lined the road were seared and twisted into grotesque skeletal shapes that assumed even more dramatic outlines in the night. Some of them looked un-cannily like ancient warriors. The wind, whistling through the contorted branches, sounded like a woman's sobbing. Both men were startled when the chariot lurched from soft earth on to what was obviously sections of an ancient stone pavement. The road twisted and opened up into a broad avenue, which led straight to the dark mass of a fort. Bricriu hauled the chariot to a halt, the horses wickering and moving uneasily. As Fergus and Bricriu watched, lights appeared in the building and then a long bar of light shafted out into the night as the gates were thrown open.

'It's a trap,' Bricriu hissed.

'If it's a trap then they've sprung it too early,' Fergus said. 'What's to stop us turning and riding away ... apart from our own curiosity,' he murmured. 'It looks more like an invitation.'

'We should turn back,' Bricriu said firmly. 'We can return and bring the rest of the troop here with us.'

'What! And have them all fall into the trap?' Fergus asked indignantly. 'No, it is our duty to press on. Then if anything were to happen to us, at least our companions would be warned,' he added, trying to keep a straight face as Bricriu's eyes opened wider and wider in fear.

Ahead of them, a shape moved in the open door of the fort and stepped into the light, casting a long narrow shadow down the path. Fergus squinted into the glare: it looked like a woman, but he couldn't be sure. 'Stay here,' he said softly, 'I'll go ahead. If anything happens, turn back and warn Conor.'

Bricriu nodded gratefully. 'Be careful,' he said, as Fergus stepped off the chariot, a spear in either hand. The dark man watched the older warrior walk down the centre of the track towards the light. Fergus might be many things – a fool, a cuckold, a drunkard – but there was no one alive who doubted his bravery.

As Fergus neared the fort, he began to make out details. The fort was ancient and obviously dilapidated. What remained of it was covered in moss and portions of the roof had subsided. It looked as if fire had raged through the building in the distant past. There was an ancient-looking woman waiting patiently in the open doorway. As he drew nearer, Fergus could see that she had once been beautiful and even now in advanced years, with her skin stretched taut across her bones, her strong features lent her face a certain natural beauty. Her hair, long and snow-white, fell to the small of her back.

The warrior bowed before the woman. 'Greetings, my lady. Our presence here should not alarm you. We are the king's men on a mission to find a princess and her maidens who were stolen from us a year past. We mean you no ill.'

'Even if you did, you would not have the power to harm me.' Her voice was frail, but crystal clear. 'A god watches over me,' she added.

'A god watches over us all, my lady.'

The woman nodded. 'Just so.'

'My companions are encamped on the hillside yonder. We would count it a great service if we could spend the night beneath your roof.'

'My roof is miserable enough, but it should provide shelter for you and your men.' The old woman bowed. 'It is a long time since warriors slept beneath this roof, though it was once the home of one of the finest families in Erin. You and your men are welcome indeed.'

Fergus bowed again and then stepped back out of the light. He was aware that something was not quite right – he had the feeling that the fort was a Sidhe fort – but he also felt that the woman meant no harm. 'I will return shortly,' he said.

'I will be waiting.'

A couple of steps took Fergus into the shadows and then he turned and raced back to where the chariot had stopped in the middle of the ancient road.

'Who is it?' Bricriu yelped, scrambling to his feet, a spear held shakily in his hands as the lumbering figure drew near to the chariot. 'Who's there?'

'It's me, you fool,' Fergus snapped. 'Why, who did you think?'

'Who's in the fort?' The smaller man blustered, ignoring the question.

'An old woman; alone, I think. The fort's a ruin, but she's offered us shelter for the night.'

'She's alone?' Bricriu asked again.

'As far as I could see.'

In the gloom, Fergus didn't see the younger man smile. 'You go back then,' Bricriu said, 'and bring the others. I'll stay here and keep watch. Perhaps whoever lives within the fort will attempt to lay a trap while you're gone.' He stopped suddenly. 'Does the woman know you came with me?'

'She never asked; I never said. But I don't think she'd assume I came alone.'

Bricriu nodded again, his gaze on the distant fort. 'Head back. I'll wait for you here.'

Fergus climbed into the chariot and turned the horses in a tight circle. He knew the other man was up to something, but he wasn't clever enough to work out what. He was basically a simple warrior – it was that same simplicity that had ensured that he had lost his throne to the conniving of a clever woman – but Fergus accepted that he wasn't clever; he never pretended otherwise.

Bricriu waited until the sounds of the chariot had disappeared into the distance before he approached the fort. He wasn't sure what he expected to find, but he knew the golden birds had come to earth somewhere around here. The very location of the fort and the fact that there seemed to be only one person around was significant: it smacked of sorcery.

Bricriu lay in the long grass and watched the ruined fort. The main door remained thrown open, spearing light out into the night and he could see the same light – a peculiarly intense, vivid light – shining through a few of the windows. As far as he could tell there were no guards and the path to the main door was overgrown with weeds and grasses, evidence that it hadn't been used in a long time. Approaching the fort stealthily, the small man peered in through a gap between the ancient-looking poles that had once formed the wall. The courtyard beyond was unused, rank and overgrown, and a tall elm pushed up through the centre of the stables. There were neither chariot ruts nor footprints in the grasses. Finally, convinced that the fort was deserted, Bricriu moved around to look in through the open door. The bright light burned his eyes, and he pressed the heels of his hands to them. When he could see clearly

again, he found he was looking into a palace: rich, ornate
tapestries decorated the walls, fresh herb-scented rushes on
the floor, the walls lined with brightly polished weapons and
old pennants, the symbols of victory. Down the centre of
the room ran a long polished table that was bright with
glittering cutlery. There was an enormous log fire blazing
against one wall. Blinking tears from his eyes, Bricriu
suddenly realized that a tall, elegant woman, carrying a tiny
child in her arms was approaching the door. The small man
scuttled back into the shadows, trying to make out her
features, wondering why Fergus had lied. Why had he said
it was a ruined fort inhabited only by an old woman? He slid
his knife from its sheath.

'Put the knife away.' The imperious voice was used to
command. 'Aaah, it's Bricriu ... I know you, Bricriu,' the
woman said, her voice vaguely familiar. 'Why are you
skulking there in the shadows. Come in the light, so that I
may see you clearly.'

The small dark man straightened slowly, reluctantly
sheathing his knife, but keeping his hand on his belt.

'You have no need to fear me,' the woman said.

'Fergus said that this was an abandoned fort inhabited by
an old woman.'

'And what do you see?' the woman asked.

'I see a palace.'

The woman nodded, and the child in her arms moved
slightly. 'You see what you want to see. You take from this
place what you bring to it. Fergus is a simple man, without
greed, without covetousness. That coloured what he
expected to see. He was expecting to find nothing more
than a ruined fort in any case ... and that is what he found.
His intellect told him that such a fort would be occupied by
an aged crone ... and that is what he saw. But you, Bricriu,
you expected to find here a place of magic and mystery, a

fort filled with hidden wealth ... and that is what you found.'

'Who are you?' Bricriu asked, moving closer to the woman, squinting against the blinding light.

'Surely you know me, Bricriu?'

The small man started to shake his head and then turned as hooves rattled on the stone road, and Fergus, with Conor and the rest of the troop, rode down the ancient track that led to the fort. Turning away, he went to meet the king.

'I'm told it's nothing but an ancient woman living in a ruined fort,' Conor said, drawing Bricriu to one side.

'Yes ... and no, lord. It's more than that. Fergus saw only a ruined fort; I looked upon it and saw a palace. There is magic here, lord, be careful, powerful magic. The crone that Fergus saw is a beautiful young woman. She knew me and Fergus by name and there is something tantalizing about her voice. She is carrying what looks like a babe in her arms, but if she is a witch, then it could just as easily be her familiar.'

The king turned to look at the shining fort. Light was now seeping through every crack and cranny, long slivers and darts of light piercing the night. 'And the golden birds we saw ...?'

'I haven't had time to look for them, lord, but if they're anywhere to be found, then they're here.' His hand closed into a tight fist. 'I can almost taste the magic in the air.'

Conor walked toward the fort. Amergin and Fergus were standing before the woman, talking quietly to her. His suspicious nature aroused, Conor hurried to join them, determined to hear what the Sidhe woman had to say.

Striding up to the woman, blinking furiously as the light blinded him, he could only vaguely make out her features.

'I am Conor, King of Ulster,' he began.

'I know who you are,' the woman interrupted him.

'I understand you have agreed to allow us shelter in your fort this night.'

'I would be a poor sister indeed, if I were to refuse my own brother shelter!'

Even as she was speaking the light behind the woman was fading ... and Conor and his troop found they were looking at the missing Dechtire. As they watched, the fifty missing women also appeared from out of the shadows behind the woman. Finally, Moriath stepped up to join her mistress. She took the child from Dechtire's hands and passed it across to Conor. 'Behold your nephew, Conor. This is Setanta, son of god and mortal woman! Behold a hero!'

CHAPTER SEVEN
The Fostering

'It is easy to say now that I knew, from the moment I first set eyes on the babe, that his fame would live on and echo down the years. Many have said this, claiming that they recognized the aura of power that clung to the boy, and perhaps they are telling the truth, for as he grew his extraordinary talents became obvious. But I doubt if any of those who stood before Dechtire in the Sidhe fort on that night realized that they were standing in the presence of greatness. If they claim otherwise, then they are liars. I am Amergin the mage; I have no need to lie, and let any man who doubts my word stand before me now and say it to my face. From the very beginning, from the moment I first saw the child who would one day become the hero Cuchulain, I knew that he was destined for greatness.

'I have the Sight: I can see the power that flows from all living creatures.

'And the light radiating from that tiny babe was blinding ...'

By morning the euphoria had worn off and Conor rode back to Emain Macha in a foul temper. He had found his sister and the missing women, and that in itself was a great coup, but what had he actually found: he had discovered that the

51

woman who had been missing for a year had borne a child – a fine, strong-looking boy, it is true – but a boy nonetheless that had been born out of wedlock. Dechtire claimed that the god Lugh was the boy's father ... but Conor knew that she was only saying that because she thought it might get her and her bastard son better treatment at court. The woman was still married to Sualtim ... what was he going to say when he discovered that his virgin bride had been despoiled and had birthed a child?

He had attempted to reason with her late last night, as the troop had eaten and drunk their fill from the feast which had been prepared and made ready for them. He had asked her about that too, but all she would say was that it was a gift from the boy's father, which only reinforced his opinion that some petty chieftain had fathered the child. He had suggested – quite reasonably too, he thought – that perhaps Dechtire should claim that the child belonged to one of her maids. But Dechtire had refused. Conor had then suggested that their elder sister Fionnchaomh, who had been married for several years and had borne three sons, might take the child for her own. Again Dechtire had refused. There was no shame in bearing a god's child, she had said proudly, and then turned and walked away.

Conor was worried about what his mother was going to say.

Ness's face, which was capable of masking all of her emotions and thoughts, was a study in rage. She had spent her whole life scheming and plotting to place her son on the throne, to place herself in a position where she was, in effect, the virtual ruler of the most powerful kingdom in Erin. And she wasn't going to see it all come crumbling down around her now. No stupid girl, and no ill-born whelp was going to stand in the way of her ambition.

Ness didn't care about the child; the child was an

unfortunate mistake. What she was more concerned about was Sualtim's reaction. She needed the chieftain, his men and their loyalty to keep her son on the throne. Maeve, Queen of Connaught, was watching Ulster with envious eyes and Ness knew that, sooner or later, the western queen would look on Ulster with more than a speculative gaze. And Maeve was ruthless in her ambition: that was probably why Ness respected her so much.

There was movement behind her as, one by one, her children and their chief advisers filed into the room. Ness would have preferred to keep this within the family, but unfortunately too many people knew of it already, including Bricriu Poison-tongue; undoubtedly, he was already taking great delight in spreading salacious tales around the fort. Or perhaps not. His evil nature was tempered with a highly developed sense of self-preservation.

Taking a deep breath, Ness turned away from the window. She was momentarily surprised by the amount of people in the small room.

'Why did we not hold this discussion in the Great Hall?' she asked sarcastically.

'Why did we have to hold it here in the first place, mother?' Dechtire asked quickly. Ness was surprised to find that Sualtim was standing behind the woman, his face set in a grim mask.

'We are here to discuss your shame,' Ness snapped.

'I have brought no shame to this house,' Dechtire said proudly. 'Instead you should be proud of me. I am the chosen of Lugh, and he has gifted me – and thus the whole kingdom of Ulster – with a child, a hero.'

'So you say.'

'Are you doubting me, mother?' Dechtire asked quickly.

'It would be unwise to call my wife a liar,' Sualtim said suddenly, startling them all.

Ness looked around, confused. She had expected the old chieftain to be enraged and she had been prepared to react accordingly, but ...

Amergin, the ancient druid, stepped forward. The old man's eyes were sparkling and, when he reached out and placed his hand on the babe's head, there was a reverence in his touch. 'This is the son of a god,' he said simply. 'I can feel the power that flows from his body.'

'We have come here today, mother, to decide the boy's guardianship,' Dechtire said. 'Lugh himself told me that the boy was destined for greatness. He must be taught by the best of the men of Erin, he must be made proficient in all the arts and crafts that make a warrior great.'

Ness looked from face to face, startled by the extent of the opposition. Events had moved too quickly. She had been prepared to shame and humiliate her daughter and dispose of the child to one of the serving wenches or, failing that, to a niece or cousin, so that it could be raised in comparative comfort. Now, she was faced with some of the most powerful nobles in Erin – Morand the Judge, Amergin the Druid, Sencha the Poet – and her husband, Fergus, Conor and Sualtim. She had a feeling that all she had worked to achieve, the power she had craved and coveted – and achieved – was subtly altered this day. She would never again be as powerful.

'You have obviously reached a decision,' she snapped. 'Indeed, that decision would seem to have been made before you came to me. I'm not even sure why you're here.'

'You are the child's grandmother,' Dechtire said with a tight, bitter smile and, in that instant, her face resembled her mother's. 'It is the grandmother's place to advise upon the child's training and education.'

Ness's twisted smile matched her daughter's. There was a game being played here. She was sure Dechtire didn't want her advice ... and she was equally certain that she wasn't going to give it either. 'Since this child is the son of a god and mortal woman,' she said slowly, 'perhaps it would be better if wiser minds than mine were to pass judgement.' She looked at the ancient judge; 'Morand, what would you advise?' she asked. When she saw her daughter's triumphant smile, she realized she had fallen into the trap Dechtire had prepared for her.

The old man ran his fingers through his snow-white beard. 'It would be better if the boy were to be treated as a normal youth,' Morand began. 'If he is truly god-touched then his special qualities will soon make themselves apparent. When he has come of age and when there are clearer indications of his talents, for all I can see now is a newborn babe,' he added with a toothless smile, 'then let him be trained by the best men in Erin.' The stooped old man turned to look around the room. 'There is no wiser man in Erin than Amergin: let him teach him wisdom. Sencha is the greatest of poets: let him instruct the boy in the lore and legend of our land. Fergus is the most loyal and courageous of men; let him instruct his grandson in these qualities. And I', he added modestly, 'will teach him patience, foresight and judgement.' He bowed to the king and then turned to look at Ness. 'That is my judgement.'

'And what about me?' Sualtim demanded. 'Am I not to be included in your list?'

The old judge smiled. 'Yours is the most important task of all, Sualtim. You must raise this child as your own; teach him what you have learned, so that when the time comes, the experiences and knowledge of these others will find a fertile ground to grow and flourish.'

The warrior stepped back, nodding in agreement.

'Then it is finished,' Dechtire said, coming to her feet, walking towards the door.

'Tell me,' Ness said suddenly, 'have you named this child yet?'

Dechtire looked back over her shoulder, her eyes sparkling. 'Lugh said he should be called Setanta ... though that is not the name he will be remembered by,' she added.

'What will history call him?' Ness asked, rising to her feet and approaching the cloth-wrapped child, which she hadn't looked at yet.

'The gods themselves will decide that,' Dechtire said, turning and walking without allowing her mother the opportunity to look at the babe.

CHAPTER EIGHT

The Boy Setanta

'As the boy grew up, I was concerned that Sualtim, my husband, would not be able to treat Setanta as he would a natural son. I grew even more fearful when I discovered that I was barren after the birth of the boy. Those who love the gods must give much of themselves.

'But I, who had resented my marriage to the aged chieftain, grew to love the old man, when I discovered that he never resented not having sons of his own loins to carry on his name, and that he had found a place in his heart for the boy, Setanta ...'

Sualtim loved the boy Setanta. And no one was more surprised than he was. At times he imagined that perhaps Lugh, the boy's father, might have cast a spell on him, to make him care for the boy, but he liked to think that his feelings for the boy were natural. It was also true that Setanta was a boy that would make any father proud.

The old warrior was equally surprised to find that he had actually fallen in love with Dechtire.

He had accepted the young woman as his right when Ness had offered her daughter in return for his loyalty, but he had no feeling for the girl then: indeed, he had never even set eyes on her until the day before they were due to be married. Though he had often thought about marriage as he advanced in years, there had never seemed to be either the time or the opportunity to wed. And then the offer had come from Ness. It had come at the right time: after years of wandering and selling his sword to the highest bidder, Sualtim had settled and decided to raise a clan about himself, hiring others to do what he had formerly done himself. He had observed that it was the chieftains who lived to become old men, not the warriors.

This marriage suited him. It brought him closer to the throne: closer to the heart of things. There were dangers of course: in the land of the Britons if a king was deposed, often his entire family – including brothers and sisters and their families – were slain, simply to remove a focus for rebellion at a future date. But the aged warrior hadn't survived so long without learning some lessons: and the greatest lesson he had learned was when to fight and when to run. And being close to the throne meant that he would have plenty of warning of impending danger, for the king's network of spies was widespread and there were few courts which didn't conceal a king's man. So Sualtim had weighed up the pros and cons and decided that the advantages to being the brother-in-law of the king of Ulster far outweighed the disadvantages.

For a few brief days his future had been assured ... and then his wife had been stolen on their wedding night, and everything had fallen apart. He had been too drunk at the time to even notice, and it wasn't until early the following morning that he had awoken to the cries of consternation as the women were discovered to be missing. It was initially assumed that they had been kidnapped – possibly by Maeve of Connaught – but when the women's clothing was discovered in numerous bundles around the room, another explanation was looked for. Amergin the

Druid had smelt the stink of ancient magic in the air and Sualtim had been somewhat mollified: what could a mortal man do against magic? A warrior was expected to fight man and beast: he was not expected to fight a god's power. He was also more than a little relieved that he hadn't found himself in a situation where he was forced to wage war on Maeve: that was tantamount to suicide.

And if the truth were only known, Sualtim was not entirely displeased to find himself married but without a wife. He enjoyed the privileges of being close to the throne, without the disadvantages of a wife. From the little he had seen of Dechtire, he remembered her as being a pretty, but shrewish young woman. And all he had to do was to look at Ness to realize how she would look in ten years' time; nor was he arrogant or stupid enough to think that he would not be manipulated in the same way that Fergus had been used by Ness. Many men chose to mock Fergus, but these tended to be the younger, unmarried men, who had yet to experience a woman's wiles. Only a fool thought himself above a woman's stratagems.

He had patiently bided his time, waiting a year before bringing his complaint back to Conor: he had given his support to the king in return for a position of honour and a bride. Conor had enjoyed all the advantages of Sualtim's support ... but Sualtim had received nothing in return. The old warrior hadn't been expecting Conor to agree to go in search of the missing women, he had been quite prepared to trade for cattle or gold.

Sualtim had been surprised and confused when Dechtire had returned with a child, whom she claimed was the son of Lugh. He didn't know how to react. If his wife had borne the child of another man, he knew he would have taken both their heads to avenge the insult to his honour and set them on stakes over his fort as an example. But then Amergin had spoken to him, and the druid had only added to his confusion. The ancient druid had pointed out that Sualtim had, in fact, been honoured by the god because Lugh had chosen his wife to carry a child. Amergin had pointed out that it was a unique honour, and that the child of such a union would be blessed indeed.

And when Dechtire had returned she had been different. But then all the legends said that it was not possible to go into the Otherworld and return unchanged. She was gentler, she seemed more caring, almost loving, and the son she brought with her, the boy Setanta, was all that a man could ask for in a son. He also bore a startling resemblance to Sualtim – with the same fiery red hair, the same grass-green eyes – so that he could so easily pass for the warrior's natural child.

And in truth, from the moment Sualtim had laid eyes on the boy, he was lost.

Even as a very young boy, Setanta showed himself different from the other children in the fort. He was faster, stronger, quicker than any of them, but he was also quiet, attentive and, when Fergus or Amergin came to talk to the child, he listened to them with an attentiveness that went far beyond his years. Though he had never been told that Sualtim was not his natural father, the old warrior guessed that the boy must have heard the stories, but he never asked, never questioned. If the boy had a fault, it was his temper, which though it rarely surfaced was savage and unpredictable. Because of the boy's strength and speed it often took two adults to control him.

Sualtim guessed that by the time Setanta had reached his tenth year, he would be a worthy opponent for any man: he was wrong. By the time Setanta had reached his eighth summer only the strongest or most cunning of warriors would go up against him in games or at training. The boy was still often defeated at this time, but only because of his inexperience. With proper training they all knew he would be invincible.

Sualtim walked across the plain of Muiritheme with Setanta by his side. The boy was eight summers old, but looked and acted older. Sualtim guessed that he might pass for a boy of twelve or fourteen summers.

It was close to the turn of the year. The days were shortening and the forests that surrounded Muiritheme had already turned gold and bronze. With the sun slanting low across the horizon, casting long shadows out across the scorched grass, washing their red hair and beards to blood-red, bronzing their already golden skin, the man and boy looked almost like brothers.

Setanta stopped and looked into the sun, shading his eyes from its glare. 'I've heard it said that if one were to look into the sun then one would see Lugh, the Lord of Light.'

Sualtim nodded slowly. He was not an especially religious man: he followed the observances, believed in them without question, but was also mindful that he had never seen or heard anything that he could not put a natural explanation on. Except the boy.

'I've also heard it said that Lugh is my father,' Setanta added gently, not looking at the older man.

Sualtim shaded his eyes and stared at the bronze ball. 'So I've heard,' he said gently. 'I've also heard that if one were to look into the sun too long then one would go blind,' he added.

Setanta looked at him quickly, not sure how to interpret the ambiguous answer.

The boy and man stood in silence for a time and then Sualtim said, 'What do you want to know?'

'The truth.'

'I don't know the truth,' the old warrior said gently. 'I raised you as my son ...'

Setanta reached up and squeezed the old man's fingers tightly. 'You are the only father I have ever known. You are my father,' he said fiercely. 'Amergin has taught me that the only truth is the truth which lies within. He showed me how to look beyond the surface, to see the deeper meaning, and to trust to intuition and what he calls the natural understanding that all men have, but which only few use.'

Sualtim nodded. 'Amergin is one of the wisest men in Erin. I don't profess to understand all he says, but I will accept what he says without question.' He attempted a smile. 'So what does all this understanding tell you.'

'It tells me that you have loved me as a son.'

'I have.'

'So no matter what you tell me now, father, it will have no influence on how I regard you.'

Sualtim squatted down until his head was on a level with the boy's. He put both hands on his shoulders and looked into his grass-green eyes. 'Ask me what you will.'

'Tell me the story of my birthing.'

Sualtim shrugged. 'In truth I don't know. I'm sure you heard how your mother was taken by the god Lugh into the Otherworld. She stayed with him in Brugh na Boinne, where she conceived you. And I have never blamed her for it,' Sualtim added quickly. 'For what mortal can resist a god?' he asked with a smile. 'When she returned to this world, she had just given birth to you.'

Setanta nodded. 'That's what I heard. Did Lugh never say what was to be my destiny?'

'No, every man must find his own destiny. But I think that yours must surely be great.'

'What would you advise me to do?'

'I have taught you all that I can. Perhaps it is time for you to continue your training.'

'How? Where?'

'Go to Emain Macha. Seek out your uncle, Conor. He has a duty to you. But be careful of him; he is wily and dangerous. If he can avoid his obligations to you, then he will. You must put him in a position where he cannot afford to ignore you, where he is forced to recognize you as a relative.'

'How will I do that?' Setanta asked.

'You are the son of a god. You will think of something.'

CHAPTER NINE
To Emain Macha

'I have listened to the bards tell the tales of how my nephew Setanta came to Emain Macha. And I have listened to the multitude of stories that abound about Setanta's life and deeds. Perhaps because Setanta's deeds are wondrous, it is necessary to make everything he did seem magical. I have heard for example, that he came to my court with a dozen heads on his chariot, but that is simply not true.

'Why is it, I wonder, that those who accept the more fabulous deeds – some of which are so outrageous as to be nearly an insult to the listener – find it difficult to comprehend or believe the tale of the first time the boy Setanta came to court ...?'

'The man is often the mirror of the boy. You can tell the type of warrior a man will become by the way he plays as a boy,' Conor said slowly to no one in particular. He was more than a little drunk.

Fergus, who was standing alongside the king, nodded absently. He ran his forearm across his forehead, wiping off the sweat. Both men were standing beneath the shade of a copse of old oak trees and, though the trees provided some shelter from the blistering sun, the intense heat sapped strength and energy. The druids were calling this the warmest summer in living memory, and opinions were divided between those who claimed it was a gift from the gods and those who claimed the gods were displeased.

The two men were watching a game of hurley being played by twenty-two of the young princes and nobles in the fort. Two teams of eleven boys, each with a curved hurley stick, attempted to manoeuvre a ball past the other team's keeper. Conor and Fergus looked at the young boys almost enviously, remembering the days when they had had the energy to run and play without heeding the weather.

'That one ...' Conor raised an arm and pointed to a tall, stocky boy, a particularly aggressive player, who pushed and shoved his way through the opposition, using his hurley stick as a weapon, hacking legs, ankles and shins as he brushed past. 'That one now. There's a future fine warrior.'

Fergus disagreed. 'He's not a good team player. He keeps the ball to himself and he relies too heavily on his brute strength to carry him through. A more skilful player will take the ball from there ... just like that!' He pointed as a smaller, slimmer boy snatched the ball out from under the bigger youth's feet.

Conor grunted in disappointment. He had never been a great hurley player as a young man, and he had the greatest of respect for those who could handle the small hard ball, deftly manoeuvring it along on the curved stick. He drank some more wine, grimacing because it had become warm and bitter. When he turned back to the game he noticed that it had stopped. Shading his eyes against the sun's harsh glare, he asked Fergus, 'What's wrong?'

His stepfather shook his head. 'I don't know. I'm not sure. There seems to be another boy on the pitch.'

'Who is it?' Conor demanded querulously. 'Why have they stopped the game?'

Fergus shook his head again. 'I don't know. They seem to be arguing with the newcomer.'

Conor squinted into the distance. 'Which one is he?'

'The boy with the bright-red hair.'

The discussion over, the boys resumed their game and the newcomer went to stand on the opposite side of the field.

'Ah, they're starting again ...,' the king began, when the game dissolved into chaos as the slender red-haired boy raced across the field, caught up the ball on his hurley and wove his way through the crowd. He was at least twenty paces from the keeper, who was standing between two trees, when he fired the ball right between the boy's legs.

Fergus nodded in approval.

The keeper struck the ball a terrific blow, sending it practically to the other end of the field, but the red-haired boy had reached it before it struck the ground. Two bigger, older boys crowded in on him, but he twisted past the first and shouldered the second aside, sending him crashing to the ground. He struck the small black ball high into the air, gauging the angle perfectly so that the keeper had to look up into the sun, and was temporarily blinded. The ball dropped down directly behind the keeper and rolled between the trees.

'He's good, whoever he is,' Conor said, sipping the tepid wine again, not tasting it this time though.

Singly and in groups, people began to wander down from the fort as word of the red-haired player's prowess spread. The boy raced from one end of the field to the other, tackling the twenty-two players, putting balls past each of the two keepers in turn. His skill, speed and strength were phenomenal and, though he was only one against twenty-two, none of the others – either singly or as a team – could stand against him. And as the crowd gathered on the sidelines began to cheer the red-haired boy, so did the other players' frustration turn to anger. The large, aggressive boy whom Conor had remarked upon earlier struck the red-haired boy across the shoulders with his hurley, felling him to the ground. He then stood over the fallen boy and planted his foot on his chest. But the smirk on his face turned to a howl of pain as the fallen boy caught and twisted his leg, sending him sprawling. The red-haired boy surged to his feet, dragged the other boy off the ground and then struck him a single blow to the forehead which rendered him unconscious.

Now the rest of the boys surged in, hurley sticks flailing, but the red-haired youth held his own, using their own numbers against them, quickly winnowing through the group, knocking half a dozen unconscious, removing another dozen from the mêlée with bruised fingers and bloodied knees. Now only four of the older, more experienced boys remained, and these circled warily around the red-haired youth, who didn't even seem to be breathing heavily.

'Stop it, stop it quickly before someone is killed,' Conor commanded, 'and bring the boy to me.'

Fergus raced across the field followed by two of Conor's personal guard. The four boys were closing in on the stranger and now they had knives in their hands. All the red-haired boy had was his hurleystick. Fergus grabbed the nearest boy and flung him backwards. A blow to the side of the head sent another sprawling, while the guards grabbed the remaining two boys, knocking the knives from their hands. To raise a blade against an unarmed opponent was considered disgraceful.

When the red-haired youth turned to look at Fergus, the old man was somehow unsurprised to discover that it was his stepdaughter's god-born son, Setanta.

'What are you doing here?' he asked stupidly, standing in the centre of the field strewn with groaning and weeping boys.

'Sualtim told me that I would have to do something to get Conor's attention. Will this do?' Setanta asked innocently.

'It'll do,' Fergus nodded. 'Come and meet your uncle.'

Conor greeted the boy warmly enough until he learned his name and lineage. He had had little enough to do with his sister in the years since her return with the child from Brugh na Boinne. Ness had conspired to poison his mind against her and, in truth, he feared the boy she had borne. Perhaps he was the son of a god; if he was, then that in itself was reason enough to fear him, but even if he wasn't, then he was still too close to the throne for comfort. When the boy had reached manhood, what was to say that he would not turn his envious gaze upon Conor's throne? As the king's nephew, there were bound to be some that would follow his banner.

'Why have you come to Emain Macha?' Conor asked.

The red-haired, green-eyed boy stared into the King's pale grey eyes. 'I am claiming no more than is my right,' he said proudly, his voice echoing across the now silent field. 'My mother is the Princess Dechtire. I am due the training and education as befits a prince.'

Conor fidgeted uncomfortably. He was aware that the crowd which had gathered to watch the boy on the playing field now stood around, watching him intently, and he knew that if he were to deny him his right, he would have to have a very good reason.

Secretly enjoying his stepson's discomfiture, Fergus leaned forward. 'Better to have him at court where you can watch him than to send him back to Muiritheme angry and upset. You've seen what he could do against a far superior force. You want this boy as a friend – not as a foe.'

Conor nodded slowly. What Fergus was saying made sense ... and besides, if he were at court, away from his family, a serious accident could always befall him.

Watching the smile that twisted Conor's thin lips, Fergus knew what the king was thinking. 'It's agreed then?' he asked quickly.

'Agreed. The boy can stay.'

Fergus stretched to his full height and called for silence, his powerful voice echoing across the field, the heavy atmosphere robbing it of all inflection. 'We are honoured today to be joined by our king's nephew, Setanta, son of Dechtire, the king's own sister. We have seen that he has all the makings of a mighty warrior, and so we have agreed to train him in all manner of the martial and physical arts. Will any here undertake to further this boy's education?' he added quickly.

Even as Conor came to his feet, realizing what Fergus had done, Cathbad the Druid had stepped forward and rested his tiny hand on the boy's shoulder. 'I will teach Setanta all I know,' he said simply, his coal-black eyes darting from Fergus to Conor, as if reading their emotions.

Setanta turned to look at the man who stood no taller than himself. He bowed deeply. 'I am honoured to have been chosen by you. All Erin knows your name.'

The druid squeezed Setanta's shoulder with surprising strength. 'The honour is mine, Setanta. Soon, the whole world will know your name,' he promised.

CHAPTER TEN

The Naming

'When the boy Setanta came to me for training, I looked into the stars and read the oracles, as I did for all my pupils. Some had particular talents or skills that lay hidden and had not manifested themselves. Once I had established the nature of those skills, I could develop them.

'But, though the destiny of every man is written in the stars, I was puzzled because I could never find Setanta's place amongst them. Indeed, even the name didn't feature in my oracles.

'Confused and troubled, I wondered if my skill was leaving me as I grew into my dotage, for my horoscopes were always accurate.

'It wasn't until Setanta had his encounter with Culain the Smith's great dog that all became clear to me ...'

As the seasons changed, Setanta changed from a boy to a young man, and even Conor, who hadn't wanted him at court and had considered removing him, grew to admire the handsome, fearless youth. Cathbad, the tiny druid, instructed him in Erin's lore and legends, Sencha the Poet taught him the poetry and lays that told of Erin's heroes, heroines and history, while his uncle Fergus taught him weaponcraft and fighting skills, until the boy, who had not yet passed his twelfth summer, could best the cunning old warrior.

Soon it became a matter of pride for Conor to acknowledge Setanta as his nephew. He started taking him everywhere he went, as an example of the training and skills taught at Emain Macha. Having seen Setanta, some of the princes and nobles who had traditionally remained neutral in the struggle for kingship and thus avoided the court, sent their sons to Emain Macha for training. This not only ensured Conor an income, but also guaranteed that their fathers wouldn't move against the court while their sons were training there. It had also been proven that a warrior who had trained at a particular court made friends and allegiances there, and would be unlikely to side against it in a future conflict.

Once a year, Conor made a point of visiting the craftsmen who serviced Emain Macha: the carpenters, smiths, masons, potters, armourers. Ness had taught him that these were just as important to a fort's survival as the warriors who manned the walls, or the cooks who fed the same warriors.

Conor rode out with a dozen chariots on a morning close to the end of the warm season. The bite of the Cold Months was in the air and the trees had turned brown and golden in anticipation of the long sleep. The distant mountains were already capped with snow and the druids were warning that this would be a harsh winter.

Setanta was playing hurley in the long field behind the fort. As usual he played alone against a team of eleven and sometimes fifteen other boys, and such was his skill and speed that he had never yet lost a game.

The boys gathered into a line as the chariots stopped at the edge of the field and Conor raised his hand to Setanta. 'It is time to pay our respects to Culain the Smith. You should come.'

Setanta looked from Conor to the youths. 'You go on, uncle, I will finish this game and follow.'

'You don't know the way,' Conor smiled.

Setanta shrugged. 'I can follow your tracks and put some of that fieldcraft Fergus has taught me into practice.'

The king smiled. 'As you wish, but don't linger too long. There's a storm coming in. And a chill or fever will slay a warrior as surely as an enemy's spear.'

'Another goal or two at the most,' Setanta smiled.

Conor looked at the faces of the boys and nodded agreement. He knew it was a simple thing to allow these boys to continue playing on, but he had learned enough from his mother over the years to understand that it was with such small things that great kings were made. Maybe in later years these boys would remember him as a kind and generous man who had allowed them to continue their game. 'Another two goals,' he conceded. 'Then follow on as soon as you can.'

'I will, uncle,' Setanta said, already turning away, tossing the ball high in the air. Two goals then ... and maybe another two after that ...

The evening had drawn in before Setanta finished the game and suddenly remembered that he was supposed to follow Conor to Culain's fort. The wind coming in from the north was chill, flecked with rain and the promise of the storm to come. Setanta thought about heading back to Emain Macha and finding some warmer clothes, but, realizing that he had lingered too long already, set off in the direction Conor and his troop had gone. To keep himself warm, he batted the ball high into the air and raced after it, attempting to catch it before it hit the ground again.

Culain's fort lay to the south and west of Emain Macha. It was relatively easy to follow the tracks of the chariots and horses even in the fading light ... until the rains came down. Thunder rumbled almost directly overhead and the heavens opened, the sudden deluge churning the earth to mud, instantly obliterating all signs and tracks. Lightning flickered and the boy made the Sign of Horns with his fore and little fingers, wondering what had angered the gods and roused them to such a fury. The rain came down in a solid sheet, reducing visibility almost to nothing, forcing him to seek shelter beneath a broad-leafed bush, knowing the dangers of standing under a tree. It was dry in the heart of the bush, and he waited patiently while the thunder boomed and crashed overhead and the lightning crackled across the skies. A tree close-by was struck by the god's spear, torn apart like a length of cloth, sparks and flames shooting upwards, only to be immediately doused by the deluge. That was the only time the boy felt even the whisper of fear. But he knew that the gods wouldn't take his life that day in this way: from the little he knew of his background, he was aware that he was destined for greatness. Dropping his chin on to his chest, he closed his eyes and fell into a light doze.

It was night by the time the storm passed over, and Setanta emerged from the bush cold and shivering. He knew he should return to Emain Macha, but he felt almost honour-bound to continue on after the king. If he didn't turn up what would Conor say: that Setanta had been frightened off by a little thunder and lightning?

Following the tracks was much more difficult now. The storm had cleansed the earth, and the wind and heavy rain had disturbed the disposition of the leaves, branches and tall grasses, all of which would have given him clues to the direction Conor and the troop had gone. Setanta stood in the centre of a muddy track, listening to the night sounds, the hiss and rustle of animals moving stealthily through the undergrowth, the creaking of branches and rattle of leaves. Tonight the usual night sounds included the musical addition of the dripping and plinking of the rain off the leaves. The boy knew they had been heading south and west, so he set off through the undergrowth, using the few scattered stars to guide him. The wind was blowing from that direction ... and that gave him his first clue. Born and raised in the countryside, Setanta was sensitive to the odours of the countryside; his sense of smell had not yet become blunted by the odours of living close to a fort. So Sualtim had taught him how to develop that sense, how to track animals by their scent. Setanta knew the odours of fox and deer, elk and boar.

And man.

And faint and foul on the fresh night air was the unmistakable odour of too many men crammed together in one spot.

Moving more quickly now, confident of his destination, Setanta followed the course, climbing a tall tree only once to confirm his suppositions, when the wind shifted, carrying away all traces of a scent. He spotted the lights of a fort atop a distant hilltop. It could only be Culain's.

Setanta slowed as he neared Culain's fort. The Smith was a powerful warrior and chieftain in his own right. His knowledge and skill in the forging of weapons gave him authority and ensured that he was respected. His skill had also made him wealthy, and his own troops were counted amongst the best in Erin ... and they were certainly better armed and armoured than most other troops.

Culain's fort was perched atop a hilltop. It was a solidly constructed building of wood and stone, with the majority of buildings roofed with thick slabs of turf. The entire fort was ringed by a palisade of tall, sharpened stakes. The ground around the fort had been cleared of trees and vegetation so that it was virtually impossible to approach too closely to the fort without being spotted by the sentries ... except that Setanta with his sharp eyesight and acute hearing could neither see nor hear anyone. Nor were there any sounds of revelry coming from within the fort, and the boy suddenly looked to the sky, gauging the position of the moon and stars. There were clouds scudding quickly across the sky, but, judging from the position of the few stars he could see, he guessed that it was very late indeed. Thunder rumbled threateningly in the distance.

Gripping his hurley stick tightly, moving as quietly as possible, Setanta neared the fort. Should he walk boldly up to the main gate ... or approach it stealthily? Both approaches were dangerous. A lone figure boldly approaching a fort at dead of night was suspicious enough: if he were on guard duty, he would immediately come to the conclusion that the figure on the road was a diversion, while others crept around from the opposite direction. Any trained and experienced guard would probably kill the figure and sound the alarm. The alternative was to approach stealthily, but if he were spotted, it would be immediately assumed that he was up to no good and he'd probably end up with a spear in his belly. He could of course spend the night where he was and enter the fort when the gates opened with the dawn. Thunder rumbled again, closer this time, helping him come to a decision. The palisade was about twice the height of a tall man: he should be able to climb it.

Setanta approached the fort cautiously, still puzzled by the apparent lack of guards. But if there weren't obvious guards, then there must be traps of some sort. When he found none, he began to suspect that something was wrong within the fort. Tilting his head back, he smelt the air, concentrating on the individual odours, identifying and then dismissing them from the catalogue of smells he knew. There were human and animal smells aplenty, food, midden and manure odours predominating. He smelt fresh straw, cooking spices, alcohol and turf smoke. But he smelt neither blood nor death on the air.

He was concentrating so intently on the fort that he didn't hear movement in the grass behind him.

Setanta came around the fort, so as to approach it from the side. The clouds were massing from the north, the wind blowing in from this direction also, and he knew that even if there were guards, they would be reluctant to stand with a bitter wind blowing into their eyes. He was surprised to find no pit around the fort, no stakes driven into the ground. He touched the wall of the fort, expecting to find it polished smooth without hand or foot hold, but the logs were rough hewn, tree-trunks still bearing the stumps of branches. The only reason for such stupidity, Setanta reasoned, was magic. The fort was obviously protected by some powerful spell ...

Even as the thought crossed his mind, he heard the scrabbling behind him. Instinct drove him down and to one side – just as a beast crashed into the wall where he'd been standing. Setanta used the slope of the hill to roll rapidly away from the wall and the creature. He came quickly to his feet and faced the beast.

With the clouds scudding across the sky, it was impossible to make out details, but he formed the impression of a long-haired, four-footed creature, with a narrow head, which was on a level with his. Rows of white teeth gleamed in the starlight. The beast padded towards the boy, moving completely silently now. When it was still at least fifteen paces away from him, it leapt, powerful muscles carrying it up and forward. Setanta threw himself *towards* the creature, rolling beneath it, coming to his feet behind the beast. The creature stumbled, confused by the sudden disappearance of its prey. As it turned, lightning flashed overhead, illuminating the beast for an instant: it was a dog, an enormous hunting-dog, the biggest Setanta had ever seen. There was a thick spiked collar around its neck and a similarly spiked leather jerkin across its back. Its teeth were massive, its eyes a dull sulphurous yellow. Dropping low on its belly, it crept towards the boy.

Setanta backed away from the beast. He knew he couldn't outrun it, nor could he hope to dodge it indefinitely. He was unarmed except for the knife on his belt and the hurley stick in his hand. But this creature would snap through the stick and the knife would probably slide off its leather-covered hide.

Thunder boomed again, but the beast didn't even flinch. In the split second that the lightning seared across the sky, the beast leapt, jaws gaping.

Setanta had guessed that the beast would jump with the lightning, muscles and nerves reacting to the sudden light. In the instant the lightning flared it would be momentarily blinded. He would only have one chance: in the instant before the lightning cracked, he tossed the hurley ball high into the air. His timing was perfect: the lightning painted the night in sharp black and white at the precise moment he struck the ball with the hurley stick. The ball struck the huge dog in its gaping mouth, smashing through teeth before erupting outwards through the back of its skull. The dog was dead before it hit the ground at Setanta's feet.

At that moment the fort came to life. Light lanced out into the night as the fort's gates were thrown open and a dozen chariots followed by fifty armed men raced out into the night.

The first chariot skidded to a halt before Setanta and Conor jumped out, ashen-faced, into the flickering torch-light. He looked from the boy to the dog and Setanta could see the conflicting emotions race across his face. Conor may have come to accept Setanta, but he would never forget where he came from, and while he remained at court, he was a symbol of the king's disgrace and a focus for any disaffection that might arise amongst the younger nobles. But if anything were to happen to the boy then the allegiance of Sualtim would founder and Lugh himself might move against the king. And no man could stand against a god's wrath.

A tall, brawny man wearing studded armour came running up. He looked from Setanta to the dog and then knelt by the beast and cradled its shattered head in his arms. 'I raised this dog from a pup,' he said thickly. 'I bred its sire and dame, my father bred their sires. For three generations the hounds of Culain have guarded this fort, and with every generation the hound became bigger, stronger, fiercer. And you killed it. How?' he demanded.

Setanta shrugged. 'With a hurley ball.'

Culain the Smith ran his huge hands down the dog's matted coat. 'There is an ancient prophecy that when the hounds of Culain die, then so too will the clan of Culain. You have doomed us, boy.'

Setanta knelt by the Smith. 'Not intentionally.'

'Nevertheless, you have doomed us.'

'Is there no other hound?' Setanta asked.

'A pup, born ten nights past.'

'Then let me be your hound, let me guard your fort until it is raised to maturity.'

'You?' Culain asked, looking from the boy to Conor.

'He did kill your hound,' Conor reminded him.

'So he did. Then this must be the boy Setanta, son of a god and mortal woman.' The Smith nodded. 'You will be my hound, you will be the *cu culain*, the hound of Culain.'

'Cu Culain,' Setanta said quickly. 'Cuchulain, yes, I will guard your fort.' Coming to his feet, he announced to the assembled warriors, 'Setanta died this night. Henceforth, let me be known as Cuchulain, the Hound of Culain!'

CHAPTER ELEVEN

To Take Up Arms

━━━━━━ ♣ ━━━━━━

'While Cuchulain was my pupil, I discovered that he was not perfect, as I imagined that the son of a god would be. He had many faults – he was vain, he was aggressive and often ill-tempered – but these faults only served to emphasize his other qualities, and he could be extraordinarily kind and generous.

'His greatest fault was his impetuosity. He reacted rather than acted, and he was often forced to pay the price.

'He took up arms for example, simply because he had overheard me giving a piece of advice to another pupil. He did not consider the ramifications of what he was doing. But, by doing what he did, he set in place a course of action that was to forever influence not only his own life, but also the future of Erin ...'

In the days and months following his killing of the hound, Cuchulain, as he insisted on being called, patrolled the fields around Culain's fort every night. Thieves and bandits who laughed at the story of a young boy guarding the fort, and who attempted to steal the cattle and corn, quickly discovered that only an extraordinary boy would have been able to defeat the hound. And now that same boy guarded the fort. Stories about the boy grew, enhancing his legend ... especially since he was never seen. During the day

Culain's fort was well guarded by the Smith's own warriors, but at night the guards retired and the mysterious boy took up his duty.

Poachers and cattle rustlers found themselves coming under a hail of fire from slingshots and spears; their traps were destroyed, or they stumbled into traps which had been prepared for them. Occasionally, they were trailed back to their lairs and their own forts and huts were burnt to the ground around them. Rumours spoke of an entire magical army guarding the fort, while others said that there was a boy, but that he wasn't entirely human, he was a half-beast, as his name suggested, one of the were-creatures.

And though Cuchulain spent most of every night guarding the fort, neither his studies nor his training suffered. He excelled in all the martial arts, his knowledge of folklore and history was prodigious and his memory was phenomenal. If he had a fault it was perhaps his uneven temper, which his teachers ascribed to the fiery nature of his unnatural father. Lugh was the Lord of Light and the blazing sun was his symbol. Was it any wonder then that his son burned with a passion that could be as fierce and unrelenting as the sun on a summer's day.

Every morning Cathbad the Druid instructed the class of nobles' sons in the ancient lore of Erin. This was an ancient tradition: if a warrior were to fight for his clan and country, then he should know the customs, history and glories of that clan to be aware of what he was defending. The tiny druid with the coal-black eyes would also instruct the group in signs and portents which were equally important for both warrior and herdsman alike. Though the gods rule the world of men, they rarely interfered, preferring instead to allow man to make his own mistakes and thus learn by them. However, they often left subtle signs for those with the knowledge to understand and interpret them. Knowledge of such signs was considered essential for every educated man. There were days when to venture forth on to the battlefield was tantamount to committing suicide, days when seed sown was sure to flourish, days when the bull could be brought to the cow. If a crow flew left to right across a battlefield, then victory was assured; if it flew in the opposite direction however, then all was lost. A red sky at night promised fair weather on the morrow, a red sky in the morning was a warning that the day would end in rain.

'Every day is full of portents, which the wise man can read and profit from,' Cathbad said.

'And what of today?' one of the young princes asked. 'What are today's portents?'

Cathbad sprinkled green powder on the fire. Blue-green flames flared and danced and the odour of bitter herbs wafted around the long open room.

'If a young man were to take up arms this day then his name would be revered through the land of Erin and beyond for a hundred generations and more.'

The youths laughed amongst themselves.

'However,' Cathbad added with a grim smile, 'though this youth will achieve fame, his span of years will be short upon this earth. Like the fire which blazes brightly, but is quickly consumed, it gives off great heat, but it cannot last too long for it is burnt out by its own fierceness. Better to be like the fire which burns slowly, and last a long time.'

'But there is always the need for a blaze,' Cuchulain said from the back of the group.

Cathbad nodded and smiled. 'Often it is the blaze which starts the fire.' He looked up into the heavens, gauging the time. 'It is close to noon. We shall end our class now. A day like this is too good to waste.' He nodded towards the clouds massing on the horizon. 'And I need no second sight to prophecy that we shall soon have rain.'

♣

Cuchulain found Conor in the stables watching Culain the Smith shoe the horses. The air was heavy with the sweat of horses and men and the metallic tang of burnt metal. Conor nodded to the boy. 'On the day that you take up arms,' he said, 'I will give you the pick of my horses.'

Cuchulain smiled. 'Then the gods must have put the words into your mouth, uncle, for I have decided that I shall take up arms this very day.'

Conor nodded, surprised, but not altogether displeased. The boy was fifteen, already a man in many respects. And when he took up arms, he would no longer be considered a boy – and no longer Conor's responsibility. Whatever happened to him thereafter would be the result of his own actions. 'I am a man of my word. I will honour my promise. You may take your pick of the beasts and chariots in this stable and take your choice of the weapons in the great hall.'

Cuchulain walked down the length of the stables looking at each horse in turn, running his small hands over the beasts, peeling back their lips to examine teeth, staring into their serious eyes. He finally patted two coal-black horses. 'These two.'

It was only with a supreme effort of will that Conor kept his temper. 'They're my personal beasts,' he said through gritted teeth.

'I did not know,' Cuchulain said immediately. 'I'll choose another pair.'

Conor shook his head. 'I made you a promise. I'll keep it. You may keep the beasts.'

As they walked back into Emain Macha's main hall, Conor asked, 'Why did you choose today to take up arms ...?'

'Because Cathbad said it was an auspicious day for a warrior to take up arms and become a man. He said that whosoever took up arms on this day would be remembered for ever.'

The druid stepped out of a doorway before the surprised

pair. His thin face was a mask of anger and despair. 'And I also said,' he hissed, 'that whoever took up arms today would live a short life.'

'I know that,' Cuchulain said, walking past the druid into the great hall which was lined with weapons.

'When you lift a weapon off that wall,' Cathbad warned, coming up behind him, 'you become a man. And your days are numbered from that moment. Think before you act. You are a young man, you could achieve so much. There is a great future ahead of you, if you choose to accept it.'

Conor looked at the druid. 'You know the future. Surely you know what choice he makes?' he asked.

'The future is mutable. There is always choice. I know what the future holds in store if he continues with this course of action. If he changes his mind and makes another decision, then that future will change.'

Cuchulain turned back to look at him. 'And if I take up arms today, will I still not achieve much?'

'You will.'

Cuchulain looked from the druid to his uncle and back again. 'Well then, how should I choose? Should I choose a short life which will be honourable, or a longer, safer life? And if I choose the latter, will I not spend the rest of my days wondering, "What if ..."'

'At least you will have the consolation of having the rest of your days to live,' the druid said curtly. 'Beyond the veil of death, there is only eternal sleep.'

'I don't want to be a fire that smoulders,' Cuchulain said, lifting a short stabbing spear off the wall. 'I want to be the fire that blazes.'

The druid nodded and bowed his head. As he turned away, he added, 'Then have a care, Cuchulain, lest your fire consume all Erin.'

Conor looked at the fifteen-year-old boy. 'Today you have become a man.'

CHAPTER TWELVE
The Bloodying

'The first deeds of a fledgeling warrior were called the bloodying. Such deeds would have repercussions down the years. A warrior who achieved a great or grand bloodying would have gained a reputation that could be enhanced, but if a warrior's bloodying was a poor, ineffectual thing, then it would take him many years to expiate the shame of it.

'Cuchulain's bloodying was magnificent ...'

There were no doubts in Cuchulain's mind. He felt the rightness of the decision. He had no fear of death, for had he not been born in the Otherworld, which some men claimed was one of the places of death? Death was no enemy to be feared; death was every warrior's companion, and if one respected death, then surely one's own death would be all the more peaceful for that. Even though he was still a boy, Cuchulain had heard warriors tell of men who had feared death, feared the loss of all they had achieved. And so they had died without their dignity, squealing and crying their shame. Where was the honour in that? What was there to be afraid of?

No. This was the right decision. A decision that befitted the son of a god. His father's name would be remembered down through the land of Erin for generations to come. Well then, so too would his name: he owed it to his immortal

84

father, and he felt he owed it to his mother and mortal father. They would be proud of him. Of that he was determined.

Cuchulain lifted a short sword off the wall and hefted it in his hand. It felt too light and the balance was wrong. The next weapon was too heavy, but the third was perfect, a light sword with a razor-sharp blade and a hilt long enough for him to wrap both hands around for a two-handed swing.

'This one,' he whispered. He glimpsed the expression on Conor's face. 'Is something amiss?'

'That was my father's sword, aye and mine too ... but no, but no, you chose it, you use it until you find yourself a better weapon.'

Cuchulain turned the sword in both hands, the keen edge cutting the air. 'I doubt if I'll ever find another sword like this.'

Conor smiled in agreement. 'I doubt it.'

'I'll wear it with pride and honour it with blood.'

Conor nodded absently. He had no real interest in the sword; it had been three years since he last held one. 'Now that you are a man, tradition dictates that you must distinguish yourself.'

'How?' Cuchulain asked.

'In the old days a young warrior was expected to bring back his first head taken in battle,' Conor smiled. 'But in these more enlightened times, a trophy of an elk or bear will suffice.'

Cuchulain looked at his uncle and the older man saw a curious change come over the boy's face. His eyes turned glassy as his breathing deepened, and the smile that twisted his lips was anything but pleasant. Without saying another word, he bowed and turned away.

Conor hurried after the boy. 'Where are you going?' he demanded.

'I am going to my bloodying.'

'Now? Immediately?'

'Yes, now.'

'But you're still a boy,' the king protested.

'Today I am a man.'

'You cannot go alone. Ibar, my charioteer will accompany you.'

Cuchulain considered before replying. 'I will allow it. It is fitting that I should have my own charioteer,' he said arrogantly.

'In the past many warriors did not survive the bloodying,' Conor said carefully, raising his hand to attract the charioteer's attention. 'It would be better if you were to take care.'

Cuchulain glanced sidelong at his uncle. There was no doubt in his mind that he would survive.

'Cuchulain has taken up arms this day,' Conor said to Ibar. 'Now he wishes to go in search of a trophy. Take him to the hunting grounds; let him slay a boar or elk.' When Cuchulain had moved out of earshot, he added, 'He is young, impetuous; ensure he comes to no harm, lest we raise the wrath of Lugh. Take him anywhere he wants to go, but do not lead him into danger.'

'What do I do if he orders me to take him some place dangerous, where he might be injured or mortally wounded?'

'Well ... warn him of the possible consequences of his action,' Conor said slowly, and then added with a wry smile, 'But if anything happens to him, then make sure that neither you nor I is involved. And we shall of course hound his murderer to the ground.'

'Of course.' Ibar bowed to his king, schooling his face to a rigid mask. He had been with Conor long enough to realize the implications behind what he was saying. Conor feared Cuchulain, feared what he was, and was terrified by what he might become. If Cuchulain were to have an accident, then Conor would not be unduly upset ... so long as he wasn't involved.

Ibar had heard the stories about this boy Cuchulain. By all accounts, the boy was a prodigy – but he still felt quite insulted that he should have been chosen to look after him. If Cuchulain felt himself man enough to take up arms, then he should be man enough to control his own chariot.

The boy swaggered up, walking with an arrogance that befitted a more seasoned warrior.

'Where to, my lord?' Ibar asked, unable to keep the sarcasm from his voice.

'South and west of here,' Cuchulain said, without even glancing in his direction. He raised his right arm in salute to Conor as they rode out of Emain Macha, and then immediately forgot about the king the moment they rode past.

The day was hot and they were still in sight of the fort when Ibar was coated in sweat. The white dust of the road stuck to his damp flesh, giving him a ghostly appearance. By contrast, only Cuchulain's clothes were touched by the dust. 'Why don't you sweat?' Ibar demanded.

'I am the son of a god,' Cuchulain said simply. 'Are there places hereabouts that you would avoid?' he asked in the same breath.

Ibar nodded. 'There are some tracks I would prefer not to cross.'

'Perhaps you should tell me so I will know what to avoid?'

The charioteer shrugged. 'Conor has rid the lands hereabouts of those who would have opposed him. There are some lordlings who brag and boast, but when put to the test they will stand with Conor, if only because they could not oppose him. They would not stand in the way of a large troop, but a single warrior or a chariot crossing their land might have some difficulties.'

'What about their oaths of fealty to the king?' Cuchulain asked sharply.

'All the lords have sworn fealty to him ... all except the Clan Nechtain,' he added.

'And why is that?' Cuchulain asked.

'They are a proud, strong clan and the three eldest sons, Fothad, Tuathal and Faithleann, jealously guard the family honour and lands, killing all who stray on to their fields.'

'They are fine warriors?' Cuchulain asked.

Ibar nodded. 'Amongst the best in Erin.'

'So, their heads would be accounted a prize indeed, eh?'

Ibar threw back his head and laughed. 'Why – what are you thinking, that you will be the one to take them? I've seen older, wiser, stronger warriors than you will ever be fall before them.'

'Take me there,' Cuchulain demanded.

The charioteer shook his head. 'I will not. Your uncle the king will have my head if any harm befalls you.'

Cuchulain's right arm moved – and suddenly the point of his knife was at Ibar's throat. 'And I will have your head if you do not help me.'

'I could kill you for this,' Ibar said through gritted teeth.

'You could try,' Cuchulain smiled. 'But I don't think you'd succeed,' he said calmly.

For a moment it looked as if Ibar might try, but, looking into the young man's eyes, he saw a dangerous light glittering deep in their depths. And then he realized with a shock that Cuchulain actually wanted him to attack. The boy was keyed up to such a pitch of excitement, his grin a fixed rictus, his lips damp with spittle, that it looked as if a battle frenzy might overtake him at any moment. Ibar turned away, surreptitiously making the Sign of Horns with fore and little fingers to ward off evil. There hadn't been a berserk warrior in Erin for generations, though he knew they were not uncommon in the colder northern climes. He glanced sidelong at the boy; berserkers usually needed to work themselves up into a battle-frenzy. While the frenzy possessed them, they fought with total savagery and were able to take killing blows without feeling any pain. Some of them fought on until their bodies had been hacked to pieces. But Cuchulain didn't need to work himself up into a frenzy; the blood-lust was high in him, rank and bitter on the dry, dusty air. And Ibar, who had thought him no match for the Clan Nechtain, wasn't quite so sure anymore.

As he was turning the chariot, he said softly, soothingly, adopting the same tone he used to calm a maddened horse, 'There is a band of brigands to the south of here; I know where their camp is. Perhaps you would prefer to fight them,' he suggested.

'Take me to the Clan Nechtain,' Cuchulain said, blood foaming on his lips where he had bitten the inside of his cheeks.

They rode in silence for the rest of the journey. Finally, Ibar pulled the chariot to a halt before a narrow wooden bridge that had been built over a fast-flowing stream. On the opposite side of the stream, a long, low, narrow hut had been built close to the trees. The ground before the hut was studded with swords and spears driven into the earth. Atop each weapon was a skull. Some were obviously ancient, while others still bore strips of decaying flesh. Ibar cast an experienced eye across the field of skulls: there were at least a dozen newly taken heads since he'd last seen it. That brought the total to nearly one hundred. No one knew what happened to the rest of the bodies; there were rumours that the three brothers of the Clan Nechtain ate them.

Cuchulain looked calmly at the field of skulls. The battle-light had gone out of his eyes and had been replaced by a cold anger. 'Tell me about this clan,' he said.

'There are three brothers,' Ibar began, 'Fothad, Tuathal and Faithleann. Fothad is the eldest. He is a tremendously strong warrior and he wields a sword carved from a slab of stone. No sword or spear can withstand a blow from it. I've seen it cleave through shields and cut a man in half. He will have to be fought from afar.

'Tuathal is the middle brother. He is cunning indeed. He has trained in most of the martial arts with the greatest warriors of our day. It is said that he can analyse a warrior's style simply from the way he approaches a field of battle, identifying the teacher and hence the tricks and moves that the warrior has been taught. His cunning will have to be matched.

'Faithleann is the youngest of the brothers. He would be about ten years your senior. He will probably want to wrestle and he likes to fight in the water,' Ibar added. 'This stream is chill and its very coldness will rob a warrior of his body heat and strength in a matter of moments. However, Faithleann swims in this river twice a day, at break of day and sunset, and is well used to the water. He also knows the lie of the river and the shape of the riverbed.' Ibar paused and added, 'It is said that they are flesh-eaters.'

Cuchulain, who had been listening intently, glanced back over his shoulder at Ibar. 'Would you have overstated these warriors' prowess just to frighten me?' he asked.

The charioteer shook his head. His lips twisted in a cold smile. 'If anything I have understated their prowess.' His arm swept out, encompassing the field with its bizarre trophies. 'Look around you; you're looking at some of the finest warriors in Erin and Britain. Let that tell its own story.'

Cuchulain looked at the field again and nodded. 'There is obviously much truth in what you say.'

'There is,' Ibar said sarcastically, but Cuchulain didn't react.

'How do I summon the brothers?' the boy asked.

Ibar nodded towards the bridge. 'Walk out there – they will come to you.'

Without another word, Cuchulain strode boldly out on to the bridge. It rattled almost musically as he walked on to the swaying wooden structure, tiny plinking, clacking sounds. Looking over the side, he saw that countless tiny bones – finger bones, toes, pieces of ribs – had been tied on strings beneath the bridge. They clattered together with the movement on the bridge. When the boy looked up again, he saw that three men had appeared from the long wooden hut. Even from a distance, Cuchulain could see the re-markable family likeness: the three brothers were dark-haired, dark-bearded, each wearing a leather kirtle. The eldest of the three brothers approached the bridge. He looked past Cuchulain to glare at Ibar. 'What is the meaning of this, charioteer?'

'This day the boy took up arms and became a man. This is his bloodying.'

Fothad threw back his head and laughed, revealing teeth which had been filed to points. 'There will be a bloodying, aye, but it will be this boy's. Take him away, Ibar. I will not kill him today.'

'I had heard that the Clan Nechtain were great warriors,' Cuchulain said coldly, 'not full of hot wind.'

Fothad looked at Cuchulain and sighed. 'As you wish. If you are so eager to die then let me accommodate you.' He walked back to where his brothers stood. One of them handed him an enormous sword that was a uniform silver-grey in colour. The warrior returned to the bridge, the sword resting across his right shoulder. When he stepped on to the swaying, whispering bridge, he hefted the sword and spun it around his head, the wind whistling and sighing across the grey stone blade.

'I will cut your heart out, boy,' he laughed.

Cuchulain hefted the hurley ball he had brought with him. Tossing it high into the air, he struck it a tremendous blow with the hurley stick as it fell.

Fothad saw the ball coming towards him and attempted to cut at it with his sword. He missed. The ball struck him in the throat, crushing the soft tissues. Fothad dropped his sword and clutched at his throat, his face mottled a deep purple. Cuchulain strode up to him and, with the hurley stick clutched in both hands, struck him with all his might. The curved hurley stick struck Fothad beneath the chin, actually lifting him up off the ground, driving him backwards. The snap of his neck was clearly audible and he was dead before he hit the ground.

Cuchulain stooped and lifted the fallen sword. The stone felt cold and slick in his hand. He swung it experimentally, listening to it wail.

The two remaining sons of Nechtain looked at the still-quivering corpse of their brother, and then Tuathal strode forward to where the nearest skull was perched atop a short-handled boar-spear. Batting the skull aside, he wrenched the spear from the earth and approached the bridge.

Cuchulain swung the sword around his head, the edge keening the air with an almost-human sob. He then began curling it in the air before him in an intricate figure of eight, concentrating on the sword rather than the warrior who was now racing towards him, the large-headed boar-spear tucked beneath his arm.

Cuchulain waited until Tuathal had stepped on to the bridge before he released the stone sword, launching the sword underhand towards the warrior. The stone blade struck Tuathal point first in the centre of the chest and erupted outwards from the middle of his back. When he fell, the point of the blade which was protruding from his back bit deeply into the soft turf, impaling him on the ground.

Faithleann, the youngest of the sons of Nechtain, looked at the bodies of his two brothers and then at Cuchulain. For the first time, something like fear showed in his eyes. He had seen five and twenty cold, hard winters and had killed eight times that number, so he knew death as a constant companion, something to be respected, but accepted. He knew the harbingers of death, the tools of killing. He had come to recognize the warrior who could kill and those who could be killed simply by the way they moved, walked, even held themselves. Now, looking at the boy Cuchulain, he realized he might be looking at his own death. He saw it written clearly in the boy's grass-green eyes. There was no anger in them, no fear, merely a simple acceptance of the fact that killing Faithleann was something he could do.

Faithleann approached the young warrior with his arms spread wide. 'I have no weapons,' he said loudly. 'If we are to fight, then let it be man to man in yon fast-flowing river.'

Cuchulain glanced down into the river that foamed beneath the bridge. 'You are older, taller, stronger than I,' he remarked softly.

'Does that make a difference?' Faithleann asked.

'Not in the slightest,' Cuchulain said with a laugh. He vaulted over the side of the bridge to land in the icy water.

Faithleann dived into the water beside him. As his head broke the surface, blinking and sputtering, Cuchulain caught him by the chin and twisted his head sharply, thereby snapping his neck.

From the moment Fothad had stepped on to the bridge until Faithleann's lifeless corpse floated in the water had taken less than a hundred heartbeats.

The young man dragged the corpse out of the river and lined it up alongside his brothers. Pulling Fothad's stone sword from Tuathal's body, he neatly severed their heads with a single blow apiece. Tying the heads by their long braided hair to the boar-spear Tuathal had intended using, Cuchulain marched back across the bridge, the spear on his shoulder, the heads dangling behind him. He turned so that Ibar could inspect his spoils.

'Will this do?' he asked.

'There hasn't been a bloodying like this since the last great battle between the Tuatha De Danann and the sons of Mil.'

Cuchulain smiled boyishly. 'Cathbad said that this was a day for a warrior to take up arms. He said that the warrior would be known all across Erin and remembered down through the years.'

Ibar looked at the three dripping heads and nodded firmly. 'There's no doubt about that,' he said feelingly.

CHAPTER THIRTEEN
The Battle-Spasm

'I was the first to see the battle-spasm twist Cuchulain's body.

'From the moment I had looked into his eyes and saw the madness lurking there, smelt the metallic tang of his un-natural sweat on the air, I knew he was possessed.

'I have seen berserk warriors before, but the battle-spasm that warped and twisted Cuchulain's body was the most horrific I have ever seen. It turned a handsome boy into a bestial creature.

'I knew then that he was doomed ...'

The boy was quivering as he climbed back into the chariot. Ibar could feel the heat flowing off his body, could see the power crackling through the boy's hair, sparking on to the chariot's metal fittings. Bloody froth covered the young man's lips, and his muscles and veins were clearly deline-ated beneath his skin, his eyes were bulging slightly and he seemed incapable of speech. The air was foul with a rank odour, the battle-sweat that accompanied the berserker rage.

Ibar shuddered. This was no berserker, this was some-thing far worse, something far more deadly. He had seen berserkers fight, he knew many tales of warriors afflicted by the battle-curse, but he had never heard it happening to one so young. Conor would have to know, aye, and Amergin too. But if this wasn't a berserker rage ... then it could only be a battle-spasm.

Without saying a word, Ibar turned the chariot around and headed back towards Emain Macha. The horses were difficult to control, but it was not the smell of blood which had made them skittish ... they were battle-trained, well used to the blood and death – rather it was the almost tangible aura of power that flowed from the boy and the rank animal odour he exuded. The charioteer glanced at the boy: it looked as if the features on the boy's face had coarsened, the planes and angles of his face had sharpened and deepened, and the ridge of bone above his eyes seemed more pronounced. His hair had thickened and changed texture; a thin film of grease now coated it. Strands of coarse hair had sprouted on the backs of his hands.

Ibar looked away quickly: this was the battle-spasm.

In the history of Erin, less than a dozen warriors had been afflicted by a genuine battle-spasm. In the past there had been berserkers aplenty on the battlefields. These were men who, in the heat of battle, found themselves acting and behaving with complete disregard for their own safety. There were others who were able to assume the attributes of their totem animal before a battle and, during that battle, they would act with all the ferocity, courage and strength of the animal they had called down to possess their bodies – bears, wolves, boars. There were still others, wilder berserkers who offered themselves to their dark gods, inviting the gods into their bodies, offering them the blood and souls they slew on the battlefield as sacrifices.

A single man could change the course of a battle. Two alone could guarantee victory.

Ibar looked at Cuchulain and wondered what category he fell into. However, he also knew that whatever spirit or demon possessed him had not yet left his flesh. The boy was liable to attack and rend whatever stood in his way now, taking offence at the slightest imagined insult. He needed to work off some of his berserk energy.

Ibar took the long way back to Emain Macha, slowing the horses to a trot, but Cuchulain showed no signs of shedding his battle-spasm and his face remained twisted in its bestial attitude. As they rode through the portion of the great forest which still covered the heart of the island of Erin, Ibar spotted movement through the trees. As he watched, two enormous stags moved majestically into the light. The charioteer pointed the creatures out to Cuchulain. 'Now, they are proud and mighty beasts. Kings in their own right. They'd be a worthy gift to your uncle Conor on this, the day of your bloodying.'

'I will take their antlers,' Cuchulain growled, his voice hoarse and raw.

Ibar shook his head quickly. 'No, no, you must not do that. Capture them alive, bring them back to Conor docile so that he might free them into his own parkland to breed with his own deer. In seasons to come men will look on them and remember your feat, and the memory will linger long after they have forgotten those heads you took.'

'How will I capture them?'

'You must run them to earth. Chase them until they can run no further and when they stand shivering with exhaustion before you, then you can bring them in safely. Do you understand?'

Cuchulain nodded ... and then he simply leapt off the chariot and raced through the thick undergrowth towards the stags, making no pretence at concealment, no attempt at stealth. The raw energy, the spirit that possessed him drove him on. The noise and the bitter stench of blood and power that clung to him alerted the stags, and they turned and ran, taking great bounding leaps that carried them deep into the wood.

Ibar attempted to keep up with the chase, but the track narrowed to little more than an animal run, and the charioteer was forced to turn back and follow the wider tracks. It wasn't that difficult to follow Cuchulain. His passage was marked through the forest by the rending of branches and the snap of saplings as they fell before the stags' flight. Birds rose cawing and screaming into the air along the route, and when Ibar was certain of their route – they were obviously heading towards the lake – he whipped up his horses to a gallop and cut across country, hoping to reach it before them.

Ibar raced out of the forest track on to the sandy strip of ground that bordered the lake just in time to see Cuchulain leap on to the back of one of the stags, wrap his arms around its neck and, with his unnatural berserk strength, wrestle it to the ground. The second stag raced into the bitterly cold water and stopped, its once-proud head drooping in exhaustion, foam and spittle dripping from its lips.

Cuchulain rolled to his feet, leaving the stag shuddering on the ground and stamped into the waters after the second beast. The cold lake waters hissed and steamed around him, wreathing him in steam. The beast raised its head to look at him and then lowered it again, threatening him with its massive antlers. Its foreleg pawed the ground, churning the shallows to mud.

When he was close to the creature, Cuchulain threw back his head and screamed: an unearthly howling that startled Ibar's battle-trained horses into prancing and rearing. The stag raised its head in surprise and Cuchulain struck it a single blow between the eyes with his fist, dropping it to the waters. The boy stooped and lifted the enormous creature and, without any apparent effort, carried it back to its companion which was still lying on the strip of beach, sides heaving.

Cuchulain turned to look at Ibar, and the charioteer was shocked that the battle-spasm hadn't left the boy. His face was still warped and twisted into its beast-like grimace. 'Alive,' he grunted.

Ibar nodded. 'It is a mighty deed, Cuchulain, worthy of a great hero.'

There was a sudden movement overhead – a shadow raced along the ground – and both man and boy looked up in time to see two elegant swans flying slowly towards the lake. Cuchulain's reaction was instantaneous. Stooping, he grabbed two small rounded stones and hurled them upwards. It happened so fast that Ibar wasn't able to follow the flight of the stones, but he distinctly heard them strike the swans, saw the birds wheel in confusion, the rhythm of their wings broken. The two birds tumbled into the dark waters of the lake. Even before they hit the water, the boy had dived in after them, striking out strongly for the two creatures which were now swimming dazed and confused. They reared up as he approached in a welter of hissing, steaming water, striking at him with their beaks, but Cuchulain batted their heads aside. Wrapping an arm around their bodies, he pulled the stunned creatures in towards the shore. When he had wrestled them up on to the beach, he pulled off his cloak and ripped it up into long narrow strips with which he bound the birds' wings. When he looked at Ibar, the charioteer was relieved to discover that the boy's features were no longer as bestial. The planes of cheek and jaw had softened, the ridges over his eyebrows had receded. The battle-spasm was finally leaving him.

Cuchulain walked around the chariot, running his slender fingers across the three severed heads, patting the flanks of the exhausted stags, touched the swans' soft plumage. He turned to look at Ibar and his eyes were wild. 'Are these a hero's spoils?'

'They are.'

'Then let us take them to Emain Macha. Let all Erin know, then, of how Cuchulain fared when he went to his bloodying.'

'There will be those who will envy your prowess,' Ibar advised him, 'and some may challenge you.'

'Let them challenge me: will they prevail?' he demanded.

'No one can stand against you, Cuchulain,' Ibar said seriously.

CHAPTER FOURTEEN

The Women of Emain Macha

'I had attempted to work off some of the power that still flowed through the boy's body by having him chase the stags. I never thought he would catch them.

'But when he'd captured them and struck down the swans, he insisted that we return to Emain Macha. With the berserker rage still in him, I could not refuse, but I was terrified that I was bringing doom to the court.

'But when all my wiles had failed, when neither spell nor sword could have stood against him, the boy's own modesty proved his undoing ...'

News of Cuchulain's approach reached Conor long before the chariot came in sight of Emain Macha. Ibar had deliberately chosen the longest route to the fort, allowing time for the battle-spasm to wear off the blood-crazed young man. It was a dangerous game he played; if Cuchulain were to even suspect that something was amiss, then his emotions, already fired and heightened by his blood-lust, would set him against the charioteer ... and another head would join the trio Cuchulain was already carrying to Conor.

Finally, when Cuchulain was beginning to become restless and Ibar noticed that he was watching the position of the sun in the heavens, the charioteer was forced to give the horses their head, and allow them to find the route to their stables.

Though a battle-spasm usually took and possessed a warrior only briefly, the energy burning through his body, leaving him exhausted and weakened, the berserker fever that had possessed the boy was still surging through his blood.

When the walls of Emain Macha rose before them, Cuchulain's fever, instead of lessening, seemed to intensify. He began to shiver as if he were chilled, but he was radiating heat, and his hands clutched at the wicker rim of the chariot, shredding it, the veins clearly visible beneath the pale blood-spattered flesh.

When Cuchulain came in sight of Emain Macha, his excitement only increased, sizzling through his skin, lifting his hair off his head in long crackling streamers. The horses reared with the heat and the bitter stench of magic, and even the exhausted stags, who had been trotting alongside the chariot, roused themselves, revitalized by the power in the air. The swans began to twist and turn in their bonds, the long sinuous necks snapping at one another.

Cuchulain, realizing what was happening, leapt from the chariot and raced towards the fort. As he ran, his footprints seared and blackened the grass.

Amergin and Conor watched the approach of the youth.

'Battle-spasm,' Amergin said softly, 'and the boy has not yet been trained in how to control the wild magic.'

'What are we going to do?' Conor asked. He knew what a berserk warrior could do to a man while he was still possessed. 'Your magic?' he suggested.

'He's immune to all but the most powerful of spells,' Amergin muttered. 'Cast a spell at him now, and the magical aura that surrounds him will simply cast it back at the sender.'

'What are we going to do?' Conor repeated.

Amergin shook his head. 'I'm not sure.'

'My lords?' Both men turned. A tall, sharp-featured woman was standing behind them, her hands folded into the long sleeves of her gown. A hood concealed most of her face. 'My lords, there is a way to cool the boy's passion.'

'Who are you?' Conor demanded.

The woman raised her head and looked into his eyes. 'My lord, do you not recognize me? I am Levercham, one of your wife's attendants.'

'I know you,' Conor said shortly. He remembered seeing the hard-faced, almost masculine-looking woman around the court. Though he hadn't spoke more than a dozen words to her, he instinctively distrusted her. 'What do you want?' he demanded.

'I can help Cuchulain.'

Conor grimaced. He turned to point to the approaching boy. 'So, you can defeat the battle-spasm? How?'

'Before I answer, I need to know if the boy is still a virgin.'

Conor and Amergin looked at one another in astonishment.

'My lords?' Levercham persisted, her thin lips curling in a smile, amused by the king's reaction.

'Well, yes ... yes, I suppose so,' Conor said.

'Good. Now, my lords, I need five naked women ... and at least three barrels of ice-cold water.'

'What foolishness is this?' Conor started to shake his head. 'I don't see ...' he began.

'I do,' Amergin said with a smile. 'It is a worthy plan, my lord.'

Conor shook his head. 'If you think it would work, then do it. But do it quickly. The boy's approaching.'

♣

Cuchulain reached the gates of Emain Macha just as they opened to allow five women to pass through. Even in his maddened state, he noticed that they were all beautiful and that they were each wearing long, enveloping woollen cloaks.

He was drawing alongside them, when the first woman allowed her cloak to fall to the ground. She was naked. The boy's mouth opened in astonishment ... which turned to shock as the second and then the third, fourth and fifth women opened their cloaks, revealing that they too were completely naked. Cuchulain felt the blood rush to his cheeks and his breath catch in his throat. Ashamed and confused, he looked away ... and twenty of Conor's strongest warriors dropped a net over him, quickly bundling him up into the fine mesh. The net immediately began to smoke and burn with the passion still running through the boy's body. They carried him to the first of the large barrels which had been filled with ice-cold water and plunged him into it.

The water hissed, boiled and bubbled ... and then the wooden laths burst asunder under the force of the boiling water.

Cuchulain, still wrapped in the net and accompanied now by the naked women, was then dropped into the second barrel; this too burst asunder as the water bubbled and boiled.

The struggling boy was then dropped into the third barrel. The water hissed and steamed, overflowing the sides, but the barrel did not explode under the pressure. When Cuchulain raised his head, the battle-spasm had left him and his features had resumed their usual planes, the muscles and veins no longer pronounced.

Conor came and lifted the dripping boy from the barrel. 'Today you became a man, Cuchulain. You acquitted yourself like a true warrior. But at least now can you admit that you still have much to learn?'

Cuchulain nodded. 'What happened to me, uncle?'

'It is called the battle-spasm,' Conor said quietly. 'I don't understand it, but Amergin will teach you about it and show you how to control it, rather than allow it to control you.'

'Uncle?' Cuchulain asked, smiling shyly.

'What?'

'Do you think he could teach me about women?'

The king laughed aloud and then, leaning close to Cuchulain, he whispered, 'No man can teach you about women. That knowledge is earned through experience.'

CHAPTER FIFTEEN
Amergin's Tale

After the events of his bloodying, I found myself watching the boy all the more closely, berating myself for a fool because I had not paid more attention to him during his formative years. He was the son of a god and mortal woman: it was right and proper that he should be more than a man, but less than a god, and I felt that I should have known that he would possess some extraordinary powers.

Perhaps if I had taken care to train him properly at an earlier age, instead of leaving him with Sualtim and Dechtire, perhaps he would have been able to control the battle-spasm, and hence the butchery of the Clan Nechtain would never have taken place, and then the catalogue of events that followed might have been different ... or then again, perhaps not. After all, he had chosen to take up arms on a date that was indeed auspicious.

Over the seasons that followed the day of his bloodying, as the boy pursued his training, his reputation grew until the bards were beginning to sing of the red-haired boy as the greatest warrior in all Erin.

There was danger in this of course. Cuchulain was indeed amongst the greatest of the warriors, but there were others who were better than him in many ways, warriors who had tempered their skills with sword and spear, with courtliness, gentleness and courtesy. The boy had none of these and, with the arrogance of youth, imagined that he needed none of the gentler traits.

With Cathbad, I showed him how to control the battle-spasm that twisted and turned his body when his blood-lust was aroused. Fergus taught him how to fight coolly and calmly, how to ignore the taunts of enemies and not to allow them to rouse him to anger.

But despite his great feats and his prowess as a warrior, Cuchulain was feared and distrusted by many in Conor's court for numerous reasons ... but principally because he had inherited his immortal father's beauty. As he had grown taller and his boyish features had firmed into manhood, he had indeed become handsome – some of the women of the court even called him beautiful – and the men, seeing how their wives and daughters looked at the young man, grew envious.

And I knew from bitter experience that a woman's jealousy is far more dangerous than a warrior's sword.

I finally brought my fears to Conor. Choosing my moment carefully, I waited until there was a game of hurley in the broad fields below Emain Macha. As usual Cuchulain was playing alone against the rest of the field and, though the spectactors comprised the women of the court, with husbands, sons and lovers in the opposing team, they only had eyes for the red-haired young man.

Touching Conor on the sleeve, I pointed first to the women of the court – and his own wife was amongst them – and then to Cuchulain. 'Either send the boy away or find him a wife,' I said bluntly. 'Otherwise some foolish lord will challenge him to a duel ... and, when Cuchulain inevitably kills him, you will find that you have not only lost a lord, you'll also have lost his followers and their support. And Cuchulain will spend the rest of his life killing off the family and loyal followers of the lord who wish to avenge their master's death,' I added, painting as dark a picture as I could.

'What do you suggest?' Conor asked sourly. 'Everywhere I go all I hear is the name of this accursed boy. I tell you, Amergin, if he wished it, he could claim this throne!' I noted how his hand fell automatically on to the knife on his belt. 'Tell me what to do.'

This was what I had been waiting for. 'Marry him off,' I said quickly. 'Find him a wife.'

'Who?' he asked.

'Does it matter? She must be beautiful and intelligent, clever and cunning: only thus will she be able to control Cuchulain. And once he is married, the other women in the court will not look on him so enviously.'

'Why not?' Conor asked, surprised.

'Simple,' I smiled. 'They will spend their time arguing amongst themselves as to how this one woman was able to trap Cuchulain when all their wiles failed. If they harbour any jealousies, then they will direct them towards the woman. And though they may continue to watch him, they will always be aware that she is watching them.'

The king considered the plan for a few moments, looking for a flaw in it, but he was finally forced to concede that, on the face of it at least, he could find nothing wrong with it. 'Do it,' he said tiredly. 'Find Cuchulain a wife.'

In the days and moons that followed, I travelled the length and breadth of this land looking for a maid who might serve Cuchulain as a wife.

Now I have heard these modern scribes tell how Cuchulain himself went and questioned Emer and she him, and I have listened to the poets declaim the courting speech of Cuchulain and Emer. The truth of it was far different. As was customary at the time, once we had ascertained that the girl Emer had all the attributes we desired in a wife for the young man – that she was cunning and resourceful, strong-willed and intelligent, and beautiful too, though the men of Erin put more store in a woman's character than any comeliness – I approached Forgal, her father.

Forgal was a small, stout, ill-favoured man who had nonetheless managed to sire two of Erin's loveliest women, Fial and Emer. He was ill-liked by his neighbours because of his cunning, and no faith could be put in his word. But he held the northern approaches to the Ford of the Hurdles, just above the black pool where one of Erin's oldest rivers rises. There was an important bay here, deep, secure and sheltered, and those who used the bay were forced to deal with him, and the tithes he charged had made him wealthy.

He was commonly known as Forgal the Wily, though sometimes less pleasant names were used.

We met in the large orchard behind his fort. I remember the day clearly; the sun was high in the heavens and it was close to the end of the hot season. The air was rich and redolent with the smell of the apples ripening in the trees, and flies and bees buzzed everywhere. Forgall had carefully positioned his two daughters at one end of a long grove, with Fial sitting a little in front of her younger sister.

'You know why I am here,' I said, without preamble. I did not like this man, for he had scant respect for me and my calling and, in his arrogance, he assumed he was cleverer than I.

'I have heard that my lord Amergin is looking for a wife for the hero Cuchulain.' His voice was little more than a whine, irritating and disturbing.

'You have heard correctly.'

'I am honoured that you should have chosen to come

here. My daughter Fial is a proud and beautiful maiden, trained in the manner of women ...'

'I have not come for Fial,' I said quickly. Despite her beauty, Fial had the temper of a wild mare and a tongue as sharp as any blade. She was two and twenty summers now, already long past the age when she should be wed. Forgall had been attempting to marry her off – without success – for years. 'I am here to ask for the hand of your daughter Emer for the hero Cuchulain.'

Forgall stopped and looked down the grove at the two women. I could see that he was thinking furiously. He didn't want to give up Emer – for that would inevitably condemn Fial to a life of spinsterhood – and yet he could not refuse what amounted to a direct order from the king. Forgall depended on Conor for troops to help him defend his bay from the invaders from the land of the Britons or the dark-skinned warriors from one of the warm lands far to the south.

'I am honoured that my daughter Emer should have found favour with the king and the hero Cuchulain ...' He was unable to keep the note of sarcasm from his voice. 'But I am a father,' he added, 'and the welfare of my daughters is my first concern. I have heard much of this boy Cuchulain. A fine young man by all accounts, who will make a fine husband,' he added quickly. 'But there are only the events of his bloodying to stand to his favour. And I understand he is afflicted with a battle-spasm.' The small man shook his head in mock horror. Forgall had fought often enough to have seen a berserker's rage. 'I would like my daughter to marry a man who has been trained in all the martial arts of war and battle. A warrior with such training would be able to control the rage that exists in his body.' He turned to look at me, though his eyes never met mine. 'I am sure you have heard tales of how some of those cursed with the battle-spasm have been convulsed during the act of love-making and then savaged their wives and lovers.'

I nodded slowly. I had heard such tales. The blood-lust of battle is similar in intensity to the heat of passion during the act of love. There were indeed tales of warriors who had gone berserk and slain their wives in such a fashion.

'I would be failing in my fatherly duties if I were to allow my daughter Emer – the light of my life – to wed if there was even the faintest possibility that such an event might come to pass.'

'What are you suggesting?' I asked.

'Let Cuchulain be trained by Domhnall of Alba. He is a mighty warrior and teacher who has trained many of the finest knights in Erin and the land of the Britons.'

'I know him,' I said.

'If Cuchulain is as good as you say he is, then he will quickly master all that Domhnall has to teach him, and then he can return and claim Emer's hand.'

Looking at the man, I guessed that it would not be so easy. And yet I knew that Domhnall, who was more usually known as the Warlike, was one of the finest battle-masters in the known world. And Forgall's worries were indeed justified; no man could fault him for safeguarding his daughter's future.

'I will bring your demands to Conor and Cuchulain,' I said, turning to look at the two women again.

'They are not demands,' Forgall said quickly. 'This is part of the price I am exacting for my daughter's hand.' The man smiled, showing ill-fitting teeth.

'Cuchulain will pay the price,' I advised him. 'But it would be better for you if you were to play fair with him.'

'I am a man of my word,' Forgall lied.

It would normally take a student three sets of seasons to

complete his training with Domhnall of Alba. In the first year the student acts the part of a humble servant in the fort in order to learn humility; in the second year the student takes the part of a servant to the older students in order to learn from them; and it is only in the third and final year that the student is allowed to handle weapons and the training begins in earnest.

Cuchulain completed his training with Domhnall in one season.

The final test for a warrior who had completed Domhnall's training was when he was forced to face Domhnall the Warlike in single combat. But Domhnall was a berserker himself, though he had learned to rigidly control the bloodlust that surged through his veins in the heat of battle, and, while he was now advanced in years, he was still one of the fiercest warriors in the known world. Kings and princes had attempted to buy his sword and expertise, but the old man had sworn an oath never to lift a blade in war, and now his energies were directed towards teaching.

Fergus MacRoth had trained with Domhnall and he said that when the time for his final test came, he fought with the ancient warrior for a day and a night, and though he wasn't overcome, nor could he overcome him. Fergus also added that he thought that Domhnall was holding back for fear of injuring him. Later, I spoke to a full twenty warriors – each of them a hero – who had trained with Domhnall, and in every case their single combat with him had lasted a day and a night and sometimes a second day until they had fallen down exhausted.

Cuchulain's combat with Domhnall lasted half a morning.

I did not see it; only warriors in training were allowed to witness the battle 'twixt the master and the student. Those I spoke to said it was truly terrifying.

Cuchulain and Domhnall faced one another with sword

and knife. They moved at one another slowly at first, with what seemed like infinite caution, until those students who were watching were beginning to grow bored. However, those skilled in combat realized what they were doing. They were gauging their opponent, analysing every little move, every tiny movement. There was a sudden flurry of blows, metal sparking off metal, and then both man and boy backed away.

Like dancers in some intricate pavane, they closed with one another again, and then the blows were so swift, so sudden and so numerous that the watchers couldn't keep count of them all.

And as they fought, both warriors began to *change*.

This was not the full battle-spasm – Domhnall was too old, too experienced a warrior to allow that to happen, and I had trained Cuchulain, teaching him how to keep the change under control – but they allowed some of the berserker rage to flood to the surface, lending them speed and strength. The blows became faster and faster still, until the watching students could no longer even see them. The opponents' bodies were shifting through a controlled warp-spasm, making them seem vaguely beast-like, and those watching saw the shape of bears, wolves, dogs and horses, sometimes a mixture of all of these, and sometimes a creature that no one recognized, twist and rend the old man's and the boy's skins.

It ended abruptly. There was an especially swift flurry of blows ... and then Domhnall's sword went spinning in one direction, his knife in the other.

And Domhnall had been delighted! He said it had been fifty years and more since anyone had unarmed him.

'If you would wish to finish your weapons training,' he continued, 'then I will give you an introduction to Scathach, the Warrior-Woman of the Isles.'

'What can she teach me that you have not?' Cuchulain demanded.

Domhnall smiled. 'Scathach is not entirely human, there is Sidhe folk blood in her, making her long-lived indeed. She trained me and now I think she should train you. She can instruct you in ways that I never could. What say you, Cuchulain?'

'I would be honoured.'

So Cuchulain went in search of Scathach. When I learned that he was to travel alone through a friendless land, I persuaded two more experienced warriors – Laoghaire and Conall Cearnach – to accompany him on the pretext of continuing their training with the great weapons-mistress.

But I should have realized then that Cuchulain needed no companions. Cuchulain needed no one but himself.

CHAPTER SIXTEEN

Scathach

I am Uathach, daughter of Scathach nUanaind, the legend.

My mother trained Cuchulain in the arts of war; I taught him the art of love. He was a boy when he came to our isle; he was a man when he left.

My mother's origins are shrouded in mystery. I have heard the tales which told how she had come from some mysterious continent far to the south and across the seas. There are other stories which tell of her origins in an equally legendary land where the people have a yellow cast to their skin, and there were even some who said that she was one of the Old Gods left on this world when the others had retreated from this place.

Scathach was none of these.

She had been a woman once – when the world was young indeed – though she had been cursed with immortality. My mother learned her weaponcraft alongside her sister Aife from their father Ard-Greimne, who had been a warrior in the lands of the Greeks. They never knew their mother and, on account of their speed and strength and their ability to see into the Otherworld, they agreed that she must have been either one of the Sidhe, a spirit or a demon.

My mother had been a maiden of sixteen summers when she had gone in search of adventure. In those days, even more so than in these violent times, there was a ready demand for a sword, and my mother's skill ensured that she was never without food or a bed. She fought across the known world, down into the continent of the Dark Folk, eastwards to the land of the Brown Skins, and she even ventured northwards into the icy Cold Lands, where the folk are golden-haired and sky-eyed. She fought men and demons, commanded armies and deposed kings, and her exploits would fill a bard's memory and take a year of nights for the telling.

Scathach was one and twenty when she fell in love. The youth was alabaster-skinned, black-haired, black-eyed and achingly handsome. She met him in the dark hills close to one of the inland seas that flows into the Middle Sea. Their attraction was instant, their love immediate, and my mother swore to give up her warlike ways to settle down with the coldly beautiful stranger. They spent ten days together ... and each morning she would awake tired and debilitated after a night of passionate lovemaking. On the eleventh night she forced herself to stay awake ... and then she discovered that the youth was one of the Boban Sith, the bloodsucking demons. As he bent over her neck, long fangs dripping their numbing venom, she plunged her dagger up beneath his chin, impaling his head on the spike of metal, and then she forced him aloft. With her bare hands she broke the creature in two, and then tore him limb from limb so that his foul body might not regenerate.

My mother wandered northwards, fleeing the dark, forbidding land, but it was too late. The youth had fed his poison into her veins, making her one with him. She was doomed never to age and never to die, unless of course her head was struck from her body or her heart was torn out. Loathing what she had become, my mother fled into the Northlands, and in time she birthed me, for the Boban Sith are not barren and seedless as some have attested.

To support herself and her newborn babe, my mother returned to her mercenary profession. Her reputation grew, and in time her name entered the language as another word for sudden bloody death. Her name was used to frighten children. In time she even became confused with the dreaded Morrigan, the Crow Goddess of Battle, a dark semi-human goddess who haunts the battlefields and feeds off the flesh of the fallen warriors.

I sometimes think that my own mother might have been the source of this legend, for she once supported her need for blood by supping off the slain on battlefields, though she has sworn a great oath that she never slew an innocent man or maid and she never took the blood of one who was unwilling.

Eventually, Scathach came to this isle, which lies off the coast of the land of the Picts. A band of foul semi-human beasts were its only occupants, who preyed off the locals and lured boats to their doom on the rocks. These beasts then fed off the flesh of those they had entrapped.

The band of beasts numbered twenty, living on the isle known as Skye. It took Scathach half a morning to slay them all, and then she built a huge pyre and burned their flesh.

Settling on the isle, my mother set about building a fort. She traded her skills with the lordlings on the mainland for fish and meat and a few sheep, and she set about making the barren isle our home.

In time a warrior came to her. He was a tall red-haired, red-bearded warrior from the land of Erin who had heard of Scathach's presence on the isle and had come to beg her to train him to be a warrior.

The warrior had skill with the shaping of stone and, in return for his help with building the fort and tilling the land, my mother agreed.

A season later another warrior appeared.

By the end of the third season there were twenty warriors training with Scathach nUanaind. It pleased my mother; it meant that she no longer had to sell her sword in return for provisions, for now she passed on her skills for princely fees.

I received my training at my mother's hands. By the time I was twelve summers, there was not one warrior who could stand against me. By the time I was fourteen only my own mother could still best me in battle.

And then Cuchulain arrived.

I clearly remember the day he came. It was late in the year and the trees were beginning to shed their leaves. In the morning and late in the evenings the touch of the Cold Months was in the air.

We had not had many warriors that season ... but no, that is not entirely true, we had had many warriors, but there were few that met our exacting standards, for we did not take all comers. We limited ourselves to those whom we were confident would be worthy bearers of the training.

When a warrior wished to train with Scathach, they were first housed on the mainland off the island, where they would spend ten days in meditation and fasting. It was surprising how many of the greatest warriors lacked the patience even for this. Once they had passed this test, they were tested in their weaponcraft and skill by warriors who were already in training with Scathach, and if they passed this second test, then they had to make their way to the isle themselves and present themselves to my mother.

I remember when Cuchulain came to the mainland, the three sons of Usnach were waiting there, undergoing the trial of patience. I was unwilling to take them for I have a little of the Sight, and I had seen the doom that lay in store for them and I felt we were wasting our skills and time in training them. But my mother – whose heart was always softer than her reputation painted it – insisted that they should be allowed to train so that at least, when their end came, they might die with dignity and honour.*

Our spies had told us of Cuchulain's approach. Domhnall of Alba, who had once trained with Scathach until he had learned her secrets and stolen them for himself and then established a rival school, nevertheless took care to keep my mother informed of those he had sent on. This shabby thief lived in fear that one day my mother would seek retribution for his foul theft of her knowledge. We knew that Laoghaire and Conall Cearnach, who had left Alba with Cuchulain, had changed their minds about accompanying him to Scathach; perhaps it was the high mortality rate amongst our pupils which frightened them, though I later heard that it was Domhnall's own daughter – a whey-faced trollop – who had enticed them back. I doubt this. The girl was incapable of enticing any sighted creature into her bed.

I think I fell in love with Cuchulain the moment I saw him. Nowadays the legends make him a giant, but he was not tall, for even I stood slightly taller than him, nor was he overmuscled as many of the warriors were. But he was handsome, confident and swift. Looking at him I could see a little of the hero-light that burned around him. This is the light that burns around all living things and is visible to those with a little of the Sight. It blazes strongly around those in whom the passions burn fierce. The light of lovers can be blinding to those who can see – and even those without the Sight can sense the glow from lovers. But there is no fire stronger, no light brighter than the hero-light.

The light that blazed around Cuchulain's head was painfully

*The full story of the sons of Usnach is told in *Irish Folk and Fairy Tale Omnibus* by Michael Scott (Sphere Books, 1989).

blinding. I knew then that here was a hero whose name would live for many generations to come. I also knew that his life would be short-lived, for no mortal can sustain the passion that burned in him and live.

Cuchulain spoke to the sons of Usnach, who instructed him as to what would be expected of him. I thought for a moment that he would ignore the rules and attempt to make the crossing to the isle without undergoing the tests, but the young man simply sat down cross-legged on the beach, with his spear resting across his knees, bowed his head and fell asleep. He stayed like that, still and unmoving, for the ten days. On the morning of the eleventh day, he came smoothly to his feet and moved swiftly down the beach to where the bridge of stones had been built that connected the mainland to Scathach's isle. There were four warriors in training with us then, all of them heroes: two from the land of Erin; one from Gaul; and the fourth, a huge blond, blue-eyed northerner from the icy fastness. They stood ranged against Cuchulain. This was the second test and, though the contest was not to the death, men had been sorely wounded and some had been killed.

Cuchulain defeated them easily, with a casual, almost arrogant ease.

The men from Erin and Gaul accepted defeat with a good grace, knowing that there was no shame in being defeated by a hero, but the northerner – though he had been disarmed within a score of heartbeats – attacked Cuchulain again, slashing at him with his spear when the younger man's back was turned. The point of the spear scored a thin cut across his back.

Cuchulain's revenge was terrible. He waited until the warrior had swung at him again, deftly slipped beneath the spear and struck the northerner a terrific blow beneath the chin. The force of the blow actually lifted the big man up off his feet and dropped him heavily to the ground. While he lay there dazed, Cuchulain snatched the spear from the man's numb fingers and pinned him to the ground by his left ear. The northerner struggled wildly, tearing his ear off as he attempted to wrench the spear free. Cuchulain pulled the spear free and then drove it through the northerner's leg deep into the ground, piercing his kneecap, ensuring that he'd never fight again.

Having defeated the warriors, Cuchulain's final task was to cross to Scathach's isle to claim his right to train with the weapons-mistress. There was a simple stone bridge connecting the isle to the mainland. The middle section of the bridge was missing, so the warrior had to climb a steep curve and then leap across the gap. If he failed he could be tossed on to the rocks far below. At the very least he would end up in the bitter Northern Sea, at worst he would become a sacrifice to the rocks and the cold lords of the sea. I have heard it said that my mother's training produced monsters. But this is not true. She produced the best warriors because she took only the best there was.

Cuchulain climbed the sixty stone steps to stand at the edge of the gap. The stairs had been carefully chosen so that they were of irregular shapes and sizes, and therefore a warrior would be unable to approach them at a run and help bridge the gap. Cuchulain stood on the edge of the gap, his red hair streaming out behind him, like flames. In one quick, fluid movement, he suddenly crouched down and then launched himself forward, hands reaching for the edge of the second half of the stone steps.

He missed.

My heart almost stopped when I saw him plummet down towards the grey sea. But he managed to twist and turn in mid-air and entered the water cleanly. He swam strongly towards the shore and raced up the shingle beach. I thought he might try again immediately, but instead he stopped, pulled off his sandals and shook them dry.

For his second attempt, he stood upright and threw himself forward ... but this time he didn't even come close to the opposite side and, once again, he cleaved the waters below.

The third time he studied the approach to the steps more closely, and I could almost see the dawning realization as he counted out the steps and discovered that every third step was flatter and broader than the rest. I knew, even before he made the jump, that he would make it.

Cuchulain raced up the steps, taking every third step. When he reached the edge of the break, he simply leapt forward. His added momentum and speed carried him across without a problem. From the moment his feet touched the island side of the bridge he was Scathach's.

And mine, I swore.

CHAPTER SEVENTEEN

The Warrior

'He reminded me a little of a youth I had known a long, long time ago. Physically, they were completely dissimilar: Cuchulain was light and lithe, while the man I had once loved was dark and sere. But when I looked into Cuchulain's eyes, I realized that he was indeed brother to that long-dead child of the night.

'My daughter who has the Sight could only see the hero-light burning around the man.

'I looked into his eyes and saw the blood-lust and madness lurking within him. A thousand years and more ago, I had learned to fear that madness. When I slew the vampire, I thought that I would never again see such a terrible lust. I have fought killers, madmen and monsters, those who had sold their souls to the Dark Gods, but I had never encountered the look I had seen in my vampire-lover's eyes. Until I met Cuchulain.'

Three seasons passed on Scathach's bitter isle.

Cuchulain soon discovered that the time he had spent with Domhnall of Alba had been wasted, the little he had learned from him useless. The tricks he taught his students were nothing more than that – tricks. Scathach instructed her students in stratagems, encouraged their skills, forced

123

them to discover their own fighting styles, emphasized their strengths, showed them their weaknesses, taught them how to overcome them.

Domhnall turned out warriors. But Scathach created heroes.

He learned more during the three seasons on Scathach's isle than he had learned in all his years in training in Erin. He also met Uathach, Scathach's daughter. Slender and pale, with large dark eyes and flowing black hair, she captured Cuchulain's heart the moment he laid eyes on her. She was unlike any woman he had ever met before. Wild and warlike, her skill with sword and spear, knife and shield matched his. Taking him to her bed, she instructed him in the arts of love. At the moment of his greatest passion, when his control slipped and the battle-spasm began to twist him into a bestial creature, she whispered calming spells to him, subduing him, and she instructed him how to control the conflicting passions – those of love and hate – that surged through his body, channelling the energy away from the warp-spasm.

And Cuchulain, who was to know the love of many women in his short life, always claimed that this was the most valuable lesson he learned on Scathach's isle.

Uathach was his first love and, like many young men, he thought that there would be no other.

And then he met Aife the Warrior.

'Who is she?' Cuchulain demanded.

Scathach sat back into the shadows, her eyes taking the light from the evening fire, turning them blood red, shadows dancing across her unnaturally pale skin. Teeth flashed in a smile, her mouth quickly covered by a raised hand to conceal the razor-sharp fangs that had grown in place of her own teeth since the change had come over her.

'Aife is mother's younger sister,' Uathach said quietly. 'She is called the Warrior.'

'She claims she is better than I,' Scathach hissed, 'but I think we are equally matched. Some day perhaps we will put it to the test.'

Cuchulain lowered his head slightly, digging his nails into the palms of his hands. Though the young man feared nothing and no one, Scathach frightened him. She was non-human, a semi-human bloodsucker and his every nerve screamed at him to slay her. Her skin was sand white, her eyes bloody and the fangs that jutted from her upper jaw were those of a beast. Her skull had been shaved completely bald, save for a knot of hair that grew out of the top of her head and flowed down her back in a thick rope.

Uathach, sensing his unease, rested her long slender fingers on the back of his hand. Her ice-cold touch startled him. 'Aife is mother's younger sister,' she said again. 'Ten years and more separate them, though their lives have often paralleled one another's. However, whereas mother was tricked and trapped by a foul vampire and hence came to her own immortality in that way, Aife sold her sword to some of the most powerful magicians in the ancient world. Her fee: immortality. Now those magicians who paid her have gone, some died of natural causes, others slain by Aife or those hired by her, and now only she remains.'

'The years had warped her,' Scathach hissed. Her damaged throat and teeth made speech difficult. 'Immortality is not a boon, it is a curse. There is no joy in living forever, only sorrow. To see only death, to know that every living thing you see will wither and die, to watch all you love and care for become enfeebled and fade; there is no pleasure in that. Soon, soon you begin to kill without compunction, without thought – after all, what you are killing will die soon enough in any case – and once that happens you lose your humanity.' She laughed, a hissing, rasping sound. 'I fear I lost mine a long time ago.'

'You no longer kill for pleasure, mother,' Uathach said quickly.

'Teaching is a noble occupation,' Cuchulain added. 'What does Aife do?'

'She kills,' Scathach said shortly. 'While I moved northwards in my youth, she travelled along the lands that bordered the Middle Sea, leaving a trail of destruction in her wake. She even moved in the Dark Continent for a time, and she was worshipped there as the White Goddess. Once she had learned the dark jungle magic, and tiring of the sacrifices that were offered to her, she moved into the Desert Lands, where the sand people thought her a djinn, a demon.

'She crossed the sea and continued northwards, but more slowly now, taking her time, for she had become immortal by then. She married mortal men, had children by them, and then lived to see those children grow old and die. Men called her the Witch Queen, and many religions have grown up around her, making her part of their belief.

'Some years ago, she began to move northwards. Perhaps she had heard that I was still alive, though that may be nothing more than my own conceit. She was always ambitious. But certainly somewhere on the way north, she learned of my existence, and it seemed as if that gave her a focus.

'Over the seasons, she gathered around her an army of prodigious size, and they have fought, plundered and pillaged their way through the length of the land of the Britons.'

'Why?' Cuchulain asked.

'For the pleasure of killing, for the thrill of battle, for the booty. And now ...'

'Now ...?' Cuchulain asked.

'Now she has come to kill me.'

The young man shrugged. 'Then why do you not go out and kill her in turn? You are the finest warrior in the known world.'

'She is of my flesh, Cuchulain.' The woman drew in a shuddering breath. 'I am little more than a beast now. I am a creature of blood and darkness. But that creature that made me thus – a vampire – was even less than I, for the vampire folk oft slay their own kin and drink their blood. Apparently, such blood will give the immortal vampire almost godlike powers, make them completely impervious to ageing – for we do age a little – make them indestructible.'

Cuchulain shook his head slightly. 'I don't see ...'

'If I fight Aife and slay her – as I must – then the sight and smell of her blood will rouse the feeding frenzy in me. Once I taste that blood, I am doomed. I become a beast, an indestructible, undying butchering beast.'

'Then let me fight her,' Cuchulain said softly.

Scathach shook her head. 'I cannot.'

'Why not?'

Scathach looked at her daughter and then turned back to Cuchulain. 'I cannot,' she said again. 'I must fight Aife ... If I do not face her on the mainland, then she will come to this isle.'

'Appoint me your champion,' Cuchulain insisted. 'I will slay this woman for you.'

'She has lived and fought for a thousand years,' Scathach smiled briefly. 'She is known as the Warrior for good reason.'

Cuchulain came easily to his feet. 'And you, who have lived longer than she, have trained me.' He turned to Uathach. 'Issue the challenge. Make it loud and public. She cannot refuse me because she will lose face with her own troops.'

'And if she kills you, Cuchulain?' Scathach asked.

'I am the son of a god. It will take more than one mortal to slay me,' he said arrogantly.

'Aife is no longer mortal,' Uathach gently reminded him.

It was one of those quiet days of summer, still and silent, without the hint of a breeze. The very air felt heavy and every breath was laboured. And though there were more than a thousand warriors spread out across the flat rolling plain and up into hills, they made no sound.

Scathach, Uathach and Cuchulain stood and faced the assembled host. Scathach was heavily cloaked, her pale skin and sensitive eyes shielded from the harsh glare of the sun. She could fight in the daylight if she had to, but her skin quickly burnt and the pain enraged her. Then, like a wounded beast, she struck all around her.

Aife had accepted Cuchulain's challenge, though she had added that, when she slew the young man, she would then slay Scathach and Uathach also.

'Is there anything else you can tell me about her?' Cuchulain asked, as a chariot broke through the ranks of the assembled army and raced across the plain towards them. In the still air the breathing of the horses and the metallic jingle of the harness was clearly audible. 'What does she covet, what are her most prized possessions?'

'She covets gold and power. She delights in the fact that she is stronger, quicker and deadlier than any man. She has had a hundred husbands – more, probably – and countless lovers. She has seen them all into the grave. She delights in taking strong, proud men and subjugating them to her will.' Scathach nodded towards the chariots and the two fine-boned horses that were pulling them. 'She treats beasts the same way. She always picks the best and then breaks them to her will.'

Cuchulain looked at the chariot with interest. The wicker

frame had been covered with a thin patina of gold. The horses' bits and bridles were also gold.

'How does she prefer to fight?' he asked, still looking at the chariot.

'She can fight equally well with all weapons and in all styles. I think she will attempt to dispose of you quickly, as an example to me. She will give you no quarter; she will look upon you simply as a nuisance.'

Cuchulain smiled.

Scathach caught the look and shook her head warningly. 'You must control the battle-spasm. If it takes control of you, then you will surely lose. The battle-spasm grants you victory by means of the berserk fury that controls you; but if it takes you over completely, then Aife will use that fury and the loss of self-control against you. Use a tiny portion of the battle-spasm if you wish it to grant you strength and skill, but do not allow it to possess you. This time, Cuchulain, you must depend on your skill and swiftness and cunning.'

Aife had stepped off the chariot and strode across the plain to stand in the centre of the green field. She was a tall, muscular woman whose features were softer, more pleasant than Scathach's, though the family resemblance was still strong. Looking at her, Cuchulain would have put her age at around two and twenty years, though he knew she was more than a thousand years old.

She was wearing a simple leather breastplate and kirtle. A leather band kept the hair from her eyes, which were a bright green in colour – the same colour as his own, Cuchulain noted. There was a long barbed spear in her right hand, and her left hand was resting on a broad-bladed dagger on her belt.

'Is this your champion, sister?' Aife asked scornfully. 'Why, he is nothing but a youth. Is this a test perhaps, are you trying to gauge my skill? I have heard that you can immediately tell where a warrior has trained by how he moves, even by how he draws his weapon, but, sister dear, my skills are older than any of these new battle-masters. The skills they teach are but a diluted shadow of my own.'

'When you're finished talking, we can fight,' Cuchulain said loudly, his voice carrying clearly on the still air.

'Aaah, he is arrogant, perhaps even confident. For a moment there I pitied him, as you sent him out to die, but only for a moment. However, I will still be merciful to him, I will kill him swiftly.'

'What does she do?' Cuchulain asked, turning to look at Scathach and Uathach, 'Talk her opponents to death?' He lifted a barbed spear identical to the woman's and turned to face the warrior. 'There is a time for talk and a time to do battle. Now is the time to fight.'

Aife smiled chillingly. 'Now is the time to die.' She suddenly lashed out with the spear, the barbed head hissing for Cuchulain's throat. Still smiling, though now his grin was the merest baring of his teeth, Cuchulain moved his head back slightly and the spear point missed his face by a hair's breath.

'Too slow, old woman,' he whispered. 'Too slow.'

The young man and the ancient warrior-woman circled one another, spear and knife in hand. No blows were struck, they simply moved in an intricate dance, gauging one another's skill by tiny moments, subtle suggestions. To an unskilled warrior it looked as if they were simply looking at one another, but those who had been trained knew what was happening, were aware of the nuances of this deadly dance.

There was a sudden flurry of blows, spear off spear, knife off knife, and then they both stepped back.

'He is good, Scathach, you should be proud of him,' Aife said evenly. She looked at Cuchulain in a new light. It had been generations since any man had stood before her first blow and lived.

'You too have some skill,' Cuchulain smiled.

The second exchange of blows was longer. The barbed spears struck, struck and struck again, but the blows were always countered on both sides. Finally, the barbed heads became entangled and while Cuchulain wrenched his, Aife twisted hers ... and both spearheads snapped.

'Scathach has trained you well. You have speed, strength and cunning.'

Cuchulain bowed his head slightly. 'I have fought many warriors, but none like you,' he said admiringly. 'Truly, you are a great warrior.'

Aife bowed slightly.

'And I have never seen a finer pair of beasts,' he added, nodding to the chariot. 'Such fine-boned steeds. Where are they from?'

Aife glanced around to where her horses and chariot had stopped ... and suddenly Cuchulain was upon her. He allowed a little of the battle-spasm to possess him now, using its strength and speed. His right leg hooked around the woman's, pushing her backwards, off balance, while the point of his knife pressed against her slender throat. Aife crashed to the ground with Cuchulain atop her. The merest trickle of blood snaked down her throat where the point of his knife had pricked it.

'Yield,' he hissed.

'Never.'

'Then I must kill you,' Cuchulain said simply.

Aife had looked into the face of death often enough to know its simple terrifying truth. When she looked into the young man's eyes, she saw that he would indeed kill her without a second thought. And though she had lived for a thousand years and more, she still feared the last long sleep.

'I yield.'

CHAPTER EIGHTEEN

Emer, the Bride of Cuchulain

I am Emer, the bride of Cuchulain.

I am the reason Cuchulain went to train first with Domhnall and then with Scathach.

My father wished to protect me, I suppose, and perhaps he hoped that while he trained, Cuchulain might be hurt or killed, though neither happened. Even if he had been maimed, then my father could have refused him. Indeed, because of my father's demands, much of what would happen later – not only to Cuchulain, but also to the kingdom of Ulster – could be laid directly at his door.

I suppose it might be said that my father made Cuchulain a hero.

My sister was Fial. She was older than I and as pretty, though she possessed my father's foul temper and bitter tongue, and Forgal, our father knew that if she were not married off before I, then his chances of finding her a husband would grow very slim indeed. So when Amergin came to my father looking for my hand, he tried, without success, to make him take Fial. But Amergin refused. I was destined to be Cuchulain's bride and he would accept no other.

But my father was not about to give in so easily. He insisted that Cuchulain go to train with Domhnall of Alba so that he might learn to control the battle-spasm that sometimes twisted his body into an animal-like shape. It was a just and reasonable request and Cuchulain agreed without question. I do not know what happened in Domhnall's school, but I do know that Cuchulain went next to Scathach the Weapons-Mistress. He trained with her there, honing his skills to a level that rendered him virtually invincible. I have heard also that he became the lover of Uathach, Scathach's daughter, though I have also heard that the two women are demons, so perhaps this is not true.

What is true, however, is that he fought the immortal Aife, whom some said was the sister of Scathach, though this is possibly a lie, for Scathach was hideous while Aife was very fair indeed. But if she was not some demon, then perhaps she was a goddess. Cuchulain defeated Aife in single combat and, almost as if the combat had been a bizarre courting ritual, I know that Cuchulain went to live with this goddess and that they grew to be lovers, and I know that in time she bore a son whom she named Conlai. But by the time she discovered she was with child, Cuchulain had left to return to the land of Erin. He never knew the boy, never even knew he had begotten a son, and thus the way was paved for a terrible tragedy. When this boy Conlai had grown to manhood, he came to this land to seek his father and claim his birthright. Many tales, rumours, half-truths and lies have grown up around the events of their first meeting. Suffice it to say that they did not recognize one another, for the boy favoured his mother. There was a challenge, and they fought. And Cuchulain killed him. That was the father's gift to the son. Perhaps that was Cuchulain's bane: to kill everything he came in contact with, to destroy that which he most loved ... including himself.

There are myriad tales about Cuchulain; some true, others are simple fabrications, still more are but the earlier tales of Erin revitalized and renewed with Cuchulain in the heroic role. They can only hint at his greatness and they rarely speak of his madness.

I have been asked many times if I loved Cuchulain. And in truth I cannot answer. He was all that a woman should find acceptable in a man. He was fine and strong, handsome, wealthy and loving in his own way. But in truth Cuchulain really only loved Cuchulain. Nor was he faithful to me: he had many lovers. In the beginning I became enraged when I learned of his infidelity, but eventually I came to realize that the passion that drove him to war, the lust that burned in his body and enabled him to effect the warp-spasm, was the same lust he had for women. It was simply another part of his nature. I lived with him, loved him and I never left him, so I suppose you could say I loved him.

When Cuchulain returned to the land of Erin after training with Scathach and then with Aife, he came to claim his wife. But my father Forgal still didn't want me to marry Cuchulain. Once I believed that he thought it would bring us too close to the throne, and often those close to the seat of power were crushed when that seat toppled, and Conor's hold upon the reins of power in Erin was oft tenuous. Later I learned that my father had had his future read by a druid, and in the smoking entrails of a bird the old man had predicted my father's doom by the hand of a red-haired youth who had come to steal a valuable treasure. So when Cuchulain presented himself at our fort, Forgal refused to give my hand, saying he would never give me to some barbaric shape-changing savage.

And Cuchulain laughed, and those who were watching him swore that they saw the flesh on his face twist and shiver as if something crawled beneath the skin. 'I will come for her in three days' time,' was all he said, and then he turned and walked away.

When my father learned this, he immediately called in all

his warriors and bondsmen and, with his hoarded gold, hired mercenaries to patrol the road leading to the fort. Their orders were simple: slay Cuchulain in any way they could, and a king's ransom in reward for the warrior who brought the red-haired youth's head.

So they laid animal traps, they dug pits and lined them with poisoned spikes, they set up ambuscades, and a hedge wizard even set up a glamour on the path leading to our fort. If anyone were to approach the fort on that path they would think that it ended in a thick hedge of thorns. The same wizard chanted his dark spells across some of the poison ivy that grew thickly in this part of the wood and, as we watched, it took on a life of its own, growing, twisting, turning, snaking across the path, covering it in a thick impenetrable mass in a matter of heartbeats.

Later that same day, Forgal stood on the ramparts of the wall surrounding the fort and looked out over his domain. As well as the spells and traps, there were a thousand men waiting in the fields and forests, while another five hundred were gathered inside the fort, all of them armed and waiting for the warrior.

'I don't care how good he is,' Forgal said aloud, 'rumour oft makes men's reputations greater than they are. But no man could break through that barrier.' The troops gathered around him nodded in agreement.

But they were all wrong.

The waiting guards expected Cuchulain to ride to the fort with an army of his own, and to attack at dead of night, but they were wrong on both accounts: Cuchulain came alone in the middle of the day.

I was confined to my room until Cuchulain had been slain or driven off, and there were four southern mercenaries standing outside my door, guarding me. From my room I had a clear view out across the forest that bordered the western side of the fort. Close to noon, I became aware of a low buzzing, droning sound that seemed to be coming from the forest. Standing by the window, I watched Cuchulain appear, striding boldly out of the dark forest as if he hadn't a care in the world. He had come through the traps and enchantments as if they weren't there. There was blood on his spearhead, but he seemed to be untouched. And then I realized that the noise from the forest was the cries of the wounded he had left in his wake.

I watched the red-haired young man dart across the open space that had been cleared before the fort. Chariots burst from the forest and galloped towards him but, instead of turning and running from them, Cuchulain turned to face them. The fort gates opened and half a hundred warriors rode out to slay the young man.

What followed was slaughter.

I had heard about the warp-spasm which twisted Cuchulain's body into that of a beast. My father described it as being something akin to the were-change, as something horrific. But it wasn't ... it was something more, much more. It was terrifying and exhilarating. In the few pounding heartbeats it took for the raw power to course through his veins, altering muscles, twisting bones, turning a man into something that was neither man nor beast, I think I came as close as I ever will to understanding the powers of the gods. But the change did not make him bestial – it made him godlike. His sudden change had startled the approaching horses. They shied and reared away from the apparition, tossing riders, upsetting the chariots, sowing confusion in the tightly packed ranks of the fort's defenders. And then Cuchulain was amongst them. At times he moved too fast for me to follow: the only way I could keep track of him was by the trail of bloody devastation he left in his wake.

Lightning flared twice, striking down from a clear sky to

sear some luckless warrior standing close to Cuchulain. The white light flowed like liquid along the metal fittings of arms and armour, roasting the body, adding the stench of burnt meat to the odours of blood and offal and death on the air. The wooden frame of a chariot began to burn, panicking the horses it was still yoked too, and they galloped screaming through the packed warriors, creating even more confusion. Small fires began in a dozen places about the field.

Once, Cuchulain stopped in the midst of the butchery and confusion and looked towards the fort – and I could have sworn that he looked directly at me.

When he moved again, men fell back, stumbling over the bodies of the dead and wounded in an effort to get away from this god-driven hero.

And all the while Forgal stood on the ramparts and screamed at his men, encouraging them to slay Cuchulain, offering larger and larger rewards to the man who would kill the red-haired youth. But my father fell silent when Cuchulain turned towards the fort. The young man began to run and the battle-spasm lent him speed and strength. When he was within a dozen paces of the wall, he made a mighty leap that carried him up and on to the smoothly polished wooden stakes. He clung there like a huge quivering insect ... and then he began to climb, using his fingers and toes to dig deeply into the wood.

My father went into a paroxysm of rage. He grabbed half a dozen throwing spears and, leaning out over the edge of the fort, rained them down on Cuchulain. The young man batted them aside with one hand as if they had been straws. By the time Cuchulain reached the top of the wall, a dozen of father's battle-hardened mercenaries had gathered. Any one of them should have been able to stop the young man climbing over the wall, but they were no match for Cuchulain. He killed the first one before he had even climbed over the wall. The man had leaned out over the edge to hack at the young man with his sword. Cuchulain's left hand had shot out, grabbed the warrior by the throat and hauled him forwards, out over the edge. Before the warrior had hit the ground, Cuchulain had vaulted the ramparts and was in amongst them. The fight was brief and bloody. It lasted less than a score of heartbeats and, when it was over, Cuchulain was the only one left alive.

He turned to where my father was crouched at the other end of the ramparts.

'You should have kept your word,' Cuchulain said softly. 'You should have given me your daughter.'

'You've never even met her,' father began.

'She was chosen for me by those whose opinions I respect and trust. I have heard much about her. She must be precious indeed for you to make such efforts to keep her from me.'

Forgal lifted his spear.

'Take her then, but you must swear to spare me.'

Cuchulain laughed, the merest baring of his teeth. 'Perhaps if you had not asked me, I would have ... and then again, perhaps not. Many brave men died this day because you did not keep your word. Their deaths are laid at your door. It is only right that I should exact retribution on their behalf.'

'But you killed them!'

'I was merely the instrument of their deaths: you killed them.' Cuchulain smiled again. 'And now I must kill you.'

Forgal launched his spear at Cuchulain, but the young warrior caught it in mid-air and snapped it across his knee. Laughing, he took a step closer to my father. Forgal backed up against the edge of the ramparts ... and then he fell.

To my dying day I shall never be sure if he jumped or fell to his death. I know that he died without honour. I know that he was prepared to sacrifice the lives of good men so as not to keep a sworn oath, and I know that at the end he was prepared to trade his own life for me.

So when I am asked how can I live with the man who killed my father, I simply reply that Cuchulain did not kill my father. Forgal slew himself the moment he traded away his honour. For a man without honour is no better than a dead man.

Thus Cuchulain claimed his bride. There are other embellishments, other versions: this is the truth.

CHAPTER NINETEEN

Fergus's Tale

Someday I will tell the full story of Cuchulain.* Should I live long enough, I will collect together all the tales, both actual and mythological, that surround his life. I will tell of his many battles, of his many loves, of the friends he made and killed, of the son whom he slew through ignorance.

Cuchulain's life was short – as he knew it would be – but it was full. Indeed, he experienced more in his few years than most men experience in all their allotted span of years. Perhaps it was because his life was so short that his passions were great: his hatreds, his loves, his joys and angers were always grand passions. He placed honour above all else, and took offence at the slightest insult – when only blood would placate him – but I have seen him weep over the death of a cat-caught bird.

I loved him.

And yet there came a time when we fought on opposite sides, when we even stood face to face with weapons in our hands and death in our hearts. There is no easy way to tell this tale. Bards have made sagas from its events, for indeed it was no one event, but a score of incidents coming

---

*Fergus is credited with writing down in ogham the first full account of the events of the Tain and Cuchulain's defence of Ulster.

together to an inevitable tragic conclusion, like the twisted weave of a rug that forms a pattern. There is no one point where I can say, 'It began here' or 'Thus it began'.

If we go back far enough, it is even possible for me to blame myself. If I had not yielded my throne to Ness and her son Conor, if I had fought for my rights instead of meekly standing aside ... but there are too many ifs and buts, and how can we humans hope to fathom the motions with which the gods direct this human world.

It begins and ends with Conor's treachery. But his treachery grew out of the birthing of a baby girl eight and ten years before.

I recall that we were visiting Felim, one of his more important allies, when a girl child was born to the lord. I generally accompanied Conor when he toured the countryside, advising him which lords were friends and which were enemies, warning him about those who would sit on the fence until the battle was half decided and then throw in their lot with the victor. Usually, Conor ignored me, but this time he chose to heed my advice to spend some time with Felim. The old warrior controlled many of the harbours and bays, and his warriors kept the tracks and trade routes free of bandits and brigands.

We had arrived during the birthing of the babe and, in the silence that hung over the fort, we heard the child's first mewling cries as we sat down to the feast. The old warrior was so excited – for he was long past the age of siring children – that he broke with tradition and carried the newborn babe into the great feasting chamber and showed it to each one of us in turn.

Cathbad and Amergin, both of whom had accompanied Conor, drew back as the babe passed by their faces. Conor caught their sudden startled looks.

'Is aught the matter?'

Neither wise man spoke.

'Tell me,' the king demanded.

Amergin turned away. He feared no man's rage and was not dependent on Conor for anything. But Cathbad was an old man whose power, though still considerable, was beginning to wane. He needed the king to support him in his old age.

'This babe, this child ...' he began.

'What about this child?' Conor demanded. He leaned over and pulled aside the swaddling cloth covering the child's face. 'She is not deformed, nor is she ill-favoured.'

'One day she will be one of the most beautiful women in the known world,' Amergin said, not looking at the girl, staring deep into the flickering fire.

'Is she cursed then?' Conor asked.

'Her only curse will be her beauty,' Cathbad replied.

'She will bring pain and suffering wherever she goes,' Amergin said. 'She will sunder families, she will topple kings: better if she were to die this day than to live and destroy the kingdom of Ulster.'

But Conor wasn't listening. He looked at the child again. 'The most beautiful woman in the world,' he said very softly. 'Truly?'

'Truly,' Cathbad nodded.

'Then she will be my bride,' Conor said firmly. He looked up at Felim who had been listening to the druid's pronouncements with growing alarm. 'I will wait until she has come to womanhood and then we will be married. It is fitting that the most important king in Erin should have the most beautiful wife. And if she is my bride then no one else will have any claim on her, and all that you say cannot come to pass.'

Thus did Conor seal the doom of many.

The girl, who was named Deirdre, grew to womanhood

and, in truth, she was the most beautiful woman I have ever seen. Tall and erect, she was pale-skinned, raven-haired, black-eyed. But her temperament did not match her looks: she was ill-tempered, spoilt and wilful. She had grown up knowing that she was to be the king's bride, aware that she was beyond the reach of teachers and tutors, even her parents. Their fear of the king ensured that she got her own way. And what Deirdre wanted she got.

Close to the time when she would have been wedded to Conor, the girl met and fell in love with Naise, one of the sons of Usnach. Though Naise was a man of honour, he pitied the beautiful young woman who was to be married to the aged king, and he resolved to spirit her away before the wedding. The tale of their elopement and Conor's pursuit have been woven by the bards into one of the great tales of Erin, one of the Three Sorrows of Irish Storytelling.* The flight of Deirdre and the sons of Usnach raised passions on both sides, and I thought then that the old druid's prophecy had come to pass, and that death and destruction would follow.

But I was wrong.

Time passed and people soon forgot about the king's betrothed who had fled with a lowly warrior ... forgotten, that is, by everyone except Conor, who had put a price on their heads and banned them from ever setting foot in Erin again. But that was not the end of the matter. Conor schemed, plotted and planned to wreak his revenge, and he was prepared to bide his time and wait until the lovers had thought that enough years had gone by for them to relax their guards. His hatred twisted him, making him forget everything except his lust for Deirdre and the insult he had endured. He forgot honour, friendship, duty and loyalty: he

*The full story is told in *Irish Folk and Fairy Tales Omnibus* by Michael Scott (Sphere Books, 1989).

was prepared to sacrifice everyone and everything in his desire for vengeance.

When he judged that enough time had passed, Conor seemed to relent. He revoked the reward he had offered for the brothers' heads and agreed to allow Deirdre, Naise and his brothers to return to Erin. But they refused to believe the tales they were hearing out of Erin, and even the messengers Conor sent to Alba couldn't convince them to return home. Finally, Conor asked me to go, because all Erin knew that, despite my many faults, or perhaps because of them, I was a man of my word.

'Truly, lord,' I asked before I left, 'do you intend to allow them to return to Erin?'

Conor looked affronted that his honour had been impugned. 'Truly.'

I suppose I have always been foolish, stupid even, but I believed him then, believed him as I had believed his mother when she had told me she would return my throne to me after one year. So I went to Alba, where Deirdre and the sons of Usnach were living in the Glen Ethibe. By this time Deirdre had wed Naise, the eldest of the three brothers. The sons of Usnach, having been trained by Scathach, were earning their keep as sell-swords, and had won for themselves a formidable reputation in Alba. They were wealthy, wanted for nothing and, on the face of it, there was nothing to entice them to return to Erin. They received me gracefully, for they had no quarrel with me, and I swore to them a great oath that Conor had relented and had agreed to allow them to come home, for it was not fitting that some of the finest of Erin's warriors should be forced to live on foreign soil.

So they came back to Erin.

I thought I was bringing them home. But I was bringing them to their doom.

Conor's plan was well laid and intricate. First I was tricked and duped by a churl named Baruch into spending the night in his fort. I did not want to stay, but he reminded me of a curse a druid once levelled on me: never to refuse bread and mead at a warrior's table. Perhaps I suspected then that something was awry, for there would have been very few at Conor's court who would have known of that old geasa, that curse ... except Conor of course. Deirdre and the sons of Usnach were eager to press on to Emain Macha, for they knew that once they had been received and accepted by Conor in full sight of all the nobles of Erin, then there was little he could do about them without showing himself up as a treacherous coward. I would have preferred them to stay with me, for I knew Conor would not move against them while they were in my company. But they were determined to reach the court, so I persuaded my own two sons Iollan and Buinne to accompany them, thinking this would give them some measure of security.

I was wrong – again.

The small party had actually reached the Red Branch Hostel when Conor's men attacked them, trapping them in the round wooden building. The besieged warriors were vastly outnumbered, but the sons of Usnach had been trained by the weapons-mistress and they took two hundred and more warriors to their doom that day. Perhaps they might even have been victorious, for the five warriors – the three brothers and my own two sons – were able to watch the three windows and two doors into the chamber. If they had been able to hold out until the dawn, I would have arrived, and then there would have been a very different tale to tell.

But then Conor, ever treacherous, bribed my son Buinne – though son he is no longer – into betraying the sons of Usnach and walking away into the night. In return for his treachery, Conor gifted him with an entire mountain, though the day he set foot on its slopes the ancient forest there died, the trees crackling and falling with the sounds of a thousand moaning warriors, the grass withered underfoot, the pools turned stagnant and the fish floated belly-up in the rivers, and the mines which had once been rich in gold henceforth produced nothing but worthless granite.

Such is the price of treachery.

But there was a more terrible price paid by the three sons of Usbach and my own dear Iollan, all of whom were slain that day. And again the king was forced to use treachery to slay them, for none of his own men could stand against them. He pitted his own son against Iollan and he tricked Cathbad into bewitching the sons of Usnach, allowing them to be taken.

So they died, slain by treachery: Deirdre was taken by Conor and forced to be his bride and, in the year that followed, her beauty withered like a water-starved flower. She died a year and a day after Naise's death, some say by accident, though others, who saw what happened, claim that she took her own life.

But all that was for later.

I left Baruch's fort before first light the following morning, a chill premonition driving me on. Before I reached Emain Macha, I saw the smoke of many fires rising up into the heavens, and I could smell the stench of death and despair on the fresh morning air. I knew then that something was terribly wrong, though I was still unprepared to admit that Conor would renege on his sworn oath-given word. A party of my own retainers met me on the road. They were armed for battle and I knew, even before I reached them, that the news would be bad. I hadn't been expecting how bad.

I have no magic, no skill at spells or wizardry: there is no magical power in these old bones. Unlike Cuchulain, I was never afflicted by the battle-spasm, but I think something like the warp-spasm twisted me that day and the days that followed. I have no memory of those terrible days, though I am told that, along with Conor's own son Cormac, who had grown to despise his father's treachery, we raised an army and sacked Emain Macha, burning it to the ground. Conor barely escaped with his life. My vengeance on the man who had forced me to eat in friendship with him is beyond description. And Cathbad, who had been tricked by Conor into helping him destroy the sons of Usnach, cursed the name of Conor, and swore that none of his sons would rule in the troubled halls of Emain Macha.

And so it was.

With Cormac and his warriors and bondsmen, and my own followers, we left Ulster, swearing never to return. We headed into the west, to the kingdom of Connaught, where Maeve, Queen of the West, and Ailill, her husband, ruled. They were the sworn enemies of Ulster, but that was not the reason I sided with them. They were honourable and, when a man loses all else, what is left but his honour? It is the one absolute in this ever-changing world of ours.

I thought it was ended when I took up service with Maeve. I was wrong. It was only beginning.

CHAPTER TWENTY

The Tain Bo Cuailgne

_____ ♣ _____

'I am the land.

'The sovereignty of this land is invested in me by ancient rites hallowed by tradition. I have the power to sanctify kings and make princes, for any man who wishes to rule in Erin must first lie with me and receive my blessing. Those who choose to ignore the ancient ways oft find that their reigns are short indeed.

'I am Maeve of Connaught.'

She was the high priestess of an ancient rite, the last of her kind. It was said that she could trace her lineage in an unbroken line through the female line back to the Three that were One, Banba, Fodla and Eriu, who had greeted Amergin when he had landed on the isle that would one day become Erin. She was Maeve of Connaught. Tall, with strong, almost masculine features, a flaming crown of amber hair flowing to her waist, the woman possessed the last remnants of the wild magic that was deeply rooted in the land. Tradition had it that when a king was elected to rule, he had first to receive a blessing from the keeper of the old magic. The future kings would first undergo a ceremony that would wed them to Maeve, then they would feast throughout the day, and in the evening they would lie together as man and wife; then the king would become one with the land, and the land would impart a little of the wild magic into him. When the magic was stronger, it was said that if an unworthy king lay with the land, then the land would blast him like a lightning-struck tree, but it had been a long time since that had happened.

Maeve had blessed seven kings thus. The tributes in gold, cattle and land that the kings had paid to receive her blessing had made her wealthy, and her magical powers had made her feared. But though she had lain with seven kings, she had only ever made one of those – Ailill of Connaught – her consort. Together they ruled the wild western seaboard and, though Maeve was twenty years and more her husband's senior, theirs was a good marriage, full of honour, a great deal of respect and more than a little love.

Perhaps it was the years that lay between them that kept them together; Maeve claimed that Ailill kept her young, while Ailill took comfort from Maeve's knowledge, experience and power. They had both come late to marriage and had been independent for far too long to give up a measure of that freedom to a spouse, so they kept separate households in the huge fort of Cruachan on the plain of Magh Ai. And, in an age where wealth was measured by cattle and gold, they both shared a passion for breeding the beasts and the acquisition of gold. Much friendly rivalry existed between the couple as they each strove to increase their wealth and improve their herd, though in time this rivalry was to turn into something darker.

The argument had begun simply enough, over something which, later, neither of them could remember. But, as is usual with such arguments, it grew bitter and prolonged. Family and friends' names and reputations were dragged into the argument, until it turned into a series of petty boasts.

'You were a lazy and ignorant youth when I met you ... and you're still the same ignorant youth today,' Maeve snapped, her amber hair billowing out behind her with the suppressed force of her arguments.

'I was your last chance for a husband,' Ailill countered. 'If I hadn't taken you, you would have died bitter and alone. This was a poor backwater when I came here. I brought wealth and cattle with me. I am responsible for making Cruachan what it is today.'

Maeve opened her mouth to reply and then deliberately closed it again. She could feel the rage building up inside her and, though some of what he said was true, she still possessed enough of the Old High Magic to be able to strike him down where he stood ... and, for all his many faults, she still loved him.

'Everything you brought to this marriage, I matched,' she said evenly.

'Prove it,' he snapped.

'I will.'

'How?' he demanded.

'We will have an accounting of our possessions. We will see then whose wealth is the greater.'

'Then Fergus of Ulster must oversee the counting: since he is neither of your camp nor mine, and his honour is without reproach, he will give us a true figure.'

'Agreed!'

For a day and a night a group of scribes and scholars ranged through the fort tallying the possessions and treasures of the households of Maeve and Ailill. By the morning of the following day, it became apparent that their treasures were evenly matched ... in every respect, but one.

Maeve and Ailill met Fergus on the edge of the enormous fields of Magh Ai that bordered the fort. Early morning mist curled and twisted sinuously in the cold air, and they were all warmly wrapped against the winter chill. Water droplets glistened like pearls in Maeve's amber hair.

'Well?' the queen demanded, striding up to the old warrior.

Fergus looked at the ogham reeds in his hands. These contained the valuations that were the results of the druid's deliberations. 'A day and a night past and you asked me to determine your individual wealth ...' he began.

'Why did we have to meet in this place at this ungodly hour?' Ailill demanded.

Fergus ignored them both. 'I have checked these figures myself,' he said slowly, 'and perhaps it would be better if you did not know the answer ...'

'Tell us,' Maeve and Ailill said together.

'Your treasures and possessions are almost identical ...'

'Almost?' their voices echoed.

'Almost,' Fergus repeated. He suddenly nodded out across the fog-wrapped field. A white-horned bull – ghostly and ephemeral in the early morning light – lifted its huge head and looked towards the sounds of the voices. 'Tell me about that animal,' he said suddenly.

Maeve bared her teeth in a savage grimace. 'That bull was calved in my herd five seasons past. When it was barely one season old, it wandered from my herd into Ailill's. We brought it back, but the following day it had wandered back to Ailill's herd. Again and again, it was returned to my herd, but only to return to my husband's herd at the first opportunity. Finally, we saw the hand of the gods in it, and I formally gifted it to him.'

'The finest bull in all Erin,' Ailill said proudly.

Fergus nodded towards the white-horned bull. 'And that is the only difference between your possessions.'

Ailill threw back his head and laughed. 'So it is settled,

wife: my wealth is greater than yours ... and the irony is that you conspired to make it so by gifting me the bull.' Shaking his head, he turned and walked back towards the fort, the morning mist robbing the humour from his laughter, turning it flat and ugly.

Maeve turned to look at the bull again. Her eyes were cold and calculating, and Fergus realized that here indeed was a dangerous opponent. 'I am the land,' Maeve said very softly, her breath pluming whitely on the chill morning air. 'I am the sovereignty of Erin. It is not right that I should have been slighted thus.'

Fergus said nothing. The woman's eyes were glittering with a strange madness and her breath was coming in great heaving gasps. It was something akin to passion, but there was no love in this, only lust.

'Is there a finer animal than that bull in all Erin?' she asked.

She was surprised when Fergus nodded. 'There is. The brown bull in the possession of Daire of Cuailgne is twice the size and more of that poor white-horned specimen.'

Maeve rounded on him, her eyes hooded and distant. 'In Cuailgne?' she asked.

Fergus's smile was humourless. 'Aye, in Ulster.'

When Fergus had ridden out of Ulster, he never thought he would one day be returning, especially on so bizarre a mission. Maeve was determined to possess the brown bull. She would put the bull to her own cows and hopefully breed a herd of prize bulls that would put Ailill's single specimen to shame.

The queen had questioned Fergus carefully about the possibility of buying the bull from Daire, but the old warrior had been convinced that Daire would never sell. A good bull could sire an entire herd and such animals – especially such a prize as the Brown Bull of Cuailgne – would never be sold.

'I want it,' Maeve had said coldly. 'I will take it if I have to.'

'Do that and there will be war,' Fergus advised.

'Then so be it.'

'At least let me bargain for it first. Offer a reward – a substantial reward – for the use of the bull for a year and a day.'

Maeve looked at Ailill's white-horned bull and finally nodded. 'So be it.'

The next morning, Fergus set off with a handful of retainers, following the old familiar road to Ulster.

Fergus's reputation was enough to ensure that he was respectfully welcomed by Daire, who possessed the Bo Cuailgne, the Bull of Cuailgne. The intricate code of hospitality was observed first and it wasn't until late in the evening, when the remains of the feast had been cleared away and much drink had been taken, that Fergus and Daire sat down to discuss the reason for the old lord's return to the lands of Ulster.

'I have come to make you wealthy,' Fergus said, sitting across the fire from the younger lord. Daire was more than a little drunk and his beardless face was sheened with sweat. In the flickering firelight, his eyes were moist and unfocussed.

'I am wealthy now, Fergus.'

'I have an offer from Maeve of Connaught that will increase your wealth, both in gold, land and beasts, tenfold.'

Daire's face twisted at the mention of Maeve's name. 'I have heard tell that she is a witch, an immortal man-eating witch. Is she a witch?' he asked drunkenly.

'I do not think so,' Fergus smiled. He had been careful to eat and drink sparingly, and, though his movements seemed drunken and his speech was slightly slurred, he was completely sober. 'Though, in truth, Daire, I would prefer not to be wed to her myself. She is a good woman, but strong-willed. Why, even now she is arguing with her husband, Ailill.'

'A good man,' Daire interrupted.

'Aye,' Fergus agreed, 'a good man. But they argued recently about whose wealth was the greater, and Maeve was outraged when she discovered that Ailill possessed the White Bull of Cruachan, and that the sum total of his wealth was greater than hers because of it.'

'A good beast,' Daire slurred, 'though not as good as the Brown Bull.'

'Indeed,' Fergus said through gritted teeth, trying to keep his temper in spite of the interruptions. 'And that is why I have come to you. Maeve wishes to breed a new herd and she wishes the finest bull in Erin to sire the stock. I told her that there was no finer bull in all Erin than the Brown Bull of Cuailgne. And', he continued, raising his hand when he saw Daire opening his mouth, 'she is prepared to pay handsomely – very handsomely – for the privilege and honour of putting the bull to her beasts for a year and a day.'

Daire nodded. 'A man would be churlish to refuse a generous offer, especially since it has been so courteously presented.'

'Then you agree?' Fergus asked, surprised that Daire had agreed to the terms so easily. 'Do you not need to consult with someone lest Conor becomes angered because you have hired out the Brown Bull?'

'He is a man without honour – why should I worry about what he says or thinks. And the bull is mine,' he added. Leaning forward, he tapped Fergus on the knee. 'This payment . . . how handsome is it?'

'Handsome,' Fergus smiled. 'A man could keep an entire

household with servants and retainers for ten seasons with what Maeve is willing to pay.'

Daire nodded again, his eyelids drooping. 'Tomorrow. We will discuss it tomorrow. You can take the beast then.'

Fergus waited until Daire was snoring loudly, and then he called one of his men who had been waiting at the far end of the room. 'Make ready to leave at first light on the morrow.'

The warrior looked at Daire. 'So he has agreed, lord?'

'He agreed.'

'A wise man,' the warrior smiled, 'otherwise we would have been forced to take it from him, eh?'

'Enough of that talk. He gave it willingly.'

'Did the drunken fool know what he was doing though?' the warrior wondered.

'He knew what he was doing, and he also knew that if he had refused me the Brown Bull then there would indeed have been war between us and Ulster. He may be drunk, but he is no fool.'

'We would have crushed them,' the warrior boasted.

Fergus shook his head. 'Don't be too sure of that. Making war on Ulster means making war on Cuchulain. And that is something you do not want to do.'

Daire awoke shivering in the chill pre-dawn, his head pounding, his every muscle aching. His last conscious memories were of talking to Fergus about ... about what? Something about hiring the Brown Bull to Maeve of Connaught. The young lord looked up as the door opened and his chief steward appeared. Without a word he handed Daire a cup of foaming mead. The potent drink which had tasted like nectar the night before now tasted foul and sticky. It was a shuddering effort to swallow it. Its bitter taste helped take his mind from his other pains.

'How are our guests?' he whispered hoarsely.

'Treacherous guests, my lord,' the steward said softly.

Daire looked at the old man.

'You promised them the Brown Bull,' the steward continued.

Daire nodded. 'In return for payment.'

'I heard them talking: if you had not voluntarily given the bull, then they would have taken it by force. They called you a fool.'

Daire's face reddened with anger.

'And what will the men of Ulster say, my lord? They will say that you gave the bull for fear of the army of Maeve of Connaught. No true man bows to a woman's threats,' the steward added softly.

Daire nodded, eyes squinting closed against the throbbing pain. 'You are right. Where are they now?'

'Fergus had arisen and was washing when last I saw him.'

'I will not see them again. Send them on their way. Tell Fergus I have reconsidered his offer. Tell him I do not want the witch-queen's gold. Tell him the bull stays here. And tell Fergus that he is not welcome in my fort again.'

'And if they refuse to go?'

'Slay them.'

'First he agreed, and seemed willing, indeed almost eager, to agree. But by the morning he had changed his mind.' Fergus sat across a round wooden table from Maeve. The queen was toying with a goblet of mead. Fergus could smell the cloying sweetness on the dry air.

'What made him change his mind?' Maeve asked.

Fergus shrugged. 'Perhaps he feared the consequences if Conor learned that he had traded the bull for a year and a day. Perhaps he thought there was a possibility that you would not return the bull ... though that is unlikely,' he added quickly, seeing the sudden flash of anger in Maeve's eyes. 'All Erin knows that your word is good.'

'Then let him know the consequences of mocking me and my messenger. I will have that bull now – it has become a matter of honour.'

'If you send men into Ulster on a cattle raid, it will mean a war,' Fergus advised.

'Wars have been fought over more trivial reasons. And I will send such an army into Ulster that has never been seen before.'

'Be very sure what you are doing, Maeve of Connaught,' Fergus said quietly. 'If you move against Conor, you move against Cuchulain.'

'I am the land,' the queen said. 'The ancient power of the Three that were One flows in my veins. Justice and right are on my side.'

Fergus carefully schooled his face to an unreadable mask.

'You doubt me, Fergus?' the queen looked up and the guards at the far end of the room straightened. 'Bring Fidelm, the seeress to me,' she commanded, her voice echoing flatly off the stones.

The queen and Fergus sat in uncomfortable silence until the beautiful blind seeress was brought before them. The girl had once looked into the Otherworld and had been stricken blind as a result. Now the World of Men was a blank to her, but she could see into the Sidhe world, and could penetrate the veil of time.

'I go to war with Ulster,' Maeve said shortly. 'Tell me what you see?' she demanded.

Fidelm threw back her head, her sightless eyes opening wide. 'I see red,' she said simply.

'Ulster's forces,' Maeve said quickly.

But the seeress shook her dark-haired head. 'Blood and fire, wounding and death on all sides. I see a host laid low. I see red.'

'Tell me that you see victory for my troop,' Maeve demanded.

'I cannot see that, queen, nor can I see defeat. I can see death aplenty.' Her brow furrowed as she concentrated on a particular image only she could see. 'I see a single man facing a host. There is a lake of blood about him, rivers of blood flowing from him, but he is blazing with a cold white light.' She took a great shuddering breath and then shook her head. 'I can see no more.'

'The man you saw ...,' Maeve urged. 'Describe him.'

'There is no need,' Fergus said shortly. 'It could only be Cuchulain, the Hound of Ulster.'

CHAPTER TWENTY-ONE

The Defence of Ulster

Do I regret what I did?

Do I regret destroying the lives of countless young men and aged warriors? Do I regret the death of the Hound of Ulster?

No.

I am the living representative of the land. I am Erin. I did what I had to do for the sake of the land. It was my duty to increase my herd, for to do so only honoured the land. If Daire had given the Brown Bull – as he had promised to do – then none of this would have happened. If there is blame to be laid, then blame him.

And let those who say that if Connaught and Ulster had not fought over the Bo Cuailgne, then we would have fought for another – equally trivial – reason, let these people say it to me now, to my face. I will take their heads for their foul slander. This was now a matter of honour and wars have been fought for less.

Connaught prepared for war. I was confident of victory. As well as my own bondsmen, warriors and mercenaries, all my six sons, the Maines, came with their armies; Ailill, my husband lent me his forces, for it is a husband's duty to support his wife in all things, even when it is not to his advantage; Cormac, son of Conor, who had come out of

Ulster with Fergus, joined with my forces; and Fergus too joined forces with me.

I do not know how many men went to war with Ulster on account of the Brown Bull ... but I know that far too few of them returned.

Despite the advice of many of my lords, I put Fergus in charge of this enormous army, deciding that he best knew Ulster's strengths and weaknesses, and a former friend is oft a bitter enemy. My advisers said that he had been too long an Ulster warrior and Conor's kinsman: he would not move against him, despite their past disagreements. I ignored them, but I feared they were soon proven right as Fergus took a long circuitous route to Ulster. My lords whispered to me that he was allowing his old friends time to prepare for battle. Fergus never denied this, but countered by saying that Conor's spies would have informed him almost immediately of the huge movements of men through Connaught. Only a fool would ignore the signs.

I often wondered if he had warned Ulster.

I wonder too would it have made any difference.

Cuchulain reached up and plucked the fat grey dove out of the air. He had seen it coming when it was still a long way off, and his sharp eyes had caught the glint of metal in its beak. It had swooped low over the frost-locked land, flown past him and then swung around by him again. He had caught it on its second pass. There was a ring in its beak, a thick, battered gold ring.

'Fergus,' Cuchulain whispered. He had made the ring for the old warrior himself, pushing through the soft gold with his fingers, shaping the metal with his hands. It was a poor thing indeed, but Fergus had worn it as if it were a finely wrought example of the goldsmith's art. Cuchulain looked closely at the ring, finally noticing the scratches on the inside of the golden circle. Perhaps the bird's beak ...? Turning the ring upside down, he suddenly realized he was looking at ogham script. Tilting the ring to catch the light, he slowly made out the scratched words: *'Maeve rides for the Brown Bull with an army. Beware.'*

Cuchulain turned and raced for the fort. All Ulster knew that Maeve would one day ride into the north with her army: she had long looked on the lush land of Conor's kingdom with envious eyes, and all she needed was the excuse ... any excuse. Cuchulain had heard how Fergus had attempted to hire the Bo Cuailgne from Daire, but he never thought the witch-queen would go to war on account of it.

The young man slowed when he reached Emain Macha. There was something wrong. There should have been guards on the gates, warriors on the walls ... but he could see no movement. Throwing back his head, he drew in a deep breath of the chill morning air; but he could smell nothing untoward on it – neither blood nor death tainted the air. Moving cautiously now, he entered the fort. The streets were surprisingly deserted, only women hurrying to and fro. They looked at him with something like horror and backed away. While Cuchulain had become well used to the varying reactions of people to him, rarely had a woman walked away from him with an expression of disgust on her face. He was one of the most handsome men in all Erin – and he knew it. He touched his smooth hairless face with his hands: was there something wrong with him, some blemish on his face?

Shaking his head, he continued on into the fort. But there were no guards in the rebuilt palace; indeed, he encountered no men in the fort.

What sorcery was this?

When he strode into the Great Hall, he thought that it too was empty, but then he saw Amergin's tall form slumped in a darkened corner. Cuchulain knelt on the rush-covered floor beside the druid. He suddenly realized how old the man looked and, though Cuchulain knew that he was almost immortal, he had always had the appearance of a man in his prime. No longer.

'What has happened, Amergin. Sorcery?'

The ancient druid nodded. 'Something like that, Cuchulain.'

'Where are the men, where are our warriors? Maeve approaches with a vast army.'

Amergin nodded. 'Aaah, that explains it then.'

'Explains what?'

'Do you not know the legend of Macha, the daughter of Sainraith, wife of Crunniuc?'

Cuchulain shook his head. 'But what has this to do with ...?'

The druid raised a hand, silencing him. 'In time past, a foolish man Crunniuc boasted that his wife Macha could outrun a chariot. For honour's sake he was forced to put it to the test, even though his wife was heavy with child and close to her time. So as not to shame her husband, Macha raced against the chariot and won, but at that moment the pangs came upon her and she gave birth to twins there in the middle of the field. And then, with her dying breath, she cursed her husband and his boastfulness and the men of Ulster who had forced him to make good his boast. For nine times nine generations, she said, at the time of their greatest danger the men of Ulster would be as women in the throes of birth, unable to move, unable to rise up from their beds or lift a sword in their own defence.' Amergin looked up, his eyes wide and frightened. 'Now there is only you, Cuchulain. Only you stand against Ulster and Maeve's army.'

'How long will this affliction last?'

'For four nights and five days.'

The young man nodded. 'But will this curse not afflict Fergus and his troop?'

The old druid shook his head. 'They have given up Ulster. They no longer have the right to call themselves Ulstermen.'

'How will I hold an entire army?' Cuchulain asked, his eyes glittering with excitement at the thought of the greatness of the deed. Here was his destiny.

'In single combat. Challenge them to send forth their champions in single combat to face you. And, Cuchulain, do not slay them too quickly. You must hold them for four nights and five days. After that the army of Ulster will arise and fall upon this Connaught rabble.'

'I think I should go and look at this rabble first,' the young man said. 'Where should I make my stand?'

'End it where it begun ... in Muiritheme.'

And so we went to war.

This wolf's-head, this Cuchulain, began harassing my troops, though he had not had the courage to come and face us. He left his messages though, proud and boastful ogham scripts cut into woven branches and left in our paths to frighten and discourage my men. I lost scouts and their chariot drivers, their heads set on stakes in the track to further demoralize and dishearten my troops. And though Fergus insisted that this is all the work of one man, I was doubtful.

And he grew bold and daring, this Cuchulain. One evening as I sat to my evening meal outside my tent, with my dog at my feet, a slingshot fell from the night sky and killed the dog. I thought that the stone had been meant for me, but Fergus swore that if this were the case then I would be dead. But one of Cuchulain's proudest boasts was that he did not kill women.

He slew my son Orlam, but he spared the chariot driver, so that he could bring me the bitter news, thinking it would daunt or perhaps even frighten me. However, if that was his opinion of me, then he was badly mistaken. I am no milksop maid frightened by blood, though I grieved – and grieve still – for the loss of a son. But it is the same grief as losing a friend and companion, to know that never again will one hear that voice raised in laughter or song. I know there will be more sons and my children have brought me nothing but honour during their lives, and there is no shame in dying in battle.

Finally, I decided to meet with this Cuchulain. I wanted to look into the face of this single man who had brought such consternation on my army.

Cuchulain awoke from a deep and dreamless sleep.

The forest was silent, no creatures moved through the undergrowth, no insects rustled beneath the leaves. And that was wrong. Scathach had developed Cuchulain's extraordinary sight and hearing to such a degree that he was able to bring the night alive, identifying every rustling sound and musty odour.

It had snowed earlier in the night, the flakes turning the forest ghostly, moonlight sparkling off the flakes, bringing them to spinning life ... and then Cuchulain realized that there was no moon that night.

Easing himself upwards, he pulled out his knife and laid it in his lap. He had slain many brave warriors that day; perhaps the shade of one of them was coming to dispute with him.

The creature appeared in the air before him, a shape of ice and crystal, of black shadows and wind-blown leaves. Snowflakes stung Cuchulain's eyes, making him blink back sudden tears and, when his vision had cleared again, he found he was looking at a tall white-faced, raven-haired woman. She stretched out a bone-white hand to Cuchulain, and he discovered that the snowflakes formed her flesh, the leaves and shadows her enveloping cloak.

'I am the Morrigan.' Her voice was something like a crow's caw, harsh and strident.

'I know you,' Cuchulain said simply. He had often glimpsed the Crow Goddess as she haunted the battlefields in her bird shape, feeding off the flesh and souls of slain warriors. 'Have you come for me?'

'Not now, Cuchulain. But soon perhaps.'

'Perhaps,' Cuchulain smiled coldly.

'It can be otherwise,' the ghostly shape cackled.

'How?'

'You are a hero, Cuchulain. Once in every generation, I allow a hero to lie with me. I can give you what you most desire in return for this night of passion. I could slay this army for you.'

'And you, what would you get in return?'

'A child. A human child.' The creature smiled, and for an instant her face assumed a vaguely bird-like appearance.

'And what would Death want with a human child?' Cuchulain wondered.

The Morrigan settled in a welter of leaves in front of Cuchulain. Her face was close to the ground, but the young man could see now that it was composed of snowflakes. As he watched, the crystals were slowly melting, making it look as if her flesh was liquefying off her skull. 'You cannot know what it is like to be inhuman, Cuchulain, to know only the Otherworld, to know only death and destruction. Give me a child, I beg you. Give me a child and I can give up this foul form.'

'And do what?' Cuchulain interrupted. 'Take up the form of the child? Possess your own child's body?'

The Morrigan knelt up, facing Cuchulain. Her snow-white hands pulled at her leafed cloak, opening it and revealing her flawless body. 'Lie with me, Cuchulain.'

Cuchulain flung his knife at the creature. It struck her below the breast and hung there for a single moment before the snow-flesh began to melt, flowing away from the metal which was anathema to those of the Sidhe world. The Morrigan opened her mouth and screamed aloud in a voice that echoed and echoed through the forest, bringing the birds awake and cawing, rousing Maeve's sleeping army, bringing dark nightmares to those who managed to remain sleeping through the sound. 'Then you are doomed, Cuchulain. There are no more chances and, when you lie dead and bloody, I will come and taste your flesh, Cuchulain, and I know that flesh will be sweet.' The snow dissolved into liquid and the leaves slowly rustled to the ground.

Shaking his head, Cuchulain settled himself to sleep. From the day he took up arms, he had known his life would be short: the Morrigan and the death she represented held no fears for him.

I was disappointed the first time I met the Hound of Ulster.

Fergus had spoken often about him, telling us the tales and exploits of his boyhood and how he had come to manhood. I had been expecting a hero, but I found myself looking at a young man who had only recently learned to shave. Even though I found it hard to believe that this single youth had been causing my army such distress, I still offered him wealth – a king's ransom – if he were to allow us passage through the land to take the bull. But he refused and, in his refusal, he insulted me. I was tempted to strike him down where he stood like some mischievous whelp and, yet, I knew there had to be more to the boy: he had slain many warriors and I knew I could not allow this to continue. Already, men were beginning to talk about the advisability of raiding into Ulster, for when a warrior fights an invisible enemy who strikes and slays, but cannot be struck and slain in turn, then frustration takes hold and nothing can destroy an army quicker.

So an agreement was reached: Cuchulain would face the finest of our warriors in single combat: if he slew them, then we would not pass and, if he were slain, then all Ulster was ours for the taking.

So I sent the best of our warriors against him, while the army of Connaught rested on a hill and watched ... though if the truth were to be told, I also sent a small raiding party ahead to steal the Brown Bull while the single combat raged ... and in this I was not breaking my oath to Cuchulain, for the army of Connaught did not pass, merely a few men.

There is a tale to be told in the battle of each warrior against Cuchulain, and I have heard the bards sing of those warrior fights, of blows traded and wounds taken. Only the best went against Cuchulain and, possibly for the first time in his life, the Hound of Ulster was wounded. None of the wounds were serious, but taken together they gradually weakened him.

I only have two regrets about those last terrible days of the Tain Bo Cuailgne: I regret sending Fergus to fight his own nephew and I bitterly regret sending Ferdia MacDaman to do battle with Cuchulain, his one-time friend and companion.

Cuchulain had raged against the Connaught forces. He slew all whom they sent before him, exulting in the warp-spasm that twisted and tore through his body. The finest warriors, even those trained by Domhnall of Alba, could not stand against him, though they fought bravely and managed to wound him in a dozen places. Once, while the spasm still twisted through him, he had leapt into his battle-chariot which Laeg, his charioteer had fitted out with spikes on the wheels and slivers of metal set into the wickerwork, and he rode the chariot through the massed ranks of Maeve's army. His two battle-horses, the Black of Sainglenn and Grey of Macha, had been draped with spiked blankets, and even the bridle had been studded with nails. The maddened warrior wrought havoc in the thickly packed ranks. Those who attempted to grab the horses or chariot found their flesh slashed by the blades, and the horses themselves, with teeth and hoofs, were as dangerous as their master. Finally, tiring of the slaughter, Cuchulain retreated, leaving behind a scene of such carnage that many of the warriors lost their taste for battle and would have walked away then, but for their sworn oaths to Maeve.

The battle had been raging for two or three days – Cuchulain had lost track of time – when Fergus approached him. The old man was armed with his battle spear and sword, his thinning hair scraped back off his face, and held in place with a thin circlet of gold.

'So it has come to this?' Cuchulain asked.

Fergus nodded.

Cuchulain lowered his sword. 'I cannot do this. You are more dear to me than Sualtim, my own mortal father. Please, Fergus, do not make me fight you.'

'I must, Cuchulain, for honour's sake.'

'There is no honour in this. You know I will kill you.'

'I know that.'

Cuchulain looked at the waiting army and then back to Fergus. 'I will not fight you; I would rather walk away than cross swords with you.'

'Walk away then.'

'I will. And if I do this for you today, then some day you

must give way to me or Conor's troops.'

Fergus nodded. 'I swear it.'

And Cuchulain bowed and walked away. Maeve was enraged, though there was nothing she could do: Fergus had fulfilled his oath and gone forth to face the Hound of Ulster, and the Hound had retreated before him.

Then Maeve, thinking Cuchulain was weakening, sent another score of warriors after him ... and he slew them all. Finally, there was only Ferdia. He had first met Cuchulain on Scathach's isle, where he had been training in weaponcraft. He was about Cuchulain's age and the two young men had formed a firm friendship. They had also sworn never to fight one another. But Maeve tricked Ferdia, swearing that Cuchulain had insulted him and impugned his honour, and eventually Ferdia relented and went out to do battle with his old friend.

I regret sending Ferdia to fight Cuchulain.

Neither I, nor any of those who rode with me, had ever seen anything like that battle. They had both trained in the same school, they had fought side by side and vanquished some terrible foes, and so they knew one another's tricks. The muddy waters of the ford that ran along the field of battle ran red with the blood of a hundred wounds and, though Cuchulain had allowed the battle-spasms to possess him while he fought the other warriors, he kept his human form during the course of his fight with Ferdia. Unlike every other warrior whom he had slain in a single day – often with the first few omens of battle – the combat with Ferdia was continued over a second day, and on into a third. On the morning of the third day, both men, terribly exhausted and weak with their many wounds, some of which would certainly have been fatal to lesser men, faced each other for a final time.

I have listened to the bards sing of this great battle –

though I have banned it from my halls, for the stanzas do not tell the truth. This was a heroic fight, but there was nothing beautiful about it: it was bloody and brutal. Here were two men, who had once been closer than brothers, now hacking and slashing at one another like trapped animals clawing at their own flesh to escape, brutally attempting to destroy the other. Where is the beauty in that? When they went out to do battle on that third day, they no longer looked like heroes: they were tired old men.

They began to fight at first light, using knives, swords, spears, shields and javelins in an attempt to get past the other's defences. The fight moved back and forth across the bloody waters of the ford, like a bizarre dance, and though they both gave and received wounds, neither seemed to have the advantage.

We thought it was over around noon.

Ferdia was fighting with a sword, a broad-bladed, razor-edged weapon that had a foreign appearance about it. A blow – lucky or skilful, I do not know – slipped past the edge of Cuchulain's shield and sank deep into his bowels. Cuchulain stood transfixed, looking at the length of metal penetrating his body and, when Ferdia wrenched the sword away, Cuchulain fell back clutching his stomach, holding his innards. Ferdia should have slain him then, but he did not. He backed away and allowed Cuchulain to be attended to.

Cuchulain's charioteer, Laeg, bound up the terrible wound and, when the young man returned to the battle, he was holding a long metal spear unlike anything I have ever seen before. Its massive head was triangular and barbed.

Fergus, who was standing beside me, shook his head when he saw the spear. 'It is the *gae bolga*,' he said turning away. 'It is over now.'

Ferdia had given him a mortal wound. Cuchulain could feel

it burning deep in his core, feel the energy and power draining out of him. Blackness began to creep in around the edges of his vision.

Laeg, the charioteer, bound the stomach wound with thick strips of cloth, pressing his bulging entrails back into his body and pinching the cut tightly closed. The bandage would allow Cuchulain to fight on for a short while, but after that loss of blood alone would kill him.

'End it now,' Laeg whispered. 'He has bested you, cry off. It is a heroic defence you have made.'

Cuchulain shook his head stubbornly. 'Never.'

'Then you will die.'

'I am going to die in any case.' Cuchulain struggled to his feet, leaning heavily on the charioteer's shoulder. 'Give me the *gae bolga*.'

Laeg left Cuchulain leaning against a rock while he went for the spear that was Cuchulain's weapon of last resort. It was an inhuman weapon, taller than a man and made from a curious metal that was unlike anything the charioteer had ever seen before. The broad head was barbed and set with a dozen narrow slits. When the spear entered a body, twelve hooked barbs slid out from these slits and impaled themselves in the body of the enemy. The only way to remove the weapon was by cutting it from the flesh of the fallen warrior. It had once belonged to Scathach and she had found it in the tomb of an ancient half-human king. She had carried it for a thousand years, until her daughter had looked into Cuchulain's future and said that there would come a day when only the magical spear would be able to save him.

Ferdia was leaning heavily on his sword when Cuchulain staggered up, one hand pressed across his stomach, the other clutching the spear.

'So this is how it will end?' Ferdia asked sadly. He knew

the *gae bolga*, knew its fearsome reputation.

Cuchulain nodded. 'There is no other way. You have given me my death wound.'

Ferdia slashed at him suddenly, the sword hissing past Cuchulain's face. Instinctively, Cuchulain flung the *gae bolga*. The spear burst through Ferdia's shield, shattering it, and bit deeply into his body, the razor edges slicing effortlessly through flesh, muscle and bone. Cuchulain jerked the spear back and the hooked barbs opened. Ferdia fell without a sound.

Cuchulain knelt on the bloody ground beside Ferdia and cradled the latter's head in his hands. 'I never thought it would end this way,' Ferdia whispered, bloody froth bubbling on his lips. 'I will die now.'

'I will follow you,' Cuchulain muttered, feeling the fire blossom in his belly.

'A man should not die at the hand of a friend.'

'You died honourably.' Cuchulain attempted a smile.

Ferdia nodded. 'Aye, killed by the finest hero in Erin.' His last breath was a wracking shudder.

Cuchulain bent his head and wept for the death of the friend he had killed. When he had taken up arms on that auspicious day, he had done so knowing that he would become a hero, but he hadn't realized the cost. He wondered then if it had been worth it.

CHAPTER TWENTY-TWO

The Final Battle

And so now it ends.

This day I will die. I have seen the signs, read the omens. Misshapen beasts haunted my dreams this last night; the shades of old friends, fallen enemies walked through my nightmares. And this morning my own two horses wept blood as they were prepared to bring me to this place. They know the end is close now. I have seen enough of death; the dread Morrigan is an old companion, I have often smelt the mustiness of her crow's wings; I know when she is close. I have been sorely wounded in this battle, too many wounds and not enough time to recover from any of them. A lesser man might have succumbed to any one of them, but I am not a lesser man. I am the son of a god ... that is why I have survived for so long.

And now I go to meet my father.

I have no regrets ... save the death of Ferdia.

I have killed friends and foes alike over the past few days. But I did what I had to do and my reasons were just. And in this life when man is faced with many choices, some of which are neither right nor wrong but something in between, then so long as he can say that he did what he thought was right, his conscience is easy.

Do I regret the deaths of men I called friends?

I don't think so. I was proud to have fought with them on occasion, and I am proud to have been the one to have slain them. There is no disgrace in dying by the hand of a hero.

I know now that I am a hero.

When I am gone my name will live after me, long after me.

See how the army of Maeve draws back from me, see how they fear me. Even amber-haired Maeve herself is frightened of me, though she will not admit it. I can smell the perfume of their fear on this tainted air. Aaah, would that things have been different, would that I did not have to die this day. There is still so much left to do. Perhaps I could have sided with Maeve like Fergus, perhaps I could have fought with her. The Connaughtmen would have triumphed and I would have become King of Ulster. But I chose another road. I chose to become the Champion of Ulster. I will die the Champion of Ulster.

And I wonder, would Maeve and her army have reached this place if they had not had that ancient spell, the doom of Ulster, to rely on? If the men of Ulster had been in the full of their health, then I would not have had to face the entire force of Maeve's army alone. Then the armies of Ulster and Connaught could have fought in one decisive battle.

And would the ending have been any different? Probably not. If Ulster had gone forth in all its might and majesty to meet with Connaught and if I had fought on Ulster's side, then Ulster would have won. As simple as that.

Even now warriors of Ulster awaken from the ancient spell, even now they regain their strength. And now they will carry the battle to Maeve's army. And what army is it now that I have slain the best of it? Ulster will win.

But I am tired now, so tired.

I will tie myself to this pillar, which will hold me upright until the army of Ulster arrives. The Connaughtmen will not approach while I still stand, they will not dare to pass. And every moment I stand is a moment for the army of Ulster to draw nearer.

I will just rest against this pillar for a moment, and then I will carry the battle to the enemy.

There are faces before me now, people from my past, most of them dead and gone now. Some of them I slew, others died because of me. Strange that I have not thought of them before. Faces, faces, faces. Friends, foes and lovers. Always lovers. What attracts a woman to someone like me, who can offer them only pain and suffering and even death, for though I have never killed a woman, I have caused the death of some.

Do I regret any of their deaths?

No, there is no shame in dying by the hand of a hero.

And am I a hero?

The greatest in all Erin. But now I am tired now, so tired. Rest. Rest. I will rest for a moment.

The gathered army saw Cuchulain slump against a pillar, but none dared approach him. Towards noon, a black-winged raven – the Morrigan, the Crow Goddess of Battle – spiralled slowly downwards and perched on the warrior's shoulder. Opening its beak, it threw back its head and cawed aloud, a long piercing scream that those who heard it swore was the anguished cry of a woman.

And then an otter crept up out of the ford, and twisted and turned through Cuchulain's legs, finally pausing to lap at the tiny trickle of blood that was pooling around his feet. Thunder rumbled in across the skies.

The watching army knew then that Cuchulain, the greatest of the Irish heroes, was dead.

But the legend was only beginning.

CHAPTER TWENTY-THREE
The Test

When he had been a simple warrior, selling his sword to the highest bidder, he had thought himself poor and yearned to be a king.

Now he was a king, the King of Kings, the Ard Ri, the High King. He was the ruler of all Erin ... and he realized now that, though he could have much, he could never have his freedom.

Men called him Cormac MacArt, King of Erin, but he knew he was nothing more than a slave. A slave to tradition and position. When he had been a warrior he went where he wanted to go, did what he wanted, and there was no one there to whisper that he was giving a bad example, no one to advise him that he should retire to bed because there was something of import happening on the morrow, no one to wake him and list his duties for the day. He had once commanded armies: now he was barely in command of himself.

But life had still been good to him; he had a wife whom he suspected actually loved him, even though theirs had been a marriage of convenience arranged by other people. She had borne him two lovely children whom he was immensely proud of. He wanted for nothing, needed nothing ... except perhaps a little time for himself.

When he had been young, he had loved his food and mead, and one of his finest pleasures was waking early to walk the damp fields and breathe the air that was almost magical in its purity. Nowadays, his stomach growled and griped if he ate too much spicy food and his advisers wouldn't allow him to drink, so the only pleasure left to him was his early morning walk.

And no one was going to take that away from him.

The king walked down the long white road that led from Tara, childishly pleased because he had 'escaped' again. While the guards had stood sentinel outside his door, he had left the palace through the window and made his way across the roofs to the safety of the ground beyond the walls. There would once have been a guard on duty, but it had been a long time since one of the chieftains had attempted to storm Tara's walls, and the guards had been given other duties.

It was early morning, the sun was still low in the sky and the dew still sparkling on the grass. Cormac breathed in deeply, almost tasting the air. It was fresh and sweet and clean.

The king stopped and turned back to look at the fort ... his fort now. Tara held such a special place in his heart at this time of the day. The early morning sun touched its white walls with a soft pink light, and its golden-tiled roof shimmered warmly. It had been on a morning such as this when he had first come to Tara as a roving warrior. From the moment he'd first laid eyes on the sprawling building, he had sworn that it would be his, and that he would never rest until he had taken the crown from Fergus the Black Toothed.

It had taken him many seasons, there had been many adventures and much blood had been spilled on the way. But it was his now. And he sometimes wondered if it had been worth it.

Despite the constraints placed upon him by his advisers and guards, Cormac always managed to take his long walk every morning just before he broke his fast. He was no longer a young man now – he had seen some five-and-forty summers come and go – but he was still fit and healthy, not yet afflicted with the stiffness and slowness that troubled many of his contemporaries. The only definite sign of age that he was aware of was that his sight was not as sharp as it had once been. Also, his hair, which had once been a bright red, had now dulled a little in colour, and there were strands of grey and silver in it and his bushy beard. His skin was the colour of a ripe nut and, against the shading, his eyes seemed much too blue in his face.

The king reached the outer limit of his walk – an ancient tree stump on the long road up to Tara – and stopped. It was his custom to rest for a few moments until his heart had resumed its more even beating. Only then would he start off on the dusty white road back to Tara. Cormac leaned back against the pale dry wood, the morning sun warm on his face, and looked on down the road – and quickly sat up again.

There was a figure walking up the road towards him! A stranger.

Cormac stood and pulled out his knife. He wondered how this man had got past the sentries and guards. Tara was ringed with warriors who kept watch on all the approach roads. Cormac had remembered how he, as a young warrior, had simply marched up to the white walls ... and decided then and there that he wanted it. Now that he was king, he wasn't going to allow that to happen again.

The lone figure stopped well away from Cormac. The king's immediate impression was that the man was tall and thin, but he was also wearing a dusty, travel-stained hooded cloak that effectively concealed his features. Cormac's fingers tightened on the hilt of the dagger. He hadn't worked to achieve all that he had simply to fall to an assassin's dagger in sight of his own fort.

The stranger brushed the hood back off his head and bowed slightly. 'I bid you greetings, Cormac, son of Art, Ard Ri of Erin,' he said, his voice soft with a lilting musical accent. He was a tall, thin old man, with long grey hair and a thick flowing beard. His skin was very pale and green-tinged in the early morning light, and his eyes were completely black, with neither white nor pupil visible. The old man raised a hand and Cormac caught the briefest glimpse of a gossamer web of flesh between the stranger's thumb and forefinger.

Cormac bowed slightly. 'You have the advantage of me,' he said very softly. The stranger seemed to be unarmed, but of course no one travelled Erin's roads without carrying some weapon. The Fianna, under the command of the hero Fionn, had succeeded in ridding the land of many of the thieves and bandits, but no road, not even the great road to Tara, could be truly called safe. 'Who are you?' Cormac asked eventually. 'Have you travelled far?'

The figure stepped forward, pushing the cloak back off his shoulders. The king's hand tightened on the small knife, thinking the man was reaching for a weapon. Beneath the cloak, Cormac saw that the stranger was dressed in a long tunic of white linen that had strands of gold thread running through it.

'My name is unimportant at the moment,' the old man said quietly, his lips barely moving as he spoke. 'I have come from a magical land, a land where there is neither sickness nor death, where there is only happiness and truth.'

'It must indeed be a magical land,' Cormac said quietly, realizing then that the stranger was either from the Sidhe or mad. 'I wish this land could be as happy as yours.'

The stranger nodded. 'It could be. A strong ruler – if that reign is tempered with justice and kindness – makes for a happy land.'

'Truly said,' the king murmured.

'What would you give to make your rule a just and wise one, remembered for generations to come?' the old man asked.

Cormac shook his head. 'It's not important that it should be remembered in future generations,' he said. 'I would be happy if my reign was considered honest and just.' A ghost of a smile touched his thin lips. 'It's an ideal I strive for, though I fear I don't always achieve it. I took this throne from a tyrant,' he added, 'and I am determined that when I pass on this throne, it will be done peacefully and without bloodshed.'

The stranger nodded again. 'If it comforts you, then let me tell you that I have a little of the Sight, and you will get your wish, though your successor's reign will not be as accomplished as yours.'

Cormac bowed. 'Your words comfort me.' He paused and then added, 'But you still haven't told me why you're here.'

The old man then put a hand under his cloak, and pulled out a long silver stick no thicker than a man's forefinger. Clustered about one end of the stick were seven golden balls. The stranger shook it gently and delicate, ethereal haunting music shivered on the early morning air.

'What is it?' the king whispered.

'It is a branch from one of the seven Trees of Knowledge,' the old man said, lifting up the stick. Cormac looked again and discovered that the stick bore a vague resemblance to a branch of a tree, and that what he had originally taken to be seven golden balls were actually apples – golden apples.

'It is very beautiful,' Cormac whispered.

'And it can be yours,' the old man hissed, 'but you must first promise to give me something for it.'

'Anything,' Cormac said absently, his eyes riveted to the silver stick.

'You can have this branch now, but I will come back in a year and a day's time, and I will ask you for three treasures from your fort. Promise me now that you will give me whatever I ask of you.'

'I promise,' Cormac said, reaching out for the branch.

'Good.' The old man handed over the stick. 'Now, listen very carefully to me, Cormac, son of Art,' he said. 'That wand has the power to heal all ills, to cure all sorrows.' His long, slightly webbed fingers touched one of the apples. 'If someone is sick, you must touch this apple and then shake the wand over them. The magical music will cure them. Touch this apple here and everyone who hears the music of the wand will fall into a deep sleep.' He touched a third apple. 'This one here will make the listeners forget whatever sorrows or troubles they have ...'

Cormac lifted the branch and was about to shake it when the stranger's hand closed around his wrist in a painfully strong grip. 'Don't waste its powers, Ard Ri. This is no child's plaything; with this you could rule the world.' The old man smiled humourlessly, showing long narrow teeth. 'Men have died trying to possess this branch, but they were unworthy of it. Prove to me that you are indeed worthy to possess this magical talisman.'

'Why are you giving this to me?' Cormac suddenly wondered, the realization of what he held in his hand beginning to sink in. 'Who are you?' he demanded.

The stranger backed away. 'Remember your promise: in a year and a day, Cormac, son of Art, we shall meet again.'

'In a year and a day, lord,' Cormac promised, entranced

by the golden apples. When he looked up again, the stranger was gone. When he turned back to the fort, he saw a long line of guards trotting down the dusty road.

The king allowed the silent guards to escort him back to the fort. The stranger had obviously been one of the Sidhe: his coloration alone suggested that. Cormac had heard tales of the Sidhe dealing with the human world ... but always at a price. He wondered what the price for the talisman would be. And then he remembered the promise he had foolishly made. The stranger would return in a year and a day.

The king left the guards at the gate, only the sullen captain accompanying him as far as the dining hall. The captain knew his own position was in jeopardy; the nobles and lords who advised the king had replaced four previous captains of the guard solely because they had been unable to keep a closer watch on the king. Cormac strode into the long, draughty dining hall where his wife Aeta, his daughter Grainne and his son Cairbre were breaking their fast with those lords and nobles who had business at court.

'Cormac, what kept you?' Aeta demanded sharply.

His wife's constant whine usually roused Cormac's ire, but he didn't even hear her this morning. He needed to speak to some of the druids. The king pulled the magical wand from his cloak, accidentally touching one of the apples as he lifted it. The sweetest music filled the air ...

Instantly, the assembled lords and ladies, servants, guards – even the dogs – fell into a deep sleep, toppling from chairs, sprawling across the table, scattering bowls and mugs to the floor.

Cormac looked at the wand. He shook it deliberately, but now it made no sound that he could hear. He touched one of the apples, flicking it with his forefinger, and then he shook the branch again ... and this time it chimed and tinkled softly, and very beautifully ...

And a group of guards, who had heard first the noise and then the sudden silence, and who had been running into the room, fell asleep on their feet and tumbled in a clatter of armour and weapons to the ground.

Startled, the king shook the wand again. No sound came out. So, now he knew that the apples had to be touched before they chimed, and then they only chimed once. He lifted one of the apples and looked at it closely. It looked identical to an ordinary apple – except that it was made of solid gold and was very, very heavy. Afraid to use the wand again, at least until he had had an opportunity to learn its powers, he shoved it back into his belt … and the music tinkled again …

And the cooks, who were carrying in large trays of gruel and porridge, fell asleep as they walked and crashed to the floor, the wooden and earthenware bowls shattering, splashing porridge everywhere.

Cormac looked around the long chamber at the scores of people, many of them now splashed with quickly cooling porridge, and wondered how he was going to explain all this …

Under the tutelage of the druids and by careful experimentation, Cormac discovered what each of the seven apples did. He could cure and heal, ease a troubled mind, salve a broken heart. News of the magical wand spread quickly and soon people came from all over Erin to be cured of their sicknesses and sorrows.

And the High King quickly forgot that the stranger who had given him the wand had promised to return after a year and a day …

Cormac stood in the lee of Tara's huge walls and looked down along the road and out over the land, trying to decide whether or not he would take his morning walk. It was raining heavily and the wind blowing in from the north was tipped with ice.

He had almost decided that it was not worth going out and getting soaked when he spotted a figure on the road. He was simply standing by the bone-white tree-stump on the road. There was something familiar about the figure – and something strange too – but Cormac couldn't make up his mind what it was. Squinting out into the pouring rain, he tried to distinguish the tall traveller's features. But all he could determine was that it was a man, an old man, with grey hair and a long grey beard ...

Cormac remembered. It was the stranger, a man he was convinced now was one of the Sidhe. He remembered the promise he had made, and he realized then that a little more than a year had passed since he had last seen the old man – a year and a day to be exact.

The old man walked up the long white ribbon of a road, approaching the fort. He stopped a few paces from the huge gates and called Cormac forward with a bent finger, like a teacher beckoning a student.

'Why can't you come over here and talk?' Cormac shouted, remaining in the shadows.

'Come here,' the old man said, his voice soft, almost gentle, though the king heard him clearly.

'No. You come here,' Cormac insisted.

'Come here!' the old man snapped and, before the High King realized what he was doing, he had walked out into the driving rain and was standing before the tall stranger. He discovered then what had been puzzling him when he had first seen the stranger – there was no rain falling on him. The rain was falling all around him, pounding into the wet earth, churning the white road to a muddy swamp, but above the old man, and in a circle around him, no rain fell.

Discovering that was surprising enough, but it was as nothing to the shock he received when he discovered that the stranger was floating just above the ground, presumably so as not to get his feet dirty.

The stranger looked down at the king with his sharp black eyes. 'Your time is up,' he said in a whisper, 'a year and a day have passed, and now I have come to claim one portion of my three wishes. You do remember the promise you made me?'

Cormac nodded. 'I remember.'

The stranger nodded. 'Good. I had thought you might forget.' A ghost of a smile twisted his lips. 'I claim your daughter Grainne,' he said.

'My what!'

'You heard me,' the stranger continued evenly. 'You must give me your daughter. We have a bargain,' he added.

'You can have anything in my kingdom,' the High King said, 'but you cannot have my daughter.'

'I want your daughter,' the old man persisted. 'Now, you have a choice. You can honour our bargain and give me your daughter, or I can go and take her.' His flat black eyes shifted upwards and he stared at Tara's walls, and then he looked back down at the king. 'And if I have to take her myself,' he said, 'I will not leave much of Tara standing.'

'Do I have a choice?' Cormac asked.

'As much of a choice now as you had a year and a day ago when you accepted the golden branch.'

'However powerful it is, it is not worth the price.' Cormac shook his head sorrowfully. 'You can have her,' he said finally, in a defeated whisper.

The old man nodded. 'I know that.'

'I'll call the guards ...,' Cormac began, but the old man shook his head. 'There's no need.'

Grainne arrived a few moments later, still clad in her

night-shift, moving slowly, eyes wide and unseeing. Cormac pressed his lips to his daughter's forehead, his tears falling to her cheeks. 'I'm sorry,' he breathed. 'I'll come for you.'

The white-haired old man shook his head, the smile on his lips twisted into a sneer. 'Don't, Cormac. Erin cannot afford to lose a king such as you.' Grainne stepped past her father and the old man swept out his cloak, wrapping the young woman in its silver folds.

A sudden flurry blew icy rain into Cormac's face, making him turn away ... when he looked again, they had both disappeared without a sound

The news of Grainne's disappearance quickly spread through the palace. To relieve the heartbreak that followed, Cormac went around the fort, shaking the magical wand, banishing his family's sorrow, making them and the servants forget that Grainne had ever existed.

And when he had done that, the king put the wand away, locking it in a deep chest, swearing that he would never use it again. He wondered why an instrument which had such potential for pleasure should have brought such sorrow.

In the days and weeks that followed Grainne's disappearance, Cormac wandered the palace in despair. He refused to sit in judgement, refused to see some of the lesser kings who had travelled from other parts of Erin and abroad to ask his advice. His intransigent ill-humour so angered them that a group of them met in conclave. Individually, none of them was powerful enough to go to war against the Ard Ri. But an alliance might stand a chance ... especially when it was apparent that Cormac had forgotten the duties of kinghood, and that the lesser lords would be sure to support them.

Cormac remained unaware of the growing threat. Unable to sleep because he heard his daughter's voice in his dreams, he wandered the fort, unwashed and unshaven and frightened ... terrified because he remembered that he had promised the stranger three things. The old man had claimed one: what would he look for next?

A month and a day passed before the Sidhe lord reappeared. Cormac was sitting in his huge throne that had been carved in the distant past by some of the first invaders to come to the land of Erin. It was made from a single piece of stone that had been carved into a tall-backed, high-armed chair. There were little markings along the arms of the chair, running down along the sides, showing the coming of Banba, the Egyptian princess, and her followers to the tiny island that would one day become Erin. Another set showed Partholon, the next invader and his people being washed ashore in their battered craft. Down the back of the chair, the battles these two peoples had had with the terrible Fomor demons were shown. There was a small patch close to the floor that was bare – no one knew why, though some said that the mason had died before he had finished the task, but others said that it would not be finished until the last High King of Erin had sat in the throne.

Cormac was lying in a drunken stupor, sprawled across the chair, one leg dangling over the arm, a broken jug of mead lying on the floor, flies buzzing around the sticky sweetness. The long chamber was deserted. This was the quiet time before the dawn, when sleep is deepest, and the doors between this and the Otherworld swing wider. The doors at the far end of the room swung silently open, and a deeply cloaked and shadowed stranger entered. Cormac immediately knew who it was.

'What do you want now?' the High King demanded, as the Sidhe lord floated towards him.

'I have come to claim the second part of our agreement.'

'What do you want?' Cormac repeated, wondering if it were possible to kill one of the Sidhe.

'I want your son, Cairbre.'

Cormac stared at the figure. 'Why?' he asked eventually. 'Why do you want my son? First you take my daughter and now you want my son. What will you want next – my wife?'

'I want your son,' he repeated, the smile on his lips giving his face an evil, demoniac cast. The king felt the small hairs on the back of his neck rise, and his breath caught in his throat.

'You can't have him,' he said quietly. 'Guards!' he suddenly shouted, 'Guards!' He smiled triumphantly at the old man. 'Perhaps we will do a different trade, you and I,' he continued quickly. 'I will trade you in return for my daughter. Guards!' he screamed.

The Sidhe lord smiled again, showing long, almost pointed teeth. 'Save your breath, Cormac. You're wasting your time calling for your guards. I am afraid they are all ... sleeping,' his voice fell to a whisper.

'Sleeping!' Cormac staggered to his feet and lurched past the stranger. Wrenching open the door he strode out into the corridor. All his guards were still in position. But like his daughter, they were asleep standing up, with their eyes open. He slapped the nearest guard across the face, but the man didn't even blink. Stepping back into the throne room, Cormac closed the door and stood with his back to it. 'What have you done to them; if you've harmed them in any way ...'

'They are unharmed. They are merely sleeping. They will awaken when I go.'

'Then go!' Cormac shouted. 'Go now!'

'Not without Cairbre.'

'And if I don't give him to you?' Cormac asked, though he already knew the answer.

The stranger shrugged his bony shoulders. 'You don't have a choice, Ard Ri. Now, give me the boy, or I will pull Tara down, stone by stone.'

'Take my son,' Cormac said, turning away. He heard cloth rustle as the stranger bowed, and then he asked. 'Will you be back?'

'A month and a day from this day,' the stranger said, 'for the third part of our bargain.'

'And what is that?' Cormac asked, turning around. But the Sidhe lord was gone.

Cairbre's disappearance devastated the fort. The young prince had been a great favourite, and the wailing and keening so incensed Cormac that he retrieved the magical wand and used it again to banish the palpable aura of sorrow that hung over the fort. Using the stranger's gift, he made everyone – even his wife – forget that there ever had been a prince.

Only he remembered the daughter and son that everyone else had forgotten.

The month and a day until the Sidhe lord's return dragged by slowly. Every clear night Cormac would stand on Tara's walls and stare up into the sky, watching the moon as it grew from a thin sliver to a large rounded ball. He watched as little pieces began to be chipped out of it, counting the days until the stranger's return.

The Sidhe lord was mocking him. But he had made a mistake: he had forgotten that Cormac had come to this throne the hard way, by virtue of his wits and the strength of his sword arm. Time and easy living might have softened him, but whereas once he had directed all his energies into gaining the throne, now he would throw the same energy, the same guile into retrieving his children.

The stranger would be back soon ... and Cormac had a very good idea what he would ask for. This time however, he had a plan ...

The stranger appeared on the first night of the new month. Cormac was walking the battlements of Tara, watching the stars sparkling in the heavens, wondering if the tales the druids told were true about those stars being holes in the sky through which the gods looked down. He had once spoken with some sailors, dark-skinned men with strange accents who hailed from lands that lay far, far to the south of Erin, who had told him tales about the stars. They said that each star told its own story and, if you only knew where to look, you could stare up into the heavens and pick out the tales of all the human heroes written across the skies.

'What do you see?'

Cormac spun around and pulled out his sword at the sudden voice. The Sidhe lord was standing behind him. 'I could have killed you,' Cormac said, angry that he had managed to creep up on him. 'What do you want now?' he demanded.

But the old man seemed to be in no hurry this time. He pointed up into the sky with a long-fingered, long-nailed hand. 'What were you looking for?' he asked, in his soft lilting voice.

Cormac shrugged. 'Nothing. I was just trying to remember some of the stories I have been told about the stars. My father Art told me some of the stories and I used to know their names, but I'm afraid that I've forgotten them now. I can only remember that star there.' He pointed up to one hard shining point of light in the northern sky.

The stranger nodded. 'The North Star, sometimes called the Sailor's Friend. Unlike the other stars it never moves, and mariners use it as a guide.'

'Are the stars really holes in the cloth of heaven?' Cormac asked suddenly. If anyone knew the truth, then the stranger would.

But all the Sidhe lord would say was, 'No.' The old man continued staring into the night sky for a few moments longer, and then he turned and looked down at the king. 'Now, we must complete our bargain.'

'What do you want this time?' Cormac repeated quietly.

'I want your wife, Aeta,' the stranger whispered.

Cormac nodded. 'Yes, I thought you might. Will you take anything else instead of her?' he asked sadly. 'She is all I have left. You have taken my daughter and my son. If you take my wife, what then will I have?'

'I must have your wife,' the Sidhe lord said, his dark eyes shining with tiny spots of starlight.

'Will I ever see her again?' Cormac asked then.

'That depends on you,' the stranger said, and then he faded back into the night and disappeared.

Cormac raced down the stone steps into his wife's bedchamber, but the bed was empty. She was gone.

Cormac rode out from Tara the following morning in the grey, gritty dawn light, just before the sun rose up over the horizon. He was accompanied by a hundred of his finest warriors – and Buan the Druid. Cormac wished that Fionn and the Fianna could have ridden with him, but they were far in the south of Erin, defending the coast from reivers from Gaul.

Cormac and his troop rode south and west all day, stopping only for a break around midday for something to eat and to allow the horses to rest. While the men were resting and rubbing down the animals, Cormac called together his four captains, and the huge men joined the king and his druid around a small fire, and then they listened to the king's story – of how first his daughter, then his son and now his wife had been taken by the mysterious white-haired old man. When he was finished, Cormac rested his hand on the druid's shoulder.

'This is Buan,' he said. 'He is the finest wizard and magician in the land of Erin. Last night, just before my wife fell asleep, Buan cast a spell – a tiny spell – on part of her clothing.'

'A spell on her clothing,' one of the warriors laughed uneasily. Like most fighting men, he instinctively distrusted the druid's magical powers. 'What good is that?'

The druid sat forward and looked at the four men. He was a tall, thin man, with a long face and slightly slanted eyes. He was completely bald, and his eyes were a pale, almost watery, blue. He opened one long-fingered flat hand and the four men looked down. Sitting in the middle of the druid's creased palm was a slender black stone, pointed at one end and flat at the other.

'What's that?' one of the men asked.

'What does it look like?' Buan demanded.

'It looks like a stone,' he said, surprised.

'That's because it is a stone,' the druid smiled. 'But this stone has also been touched by the same spell I used on the queen's clothing. So, look ...' The druid carefully nudged the stone with a long bony finger, shifting it around so that the pointed end was now facing his wrist. But as the men watched, they saw the stone turn slowly in the wizard's hand, until it was pointing in the same direction as it had a few moments earlier.

'It's a loadstone,' one of the men said.

Buan shook his head. 'It is similar to a loadstone, but it's not a true loadstone such as mariners use. A loadstone will always point to the north, and only to the north, but this ... this will point to the position of the queen, or more correctly, the position of the queen's clothing.'

'Have you any idea where we're going?' one of the four warriors asked.

Buan nodded. 'I think I know. But don't ask me to tell you. I cannot – not yet – not until I'm sure.'

The king stood up and looked into the sky. 'We've rested long enough. Come on, let's go.'

They rode on into the afternoon and, as night was beginning to fall, a mist began to rise up all round them. Thin, ghostly, almost threadlike strands at first, but they gradually thickened, turning from gossamer smoke to something that looked almost solid.

The fog slowed the riders to a stop, and then forced them to dismount and lead their horses along by the reins, keeping their eyes fixed on the back of the man in front. Though there were a hundred men and beasts strung out in a long line, if anyone became separated from the troop, they could easily wander lost and confused within a spear's length of the rest of the troop. In the thick fog sounds became muffled, and unclear, distant sounds – a bird calling, the bark of a fox – seemed very near, but the sound of the animals' hoofs were almost inaudible. It was chill in the fog, and every man and horse gleamed with a thousand thousand tiny sparkling water droplets that soaked through jerkins and beneath leathers, plastering hair and beards, the moisture itself brackish and unpleasant tasting.

Cormac raised a hand. 'We had better stop here,' he began, and then, realizing that probably no one could see him, never mind hear him in this dense fog, he turned around – and found he was alone!

'Hola! Hola! Where are you?' he shouted, but the fog muffled his voice, which sounded no louder than a whisper. 'Where are you?' he shouted again, turning around and around. He had stepped away from his horse, thinking someone might be close at hand ... and when he turned back to it, even that had disappeared into the mist.

Another man might have panicked and run aimlessly through the fog, calling out for his friends ... and perhaps catching and snapping an ankle in a pothole, or plummeting off a cliff, or impaling oneself on a jutting branch. But Cormac remained standing where he was, while all around him the fog shifted and twisted and turned.

After a while, he noticed that the fog seemed to be thinning out. The air also tasted cleaner. He could now see around him and the night sky was becoming clear again. The king looked up into the sky, remembering his talk with the tall stranger only the previous night about the stars ... and then the king stopped, feeling his heart beginning to beat harder and faster. The stars in the sky were not the ones he knew! He took a deep breath, forcing himself to look down, waiting until the fog had cleared away before he looked up into the sky again – and yes, the sky and the stars had changed. He was no longer in Erin.

Cormac pulled his sword free and looked around. He was standing in the middle of a flat field that stretched to the horizon in every direction. Nothing grew on this plain, no trees, no bushes. There were no stones, no roads, nothing that even looked like a track. He turned slowly, looking in every direction, seeking something that would give him a direction, or at least a point to aim for. But there was nothing visible ... and nothing he could do – except wait.

Morning came, but no sun rose up over this strange land. There was only a brightening of the sky and then the strange patterns of stars went out one by one, like candles. Cormac stretched and yawned – and then he spotted something in the distance, something which gleamed a bright warm colour in the morning light. He couldn't distinguish any details from the distance, but it didn't matter and, with a sigh of relief, he set off at a quick jog towards the light.

As Cormac drew nearer, he discovered that the light was being reflected from a tall golden wall surrounding an enormous circular fort. Over the top of the wall he could see that the roof of the magnificent palace was covered with what looked like white cloth or fur, while the walls of the fort looked as if they were sheathed with silver.

Wind rippled soundlessly across the featureless plain. Cormac shivered and drew his cloak higher around his shoulders. Turning his back on the gusting wind, he trudged towards the fort. As he neared it, he saw that the white roof was shifting and moving before the breeze, the white thatch lifting and falling in long sinuous waves. Abruptly, part of the roof pulled away and went tumbling up and over the walls to fall across the plain in a scattering of white stones. One landed a little behind Cormac and he turned and went back to it. Crouching, he touched the tuft of white thatch with his fingertip and then flipped it over.

And though Cormac knew he had gone beyond his own world – the World of Men – into the Otherworld, it was only when the Ard Ri realized that what he was looking at was a bird's wing, and that meant that the roof of the fort was covered with white birds' wings, he appreciated how far from home he'd travelled.

He was turning back to the fort when the golden walls parted like cloth tearing and a company of riders came galloping out. Cormac knew enough of the folklore of his native land to recognize the tall, unnaturally thin riders and their equally tall, thin horses: they were Sidhe folk. He thought they were coming for him, but the riders swept past, ignoring him. Instead, they gathered up the scattered birds' wings and galloped back to the fort. Moments later, Cormac saw small black manlike shapes crawling across the roof, and the silence was broken by the distant metallic plinking of hammers.

But no sooner had they got the roof thatched when another icy blast of wind whipped across the plain and ripped away another section of the roof. Once again the golden walls parted and the faerie riders rode out and began to pick up the wings ...

It took Cormac the remainder of the day to reach the fort. He was tired and hungry, regretting now the seasons of soft living. When he'd been younger, he'd often gone for three days or more without sleep and food.

The Ard Ri stopped outside the fort, directly in front of the opening in the walls. He wasn't tempted to go inside: on a score of occasions throughout the day – if indeed there was day in this wild place – the Sidhe riders had spurred their mounts past them in search of the birds' wings. But they hadn't acknowledged his presence in any way.

Cormac could see no movement beyond the walls, but a wisp of curling smoke caught his attention, and he moved forward until he was standing at the very edge of the opening. There was a raging fire burning up against one wall. An enormous, obviously ancient tree, complete with leaves, branches and roots was ablaze. It burnt silently and without giving off any heat. As he watched, the incredible heat ate through the tree, turning it into a thick grey ash. Cormac was about to turn away when a short, broad man crossed the courtyard carrying another huge tree across his shoulders. He dropped it down on to the pile of grey ash, sending sparks spiralling heavenwards. He touched the thick bark with the fingers of his left hand, and blue-white flames spiralled around the tree trunk before it burst into flame. When it was burning steadily, the broad, stunted figure walked away, never once acknowledging the human's presence.

Cormac watched the whole performance repeated three times, before he finally moved on.

Though his stomach told him that he had been walking for most of the day and that night should be drawing in, it was still bright when he spotted another fort in the distance. As he drew nearer, he found that this one was even bigger than the first and, rising tall behind the high golden walls that completely surrounded it, he could see four separate buildings.

The light was beginning to fade by the time he reached the walls, a purple discoloration seeping across the sky behind him. He wondered if the nights would be as long as the days in this Otherworld.

Cormac rested his hands against the smoothly polished, warm golden stone. From the distance, he had seen that the walls curved, but now that he was up close, it looked as if they ran in a straight line. The Ard Ri walked along the walls, looking for a gate, or some sort of opening. But the wall was featureless.

The first of the bizarre configurations of stars appeared in the purple sky. The wind dropped with the onset of night and the plain was deathly still.

The king stopped. There was a faint buzzing, like the distant drone of a bee. He moved on slowly, concentrating on the sound now; when he realized he was hearing voices, he stopped, pressed flat against the wall, his sword in his hand, wondering if the voices were coming closer. But they didn't seem to be moving at all and so the king dropped down into the long grass and crept on. He realized the voices had become louder, about the same time the ground began to dip down away from him. In the wan purple-green light of the Otherworld night, the king came to the edge of a cliff. Carefully parting the long grass, he peered down ... and felt the hairs on the back of his neck rise at the sight.

He was looking down into a broad, shallow valley which was seething with movement. There were more humans than he had ever seen in one place gathered in the valley ... and then he realized that they weren't human. They were Sidhe folk. He was looking at the Sidhe host, the faerie host. There were five different and distinctive races amongst the Sidhe, reflecting their origins on the sunken De Danann isle, the various coloured skins – warm copper, night-black, ghost-white, saffron-yellow and deep chestnut – shimmering in the deepening night. The five races – each of them armed and armoured, carrying banners of war – were encamped around a huge marble well that was set in the centre of the valley. The well was surrounded on all sides by nine tall hazel trees.

An abrupt silence fell on the gathered host – and then a tall fountain of water shot up from the well. The assembled host moaned aloud as the water rose. As the pure water fell, it cascaded into five different coloured pools at the base of the fountain. The water – coloured now by the pools – flowed in long twisting rivulets along the ground and through the assembled hosts, rust-coloured water moving through the host of the copper-skins, coal-black for the black folk, milk-white for the white-skins, lemon-coloured for the yellow-skinned folk, and a deep rich brown for the brown-skins.

Suddenly all the sounds stopped and the Sidhe folk fell to their knees and bowed their heads. Cormac leaned forward, wondering what was happening, and then he saw five huge fish moving slowly up along the rivulets towards the pools at the base of the well. The fish – they looked like salmon – disappeared beneath the exposed roots of the nine guardian trees. They reappeared moments later and then turned and swam away downstream. When the fish had finally disappeared, the varicoloured host descended on the streams and began to drink.

Cormac backed away from the edge of the cliff, stood up

and dusted himself off. He had no idea what was going on down there – some arcane ritual that held a meaning for the Sidhe, no doubt. But possibly even they wouldn't know its true meaning. The Sidhe had been gone from the World of Men for a long time. When they had finally left Erin, fleeing the new invaders from across the seas who carried with them the dreaded iron, they had gone into the Secret Places: the hidden valleys, the Land beneath the Waves, the floating islands, or to their palaces beneath the ground, and there they had re-created an image of the life they had lived on the fabled De Danann isle, before the sea had swept in and claimed it.

In time, the Sidhe world came to be known as the Otherworld, which was part of, and yet apart from, the World of Men. Time flowed differently in the Otherworld: a man might think he had spent but a day in the magical place ... only to return to his own world and discover that a hundred years had passed.

And Cormac had already spent a day in the Otherworld ...

The Ard Ri went back to the huge golden walls and started walking along them again. He knew that he must eventually reach a door. The sky grew dark, and then the strange nightstars began to sparkle and glitter, sweeps of swirling light, pinks, reds and greens vivid against the purple-black sky. Lights were lit within the fort on the other side of the wall – Cormac could see their glow over his head – but there were no sounds to disturb the chill night air. Suddenly, a long bar of light shot out across the open ground ahead of him. The High King stopped, his heart hammering, his sword clutched before him in both hands. Something stepped into the light and a tall, monstrous-looking shadow danced across the ground. Cormac immediately thought of the Fomor, the misshaped beasts who had once claimed Erin. Then the shape moved and the king realized what he was looking at: he was seeing the shadow of someone illuminated by firelight. Smiling at his fright, he put away his sword and then stepped forward, shading his eyes from the blinding light.

'Hello?' he said quietly, his eyes stinging and beginning to water with the sudden brightness.

Soft hands reached for him – women's by their size and shape – and they led him inside. 'Welcome to our home, Cormac, son of Art, High King of Erin.'

Cormac rubbed his eyes, blinking furiously before he managed to see clearly again. He was standing in a large circular room with many corridors leading off it, but the king didn't notice these: he only had eyes for the woman standing beside him. She was one of the De Danann folk, an unearthly beauty, tall and thin, with a long, sad-looking face and bright black eyes. Cormac bowed to her and then he looked up as a man came down the long white corridor. Cormac's hand fell to his sword: this was the tall stranger who had taken his wife and children.

The old man – though his white hair and beard lent him a regal dignity now – came up and held out both hands. 'You have arrived at last. You are welcome here, Cormac McArt, we have been expecting you. I see you have already met my wife,' he added, smiling at the beautiful woman. 'But come,' he added, 'there is a bath prepared for you and we eat shortly. You must be hungry.'

Unsure what to do or say, Cormac bowed slightly. He had come in search of his wife and children, prepared to kill the old man, but now that he was confronted with him, he seemed powerless.

The Sidhe lord clapped his hands and servants came hurrying down the long corridors, to stand in a silent line behind the man. The servants were strange silent people with greenish skin and hair that looked a little like moss. 'These will take you to your room. A bath has been prepared and some fresh clothes have been laid out for you. But hurry – we eat soon.'

One of the strange green-skinned servants led Cormac down from the windowless room in which he had washed and changed, into a long dining chamber. A huge white table ran the length of it, and the Ard Ri guessed that there must have been at least a hundred chairs on either side of the table – but only three places had been laid at one end of the table, close to a roaring fire.

The lord and lady of the house were already there, talking to a short fat man, with a shining bald head and a bright red face. They looked up as Cormac approached and the Sidhe lord stood. 'You are welcome to our table,' he said formally.

'This is Luan our cook,' the woman said. 'He will prepare a special feast to celebrate your coming.'

'Aye,' the short, fat cook grunted, and then he lifted up a small struggling pig in one hand and a short-handled axe in the other.

Cormac smiled as he sat down in one of the high-backed chairs. 'There hardly seems enough in that small animal to feed one, never mind three.'

Luan laughed heartily, his many rolls of fat wobbling, shaking and quivering so much that Cormac feared the man would surely fall over. The cook held up the pig in one hand and the axe in the other. 'Do you see this pig?' he began. 'This is a magical creature. I can slaughter it and prepare a feast from its flesh every day ... but so long as I keep the tail, I will find the pig whole and well in its pen in the morning.'

Cormac looked closely at the small pink animal. It looked

just like any other pig he had ever seen.

'And another thing,' the cook continued, 'no matter how much meat I take from this creature, there will still be enough left to feed not only one army, but five.' Without pausing for breath, Luan struck the pig a massive blow behind the head, killing it instantly. While the Sidhe lord and his lady looked on impassively, he gutted the animal and set it up on a spit to cook over the roaring fire.

The Sidhe folk and the human sat in silence while the cook prepared the rest of the meal. At last Cormac leaned forward and said to the cook, 'Should you not be turning the animal? You will burn one side.'

The cook smiled widely, showing great slabs of yellow teeth; Cormac also noticed that his centre tooth was missing. 'No, king, it won't burn – and I'll tell you something else, it won't even cook. For anything to cook on this spit, four fabulous truthful tales must be told. But they must be true, mind: tell a lie and all this meat will burst into flames.'

'A fabulous truthful tale,' the Sidhe lord murmured. 'We could be waiting a long time for our meal.'

Luan nodded. 'Aye, we could. Well, I'll tell you what, I'll start.' The cook continued chopping some vegetables with one hand, but with the other he lifted up the axe with which he had killed the pig. 'Do you see this axe? Do you know how I got this axe? Well, I'll tell you,' he continued. 'I came home one day to find a strange herd of cows grazing on my land. Well, by law those animals then belonged to me and so I took them in with my own animals and thought no more about it. However, the following morning, a man came to my fort, a small ancient-looking man, who looked – and smelt – more like an animal than a man. He said the cows were his and, while he knew that by law they now belonged to me, he would give me a great reward if I returned them to him. So, I thought about it and in the end I gave the animals back to him. And he gave me this.' The cook held up the small axe.

'I'm sure it must be magical,' Cormac said slowly.

'Magical? Magical? Of course it's magical. Whatever this axe cuts it multiplies.'

'I don't understand,' Cormac said.

'Do you see this fire now?' Luan asked, pointing to the blazing log fire that was burning beneath the roasting pig. 'Well now, do you know that fire was made by one log? Aye, one single small log. I cut the log with this axe, but no matter how many times I cut it, I still had a log left to cut from.'

'Does that work with animals also?' Cormac asked.

The cook nodded. 'I could take an ordinary animal and cut enough slices off it to feed an army,' he said.

'It's hard to believe,' the High King murmured.

'It is,' the cook nodded, 'but it is true. Look.' He twisted the handle of the spit and turned the pig upside down, showing that part of its underside had been cooked. 'We need three more truths,' he said.

'I'll tell you a truth,' the Sidhe lord said. 'It's a simple truth, but true. There is a field outside this fort, a long broad field, sewn with wheat. But do you know that we never sow that field? Nor do we ever till it. All I have to do is to go out in the morning and say, "I think I'll sow that field," and in the evening it will be sown, or I'll go out and say, "I think I'll reap this field," and in the evening it's done and the grain neatly stored away in the barn.'

'That's unbelievable,' Cormac murmured.

The cook turned the spit and showed that another section of the pig had been cooked. 'But it must be true,' he said. 'Two more truths,' he added.

'My truth is also simple,' the woman said. 'Did you see

the five armies of the Sidhe camped in the valley yonder?' She continued on as Cormac nodded. 'Well, would you believe that they are fed from the milk of seven magical cows, and their clothes are made from the wool of seven magical sheep?'

Cormac looked doubtful, but Luan turned the pig, and now another section was cooked. 'Your turn,' he said to Cormac, but the High King wasn't looking at him: he was staring at the Sidhe lord and his lady. 'Seven cows, seven sheep – now where have I heard that before?' Suddenly he looked up, his eyes shining. 'I know who you are!' He looked from the man to the woman. 'I know of only one couple in Irish folklore who have those magical treasures. You must be Manannan MacLir and you must be Fand, his wife.'

Manannan and Fand both nodded, but before they could say anything, Luan said, 'Quick, another truth, before three-quarters of the pig burns to a crisp.'

And so Cormac told the tale of how he had lost his daughter, his son and finally his wife, and how he had followed the Sidhe lord to the Otherworld. And when Luan turned the spit again, the pig was fully cooked.

'Eat,' Luan said, handing Cormac a huge chunk of the pig.

'Yes, eat,' Fand said, smiling strangely.

'You are our guest of honour,' Manannan added.

The High King was about to refuse, but his stomach rumbled and his mouth was awash with saliva. He took a huge bite from the soft meat – and immediately fell into a deep sleep!

When Cormac awoke, he was lying on the white dusty road that led to Tara. Beside him, snoring daintily were his wife Aeta, his daughter Grainne and his son Cairbre. He could see Buan lying off to one side and around him lay the hundred warriors whom he had lost in the fog.

The king sat up slowly, rubbing his eyes which felt gritty and sore, wondering if it had all been a dream, but knowing it hadn't. He was unsurprised when he turned and discovered Manannan leaning up against the stump of the ancient oak tree.

Cormac scrambled to his feet. For some reason he suddenly felt angry. 'Well?' he demanded.

'Well, what?' Manannan asked innocently.

'Would you like to tell me why you came to me in the first place, why you took my daughter, my son and then my wife, and finally tricked me into going into the Otherworld in search of them? Tell me why, Manannan, son of Lir.'

The Sidhe lord smiled and then he threw back his long cloak and lifted out a long-stemmed, beautifully worked golden cup which he had been hiding beneath it. 'It was all to do with this,' he said.

'What is it?' Cormac asked in a whisper, his anger abruptly forgotten.

'This is the Cup of Truthfulness,' he said. 'You see, we needed to give this cup to someone honest and loyal, someone who would only use it for good, someone who would use it properly. Everything that has happened so far was just a test to see if you were indeed as honest, loyal and as trustworthy as everyone said you were.'

'And?' Cormac asked.

Manannan nodded. 'And you were. You are indeed worthy to receive the cup.' He handed it across to the Ard Ri, who took it in both hands, surprised at its weight.

'What does it do?' he asked softly, looking in wonder at the beautiful designs worked into the side of the cup.

'If a lie is told before this cup, it will shatter into three pieces – the bowl, the stem and the base. Watch,' he said.

'Cormac is an evil man,' he said, and suddenly the cup fell apart in Cormac's hands. And while the High King was looking on in amazement, Manannan said, 'Cormac is a good king,' and suddenly the cup seemed to slide and lock together.

'So, a lie will make it fall apart and the truth will put it back together?' Cormac asked.

The tall Sidhe lord nodded. 'Just so.' He stepped away from the ancient tree and was about to turn down the road when he stopped and turned back to the king. 'Take good care of the cup, Cormac, because now that you can tell the difference between a lie and the truth, you are the most powerful man in all Erin.'

'But what about ... what about all I've seen in the Otherworld. Why was I shown that?'

'We were testing your prejudices, Ard Ri. You looked, you accepted what you saw, but you did not judge.'

'It was not my place to judge,' Cormac said, surprised.

'Not all men feel that way, High King.'

'What about this cup?' Cormac asked.

'Keep it. Use it. I will return for it when your time in this world is done.' And Manannan, Lord of the Otherworld, was gone. Only the ghostly thread of his voice remained on the wind. 'Erin will never again know a king like you, Cormac MacArt.'

CHAPTER TWENTY-FOUR
King of the Small Folk

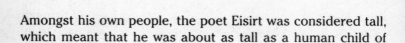

Amongst his own people, the poet Eisirt was considered tall, which meant that he was about as tall as a human child of six summers.

Amongst his own people, Iubdan, King of the Small Folk, was of normal stature, which meant that he was a head and shoulders smaller than Eisirt ... which was one of the reasons the poet had become so incensed by the king's boast.

'None of the *pure* blood', the short red-haired, red-bearded leprechaun said, turning to look at the poet, 'are as tall as I. Those who are taller should look to their pasts, for there they will surely discover the reasons for their great height. Mayhap it lies with their parents or grandparents ... or perchance their parents or grandparents lay with something they shouldn't.' A titter of amusement ran around the court, but it was a nervous laughter, for the emnity between Iubdan and Eisirt was well known. 'No,' he continued, stretching to his full height, 'a pure-blooded leprechaun should be no taller than I. Indeed, probably they should be smaller, for a king should be great in all things, including stature.'

Eisirt saw two of the guards, who were positioned behind the throne, try to look smaller.

'Kings are born to greatness,' Iubdan added. 'Greatness in all things; greatness of deed, greatness of appetite ...'

'Greatness of spirit?' Eisirt asked clearly, his trained voice ringing out across the chamber.

The king considered the question seriously, before nodding. 'Especially greatness of spirit.'

'Courage too?'

'Absolutely.'

Silence had fallen across the assembly. There was no love lost between Iubdan and Eisirt and, amongst the Small Folk, Eisirt's reputation was more secure. He had served three kings of the Small Folk and had also travelled through many of the Lands of Men. Perhaps Iubdan was the only one present who didn't realize that the unassuming poet actually had more power than the elected king.

'And in every age,' Iubdan continued fiercely, 'there is only one ruler with these qualities in abundance.'

'And you are that ruler?' the silver-haired poet asked, venom dripping from his voice.

'Assuredly,' the king said proudly.

'Curious,' Eisirt said quietly, though his voice was still clearly audible across the hall, 'I heard Fergus MacLeide, the King of Ulster, say very much the same things ... except of course that he had a body of deeds and achievements behind him to lend credence to his statements.'

Iubdan stared at the poet, his low forehead creased in a frown as he attempted to decipher what Eisirt had just said. Bebo, his consort from one of the southern tribes of the Small Folk who was a dark-haired, dark-skinned beauty with a wicked tongue and a temper to match, leaned over and whispered in Iubdan's ear.

Iubdan looked from Bebo to Eisirt, small eyes almost lost in the folds of his fatty cheeks as he attempted to sort out what the poet was getting at. He may have been stupid, but he realized when he was being led astray. 'Are you saying that this Fergus MacLeide, this humankind, is more of a king than I am?'

'More of everything,' Eisirt said softly, much to the amusement of the assembly. The majority of them had held their positions for long enough now to know that Iubdan was nothing more than a braggart. None of them expected him to remain lord of the Small Folk for very much longer. And certainly, only a fool traded insults with a poet.

Iubdan's confusion turned to an angry bluster. He glared at the poet, his mane of red hair almost bristling with his rage. 'I don't know this Fergus MacLeide, but I'll wager he is no match for Iubdan, King of the Small Folk!'

'I accept your wager,' Eisirt said immediately, and even the king, who was not renowned for his intelligence, realized that he had walked into a trap.

'Well ... yes ... well, what would you like me to do to prove myself?'

Eisirt moved through the crowd, his white robe, flowing white hair and beard marking him out amongst the multicoloured clothes and fabrics of the Small Folk. There was complete silence in the hall now, which was unbroken save for the snoring of the drunks. He stopped at the foot of the recently carved throne that had been created to celebrate the accession of the new king to the throne. The seat had been placed just a little too high though, and Iubdan's feet didn't quite touch the ground, robbing him of much of his dignity.

'Prove yourself a greater king than Fergus,' Eisirt said icily. 'Steal something from him, something he values highly, something from under his very nose ... bring us back his porridge bowl.'

There were a score of muffled snorts in the crowd, but no one dared laugh aloud.

'His what?' Iubdan demanded.

'His porridge bowl. Every morning, Fergus eats a large bowl of porridge. Bring that back, and I will be convinced that you are indeed greater than the humankind. And I will compose a lay to that effect,' he added, with a cold smile.

Iubdan nodded immediately. A lay would not only ensure his reputation amongst his own people ... but also his reputation in generations to come. 'We will do it,' he said loudly, placing his hand on Bebo's fat fingers.

'We?' she squawked in surprise.

'We,' he said firmly.

'But', she began, 'I cannot ... I mean ... I should not.'

The king patted her head again. 'No, it is fitting that you should share in my glory, and that henceforth we should be known as the greatest of the lords of the Small Folk.'

Iubdan rose to his full, though inconsiderable, height and attempted to gaze haughtily over the crowd. But, even though he was standing on a step, most of his assembled subjects were able to look him in the eye. 'We will leave you now,' he said imperiously, 'for we will need to conserve our strength for our dangerous journey into the World of Men.' The short, stout man waddled through the crowd, acknowledging their deep bows and obeisances, not realizing that most of them were bending their heads to conceal grins.

'I'll make that overgrown versifier eat his words,' Iubdan promised. 'In fact, I'll fill this bowl with the most disgusting porridge in creation and make him eat every morsel.'

Bebo flopped down with her back to the peeling bark of an alder tree and nodded. Her dark skin was flushed and she was breathless. They had been walking since sunrise and it was now close to twilight. It had been easier in the morning, but as they had approached the northern king's fort, there had been more and more traffic on the roads and

they had been forced to take to the forests, where their
short size made the going particularly difficult. They had
also been forced to spend a lot of time up a tree while a
wild boar had snorted and snuffled at their trail, puzzled by
its sudden disappearance. It had finally trotted off, but
Iubdan and Bebo had remained up the tree, terrified now by
every sound in the forest – having abruptly realized that the
forest was alive with sounds – and, to their frightened ears,
every little noise sounded hostile.

The rest of their journey was a long slow one as they had
frozen with every sound. Close to noon they had blundered
into a swarm of bees which had pursued them through the
thickets until they had both jumped into a pool. Bee stings
could be fatal to the Small Folk. And with every indignity,
Iubdan swore vengeance on Eisirt. What should have taken
half a morning took a whole day, and it was only now, with
night rolling in purple and salmon to the east, that they had
come in sight of Fergus MacLeide's fort.

They had arrived just in time to see the two massive
wooden gates to the fort swing closed.

'What do we do now?' Bebo demanded, her small face
closed and angry, her white pointed teeth giving her an
almost vixen-like appearance. 'Because I'm not staying here
all night,' she continued, without waiting for a reply.

'I'll think of something,' Iubdan muttered.

'Well, think of it fast,' Bebo nagged. 'When I came from
the Southlands, I thought I was marrying a king, not
someone who could be bullied by a poet.'

Iubdan sighed. 'Eisirt is more than a poet ...' he began.

'Eisirt is more than a poet,' she mimicked. 'He humiliated
you in front of all your people!'

'I know, I know. And when I return with this wretched
porridge bowl, I'll dismiss him from my service. You'll see,
I'll be able to do that if I defeat him at his own game.'

Bebo snorted rudely. She was having more than second thoughts about this marriage. She'd been a princess of the line in her own land and, while it was doubtful if she'd have ever become a queen, her life of comfort was guaranteed. Her father would have found a nobleman of the Small Folk for her to marry, and she would have lived out the rest of her life in idleness. She would eventually deign to give birth to the two children which were the only family that the Small Folk produced during their long lives, but these would be passed over to wet-nurses and wouldn't interfere too much with her life. However, Bebo had always been greedy and envious. When her older sister had married the western king, she had been consumed by rage and she had been determined there and then that she too would marry a king. So, when Iubdan had proposed – and it had been Eisirt who had brought the proposal, she remembered – she'd snatched at the chance without thinking too closely about it. Iubdan's star was reputed to be rising: people were saying that one day he might become the Ard Ri – the High King – of all the Small Folk in Erin. They had been married six moons now and she'd been unimpressed with what she'd seen. She looked at Iubdan, who was peering through the bushes at the fort. She could almost *see* him thinking, the wrinkles shifting on his forehead, his pudgy red cheeks almost glowing with the effort. When his forehead smoothed out, she knew he'd had an idea.

'I've had an idea.'

'Surprise me,' she muttered.

'We'll wait until after dark and then creep up to the fort, climb over the fence ...'

'And what about the guards?'

'What about the guards?' he wondered, obviously not having taken them into consideration.

'What do you think they'll be doing while you're crossing

the open area before the wall, and then climbing up the wall
– *wall*,' she stressed, 'not a *fence*? Let's leave aside the fact
that you've no climbing equipment with you: that wall is five
times your height.'

'Ah, but we don't need climbing equipment: leprechauns
are amongst the most agile of all the non-human races.'

'Well, I'm afraid I'm not climbing up that wall, and that's
all there is to it.'

'But you have to come with me,' Iubdan protested.

'When I swore my marriage oath to you, it didn't include
climbing fort walls.'

Iubdan's shoulders slumped. 'Well, have you a better
idea?'

The leprechaun queen sighed. 'Where does the fort get
its water from?' she asked.

'Why ... from the river of course.'

'And does the river flow through the fort?'

Iubdan nodded, still unsure what his wife was driving at.

'Well then, why don't we float in on the river?'

The king thought about it for a few minutes. It seemed so
simple ... and yet he was sure there was a flaw in it. 'Why
don't we?' he finally suggested.

Fergus MacLeide's fort boasted two freshwater wells, but its
principal water supply came from the river which curled
around the fort, forming part of its natural defences. Canals
had been drawn off the river to allow water to flow into the
fort itself, and this, along with its huge food and grain
storehouses, enabled it to withstand the longest siege,
making it one of the most secure forts in the Northlands.

The human guards who patrolled the ramparts were
constantly alert for raiders, especially from the west and
south, where the wild tribes still occasionally tried the might
of the king of Ulster. But there was no moon tonight and

they knew the savages didn't like to fight at night, lest they were slain and their souls became lost in the darkness of the night. Also, the wind from the north was cold, which made the guards huddle deeper into their fur-lined cloaks, and the chill flurries of rain made them less vigilant than they should have been. They didn't see the two truncated logs tumbling slowly down the river, nor did they hear the constant stream of muttered abuse that came from alongside of the logs.

'... and wet too ... my marriage vows said nothing about getting wet ... no way to treat a queen ... I should have listened to my mother ... she wanted me to marry a southerner, a grape grower, a gentle occupation, not some uncouth barbarian ...'

A stream of bubbles accompanied the second log. Though he hadn't been married long and wasn't terribly bright, Iubdan had been married long enough and was bright enough to know when to keep his mouth shut.

The two logs drifted into the narrow channel that led to the fort's kitchens. Iubdan's and Bebo's heads appeared from beneath the water as the logs bumped against the banks. The queen opened her mouth, but closed it again when they both heard voices close by, coming from the kitchens. The rich smells of cooking drifted across the water, making their stomachs rumble, and they both realized they had not eaten a proper meal since they had broken their fast the previous night.

Iubdan and Bebo remained in the water for the remainder of the night, cold and shivering, while almost overhead the kitchens – bright, warm and odorous – were abuzz with activity ... and with no sign of it abating. They discovered that they had arrived just as preparations were being made for a feast. The leprechaun king and queen both knew from experience that the cooks would probably work all night, then delegate tasks to their assistants while they snatched a few hours' sleep before returning to complete the preparations. The chances of the kitchen being empty over the coming day were nil ... and Iubdan couldn't help but wonder if Eisirt had known about the feast before he had tricked the king into heading off on this crazy quest. In the past, heroes went in search of magical swords, enchanted spears, cursed cauldrons ... not porridge bowls.

Iubdan dozed in the water, only coming awake when his head dipped below the surface, which was almost as soon as he closed his eyes. Bebo said nothing, though he could feel her eyes burning into his back.

Finally, close to dawn, he suddenly realized that there seemed to be less people coming and going in the kitchen. He nudged Bebo with his foot; she responded by kicking him solidly in the kneecap. Drifting closer, he put his mouth closer to her ear and whispered, 'I'm going to try and get the bowl now.'

Bebo looked at him balefully, saying nothing.

'There's only two of the humankind in the kitchen at the moment. They look tired. It should be possible for me to grab the bowl and make away with it.'

The queen nodded, unconvinced. Under Brehon law, it was possible for her to divorce her husband by simply dismissing him thrice in front of witnesses. Only the fact that there were no witnesses present prevented her from divorcing him here and now.

Iubdan dragged himself up out of the water and crouched behind a barrel, watching the big, ugly humankind. They were both female. They had their backs to him and were rolling out dough on a flat wooden table. He had been watching them through the night; earlier, they had been constantly twittering and chattering, but as the night had worn on into the morning, their conversation had become desultory, until finally it had ceased altogether. They were close to exhaustion, their arms working automatically, pounding the brown dough without enthusiasm. Judging that the moment was right, Iubdan slipped from behind the barrel and darted across the kitchen.

Now, he was looking for a porridge bowl ... the only problem was of course that he had no idea what Fergus MacLeide's porridge bowl looked like. It would be big, he reasoned, possibly ornate as befitted a king, almost certainly gold – the humankind liked gold.

From his position close to the floor, it was difficult to make out anything actually on the table. Even standing on his toes, his nose barely came to the top of the boards. Carefully gauging his moment, until it looked as if the two women were about to fall asleep where they stood, Iubdan grasped the edge of the table and heaved himself upwards.

And there – in the centre of the table – was the porridge bowl.

Iubdan stopped. The bowl was enormous. The king realized then that all of Fergus MacLeide's men must take their portion of porridge from the bowl: he remembered hearing something like that about the humankind. The sheer size of the bowl was one problem ... but it was also filled with thick, glutinous, steaming porridge.

Eisirt had known about this. And the poet was going to pay ...

Iubdan realized – at precisely the same moment that the women started screaming – that he had been standing on the table for far too long. He turned ... just in time for the broom to catch him across the side of the head. Iubdan screeched in surprise and outrage: these humankind had dared to touch him! Another blow swept past his face and the king hopped back. His legs hit the edge of the bowl. He staggered, arms flailing wildly, and then he stumbled backwards into the porridge! By the time he surfaced from the foul glutinous mass, the kitchen was full of the biggest warriors Iubdan had ever seen, all of them bristling with spears, swords and knives. Iubdan sighed and licked porridge from his lips. Some days nothing went right ... even the porridge was too salty.

Fergus MacLeide bore a startling resemblance to Iubdan ... except that Fergus was considered one of the tallest men in Erin. Both man and leprechaun had the same fiery red hair and beard, the same bright green eyes, the same red cheeks, a small pot-belly. The difference ended when one looked into their eyes: Iubdan's were constantly shifting and darting, while Fergus's gaze was steady and confident.

Iubdan stood dripping porridge in the centre of Fergus's long hall. Bebo, who had been fished out of the stream, stood beside him, water pooling around her tiny feet.

'Tell me, little people,' Fergus began, 'what were you doing in my kitchens?'

'I am a king of my people,' Iubdan said proudly, 'I deserve to be treated better than this.'

'A king who considers himself an equal would come to my door. He would not come skulking into my kitchens.'

'I am Iubdan, Lord of the Small Folk, and this is Bebo, my queen.'

Fergus bowed slightly, though he did not rise from his seat at the head of the table. 'I have heard of Iubdan and indeed your description matches his. But how do I know you are not a common thief, or worse – an assassin? Perhaps you were trying to poison my porridge?' he suggested, his bushy eyebrows almost disappearing into his hairline.

An angry murmur ran around the hall.

'And how do we know you are indeed a king?'

'I am the king of the Small Folk,' Iubdan said proudly.

Fergus MacLeide nodded. 'So you say. Aye, well perhaps that's the first honest thing you've said tonight. But tell me, what you were doing in my kitchens.'

'I had been set a task to steal your porridge bowl,' the king murmured.

'What?' Fergus asked, unsure if he had heard correctly.

'I had been told to steal your porridge bowl,' Iubdan said, more loudly.

'My ... my porridge bowl?' Fergus leaned forward and looked down. 'Tell me, little man, what would you use it for?'

'To bathe in,' one of Fergus's warriors laughed.

'Why did you want it?' Fergus asked again.

'I didn't want it. But I had to steal it to prove I was a worthy king.' Even as he was saying it, Iubdan realized how foolish it sounded.

Fergus frowned. 'Obviously, the customs and manners of the Small Folk differ to our own, but let me tell you, Iubdan, if any man here set me a task that was as menial and degrading as yours, I'd take his head off and impale it over my gateposts as an example to others who would attempt to mock me.'

'It was a poet,' Iubdan said quietly.

'Ah ... well of course, that's different. Poets and bards are a law unto themselves. But it's still not good for a poet to mock a king; a king loses the respect of his people that way.'

'But I had to do it to keep the respect of my people,' Iubdan said desperately. 'What was I to do?'

Fergus considered and then nodded. 'Well, there is that of course.' He laced his thick, stumpy fingers together. 'What am I to do with you, eh?'

'You should let me go,' Iubdan said fiercely, 'as one king to another, as a mark of respect.'

'But you showed scant respect for me when you attempted to steal from my kitchens. And were I to let you go, then *I* would lose face with my people. No, I think I am forced to hold you prisoner. Undoubtedly, your people will be delighted to buy your release and will pay the ransom I'll demand for you.'

'But ... but ... but this is outrageous,' Iubdan sputtered.

'I agree.'

Bebo pushed past her husband to stare at Fergus. 'Do you intend to hold me prisoner also?' she demanded.

'You came as a pair; I think you should stay as a pair and go – when the time comes – as a pair.' He paused and tilted his head to one side, considering. 'You remind me of someone ...'

Bebo's smile came on automatically. 'Someone special, someone important?'

Fergus nodded.

'Someone you loved?' she simpered

'Aye.'

With water-weed trailing down her face, her once-fine garments filthy and matted, Bebo attempted to look appealing. There was no way she was going to remain a prisoner if she could help it.

The king's eyes opened wide. 'I know who you remind me of now ...'

'Someone who was good to you ...' Bebo began.

'My grandmother. She too was a tiny woman before she died. Take them away, and find me a messenger.' He rubbed his large hands together. 'Now what ransom shall we set?'

'My lord Fergus,' Eisirt began, 'the Small Folk have listened to your request and, mindful that you have a justified complaint and in recognition of the great esteem in which we hold you and our king and queen, we are prepared to meet with your demands for ransom.'

Fergus nodded. He hadn't anticipated any problems with the Small Folk.

Iubdan and Bebo sighed with relief. They had spent thirty days – almost a moon – as guests of the king and, though they had been accorded all due respect and every comfort, they had been confined in the one room together and that had been the greatest trial of all. Divorce was now no longer a possibility, but a certainty ... all that remained to be seen was who divorced who first.

'However,' Eisirt continued, and Iubdan felt his heart sink. There had to be a 'however'. 'However, we are not prepared to meet with the particulars of your demands.'

Fergus took a few moments to work out what the poet had said. 'That would be a pity,' he said finally, 'for I would then be forced to keep your king and his queen ... but now they would not be my honoured guests, but rather prisoners. It would be better for all concerned if you were to pay the not unreasonable ransom.'

'The Small Folk pay homage to no man,' Eisirt said proudly.

Fergus nodded. 'That is as it should be; a race should maintain its honour and pride ... but where is that pride and honour when the liberty, perhaps even the life, of a king is at stake?'

'It would be foolish to threaten the Small Folk,' Eisirt said coldly.

'It was not a threat,' Fergus smiled.

Iubdan struggled free of his guard's arms. He shoved through the crowd and stood before the poet, his hands on his hips, staring up into his face. 'You got me into this, Eisirt. You get me out of it. This was all your idea in the first place.'

Eisirt leaned close to the king. 'Shut up, you fool, you'll ruin everything.'

Iubdan blinked in surprise.

The poet looked at the Ulster king again. 'We will pay a ransom of corn for Iubdan.'

'I would have thought your king was worth more than that,' Fergus said mildly.

'I am. I am. Make them pay more,' Iubdan shouted.

'I would have thought he was worth more,' Fergus continued, ignoring the leprechaun's outburst.

'He is not.'

'I want more. Otherwise I shall be forced to keep him,' Fergus shrugged.

'I should warn you, Fergus MacLeide, that it is not wise to go against the Small Folk.'

Fergus sighed. 'Then this audience is at an end. Go, go then, and do what you must, but I will not release Iubdan.'

Eisirt bowed and began to back from the room.

'But what about me?' Iubdan protested.

'You're staying with us,' Fergus said icily. 'Take him and his wife to one of the cells.'

'But you can't do this to me. I am a king!'

'Now you are our prisoner.'

The following morning all the cows of Ulster were dry, while the calves staggered around with swollen bellies. They had drained the cows dry.

The day after that all the rivers of Ulster ran red with blood, and Lough Neagh was a vast sea of blood.

On the third day, every second mill in the Northlands burned to the ground.

On the fourth day, the ears were cut off all the standing corn.

On the fifth day, all the fruit vanished off the trees and bushes.

On the sixth day, ploughed and prepared fields sparkled with salt.

And Eisirt returned on the seventh day.

Fergus was in a towering rage, his face matching the colour of his hair and beard. His bright green eyes were like chips of polished glass, and it was only because Eisirt had come in under a flag of truce and was a poet that prevented him from tearing off his head with his bare hands.

'Your people have been busy,' the Ulster king snarled as soon as Eisirt had entered the hall.

'I'm sure I don't know what you mean,' the small poet said with a mocking smile.

'Toy with me, poet,' Fergus spat, 'and I may forget your privileged position and occupation.'

The small man's smiling face turned hard and bitter. 'It would be better if you did not forget whom you are talking to, Fergus MacLeide. You may be king today, but you could be meat tomorrow.'

'Are you threatening me?'

'I have no need to threaten. If I wanted you dead, then I could slay you. Not even all your guards could protect you.'

'You boast, little man.'

Eisirt turned away. 'I will return tomorrow,' he said, without turning around. 'But I will see you before then,' he added ominously. The poet turned and marched proudly from the fort without another word.

That night Fergus doubled and then redoubled the guards around the fort. They had instructions that no one was to leave and anyone attempting to enter was to be taken or slain. Iubdan and Bebo were separated and chained to their beds, while three guards were locked into the room with them, and more guards took up positions outside the windows and doors.

Fergus himself prowled the corridors with his body-guards, unwilling to sleep in case Eisirt and the Small Folk came for him. If he had a choice he would have given Iubdan the porridge bowl: there were many things worth fighting over, but he certainly never envisioned a war between the humankind and the Small Folk over a porridge bowl. This was all Eisirt's fault ... well, Iubdan's too, for being such a weakling that he had first agreed to such an outrageous request and had then been foolish enough to attempt to carry it out. Perhaps Eisirt had been trying to determine if Iubdan was fit to rule. Now that the test had gone disastrously wrong, Eisirt was trying to retrieve the situation.

It was only as the dawn rose purple and gold over the horizon that Fergus allowed himself to relax. He leaned on the battlements, watching the mist curl sinuously across the ground, and allowed himself a smile of triumph: he had defeated Eisirt and therefore the poet had lost face ...

When Fergus started awake moments later, he discovered that his luxuriant beard which hadn't even been trimmed in the last five seasons had been completely shaved off!

Eisirt walked away from Fergus MacLeide's fort as the sun dipped below the horizon. His most recent encounter with the king had not gone well ... in fact it had been a disaster. He had misjudged the human, he realized, he had pushed him too far.

When he had turned up at noon, he was prepared to demand Iubdan's release and was quite confident that it would be granted. But when he was ushered into the hall, he discovered Iubdan and Bebo trussed up like beasts for the roasting. A pile of fresh kindling was piled beneath them and two of the fort's cooks stood alongside the trussed captives with burning tapers.

Fergus had stormed down the length of the room when the poet appeared. Without his beard, his face looked even redder and more fearsome than before. 'Tell me why I should not kill you here and now, poet?' he roared.

'I am a poet,' Eisirt said weakly.

'Not a good enough reason,' Fergus snarled.

'Kill me and the Small Folk will destroy your fort and all within,' Eisirt said confidently, although he doubted if the Small Folk would dare attack the human settlement.

'Then tell me why I shouldn't roast these two?'

The poet shrugged. 'I can't think of a good enough reason.'

'Think of one!' Iubdan shouted desperately.

'They wouldn't make good eating ...' Eisirt suggested.

Fergus poked Eisirt in the chest with his enormous forefinger. 'If you – or any of the Small Folk – come near this fort again, I will slay this pair. If any ill fortune befalls me or any of my people, I will slay this pair. If I even suspect that the Small Folk are spying on me, I shall slay this pair. Do I make myself clear?'

Eisirt nodded. 'You will slay this pair.'

'And then I will come in search of the Small Folk with fire and sword. Do you believe me?' Fergus demanded.

'Believe him, believe him,' Iubdan said in a strangled squawk.

'I believe you,' Eisirt said. He looked across to where Bebo and Iubdan dangled. 'When will you release them?'

'In a year and a day.'

The poet nodded. 'I will call in a year and a day for them. I know you are a man of your word. What ransom do you desire?'

'There is a legend that the king of the Small Folk possesses a pair of magical shoes that enables him to walk on water. Is that true?'

Eisirt nodded reluctantly. 'It is.'

'In a year and a day then, return with the shoes and I will release your king.'

As Eisirt turned and walked away, Fergus called after him, 'Tell me poet, why did you do it, why did you set the king such a ridiculous task.'

Eisirt laughed grimly. 'I was trying to turn a fool into a king. All I succeeded in doing was to make myself and my people fools.' He looked at Iubdan and Bebo. 'I think the Small Folk will be forevermore judged by the example of Iubdan ... as fools. Hencefore, that is how the leprechaun will be remembered; I'll wager that soon enough men will forget that this was once our land.'

'That is not my fault,' Fergus said gently.

'No,' Eisirt said sadly, 'it is ours. Between us – Iubdan, Bebo and myself – we have made the leprechauns into fools, into objects of fun. That is how we will be remembered.'

CHAPTER TWENTY-FIVE

The Kiss

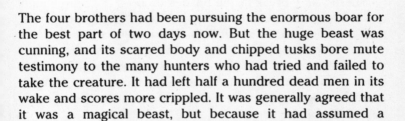

The four brothers had been pursuing the enormous boar for the best part of two days now. But the huge beast was cunning, and its scarred body and chipped tusks bore mute testimony to the many hunters who had tried and failed to take the creature. It had left half a hundred dead men in its wake and scores more crippled. It was generally agreed that it was a magical beast, but because it had assumed a physical form, it was vulnerable to physical weapons ... at least in theory.

Niall, youngest son of Eochu Muigmedon, raised his hand and his three elder brothers, who were riding single file several paces behind him, stopped, waiting patiently while he scouted the land ahead. Though not yet nineteen summers, Niall had already proven himself a brave warrior and a tracker of extraordinary ability in the previous summer when he had traced a serpent-like peist to its lair in one of the smaller rivers and then slain it himself. When the local people had dragged the creature from the bloody river and laid it out on the ground, they had found it to stretch to eight man-lengths. Niall now wore a jerkin made of the creature's skin.

The dark-haired young man slid off his mount and examined the ground which had been baked hard by an unremitting summer. Already many of the rivers had run dry, crops had burnt in the fields, and a disastrous fire had raged across the boglands in the heart of the country, which had destroyed several villages and claimed scores of lives. Niall ran his hand across the ground, but the dry, dusty, cracked earth showed no signs and he sat back on his haunches, allowing his thoughts to roam, trying to think himself into the mind of the boar, looking at the lie of the land from the creature's perspective, trying to visualize how it would see the surrounding terrain.

There was a break in the bushes there!

Niall scuttled over to the gap in the flaking hedgerow, and then he nodded in triumph. There were a dozen of the boar's black hairs scattered on the ground where it had squeezed through. Still on his hands and knees, he pushed his way through the bushes, eyes squinting in the sunlight, head turning slightly from side to side, nostrils flaring as he tested the air for scent.

The boar had come through the hedge ... and gone that way!

Niall Mac Muigmedon straightened slowly, shading his clear blue eyes from the glare of the mid-morning sunshine. With the landscape shimmering and twisting before him in a heat haze that had draped itself across the countryside like a shifting curtain of gauze, it was difficult to distinguish details, but he thought he could make out a grey thread of smoke spiralling upwards into the metallic sky.

Fethchu and Fethmac, the twins, dismounted and joined their younger brother. They were identical, dark-haired, with the pale blue eyes they had inherited from their northern mother, and so alike that even Niall had difficulty telling them apart. Both were armed with short, stout boar-spears. Maolan, the eldest brother, remained on his horse, watching the trio impassively. Though there were nearly ten years between Maolan and the twins and five more between them and Niall, there was no animosity between them, a trait they had learned from their father who had managed to weld the numerous northern and western clans together into a tribe to resist the blond, blue-eyed invaders from the Cold Lands beyond the sea.

'What do you see?' Niall asked, pointing to a pile of stones rising up in the centre of the field.

The twins squinted into the distance.

'It looks like ...' Fethchu began.

'... smoke,' Fethmac finished.

The young man nodded slowly. 'I thought so. The boar took that direction also.'

'How long ago?' Fethchu asked.

'Not long past; since the dawn perhaps.'

The twins turned as one as they raced back for their mounts, Niall following more slowly. He had seen what the boar was capable of doing; they had been following its swath of destruction across the country. He knew how defenceless lightly armed villagers were against the primeval strength of the creature, and he had no desire to look at more gored and torn bodies. In the last village they had been shown a young man – not much older than Niall – who had been gored in the belly by the beast. Though wracked by agony, the young man had managed to give a description of the beast and the direction it had taken, before finally begging them to release him from his suffering. Maolan had examined the wound, but it had already begun to putrefy. Without a word he had plunged his dagger into the youth's heart.

'The trail leads yonder, brother,' Niall said, looking up at Maolan. The eldest of the brothers nodded slightly; he rarely spoke and was nicknamed 'the Silent'.

The four brothers rode on. They moved in single file,

with plenty of space between their mounts. If the boar charged, it would only be able to concentrate on one of them, leaving the others time to attack it.

They rode across a flat open countryside, scorched amber and gold and without signs of life: neither deer nor cattle roamed the fields and no birds flew in the heavens. Without the benefit of any shade, the sun was unbearably hot and Niall could feel hot sweat moving down along the length of his spine. He was wearing a heavy leather cuirass, which was uncomfortably heavy, but, as Maolan had pointed out, better to be hot than dead.

The young man dug the heel of his hand into his eyes, and brushed away the salt sweat, blinking furiously. The grey thread that rose straight up into the cloudless, windless sky was indeed smoke, and was issuing from a tumbled pile of stones that was half buried in the ground. If he hadn't seen the smoke, they would probably have ridden past, assuming that it was nothing more than a natural outcropping of rock.

The four brothers stopped well back from the rock. While Niall and Maolan examined it closely, the twins deliberately turned away, keeping watch on their surroundings: there were more dangerous beasts than wild boars in the countryside.

'Can you see any sign of the beast's spoor?' Maolan asked.

Niall dismounted and dropped flat on the ground, his hands brushing at the burnt grass, seeking any sign. The grass was crisp beneath his fingers and, as he pressed downwards, it slowly straightened, leaving no visible mark. Resting his chin on the ground, he stared intently on the earth, finally spotting a series of indentations in the earth. Coming easily to his feet, he nodded at the tumbled pile of stones. 'It went that way.'

The four brothers moved towards the stones. There was a deeply shadowed opening close to the ground, through which the grey-white wisp of smoke was escaping. They had spread out into a long line, being careful not to bunch up. Niall stopped and pointed with his spear. An enormous boar-print was clearly visible in the dust beside a flat stone.

Maolan looked at Fethchu and Fethmac and pointed left and right. They were to go around the stones. With his spear, he indicated that Niall should go up on to the stones, above the entrance. Maolan waited until the twins had reappeared on the far side of the stones; they were both shaking their heads, indicating that there was no other entrance. Moving in closer to the island of stones, they took up positions to the left and right of the dark entrance. When his three brothers were in position, Maolan grounded his spear, butt first, on the hard earth and called out, 'You, within! Come forth. Face me.'

Niall heard a scrabbling sound from inside the heaped stones and jerked his thumb downwards, warning his brother that the primitive dwelling was occupied.

'I have tracked a savage beast to this place,' Maolan continued. 'That is all I am hunting this day.'

A shape appeared in the doorway, a bundle of grey rags, mingled with leaves, twigs and matted filth. Niall, who was above the figure, recoiled with the stench that wafted up from the creature.

'I am the son of Eochu Muigmedon ...,' Maolan began.

'Where are your brothers, Maolan, son of Eochu Muigmedon?' The cracked voice was undoubtedly female, though the features were hidden beneath a mass of twisted, tangled hair. 'All Erin knows the sons of Eochu Muigmedon are inseparable.'

'Who are you, old woman?' Maolan asked. 'What are you: witch, sorceress?'

'Neither,' the old woman cackled, 'and not so old as you might think,' she continued. Using a twisted stick, the old woman hobbled up from what was obviously her dwelling in the heart of the stones. She looked left and right, immediately spotting the twins, and then raised her head slightly to look up at Niall. 'Are the sons of Eochu Muigmedon so frightened of one woman?'

Niall slid down the stones to stand beside the creature. Though he was the smallest of the brothers, the woman only came to his chest. 'It was not you we feared,' he said easily, 'but rather what else might be within.'

'There is nothing within but memories.'

Niall nodded, concentrating on breathing through his mouth. The woman was indescribably filthy and, in the intense heat, her odour had assumed an almost physical presence. He could feel his eyes watering with the smell and he knew he'd be smelling that stench for days to come. He would have to wash at the first opportunity. 'We have been chasing a fearsome giant boar for days now. Every town, village and farm we've encountered has some evidence of its passage ... usually a dead or wounded body,' he added. 'We were afraid we'd find another such here.'

The old woman nodded. 'The boar passed this way earlier this morning. But there was nothing here to tempt it to linger.'

Niall nodded. 'We'll head on then. We must stop this beast before it wreaks more destruction and claims more lives.'

'You'll quench your thirst first though,' the old woman said and, without waiting for a reply, slipped back into the dark interior of the pile of stones. Niall looked at Maolan, who shook his head quickly. They all knew the dangers of accepting food or drink in this fashion.

When the woman reappeared, she was carrying an enormous stone jar and four polished wooden goblets. She set the goblets down on a flat stone and poured thick sweet-smelling mead. Niall felt his mouth water with the sweet richness of it. 'We must push on,' he said reluctantly, 'we are determined to catch this boar.'

'The mead is good,' the old woman said, her voice sounding suddenly tired. 'Will you not accept my hospitality?' She held out a brimming goblet.

Niall looked at his elder brother again. 'It is not that we do not appreciate your hospitality ...,' he said eventually

'You fear me,' the woman said suddenly. 'You fear me because of my appearance. Thus am I cursed. Thus am I doomed.'

'Niall,' Maolan said softly, 'we must away.'

The young man looked closely at the woman, seeing her deep brown eyes for the first time beneath the matted tangle of hair. Her eyes were magnified with unshed tears.

Before his brothers could object, Niall reached out suddenly, snatched the goblet and drank deeply. The mead tasted like nectar.

'Niall!' Maolan hissed angrily.

The young man passed back the goblet, his head reeling from the powerful drink. 'My brother worries too much,' he said softly.

'Caution is always admirable, but sometimes one has to trust one's instincts,' the old woman murmured.

'True,' Niall whispered. 'We must away,' he said, and then, leaning forward, brushed the old woman's hair off her face and kissed her lightly on the cheek. 'Take care.'

He had turned away and was walking back towards Maolan when the twins screamed a warning. Niall turned back ... and then stopped in horror.

Something was happening to the old woman ... she was changing, altering, her body twisting, turning, convulsing.

She fell to the ground, and the rags that covered her frail body crawled and moved with a life of their own as her body spasmed. A stick-like claw bit into the hard earth, blackened ragged nails tearing grooves in the dust.

Maolan's screamed warning jerked Niall around again: the boar had appeared from around the stones and was racing toward them, head lowered, strings of saliva dripping from the gaping jaws. He realized then he had put down his spear when he'd taken the goblet of mead. The beast was enormous, its head was on a level with his chest, its eyes burning with an evil intelligence. Its paws bit deeply into the hard earth as it charged towards him, snorting in a deep bass bellow.

The twins threw their spears at the beast. Fethchu's went high over the boar's back, while Fethmac's bit into the ground in front of it. The boar didn't even slow as it trampled over it, snapping it in two.

Maolan's spear thudded into the ground beside Niall. Wrenching it free, the young man turned to face the creature that was almost upon him. He knew there was no way he could stand the boar's charge: even with the heavy boar spear in his hands, the beast would simply impale itself on the spear and then run him down.

He had one desperate chance ...

Niall raced towards the beast, the bizarre action shocking his brothers speechless. At the last moment, he grounded the spear in the hard earth and used it to launch himself up and over the boar's back. He hit the ground with enough force to knock the wind from him.

Confused, the boar skidded to a halt in a cloud of red dust. It spun around and spotted the bundle on the ground. Lowering its head, its razor-sharp teeth winking in the sunlight, it charged Niall. He managed to stagger to his feet, at least determined to die like a man.

The beast bore down on him, the sunlight turning its coarse red hair to a burnished copper that also seemed ablaze in the afternoon light ... and then Niall realized the hair was alight. The beast was burning!

The boar stopped, tossing its head in confusion. Blue flames were dancing across its skin, the coarse hair crisping, curling. It opened its mouth and bellowed, and disgorged a column of flame. It staggered a few final steps towards Niall, before crashing over on its side less than half-a-dozen paces in front of Niall. It writhed in silent agony. The stench of burning hair and flesh tainted the dry air.

Niall retrieved Fethchu's spear which had missed the beast. Approaching as close as possible to the wildly thrashing animal, feeling the skin on his face and arms sear in the incredible heat, he plunged the spear deep into its body, ending its torment.

Fethchu and Fethmac helped him away from the carcass. Maolan appeared, holding the horses. He embraced his younger brother, touching blunt fingers to the young man's hair and eyebrows which had been singed by the flames. 'You were lucky,' he said simply.

'But what happened ...?' Niall asked, surprised to find that his voice was hoarse and raw. There was a taste of smoke and burnt meat in his mouth and nostrils.

The three brothers looked beyond Niall. He turned slowly to face the same direction.

There was a woman standing before the tumbled stone dwelling. A tall golden-haired, brown-eyed woman, with pale, delicate features. In his bemused state it took him a few moments to realize she was wearing the grey rags of the evil-smelling old woman. Shaking off his brother's hands, he walked forward to stand before her. He guessed she was only a few summers older than himself.

'You saved me,' he said simply.

'You saved me,' she replied.

'I did nothing.'

'Five hundred summers and more ago, I refused the attentions of an old lord. He was powerful though and versed in magic and, whilst he had once been great, he had grown spiteful in his old age. He condemned me to live ageing but alive until someone accepted something willingly from me. I've waited and tried and, over the seasons, many people came and went and none would ever accept anything I offered. Most people feared me, loathed me for what I had become, despised me for the state in which I lived, but, you see, I had been placed under a geasa – a spell – never to leave my tower. However, the same lord had had my tower pulled down and then compelled me to live in the ruins.' She smiled at Niall and reached out with her long fingers to touch his face. 'And now you have broken that spell.'

'You set fire to the boar.'

'I once kept the fire that is sacred to the sun alight. My element is fire; my magic is drawn from that power.'

'Who are you?' Niall asked. 'And who was the lord who condemned you thus?'

The woman smiled. 'I am Grian, whom you now know as legend, and the lord was Fionn, son of Cumhal, who was once man, but is now legend. Do not condemn him. When Dermot took Grainna away from him, he lost much of his capacity to love. When his son Oisin was taken away into the Tir na nOg, he became bitter indeed. Remember him instead as a hero.'

'And you?' Niall whispered. 'What will become of you now?'

'Now?' The woman's smile was radiant. 'Now I can go and die in peace.'

CHAPTER TWENTY-SIX

The Undying Lord

Death is not the end.

This I knew before the Great Sleep claimed me. There are many worlds of experience. Some are tangible and visible to us by our god-given senses, others, which are no less real, exist in our imaginations, our dreams, in myth and legend, in our faith. The ancients had a saying: faith lends substance. If one was to wish for something badly enough, long enough and with enough fervour, then that wish would one day come true ... because it had been willed into existence. Wishes can come true.

This was the basis of all the pathetic attempts to revive the ancient Craft that debased people now call witchcraft. When thirteen people gathered together in a single place and bent their wills to a single purpose, then that purpose would indeed come into being. There is no God, save that a godhead exists within all men; know this and one knows all. Accept this, and one can accept that Death is not the end, merely the beginning.

My life in the World of Men was not unhappy. It was full of purpose and I like to think that I achieved much of what I was destined by quirk of fate and nature to achieve. I was Gerald, the third Earl of Desmond, and in my time I even became the Lord Justiciary of Ireland. I was forty years old when I died and, in the rude and savage age I lived in, that was considered old indeed. I would have lived longer had it not been for my stupidity and my interest and research into things which are best left untouched by mortal humans.

But I was not without my failings and I am not ashamed to admit them. It is those weaknesses of the spirit, those foibles which made us human: without those failings we would be gods.

And my main fault was my arrogance.

In my arrogance, I considered myself apart from the race of mankind ... though this was no idle conceit, for I have it on very good authority that my father Maurice fell under the spell of a wondrous maiden he met whilst walking around the banks of Lough Gur. He was instantly smitten by her beauty. She was tall and slender, with long golden hair that trailed to her waist, and a fragile, fey beauty that immediately marked her as being from the Otherworld. My father pursued this woman for days. She always appeared at the same spot in the lake, rising up out of the dark waters as if she had been bathing, to walk upon the shores briefly before returning to the water. Her beauty inflamed both my father's passions and lusts and one day he was waiting for her when she stepped up on to the land. Who knows what happened next: I have heard both sides of the story and the woman who bore me, whose name was Aine, says that she was forced against her will, while my father said that she came willingly into his arms. Whatever the truth of it, there is no verifying it now: my father is gone, and the woman who bore me vanished shortly after my tenth birthday. She simply walked out of the castle one evening and never returned. And though my father scoured the countryside, he found no sign of her. Perhaps she returned to the dark waters of Lough Gur which had birthed her. Certainly my father thought so, for he took to keeping a vigil by the lakeside, but in his lifetime she never reappeared.

I was unlike any other member of my family, nor, I should add, did I resemble either my father or mother. My features were very fair, my skin clear, my teeth strong and straight. But it was my eyes which marked me out as being touched and tainted with the faerie blood: they were green, bright grass-green. I discovered early on as a child that the world I looked at was not the world my human companions saw. I could see the creatures of myth and legend, the Sidhe, the leprechaun, the fir dearg, the banshee, the cluricaun, the pooka, and I accepted them as *normal* and *natural* for I knew no better. I didn't realize then that these were invisible to my friends. And at night, while I was lulled to sleep by the distant sounds of the Sidhe music or the delicate shrilling of the Wild Hunt, my boyhood companions heard only the wind and rain.

I grew to manhood in a savage, war-torn land and, though my family were English, my heart was Irish. I was fluent in the Irish language, I knew its customs and manners and, even in my own lifetime, the poetry I composed in the Irish language was accepted by the bards and *fili* and judged to be of outstanding quality.

But alongside my affairs in the World of Men, my interest in the Otherworld had grown. I had begun to practise the ancient magical Craft and I had set myself the task of becoming a master of the antique lore. With my ability to see into the Otherworld, the task was far easier than could be imagined and I progressed with a rapidity that was unheard of. Mages and magicians had given their entire lives to achieve what I accomplished in months. Now I have heard the tales that I sold my soul to the Devil. However, that is not so, but it is true that if there is a Left and Right Hand Path, then perhaps some of my practices strayed on to the darker road. My power grew, and it is true that I have seen more than any man alive today, I have gone further, stood on worlds unimaginable, heard the music of the spheres, spoken to creatures of myth, legend and nightmare. I have known the creatures men call angels and devils, I have glimpsed the purity that is God ... and the absolute evil that is His dark half.

I had achieved much, but there was so much more I wanted to achieve. However, I was still human and so, even with all my power, I was seduced by a mortal woman, and thus destroyed by my lust for her and my own pride. And to my shame, I no longer remember her name.

She was the daughter of a neighbour, I do recall that. Tall, black-haired, black-eyed, with fine strong cheekbones, a typical Irish beauty. And she had more than a passing interest in the ancient Craft herself. I had heard that she was mistress of her own coven, and I was curious to meet with such a woman. Her age and beauty surprised me, for coven mistresses are invariably older, more experienced women – the experience to run a coven and control powerful energies comes only with age. But this girl – this woman – had no need to spend a long apprenticeship in the Craft: she was a natural witch.

What was her name?

I wanted this woman, desired her without sense or reason. I was happily married and my wife had given me a son and heir, John; I had neither reason nor desire to stray. But I was fascinated by this woman ... and I did stray.

She flattered me and I, in turn, boasted to her. Her eyes held a dark promise and her body hinted at even darker pleasures. She asked me to demonstrate my powers by shapeshifting, the most dramatic and spectacular of the ancient lore. Once it was the ability of most of our forefathers. When our ancestors needed to hunt the savage beasts, they would first assume the posture and attitude of the beast they sought, and then they would allow the spirit of the animal to possess them ... and thus they would *become* the animal, knowing its wiles and tricks, seeing through its eyes, smelling through its nostrils, hearing what it heard. As man's need to hunt lessened and his proficiency with weapons increased, then so did the need to shapeshift die away. Now, only a few possess the power ... and none possessed it such as I.

I sat the woman down at one end of the long dining table in the Great Hall of my island castle. I recall that it was winter, in the soft quiet hours before the dawn, at the appropriately named dead of night. The fires had been stacked to keep them burning through the night, and the walls leapt and danced with our shadows.

'Shapeshift,' she said in the Latin tongue, and though I was sitting at the other end of the table, I could see the moist glitter in her eyes, the heaving of her bosom beneath her gown. I would have this woman before the dawn, I swore it.

I drew my shoulders up, ducked my head and called upon the ancient magical power that permeated this land. Before her astonished gaze, I assumed the shape of a huge, dark bird of prey.

'*Aris,*' she muttered, reverting to her native Irish. Again.

Shaking off the bird form, I took the shape of an ancient, withered crone, allowing my features to flow and wrinkle.

'Again,' she whispered.

Now I lay down upon the smooth wooden table, with my arms pressed close to my side, and slowly, allowing the woman time to admire the process of shapeshifting, I assumed the form of a serpent, with glittering scaled skin and flickering tongue.

She nodded dumbly. I could see the look in her eyes, but was it admiration or horror? Reverting to my human shape, I asked her, 'Again?'

Her head moved, perhaps a denial, but it was too late. By then I had begun the greatest magic, the extraordinary fête of shapeshifting that only the greatest magicians are capable of.

Drawing forth from the earth the solid magic of the ground, calling the brightness of the fires, the lightness of the air and the fluidity of the waters surrounding me, I stood, rising to my full height. And then I stretched ...

The ceiling was fifteen lengths above my head, the walls on either side were twenty lengths away from me, and the woman at the other end of the table was ten lengths away. But I grew. Stretched. My body expanded, my flesh dilated, expanding to fill the entire room. Here were the legends of the mythic giants: they were no more than mortals, but shapeshifters, who had become trapped in their magical form. My arms stretched, growing longer, longer still, until I was able to touch the walls on either side. My neck grew, rising up to the ceiling, until I was looking down on the woman. I reached for her, my long sinuous arms snaking down the length of the room towards her ...

The young witch screamed with terror and, grabbing a torch from a sconce behind her, flung it at me. My concentration lapsed for a single instant ...

But it was enough.

I had called upon the elements of earth and air, fire and water ... especially earth and water, one to give me strength, the other to give me suppleness. When I lost control of them, their energies clashed. The earth split and the island shuddered as its heart was torn apart by the magical forces. Then the waters of the lake, already beaten into a frenzy by the same energy, rose up and engulfed the sundering isle.

In less time that it takes me to relate, the isle sank beneath the waves.

But Death is not the end.

Not for one who has studied the arcane arts. Everyone in the castle that night perished ... except me. Now I am doomed to exist beneath this lake for evermore. I have however one chance of redemption: I need one of the humankind to call down the blessing of their god on me, for that would shatter the occult ties that bind me to this place, and at least allow me to rest in peace. Once in every seven years I ride out on a horse drawn from my imagination and fashioned from the mud and silt of the lake bottom. Then I ride the countryside, looking for someone to say those words, but alas, I have become a figure of fear, of terror. I am considered a portent of death. Those who have looked upon me – and survived, for my mien is horrific – say I am a demon, a pooka, one of the Sidhe come seeking their souls.

I am none of these things.

All I seek is my release.

If you see me, humankind, do not fear me, but bless me by whatever god you worship. Release me.

CHAPTER TWENTY-SEVEN

King of the Cats

Malone hit the woman casually, effortlessly. The blow caught her across the side of the face, splitting a lip already swollen from a previous blow. Without looking at her, the big man moved the plate away from him. 'I can't eat this slop,' he said icily.

Peig pressed her hand against her burning flesh. She swallowed hard, gulping back tears, refusing him the satisfaction of seeing her cry.

'Well,' he demanded, 'what have you to say for yourself?'

'That's all there is,' Peig whispered. She took a deep breath and added in a defiant rush. 'You didn't give me any money this week.'

Malone raised his head to look at his wife. A smile curled his thick lips, and the red flush that darkened his cheeks matched his hair and ragged beard. 'What are you saying, woman?' His voice was soft, almost gentle, but after eight years of marriage Peig knew the danger signs.

'I'm saying that you didn't give me any money this week, so I couldn't buy food. The village shop won't give us any more tick until we settle up the bill.' She knew what she was saying would only enrage him, but paradoxically she didn't care. When you'd been beaten so often, you lost some of your fear of the beating. She had reached the stage now where

244

she'd stopped trying to hide the bruises and cuts from the neighbours in the village; they all knew what Malone was like, his temper was infamous. 'You'd better pay up.'

'I don't think I like your tone,' Malone said very softly.

'I don't care,' Peig said tiredly. She jumped with fright as something brushed against her leg. Reaching down she picked up the two-month-old kitten and held it close to her bosom. In the last couple of years she'd come to thank God every day that she hadn't given Malone any children. Once, she'd thought that maybe if they'd had children things would have been different, but deep in her heart and soul she knew they wouldn't have been. The man was incapable of change. Once, she'd consoled herself with the thought that he only hit her when he was drunk and didn't know what he was doing: but she'd forced herself to accept that he hit her sober or drunk. He *liked* hitting her.

Malone stared down at the scarred wooden table and then abruptly pushed the pewter plate away from him with the back of his hand, splashing the thin vegetable stew across the floor. Peig looked at the remains of the meal and bit the inside of her cheek to prevent her from saying anything she'd regret: she had given him her share.

'Find me something to eat,' he said quietly, his large scarred hands resting flat on the table. They were white with quarry dust, the nails ragged and broken from hauling stones, hard rigid callouses across his palms and the backs of his fingers.

'There is nothing else,' Peig murmured. 'That's all there was. Give me some money and I'll buy you something to eat.'

'I suppose you ate,' Malone said icily. 'I suppose you ate well and this is the leavings for me, eh?'

'I haven't eaten,' she whispered.

'I suppose that bloody cat's eaten better than I have?'

Peig shook her head wordlessly.

Malone lunged across the table. His balled fist shot out, swiping at his wife. The blow caught her across the side of the head, dazing her. She felt the kitten being snatched from her arms, the animal's agonized squealing as the man's iron-hard fingers bit into its soft flesh. Peig sank to the floor as the room began to spin around her. Her stomach began to bubble with nausea. She couldn't focus properly and the floor seemed to be rising and falling. She could only watch the shadows thrown by the fire and the oil lamp dancing and writhing along the wall. She saw the shadow of the huge man lift the small struggling bundle high and then throw it forward. The animal's screaming became almost human in its intensity ... and then she smelt the sickening odour of burning hair and sizzling flesh.

Peig rolled over on her side and retched on to the bare floorboards.

The wind howling across the plain was bitterly cold, tipped with ice and the promise of rain. Peig pulled the shawl tighter round her head and hunched her shoulders to suppress a fit of shivering. She could go back now; she could go back and no one would be any the wiser. She could go back now ... before it was too late.

But it was already too late. It had been too late a long time ago.

The wind changed direction, keening across the plain, the sound reminding her of the agonized screaming of the burning kitten. She knew then she wasn't going back. She'd nothing to go back to. She'd come this far; she'd see it through to the end.

Peig had awoken just after sunrise. The pale rectangle of watery sunlight was streaming through the open doorway, but the morning freshness was tainted with the foul odour of burning flesh. She sat up slowly, feeling the ache in her stomach and the agony across the side of her face. She tasted blood in her mouth. Touching the side of her face with her fingertips, she discovered that the flesh was soft and puffy. Her left eye was swollen almost shut. Clutching the edge of the table, she levered herself upwards and, as she moved, coins dropped to the floor. When she bent to pick them up, the room dipped and surged around her. Malone had obviously thrown a few coins on to her body, probably as he'd stepped over her unconscious figure on his way out to work that morning. He had always been mean with money, but he didn't hoard it; he usually spent it drinking and gambling with his cronies in the local pub on Friday night. If he'd any left over, he'd throw it to her to buy food for the coming week, though lately he'd been coming home in the early hours of Saturday morning with less and less in his pockets. For the past two weeks, he'd given her nothing.

Killing the kitten though had been the final act. Peig had had enough. Over the years he'd become more and more obsessive, his temper had become fouler, and he'd become almost insanely jealous. He'd even stopped her going to Mass on a Sunday because he was afraid she might meet up with someone.

She'd loved him once, but that had been a long time ago. Now he terrified her: she knew that sooner or later he would kill her. And the fear that had driven her from her home had brought her here, to one of the most ancient sites in Erin.

She was standing in front of the ancient burial mound known as Knowth wherein some of the old gods of Erin were said to lie in eternal sleep. Beyond the mound, just visible as it rose up out of the early morning mist, was the site of Newgrange and beyond that again, though invisible from where she stood, was the mound of Dowth.

Peig had been brought here once before as a child. She vividly recalled spending an afternoon running up and down the sun-washed hill. As the afternoon had rolled into evening, they had sat at the bottom of the hill and listened to her grandmother telling the tale of Irusan. She distinctly remembered the sudden realization that she'd been running over a grave ... and that the grave was inhabited!

'One of the beast-folk lives in that hill,' old Granny Doyle had said, and her cracked voice had silenced the children and adults alike. 'Irusan, the King of the Cats, lives here. He is a cat that walks like a man, a man that is kindred to the cat. It is said that if you stand on the top of the hill and call him thrice by his proper name and title he will appear. But you summon him at your peril, for he is a wily creature, and not easily controlled. Sometimes, if he is in a good humour, or if the cause is a just one, he will grant a wish ...'

Peig knew that her cause was just.

The hem of her woollen skirt was sodden with the dew by the time she reached the top of the mound. The countryside rolled away in every direction and she could see the mound of Newgrange more clearly now. The wind was stronger here. It plucked at her blouse and dress, the wet cloth flapping against her thin legs. It tugged her waist-long hair back off her face, exposing the swollen purple flesh.

Peig stood on the top of the mound and looked around. Should she be facing in any one direction? Or did it matter? Finally facing to the east, she stretched her hands wide and called aloud, 'Irusan, King of the Cats, come forth.'

The keening wind mocked her.

Peig turned to the north, facing into the icy wind. Her eyes watered and the tears on her swollen cheeks were chill. She stretched her arms wide and called again, 'Irusan, King of the Cats, come forth.' The wind shredded her voice, ripping the words away.

What was the point? What was she doing? Peig shook her head; she really was confused if she'd reached the stage of appealing to the King of the Cats, some shadowy creature from Irish mythology. She felt a smile curl her lips. Maybe the years of beating and humiliation had finally driven her over the edge. She knew of women who retreated into silence or found refuge in a bottle, but there were others – and she was obviously one of them – who slipped into madness. She brushed her hand across her eyes, wiping away the tears as she staggered down the hill. 'Irusan, King of the Cats, come forth,' she said bitterly.

The rain came as she trudged down the side of the mound. Icy and bitter, it hissed against her flesh, making her pull the shawl up over her shoulders. At the bottom of the mound she ducked around behind some of the scattered standing stones, looking for shelter from the driving rain ... and screamed with surprise when she discovered that there was already a figure crouching there. It was a man, squatting on the ground in the lee of the stone, a tramp by the look of his ragged clothing and the battered cap that was pulled down low on his head, throwing his face into shadow.

'I do beg your pardon,' Peig began. 'You startled me ... that is, I was startled, I wasn't expecting anyone.'

The man grunted and nodded.

'The rain came on awfully suddenly,' Peig continued, slightly breathlessly. She realized she was babbling with fright. 'I'm sorry if I frightened you.'

'You didn't frighten me,' the man said softly, his voice barely above a whisper.

'You must have heard me calling.'

'I heard you calling. Why?'

'I was ... I was looking for someone,' Peig began, and then she continued, abruptly telling the truth. 'There's a legend that if you call aloud for Irusan the King of the Cats from the top of this mound, and if your cause is just, then he will come to you.'

'I've heard that legend,' the stranger murmured. 'Do you believe it?' he asked.

Peig glanced back up the rain-swept hill. 'I thought I did.' She turned back to the tramp ... and found herself looking at a monster.

Peig instinctively knew it was night when she awoke. There was water dripping in the distance, the sound metallic and musical, and the same instinct told her that she was underground. She sat up and a thick fur blanket slid off her body.

'You're awake.'

The voice came from some point off to her left. It hissed and rasped as if it was distorted by stone and Peig decided that she was in an underground cave.

'Where am I?' She was surprised to find how even her voice sounded.

'Beneath the mound you know as Knowth.' The voice seemed to be coming closer, though it was difficult to tell with the distortion of the rock. 'I will light a torch if you wish, but you should be prepared to find my appearance disturbing.'

Peig had a brief memory of the creature she'd seen before she had lost consciousness. Already the details were beginning to blur and fade. 'I'd like a light,' she murmured.

Something snapped and a scatter of sparks appeared in the air. The dry and faintly musty atmosphere was tainted with the sharper odour of fire and the dry smokiness of burning straw. A light flared. Peig saw the hand holding the torch first. The hand was human – except that it was completely covered in a down of fine hair, and the nails were long and slender. The torch was raised, throwing light on the rest of the creature.

And Peig saw the monster once again.

It was man-shaped, completely clothed in rags and scraps, but the head was smaller than any human's, the eyes larger, the mouth wider. It was as if a cat's skin and muscle had been laid over a human skull, the result an odd and peculiarly terrifying mixture of the two. The eyes though were human. They were bright blue and regarded Peig with what looked like cynical amusement. The mouth, filled with a cat's needle-pointed teeth, opened in what she would have assumed in a human was a smile.

'Am I so terrible to look upon?'

'No, you're not,' she said proudly, meeting his gaze.

'You called me,' the creature said simply.

'You are Irusan?'

The creature nodded. 'I am the King of the Cats.'

Peig pulled her legs up to her breasts and wrapped her arms around them, propping her chin on her knees. 'My grandmother told me about you.'

Irusan nodded. 'The old folk know about me ... though as they die, the cat-lore of Erin is dying with them.'

'What are you?' Peig whispered.

The cat-man crouched down before her. The torch shimmered across his facial hair, glinting off his silky fur, turning one eye gold, the other winking amber in the reflected light. 'I am the last of the magical folk, the last of the great cats who once roamed Erin.'

'I've heard legends about huge cats ...,' Peig began tentatively.

Irusan nodded. 'I know the stories; most of them are worthless, debased versions of the truth. When the world was young and there was magic in this land – and remember this isle was born of magic – creatures that are now no more than myth once walked with man.' The huge cat's eyes closed. 'I can remember the great boars, the huge dogs, the elks, the peists, the sea horses and water cattle, the werewolves.' The cat-man reached out and brushed the back of his paw against the woman's cheek. 'The humans were the least of all the races that ruled Erin then.' Irusan stood and stepped back into the shadows. Peig could only see the two golden points of his eyes. 'The cat-people were not the most powerful of the non-humans, nor had we any ambitions to be. Luchtigern of Dunmore, sometimes called the Mouselord, and I ruled our people between us. The humans paid tribute to us, and we in turn worked petty magics for them. The black cats were the most powerful wonder workers and humans tried to ensure that they kept the black cats happy.' His needle-sharp teeth flashed in a smile. 'A human simply didn't want an unhappy black cat around them.' Irusan sighed into the darkness. 'Now, the cat-people are gone, like most of the magical folk, and the cat-lore has been debased to simple superstitions. I am the last of the cat-people.'

Peig broke the long silence that followed. 'What will happen to you?'

'When the last human stops believing in me ... then I too will be gone. We – the magical folk – take sustenance from the belief of the human folk.' Irusan came and crouched before Peig. His head was on a level with hers and she could clearly make out the human features beneath the covering of cat's fur. 'Do you know how long it has been since someone came and called me by name and title?' Without waiting for a reply, he pressed on. 'I am stronger this day than I have been in a long time ... because of your simple act of faith, because of your belief. Tell me why you called me? Tell me what you want?'

Slowly at first, haltingly, and then with increasing

passion, Peig told her tale. Irusan listened with a cat's attentiveness. Once he moved, brushing strands of Peig's long hair off her face, exposing the bruises, and he spat viciously when he heard how Malone had thrown the kitten into the fire. Peig finished numbly, surprised by the lack of emotion in her own voice, shocked by how little she cared for the man she'd married eight years ago.

'Do you love this man?' Irusan hissed.

Peig shook her head. 'Once. No longer.'

'What do you want me to do?'

The woman shook her head again. 'I don't know,' she said truthfully.

'Why did you come to me?' he purred.

Peig took a deep breath. 'I had no place else to go. My parents are dead, my brother and sister live in the north. I have no friends; Malone doesn't encourage me to have friends. I spoke to the priest, but he said I should pray for guidance and attempt to understand my husband.'

The cat-man sat back on his haunches. 'When the world was young, there were laws, simple, direct and often brutal laws, but they were fair. Under the ancient law, if a man beat a woman, she could divorce him and take from her marriage what she had brought to it. If a man killed an animal, he had to pay the value of the beast. But you do not have the satisfaction of those laws now.' His smile was chilling. 'Though I am still called the King of the Cats, the felines that I ruled – the proud, strong, magical beasts – are no more. They went the way of all the magical creatures ... but that is not to say that the cats of today do not fall under my protection.'

Peig shook her head slightly. 'I'm not sure I understand what you're saying.'

'This Malone killed one of my race. The ancient laws are very clear on this subject.'

'What are you going to do?'

The cat-man rumbled like a purring kitten. 'I am going to revive an ancient law.'

'What will you do?' she whispered.

'What the law demands.'

'Don't kill him,' Peig said suddenly.

Irusan approached her, the torchlight glistening on the animal's fur. 'What do you want me to do then?'

'Frighten him off. Ask him not to hit me again,' she added piteously.

Irusan rested his paw on her clenched fists and squeezed gently. 'I'll talk to him. He'll listen to me,' he added confidently.

The big red-haired man was surprised when he arrived home and the woman wasn't waiting for him. He was even more surprised when he discovered that the fire wasn't lit and that there was no food prepared. He laced his hard fingers together and flexed them, the joints popping noisily: he'd give her what for when she came home.

And where was she anyway? Where had she gone, who was she seeing? Malone was conscious of the rage bubbling up within him: he was all too aware that he was fifteen years older than his wife, and Peig was pretty too, there was no doubt about that. It gave him a certain grim satisfaction to realize that she was *his*, and his alone.

The big man slumped at the kitchen table and pulled the paper-wrapped bottle from his pocket. He pulled over a chipped mug and poured a measure of the colourless liquid into it. The tiny cottage kitchen was suffused with the bitter acrid odour of pure alcohol. The illegally distilled poteen was almost one hundred per cent proof.

Malone sipped the drink cautiously, his eyes watering from the fumes. It seared its way down his dust-caked throat and blossomed in his stomach in a ball of fire.

Where was she?
Where was she?

As the evening moved on into night, Malone's jealousy –
fuelled by the alcohol – grew into something darker: a bitter
resentment, almost a hatred for the woman. He knew she
didn't love him ... she'd probably never loved him ...
probably married him for what she could get out of him. He
was older than her, working in a dangerous trade. Men were
crippled, some died as they quarried the stone. Maybe that's
what she was hoping for. She was probably with another man
right now ... just wait till he got her. He'd kill her.

Malone awoke in the still quiet hours of night. The
cottage felt empty and, even without checking the bedroom,
he knew she hadn't returned yet. Fumbling for his watch, he
squinted at the pale face: it had just gone three. Jesus God!
Where was she?

The big man surged to his feet and with a heave overturned the table, sending it crashing across the room. He
strode to the window and stared out into the night-locked
town. The street was deserted, ivory moonlight lying like a
coating of rime on the roofs of the houses, dappling the
cobbled streets.

Malone didn't know how long he'd been standing there,
his forehead pressed against the cooling glass, when he
became aware of the figures moving down the street.

A man and a woman ... walking far too close together.

Malone instinctively knew it was Peig. The big man's
teeth locked together, the tendons leapt out along the line
of his jaw, and the veins that throbbed in his forehead
pulsed with an almost physical pain. Standing in the
shadows, he watched them approach. The man was tall and
thin, dressed in what looked like rags, with a broken-
brimmed hat pulled low over his eyes. It was a tramp for
Christ's sake; she was seeing a tramp!

As they approached the door, Malone stepped back into the shadows.

'Are you sure this is what you want to do?' the man said as Peig pushed open the door and stepped into the narrow hallway.

'I'm sure,' Peig whispered. She stepped into the cottage's only bedroom and stopped in surprise: she had fully expected to find her husband asleep in the bed. She walked from the bedroom into the kitchen and looked around. 'He's not here.'

'He isssss,' Irusan hissed.

Malone lunged out of the shadows, his huge fists flailing. He caught Peig a glancing blow across the left shoulder, sending her spinning up against a wall, and then he turned his attention to the tramp. 'I'll have you,' he grunted, punching at the figure.

The first blow missed and so did the second ... even though the figure hadn't seemed to move. He saw the stranger raise a hand, felt the wind as it brushed past his face ... and then, seconds later, felt the pain. It burned across his cheeks, searing his flesh like acid. Malone clapped a hand to his face, felt the moisture there. He looked at his fingers in amazement; in the reflected moonlight, the blood looked black.

'I'm going to kill you,' he grunted. 'And then I'm going to kill that bitch!'

The tramp shook his head slightly. 'No, I don't think so.' He struck at Malone again, and this time the big man felt the white fire across his ribs. Moments later, warm liquid began to trickle down his leg. He had a knife! The bastard was cutting him with a knife.

Malone jabbed a quick punch at the tramp's face. The man ducked, but the blow dislodged his hat ... and Malone staggered backwards. The tramp was silhouetted against the window, but there was something *wrong* with the shape of his head. Something terribly wrong. Common sense told him to run, but the alcohol was burning in his blood, and his temper overrode all common sense. He threw himself forward on to the tramp – and the man lifted him bodily off the ground!

Malone found himself looking down on to a face out of a nightmare. He was only vaguely aware of the pain in his flesh where the man held him ... but then he abruptly realized that it wasn't a man holding him. It was a cat. A giant cat. He abruptly remembered the kitten he had tossed into the flames the previous night. A terrifying face, part-man, part-beast, loomed up before him, the stink of cat strong in his nostrils, the rank meaty odour from its breath almost overpowering. A mouthful of needle-sharp teeth opened up and, as Malone struggled to escape, the terrifying creature spoke. 'There is always retribution, either in this world or the next. That is the ancient law. Some men will receive their just desserts in the next life. You however are destined to receive yours in this.' The teeth closed around Malone's throat and a new odour – the sharp metallic copper of spilt blood – suffused the cottage.

The old gods, the ancient folk, the magical creatures depend on the beliefs of the humankind to ensure their survival. The more powerful the emotion, the stronger the god or creature grows.

And Irusan, the King of the Cats, is said to haunt the lonely hill of Knowth, and hunt on its grassy slopes. Only now he has a mate, and those who have glimpsed the shadowy couple claim that one is a human female. In recent years, more and more oversized feral cats have been sighted roaming the wild Irish countryside.

CHAPTER TWENTY-EIGHT

The Hunters

Father Ryan listened to the flat snap of shots rolling in off the hills in the early dawn light and crossed himself. Somewhere out there a creature – one of God's own – was either being hunted for sport, poached for food, or slain because it didn't fit into some farmer's or gamekeeper's scheme of things. The excuses would be legion: man could always find a reason to kill another creature – or another man.

The priest ran a long narrow finger down the back of the tiny quivering robin sitting on his window-ledge. The creature's wings were strapped to its body with a piece of cloth, and a tiny splint had been fixed to its right leg. Father Ryan breathed gently on the creature as he cut through the threads that secured the splint to the bird's leg. Three weeks previously, he'd been writing a sermon at his desk when he'd heard a dull thud against the window. When he'd looked up he'd seen nothing, but curiosity had made him cross to the window to investigate. He'd found the robin lying shivering on the window-ledge; the tiny creature had obviously flown into the glass.

Now he carefully cut through the threads that bound the creature's wings and cut off the matchsticks tied to its leg. The bird sat on the window-ledge and cocked its head to one side, looking at him. It had become quite tame over the previous weeks, even accepting milk-soaked bread from the priest's fingers.

'Sssshooo ...,' the priest breathed, blowing at the bird. The robin hopped into the air and darted through the window. It spun around in the air outside his study window, testing its wings before darting off into the dawn.

Father Ryan closed the window and hoped whoever was shooting out on the moors wouldn't take it into their head to fire at the tiny bird.

Darcy lifted the shotgun and loosed off both barrels. The explosion sounded flat and dead on the chill morning air. Pellets whined through the leaves, spattered off tree-trunks. The hare twisted and turned, darting through the under-growth, leaving curling trails of morning mist in its wake.

'Damnation,' Darcy swore. 'The animal must be blessed.' He struggled to break the shotgun and pull out the empty shell casings, but he was still drunk from the whiskey he had drunk the night before and his fingers felt numb.

Yeates, the local gamekeeper, gently prised the shotgun from his hands and deftly removed the smoking casings. He reloaded the weapon and snapped it shut. 'There you go, sir.'

Gordon Darcy nodded his thanks. He blinked uncertainly, wishing the blinding headache that had settled in at the back of his head would shift. He hadn't felt this hungover since ... since the last time he'd come to Ireland shooting and fishing. Maybe they put something in the whiskey ... or maybe it was the poteen he'd sampled. Poteen: clear as water and one hundred per cent proof. Even as the thought crossed his mind, Yeates, a big, burly man who was completely bald but with a full bushy beard, passed him across a silver hip flask. 'The hair of the dog, sir. It'll taste like nothing on this earth, but it'll wake you up.'

Darcy accepted the flask with a nodded thanks, but sniffed cautiously first. His eyes immediately watered. Taking a deep breath, he put the flask to his lips and swallowed deeply. The alcohol seared its way down his throat and settled into his stomach with a solid fire. The Irishman had been right: it tasted like nothing on earth ... but it made the headache disappear, probably because the body couldn't distinguish between two equal agonies. He wiped his hand across his eyes and passed the flask back to Yeates. 'Surely no one drinks poteen for pleasure,' he gasped.

'You can develop a liking for it,' the big Irishman said with a broad grin, tipping the flask back, his throat working as he swallowed with no ill effects.

'I've heard that it can send you blind.'

'It can,' Yeates nodded. 'That's why you have to test it first.'

'And how do you test it?'

'You float a knob of butter on the top of a glass full of the stuff. If it floats – you're fine. But if it sinks ...,' he allowed the sentence to trail off.

'I'll remember that,' Darcy whispered hoarsely.

'Mind you,' the gamekeeper added, 'when you've been drinking this stuff for a while, all other liquor tastes like nectar.'

'I can well believe it.'

'Now sir, have you decided what you'd like to do this fine morning?'

'Where are Vaughan and Kavanagh?' Darcy asked, looking around.

Yeates pointed further down the hillside. Darcy's two companions were almost invisible in the mist.

Darcy raised his gun above his head and loosed off a shot to attract their attention. They looked up and waved, and started to push their way through the heather towards him. The Englishman sat down on a tree stump and mopped his brow with a huge spotted kerchief. He had discovered that he really was unfit ... but then banking in the City of London was not exactly an energetic occupation.

Gordon Darcy was assistant manager in one of London's smaller independent banks. Specializing in the accounts of the nobility, it offered a discreet service to those who had fallen on hard times, extending loans and mortgages on properties that the general public would have been shocked to discover were mortgaged. It numbered several of the lesser royals amongst its clients, and one of the rumours popular amongst the clerks was that Queen Victoria herself kept an account there. Darcy knew that the rumour was untrue.

However, amongst his clients was Mrs Anna Maria Hall, the renowned novelist. Some years ago she had presented him with a leather-bound edition of Hall's Ireland, an account of a journey she had made through the country with her husband, Samuel Carter Hall. Enthralled by her account, Darcy had first visited the country on a holiday in the summer of 1860. He had been visiting it each year ever since; this was his eighth visit. This year he had persuaded Jeremy Vaughan – soon to be his brother-in-law – and Thomas Kavanagh, one of the bank's junior partners, to accompany him for a fishing and shooting holiday. They had spent three days in the country and so far had done precious little fishing and shooting, though they had done a lot of eating and drinking.

'You look awful, Darcy,' Vaughan shouted, even though he was only a couple of feet away.

'I don't have your hollow legs.'

'I think I've discovered I don't have any legs.' Kavanagh's complexion was tinged with yellow. 'The local brew is powerful stuff. What is it made from?' he asked Yeates, who was standing to one side, smoking a clay pipe. 'No, don't tell me,' he amended quickly. 'I'm not sure I want to know.'

'You don't, sir,' the gamekeeper said around the pipe.

'Yeates was wondering what we'd like to shoot,' Darcy said.

'Something that doesn't move too fast,' Vaughan said quickly.

'Preferably something that doesn't move at all,' Kavanagh added.

'Hares,' the gamekeeper said laconically. 'Be doing me and the locals a favour if you potted a few hares. They make good eating too.'

'Hares it is then.'

'Well, the best shooting will be found further into the forest. We follow the stream until we come to a natural clearing almost in the heart of the wood; that's generally a good spot.'

The three Englishmen followed the gamekeeper deep into the ancient wood. Sounds vanished one by one as they followed a silently running stream. It grew colder, damper in the wood, branches dripped moisture and the ground was sodden underfoot.

'How much further?' Kavanagh wheezed. Though the youngest of the three, he was already overweight and hopelessly unfit.

'Not much,' Yeates began … and then he suddenly stopped and pointed. A grey hare was sitting perfectly still watching them, less than a dozen yards away. It was enormous, the size of a small dog, and it regarded the humans fearlessly.

'A monster,' Jeremy Vaughan whispered, bringing his shotgun up to his shoulder.

'And my trophy,' Darcy laughed, loosing off both barrels.

The animal was moving even as the forest swallowed the report of the gun. The bush behind where the hare had been standing dissolved into a flurry of whirling leaves.

'This way,' Yeates said, darting after the animal. Darcy followed quickly behind, breaking open the gun as he ran, loading in another two rounds.

'Change your load,' the gamekeeper said without looking at him, 'otherwise you'll blow the animal to pieces, and all you'll have left to mount is scraps.'

Darcy obediently broke open the weapon again and loaded two more shells filled with small shot. 'I want that hare,' he said firmly.

'Fine-looking animal,' Yeates agreed.

They spotted the animal in a clearing close to the stream. The hare's enormous ears were twitching. Darcy was drawing a bead on the animal when his two companions came blundering through the undergrowth behind him. The hare took fright and Darcy fired an instant too late. The pellets churned the water to froth.

A dozen more occasions in the long chase that followed Darcy fired at the elusive hare, usually loosing off both barrels. On each occasion he missed – even though he had frequently boasted of his shooting skill. Kavanagh and Vaughan began to talk in loud voices of Darcy's skill with a gun, reminding themselves of the tales of animals he had bagged in the past. The realization that he was beginning to lose face drove him on, until he became quite determined that he wasn't going to leave the mountainside without that hare in his pouch.

The sun was now high in the heavens and the chill damp of the earlier morning had been replaced by a close moistness. Mist coiled and twisted around the trees and in places the air tasted like a thick soup. The three men were exhausted – even the usually indefatigable Yeates was showing signs of strain – but Gordon Darcy was determined. 'The damned animal's accursed,' he wheezed.

The Irishman nodded seriously. 'It might be a were-hare.'

'A what?'

'A were-hare.' Yeates glanced sidelong at him. 'Sure you've heard of werewolves ...?'

'I've read some stories ...,' Darcy said cautiously.

'Well, in Ireland we have were-hares. They're usually witches who take the form of hares to steal milk from cows and the like.' There was no trace of irony or humour in the Irishman's voice.

'And you believe this?' Kavanagh asked. He was bent double, both hands clutching his sides, his face an alarming shade of crimson.

'Of course,' Yeates said evenly. 'And why not?'

'But, my good man,' Jeremy Vaughan protested, 'This is the latter half of the nineteenth century. What you're talking about is arrant medieval superstition.'

The gamekeeper smiled condescendingly. 'Gentlemen, just because this is the age of science, it doesn't mean that the magic has gone away. With my own ears I've heard the banshee cry, listened to the tap of the leprechaun's hammer deep in the forest, I've seen the Sidhe host ride past, felt the chill wind of its passing. Indeed, I've even smelt the scents from the Otherworld. Oh, you may smile, gentlemen, and think me nothing but an ignorant Paddy,' he added, 'but I'll wager that even you have to admit, there is a magic in this land.'

The three men looked at one another and decided that they didn't want to argue with a man who, though older, was far bigger and stronger than they were. He was also carrying an old-fashioned single-barrelled large bore shotgun.

'So what are you saying?' Darcy asked. 'Are you

suggesting that this animal isn't an animal but some sort of supernatural creature?'

'Probably a witch,' Yeates nodded.

'A witch.'

'A witch with a hat and broomstick?' Kavanagh teased.

Yeates shook his head. 'No, nothing so stupid. I'm talking about a woman able to call upon the natural magic of this world. She wouldn't be able to change you into a toad,' he added with a broad grin, 'but she'd probably be able to make you very ill.'

'Look,' Darcy said suddenly, 'this is wasting time. Let's press on.'

Yeates shook his head. 'There's no need, sir. I think I know where the hare's gone to; I think I know where it came from.'

'Well where, man, for God's sake spill it.'

The gamekeeper turned and pointed up the hill to a gap between two tall birch trees. 'The track leads through there and down into a little valley. In the valley, close to the head of the stream are the remains of a once grand house. I'll wager you my fee that you'll find the hare there.'

Darcy straightened.

'But I wouldn't go there,' Yeates added.

'Why ... because it's haunted, I suppose?' Vaughan said with a mocking smile.

Yeates shook his head. 'The ghosts of the dead haunt buildings; I reckon they can do little enough harm to you. What you will find in yon tumbled building still lives.' He smiled at their expressions of disbelief. 'I see you're determined to go on anyway, but I'll not go with you, sirs. I'll remain here ... and if you have any sense, you'll stay here with me.'

Darcy stood up, gripping the shotgun firmly. 'I left what sense I had in the bank in England.'

As the three Englishmen walked away from the game-keeper and climbed up the hill, the Irishman crossed himself and then concentrated on lighting his pipe. He wondered how many of them would come back down along the forest trail.

Gordon Darcy led the way up the hill, with Vaughan and Kavanagh trailing behind. The three Englishmen had fallen silent, chilled by the Irishman's words, which they would normally have dismissed out of hand, but here ... here in the heart of the dark, forbidding forest, where the only sounds now were those of their own passage through the undergrowth, the same words were just about believable.

The track led directly between the two tall birch trees. Both trees were diseased, their bark flaking away like old skin, fungus covering many of the branches, the leaves speckled and blotched.

As the three Englishmen stepped between the trees, they became aware of the odour that clung to the place. A stench of old dead meat, faeces and urine. The smell became stronger as they followed the path which dipped down into a hollow. All traces of a breeze had disappeared and the odour became almost unbearable, thick and cloying, clinging to flesh and cloth. The blighted trees became more common, the disease twisting some into agonized shapes, or creating bulbous leaking growths on the trunks. The ground underfoot became marshy, every step they took sinking into a glutinous mire that squelched a noxious black liquid.

Vaughan ran his hand through his thinning hair and looked around nervously. 'Spooky sort of place.'

'Rather foul,' Kavanagh agreed.

Gordon Darcy ignored them both: he had seen something moving through the undergrowth ahead and to his left. He brought the shotgun up to his shoulder and waited.

The enormous hare bolted from cover and darted down the centre of the track.

Darcy fired. The first shot struck a tree trunk directly behind the hare. The pellets bit deeply into the trunk in a score of places, and the holes leaked a dark black ichor, like blood. His second shot scattered across the track, sending up a fine black spray. A score of pellets struck the animal. The hare somersaulted in mid-air with an almost human-like scream and crashed to the ground.

Darcy's shout of triumph was cut short as the animal lurched to its feet and raced unsteadily down the track. Darcy swore briefly as he broke the shotgun and ejected the spent shells. They fell smoking to the ground and were almost immediately absorbed into the earth.

'Let's head back,' Thomas Kavanagh suggested. 'I must admit I'm not feeling too well. The smell, you know,' he added. The bright redness which had suffused his cheeks had vanished and been replaced by a pasty yellowness.

'Stay here, go back, do what you want ... I'm going after that hare. It's wonderful now; it can't go much further.' Darcy strode forward and crested the slight rise in the track and then stopped abruptly. Vaughan and Kavanagh, who were on the point of turning back, stopped when they saw his surprised start. They scrambled up the track after him.

There was a ruined house directly below them. Perhaps it had once been a Norman castle in the distant past, but multiple additions and then its subsequent ruin had robbed it of all definite style. It was now so completely enwrapped in ivy and moss that it was impossible to make out the actual shape of the building, or even to distinguish where the forest stopped and the house began.

As the three hunters watched, the enormous hare raced unsteadily down the track and through the gaping hole where the main doors had been. Darcy checked his shotgun before setting off down the track, face set into a determined mask.

'Gordon ...? You cannot be serious,' Jeremy Vaughan protested. 'This is madness. It's only a stupid hare, for Christ's sake.'

'I'll wager you it's the largest hare in Ireland ... and probably in Britain too. And I want it.'

Kavanagh grabbed Darcy's arm and pointed down into the hollow. 'Look at the house, and look at the ground around it: it's all marshland, bogland. We're already ankle-deep in muck as it is; any further and you'll probably end up sinking in it.'

Darcy rounded on his two companions, face white with anger. 'You're afraid,' he snapped. 'Afraid of a ruined house and a drunken Irishman's story. What are you – children?' Without waiting for an answer, he strode away. 'You make up your own minds. I'm going after that hare.' He continued down the track, moving determinedly towards the house. Vaughan and Kavanagh looked at one another before they eventually set off after him. They knew what he was like in this mood; it was the same dogged determination that made him such an excellent banker. One of the stories current in the bank was that he had once ordered a complete recheck of the cash in hand to find a missing sixpence. His tenacity had also walked him into trouble on more than one occasion, especially when he vigorously pursued some of the bank's customers for their outstanding interest payments. When his blood was up, he was often stupidly reckless. Both young men were of the opinion that this was one of those occasions.

The silence deepened as they continued down the track. Previously, they had been aware that, though no birds were calling and there seemed to be nothing moving through the undergrowth, they were conscious of the breeze hissing through the branches and they were aware of the insects that hummed and buzzed and bit.

Now there was nothing. Even the insects had vanished.

As they approached the building, the stench of decay intensified. The building exuded an almost palpable odour of rotten wood, damp and decay. The house itself was surprisingly large, though most of it was now completely ruined. Portions of the roof were gone and only one section, which seemed to be of comparatively recent construction, was capable of habitation, though it too was in a state of decay.

As Darcy was approaching the door, a dog appeared. It was an enormous mastiff, completely black, with pale leprous-yellow eyes. It opened its massive jaws, its lips peeling back from savage teeth. It regarded the three hunters fearlessly, its huge head turning from side to side, before finally settling on Darcy as the obvious leader.

'Why doesn't it growl?' Kavanagh asked in a whisper. His heart was thundering in his chest and he was desperately short of breath.

And Darcy abruptly realized what had made the black dog even more terrifying – if that was possible. It was completely silent. He brought the shotgun around and pointed it at the animal: the dog was easily capable of taking down a man and ripping out his throat. His finger was tightening on the trigger when the woman appeared, a vague shape in the ruined doorway.

'What do you want here?' She spoke English with a strong Irish accent.

Gordon Darcy lowered the gun and lifted his hat politely. 'We were following a hare ma'am. We thought it had run in here.'

'There's no hare here,' the woman said shortly.

'I saw it myself, ma'am ...'

The shadowy woman's head moved, looking at the dog. 'Do you think this animal would have let a hare through the door?'

'No ...,' he said doubtfully, 'but ...'

'You're trespassing,' the woman added. 'Leave this place.'

Darcy nodded. He tipped his hat again, while squinting into the darkness, trying to make out the woman's features. 'This is a lonely place, ma'am. Do you live here alone?'

'My sisters and I keep this house.'

'You've fallen on hard times, I see,' he said quietly, moving a step closer.

'We were once the lords of this place,' the woman said from the shadows. 'Now we are nothing. Please leave,' she added in the same tone, 'lest you force me to set the dog on you.'

'Darcy,' Jeremy Vaughan said urgently, 'let's go.'

Darcy ignored him and stepped closer to the ruined house. His curiosity had been piqued, and the same tenacity that had brought him up through his chosen profession now conspired to carry him to his doom. 'You must be lonely up here on the mountain?'

'I have my sisters ... and they have me,' the woman said, and then, though there had been no visible signal, the dog leapt at Darcy's throat.

Afterwards both Vaughan and Kavanagh would claim that Darcy had managed to fire one barrel almost directly down the dog's throat, and Darcy himself was convinced he'd seen the dog's head dissolve into a fine red mist, but the animal didn't even stop. As he was fumbling for the second trigger, it leapt up and struck him in the chest with its forepaws, driving him backwards to the ground. He managed to scream once as its huge yellow teeth snapped at his throat.

Vaughan darted forward, placed the barrel of his shotgun against the dog's ear and pulled the trigger. The hammer fell on an empty chamber. He pulled the second trigger and again the hammer simply clicked. Darcy was screaming continuously now, scrambling wildly to escape from beneath the dog as sticky saliva dripped on to his face.

Vaughan reversed his gun and struck the dog across the side with the wooden stock. The animal didn't seem to notice.

Thomas Kavanagh broke his weapon and checked the loads before stepping forward, gun levelled at the dog. But Darcy was writhing about so much that he couldn't get a clear shot.

Vaughan struck at the animal again, and this time the mastiff snapped at the weapon, its savage teeth tearing through the weapon's wooden stock, shredding it.

Kavanagh lifted the gun and pointed it at the figure of the woman in the door. 'Call the animal off,' he said, his voice sounding shaky and high-pitched.

The woman moved forward, the early afternoon light revealing the long, ragged grey dress she wore.

The fat red-faced man pulled back the hammers of the gun. 'Call the dog off,' he demanded forcefully, but his own breathlessness robbed his voice of any authority.

The woman moved into the light.

Perhaps she had once been pretty, but it was hard to tell that now. Long, lank iron-grey hair framed a gaunt, start-lingly pale face. The woman's eyes were deep-sunk, red-rimmed, black coins against the unnatural paleness of her face. But it was her teeth which caught and held Kavanagh's horrified gaze. Her two upper incisors had grown unnat-urally long and protruded from beneath her top lip, gouging into her chin, creating deep, scarred grooves in the pallid flesh. Kavanagh felt his heart race in his chest; he had read too many penny dreadfuls in his youth, and suddenly here he was, facing a creature that might well have been one of the semi-human beasts from the pages of the magazines. She reminded him of lithographs he'd seen of the savage South Sea Islands. And there were cannibals, he remembered.

The woman hissed in her own guttural language and the dog – which had remained completely silent while it had been mauling Darcy – backed away from the terrified man. Jeremy Vaughan dragged his friend to his feet, pulling him away from the ruined building.

The woman's lips pulled back from her teeth in what she might have intended as a smile, but which Kavanagh and Vaughan, who were looking at her, found absolutely terrifying. 'Don't come back,' she hissed.

'Tell me in your own words what happened,' Father Ryan said quietly, looking from Vaughan to Kavanagh. 'Yeates, the gamekeeper told me something, but he was terrified and not making much sense.'

The three men were standing at the foot of Darcy's bed in his room at the inn. Following his encounter in the forest, they had half-carried him back down to the village and put him to bed. The local doctor had cleansed the scrapes and scratches and given him a sedative, but when Gordon Darcy had awoken six hours later, he had been unable to speak a word. Now the man fluctuated between consciousness, when he flailed about on the bed, wild-eyed and obviously terrified, and sleep, when his dreams were obviously disturbing.

'The story – or rather, portions of it – are all over the town,' the priest said quietly, looking at the sleeping man. 'The local people are frightened in case anything happens to Mr Darcy. They're blaming Yeates,' he added.

'It wasn't his fault.' Thomas Kavanagh patted his round face with a large spotted handkerchief. 'We're not blaming Yeates; he warned us against following the track into the forest. He told us the house was haunted.' He leaned forward and stared intently at the tall grey-haired priest. 'What lives in that house, Father?'

'I've never been there myself,' the old man said softly. 'But I grew up not far from here, so I know the legends that surround it.' He crossed himself suddenly. 'In fact, I'm surprised Mr Darcy survived his encounter with the dog and the hag. Only his strong constitution saved him.'

Vaughan touched the priest's sleeve. 'Will he recover, father?'

Father Ryan shook his head slightly. 'I don't know. I will pray for his recovery though.'

Kavanagh lifted his head slightly, looking through the window to where the edge of the forest was just visible. 'What's up there, Father Ryan. What lives in that house in the forest?' he asked again.

The priest pulled over a chair and sat down, both arms folded, across the end of the bed. Kavanagh settled himself on the window-ledge, while Vaughan perched himself on the edge of the bed across from the priest.

'I don't know how old this story is,' Father Ryan began. 'My father told me and his father told him, and it was old even then. As children we were warned not to go into the forest or the hags would get us.' A ghost of a smile twisted his lips. 'The children hereabouts are still told that.'

On the bed Gordon Darcy twisted in a private nightmare.

'It is said that seven women live in that house in the forest, seven hags who were once beautiful, but who were placed under a terrible curse by their own father.

'There are stories of witchcraft and devil worship woven into this tale, but I think these are later additions to make what is a simple story all the more startling.

'There was once a family of eight children, seven girls and one boy, who was the youngest, the baby. The mother had died birthing the boy and so he was brought up by his sisters who doted on him, refused him nothing, humoured and pampered him. In return he became wilful, spiteful and thoroughly spoilt.

'The story goes that he was about eighteen when their father remarried. The woman was young, pretty, and the marriage had been arranged in settlement of a debt.' The priest shrugged. 'Such things happened ... still do.'

'What happened then?' Vaughan asked.

'There are various accounts of what occurred next. They are confused and confusing, but they all agree that it was sometime close to the turn of the year, close to Christmas, when the tragic events took place. This would have been about six months after the marriage. The father was away for the Christmas assizes and wasn't due back until Christmas Eve. However, the weather closed in and, rather than be stuck away from his family over the Christmas period, he managed to make his way home, arriving some time in the early hours of the morning. Moving silently through the house, he entered his bedroom ... and discovered his son in bed with his wife.' The priest paused and took a deep breath. Kavanagh crossed to a side table and poured a glass of wine. Father Ryan accepted it gratefully.

'Well, you can imagine what happened then. There was a huge argument. The father dragged his son from the bed and beat him with a cane. His wife – the boy's stepmother – grabbed some scissors and stabbed the father in the back, mortally wounding him. As the man lay dying, he cursed his wife, son and daughters, whom he decided must have known what was going on, and condoned it. Maybe they did: I'm sure they must have known.

'The man's wife, son and daughters then weighed his body with stones, and tossed it into the pool in the heart of the forest. Apparently, he was still alive when he was thrown into the water, because he repeated his curses as the waters closed in over his head, damning them to assume their true shapes when their mortal life was complete.' Father Ryan took a deep breath. 'There's little enough left to tell and, what there is, is confused and wrapped up in local lore and legend.

'Some time later the stepmother disappeared. She'd been acting strangely ever since her husband's death, claiming that his ghost was haunting her, following her around the house, peering at her from the mirrors. She started drinking heavily, never bathed, rarely changed her clothes. Of course, by now her affair with her stepson had ended, the boy avoiding all contact with the dirty mad woman. Perhaps that was the last straw which drove the poor wretch over the edge. One morning, she was discovered floating in the lake.

'Everything seemed to fall apart then. The estates lost money, cattle died, crops were blighted, disease and illness struck at the tenants, until they began to give up their holdings and move away. The place was cursed, it was plain for all to see. Finally, there was only the brother and the seven sisters left in a house that they couldn't afford to keep up. As it fell into disrepair, the forest closed in and claimed it, ivy, brambles and the sodden ground all conspiring to complete its ruin.'

One of the candles on the dresser guttered out, plunging one-half of the room into darkness, but no one made a move to relight it.

'It's probably nothing more than a story, but the brother is supposed to have continued the incestuous relationship he had begun with his stepmother with his sisters. But they were rarely seen and soon the tales began to circulate about travellers disappearing in the vicinity of the house. People began to avoid the track and a new way was found through the forest which bypassed the house altogether.

'Time passed, and the women grew older, uglier, each of them now with the long ragged teeth that people said were the result of their father's curse, though others said the teeth were as a result of eating the lost travellers. The brother vanishes from the story about this time, but the big black dog now comes into the picture. Naturally, people said that the dog was really the brother.'

'It made no sound as it attacked Darcy,' Vaughan said quietly.

'Some dogs are trained that way,' the priest said, 'or perhaps it's simply mute.' He shrugged. 'And that's it; that's the story.'

'But wait a moment,' Kavanagh said quickly, 'you told us this story was very old, a hundred years ...'

'Closer to two, I should imagine.'

'Well then, how come the dog and the woman are still here?' he demanded.

The priest shook his head tiredly. 'I don't know. What do you want me to tell you: that there is a family of deformed women living in that ancient house and they have been living there for generations? Maybe they breed mastiffs too ...? That's possible, I suppose. The alternative is that we have at least one woman – and remember you only saw one – who has been living in that place for at least two hundred years. And if you believe that, then you can also believe that the massive black dog really is her brother.'

'Now that's impossible,' Vaughan said too quickly, almost as if he were trying to convince himself.

'Is it?' Father Ryan asked. 'I have been a priest for thirty and more years in this country. I've seen and heard strange things; I've watched people die because they heard a banshee wail, I've seen the mangled bodies of fishermen dragged from peist-haunted lakes, I've spoken to a man who believed he'd danced with the Sidhe folk for a single night, but when he returned to his village, he discovered that twenty years had passed. And the local villagers substantiated his story.'

'What are you saying?' Vaughan asked eventually.

'I'm saying that this is Ireland. I'm saying that the Celtic magic, the same magic that lingers in the Scottish Highlands and the Welsh mountains, in parts of Brittany and Cornwall and the Isle of Man, is strong here.'

'Are you telling me that Darcy has been struck down by something ... something ancient ... something magical?' Vaughan demanded. 'This is the latter half of the nineteenth century!' he added, almost belligerently.

'Not here, not in this land,' the priest said very softly. 'Here the old magic still holds sway.'

'So what are *you* trying to say?' Kavanagh demanded.

'I'm saying I'll pray for your friend. I'll pray for his recovery.'

Kavanagh turned to look through the window towards the dark shape of the forest. 'The answer's out there.' He rounded on the priest. 'Can't you do something? These are your people,' he added.

Father Ryan stood, old bones creaking. 'The villagers are my people, the local farmers are my people. But what lives in that forest belongs to an older, wilder god.'

Father Ryan awoke suddenly, heart pounding. He lay in the sweat-soaked sheets, trying to control his laboured breathing. He crossed himself, convinced that he was about to die. The old priest had no fear of death; he had long since made his peace with his God, and few men had the opportunity to die in their own beds. He made an act of contrition and prepared to die.

He didn't know how long he lay in the darkness, but he slowly became aware that his heart was easing its terrible pounding and that his breath was returning to normal. Perhaps he wasn't going to die tonight after all. Throwing back the covers he swung his legs out of the narrow bed ... and became aware of the figure standing by the door!

This time he thought his heart was going to burst. 'Mother of God!'

'You have no need to fear me, priest.' The voice was low, rasping, with a hissing sibilance. It was difficult to distinguish the gender, but the priest thought that it might be female.

'Who are you?' Father Ryan demanded, crossing himself quickly, sitting down suddenly on the edge of the bed. 'What do you want with me?'

'Your help, if you have it in your heart to give it.'

'Who are you? How did you get in here?'

The shape moved forward, the wan moonlight revealing a long ragged dress and matted tresses, but leaving her face and head in shadow. 'I live in the house in the forest.'

'The hags ...,' he began, and then stopped suddenly. 'I beg your pardon.'

'There is no need for apologies. We are known as the hags of the long teeth.' The woman stepped closer to the priest's bed, the wan light washing across her face.

Even though he had known the legends since childhood, he was still unprepared for the woman's horrific features, the skull-like face, the flesh taut across the bones, the eyes deep-sunk and shadowed ... and the teeth, dear God, the teeth! Two long fangs grew from her upper teeth and curled down to her jaw, biting deeply into the flesh of her chin. She was a night-gaunt, a bobansith, a vampire!

As if reading his thoughts, the woman shook her head. 'I am no longer human it is true, but I am not one of the Undead.'

'In God's name, what are you then?' he whispered.

'I am a lost soul. Help me, priest. Help me and my sisters escape this living death.'

Father Ryan took a ragged breath. 'If I can help you, I will ... but only if you will help me.'

'The young hunter ...?' the woman asked.

The priest nodded. 'He must recover.'

'He will. I swear it.' Her mouth opened in a hideous smile. 'And while I may have nothing else left, I have my honour.'

'How came you under this enchantment?' the priest asked. 'I heard a tale ...'

'It is untrue ... a corruption of the truth,' the woman said. 'Our father was an evil man, who worshipped no God but the Dark Lord of this world, the one you know as Satan. His worship had made him powerful and wealthy and, whatever he wanted, he took.

'You know that there are seven sisters and one brother ... that much is true. Our brother was the youngest, a wild, beautiful boy who grew into a handsome man. He met and married one of the local women, a raven-haired beauty whom our father had coveted, but who had denied him. For a while our brother was the happiest man alive, and we, his sisters, shared his happiness.

'But gradually a change came over our brother's wife. She became quiet, withdrawn, almost fearful, and our brother's mood changed with hers. Something was wrong, though we knew not what.

'It was close to the festival you call Christmas, but whose origin is far older, when we discovered the truth.

'Our brother had been hunting when the weather had closed in suddenly, forcing him to return to the house unexpectedly.' The woman's voice died to a hissing whisper and she remained silent for a long time. When she spoke again, her voice had assumed a harder, sharper edge. She spoke in brief, clipped sentences, the pain evident in her voice. 'He discovered his wife in bed with our father. Our brother was still wearing his sword. He pulled it free and ran them through, impaling them together in the act of love. The screams and shouts drew us to the room and we helped lift the woman away from our father. Just before she died in our brother's arms, she told him that she had been forced to do her father-in-law's will. He had sworn that he would kill his own son – her husband – if she did not.'

The priest shook his head in horror.

'And then our father, with his dying breath, cursed us. He swore that we would be hideous before the sight of man and never know a husband or lover's touch. He caused our brother to undergo a hideous transformation into the shape of a huge hound. Thus we have remained for two hundred years as you measure time.'

'How may I help you?' the priest asked.

'There is a way ...,' the woman whispered.

'He's dumb,' Jeremy Vaughan said to Father Ryan. They were standing outside the door to Darcy's room. The young man was pale and shivering, his unfashionably long hair now lank and tangled. 'He can't speak.'

The priest put his hand on Vaughan's shoulder. 'Don't worry; I can help him. But first I must speak to him alone.'

'I ... I don't know ...'

'What I have to say is for his ears alone,' the priest said firmly. He gently moved the Englishman aside and opened the door. The room was a shambles. Most of the few pieces of furniture had been broken or overturned. The bedclothes were strewn about the room and some of the sheets had been torn in two, while the mattress was tossed in a corner. The window was cracked in three places. Gordon Darcy was tied down to the bed frame. His eyes were closed and he seemed to be sleeping. Thomas Kavanagh sat on the edge of the wooden bed frame, watching his friend. When he turned to look towards the door, the priest was shocked by the stout man's features. The flesh hung loose on his face, while his eyes were deeply shadowed. There was a large purpling bruise to the side of his jaw. The priest looked at Vaughan. 'What happened?'

The young man breathed deeply. 'When he discovered that he couldn't speak, he went berserk and started smashing up the room. It took four of us to hold him down. The doctor came and gave him a sedative; he said that his dumbness might be of a hysterical nature and that it might wear off ... and then again, it might not.' Vaughan looked at the priest with terrified eyes. 'I can't bring him home like this.'

'Maybe you won't have to.' The priest looked back over his shoulder at Kavanagh. 'Please leave me alone with Darcy. Go, both of you, get some rest, something to eat. You're going to need it,' he added enigmatically.

The two Englishmen looked at one another and then both nodded: they knew there was nothing they could do for their friend. Father Ryan waited until he heard their echoing footsteps disappear down the hall before he turned to the young man on the bed. There were bruises on his face and his hands were also bruised, his knuckles skinned and bleeding. The priest could imagine how terrifying it must have been for the young man to awaken and not be able to speak. He reached over and put his fingers against the Englishman's cheek, turning his face slightly.

Gordon Darcy's eyes snapped open. He shifted and twisted against the ropes.

'Sssh, ssssh, gently now, gently, gently,' the priest whispered. 'I can help you. I can help you regain your voice.'

Darcy stopped struggling. He stared at the priest, his eyes wide and pleading.

'Listen to me. Listen.'

The four men moved quickly along the forest track. Dusk had fallen and the forest had assumed a gritty, grainy appearance, the trees melding into one another, losing definition, the leaves overhead assuming a solid consistency, blocking out the purpling sky.

No word was spoken; everything that had to be said had been said earlier. Jeremy Vaughan and Thomas Kavanagh had been adamant in their refusal to return to the ruined house in the forest, but Father Ryan had been insistent, and when they had eventually appealed to the mute Darcy, asking if he wanted to go back to the house, he had simply nodded once and spread his hands. What other choice had he, he was asking.

The two Englishmen had wanted to bring their guns, but the priest had pointed out how useless they had been during their previous encounter and had insisted that they leave them behind.

'And what are we going to do when we get there?' Vaughan had demanded.

'Nothing,' the priest had said with a ghost of a smile. 'There's nothing you can do.'

'This is madness,' Vaughan had said then and now, walking along a barely visible track in the heart of a forest, he was convinced of its absolute foolishness. He looked around sharply, positive that they were being followed. But the tree trunks could have concealed an army and he wouldn't have been any the wiser.

They crested the top of a rise and found they were

looking down on the ruined house. A single wavering light burned in one of the upper windows.

'All we need now is a ghost of the headless horseman,' Kavanagh said shakily.

Vaughan glared at him.

'No further,' the priest said. 'You two will wait here. I'll call you when you're needed.'

Neither man was inclined to argue.

Father Ryan continued down the slope towards the house. Darcy followed close behind. The huge black dog appeared in the doorway before them, a solid black shape against the dark outline of the door. Darcy looked at it curiously, no longer wondering at its silence. The dog looked at the two men and then meekly stepped inside. Taking a deep breath, Father Ryan stepped into the decaying house.

The smell hit him first, a peculiar mixture of dry rot and dampness, of foul decay and the bitter-sweet odour of rotting flowers, mingled with the richer odour of fresh tallow.

The two men stood in the doorway, allowing their eyes to adjust to the darkness. Directly ahead of them, across what must have been a grand entranceway, the sweeping staircase was vaguely illuminated by a feeble light from one of the rooms above. Grasping his rosary beads, Father Ryan crossed the hall and started up the creaking, groaning stairs.

The woman was waiting for them at the top of the stairs. With the candle held high above her head, highlighting her ragged and tattered gown, but throwing her face into shadow, she looked like Death personified.

'We're in here,' she hissed.

Perhaps Father Ryan had been prepared for the sight which met them when they stepped into the room, but all of

Darcy's resolve which had carried him so far melted away when he stepped into what had once been a dining room, and found himself facing six of the long-toothed hags, who were sitting at either side of a filthy, cobwebbed table. Tne seventh creature made her way around to take up her seat at the head of the table.

'You came, holy man,' said the creature who had guided them into the room.

'I didn't have any choice.'

'There is always choice,' she smiled, the candlelight running yellow down her fangs. 'But some choices are easier to make than others. Have you reached a decision?'

'It was not my decision to make,' he said softly, turning to look at Gordon Darcy.

The Englishman nodded. Despite what the woman said, he knew there was no choice. He had been struck dumb by magic – there was no doubt of that – and only the same magic could return his voice. Stepping up to the first of the ancient women, he pressed his dry lips to hers, feeling the brush of the long cold teeth against his flesh.

The woman shuddered and her dark glittering eyes glazed.

Gordon Darcy moved on to the next woman and kissed her also. She too shuddered beneath his touch and slumped in the high-backed chair.

The Englishman moved around the table, kissing each of the women in turn. When he finally returned to the head of the table, where the last of the hags was sitting, she smiled up at him, her teeth making the smile into a mockery. 'You may not know what you have done ... but you have saved us. When our father cursed us never to know the love of a husband or lover, he added derisively that he would render us so ugly that not even a madman would want to kiss us. And then he added, in his dying breath, that even though a single kiss would be enough to redeem us, we should never receive it.'

'We have kept our promise, the priest said, stepping forward. 'Will you too keep yours?'

'We will. You will have the cure by first light. I swear it on my everlasting soul.'

The priest nodded. 'It is enough.'

Gordon Darcy leaned over and kissed the woman. 'Thank you,' she whispered as the light died from her eyes. There was a scratching on the naked floorboards behind them, and the huge black hound padded into the room. It moved from woman to woman, nuzzling each cold hand, and then it lay down on the floor beneath the table and rested its large head on its paws, its dark moist eyes fixed on Darcy.

The priest crossed himself and prayed for the souls of the seven women, and then he watched while the Englishman emptied the bottles of poteen he had carried up in his pockets around the room. The priest handed him two more bottles of the clear liquid, and he used these to soak the dresses of the hags. At one point Darcy looked up and then pointed to the dog beneath the table, but the priest simply shrugged. 'It's not real, Darcy. It's an enchantment.' The Englishman looked at the dog, which was sniffing at the illicit liquor.

When both men had retreated to the doorway, Father Ryan tossed a lighted taper into the alcohol on the floor. It popped alight and burned with a solid blue flame. Within seconds the room was an inferno. The seven women had a brief moment of illusory life as the fire ate through aged bones, sinews and tendons, and the ancient corpses jerked and twitched. The flames quickly took hold of mildewed curtains, the stinking remains of carpets, the horsehair stuffing of lopsided seats.

The heat drove the two men back. There was a crash as

a section of ceiling fell in, and then the floorboards popped and curled upwards. They raced from the house as a wall collapsed in on itself, pulling down a section of roof with it, tiles shattering on the floor of the hall, spattering them with slivers of brick and mortar.

The fire burned long into the night. The four men stood on the knoll and watched it consume the house with a voracious appetite, roaring like some feeding beast. The diseased trees around the house burst into fingers of flame, their dark sap bubbling and boiling up, bursting into long streamers of flame. The ground itself burned, grey-white smoke issuing from the noisome black bubbles that popped to the sodden surface.

By the time the dawn broke grey and gritty over the horizon, the house and the surroundings were unrecognisable.

Neither Vaughan nor Kavanagh had asked what had happened in the house, and the priest didn't volunteer the information.

They were walking back to the village when Father Ryan spotted the robin on the bush. It was the same bird he had rescued earlier in the month; he recognized it by the random speckling of black spots in its red breast. He walked on ... and the bird kept pace. He stepped closer to it. The bird remained unmoving on the branch, watching them with its tiny black eyes. There was a twist of a green leaf in its beak. As the priest approached, it fluttered up into the air and then settled on his shoulder.

The three Englishmen stopped and stared.

Father Ryan reached up and lifted the broad-leafed herb from the bird's beak. He breathed in its acrid aroma before passing it to Darcy. 'I think this is for you. Put it on your tongue.'

The English hunter put the herb on his tongue, and

immediately his face twisted as the herb spread its bitterness into his mouth. 'It tastes disgusting,' he coughed ... and then stopped in astonishment. 'I can talk. I can talk!'

'The hags kept their word,' the priest said simply.

'Father ...,' Darcy asked, looking back down the track to where the smouldering remains of the house were just visible through the trees.

'I have no answer to your questions,' the priest said quickly, interrupting him. 'All you have to do is to accept that there is magic in this land.' He stopped and pointed with a quivering finger.

The priest and the three English hunters watched seven snow-white swans rise up from the ashes of the house. They circled around the smouldering remains once before heading off to the west. Seconds later a black swan followed them, its wings snapping in the air.

'Ancient magic, wild magic,' the priest continued. 'When it touches your life, your world will never be the same again.'

CHAPTER TWENTY-NINE

The Confession

The church was completely silent, one of those rare occasions when it was empty. Father Martin peered through the grill of the confessional, looking over the pews, making a final check before he finished hearing confessions for the day.

It had been a quiet morning, four women and one man in to confess their sins and receive absolution. Three of the women were regulars. Every Thursday they confessed the same sins -- 'I listened to gossip ... I indulged in scandal-mongering ...' – and every week he would absolve them and advise them to sin no more, knowing that they would be back on schedule next week, having committed the same sins, secure in the knowledge that they would be absolved. But he had been a priest in this parish for the past thirty years, and he knew that such sins – and their absolution – were part and parcel of country life. The old priest was about to stand up when he heard light footsteps scratching on the stone steps at the entrance to the church, and then the worn wooden floorboards creaked as the person came tentatively up the aisle.

Father Martin was intimately familiar with the church. Every old building had its individual sounds, its distinctive

288

voice, especially buildings like this one, which had seen and experienced so much history. After thirty years, first as altar boy, then as priest, and now as parish priest in this church, he knew every floorboard, could even identify portions of the building by the sounds of the boards. He listened to the person approaching up along the side aisle, and immediately knew that they were heading for the confession box. He was momentarily tempted to peer out through the grill, but instead settled himself into the seat. He'd know soon enough who it was; the confessional was supposed to provide a measure of privacy and anonymity, but Father Martin could identify every person from the parish who stepped into the deeply shadowed box.

The priest took a deep breath, attempting to clear his thoughts. He heard the door open and a scuffling sound on the other side of the partition, then silence.

Leaning over against the wooden partition, Father Martin slid back the grill which separated him from the sinner.

'Bless me, father, for I have sinned ...' The voice was young and female ... and not one he recognized. 'It's been some months since my last confession, father, though I did receive confession Christmas week last year.'

'Proceed, my child. You are here today and that is enough in the eyes of the Lord. What is troubling you?'

'Father, I'm not from this parish, though my people were, and I was baptized in this church. But I didn't want to go to my own church to confess, for the priest would have known me there, and might have thought me mad or gone to my father ...'

Father Martin nodded. He caught the suppressed hysteria in the young woman's voice, and he was already putting together what had happened. When he was younger, he remembered being shocked and outraged when such things occurred, but old age had brought him understanding and understanding had brought compassion. The girl was probably pregnant.

'Priests are bound by the secrecy of the confessional,' he said softly. 'Whatever is told to us is told to God. We are bound never to divulge what we hear.'

'I know that, father, but I'm sure you know everyone who comes in here to you. When you look at them, I'm sure you must remember what they said to you?'

'Only if it's a very unusual sin,' the priest said with a gentle smile. 'And you must remember, my child, that there are few things a priest has not heard in the confessional. I doubt if you could have shocked the priest in your own parish,' he added, attempting to put the young woman at her ease.

'Well ... I didn't want to embarrass him either, father.'

'That in itself is a very laudable sentiment, and much to your credit. Now, what is troubling you, my child?'

'My family has a small farm, father. We keep goats, sheep, some cows, pigs and chickens. There are seven children in the family and we each have a particular job to do: mine is looking after the goats.'

The priest nodded patiently, aware that the young woman needed time to get her thoughts in order. He was already reviewing the options open to her ... and there weren't many. She'd probably end up going up to Dublin to live out the last six months of her pregnancy in a home run by one of the religious orders. When she gave birth, the child would be given up for adoption. Perhaps some day, young girls like her would be able to have their children without the awful stigma of illegitimacy attaching to the innocent child. But that day was a long way off. He could not condemn the girl for loving someone; he had once known love himself.

'This happened about a week ago and it's been puzzling

me ever since. I've thought and thought about it, but I didn't know what to do, and because there was a priest involved, I thought that perhaps I should ...'

'Slow down, slow down, my child. What do you mean there's a priest involved? Start at the beginning. Tell me what happened seven days ago. Take it slowly.'

'I was out on the mountains bringing in the goats,' the young woman began, her voice sounding slightly breathless. The priest squinted through the grill attempting to make out her features, but she had her head to one side, close to the thin partition. 'My father had said that there was going to be a storm, and he's always right about the weather. I was halfway up the mountain when I heard the rumble of thunder. Away off to the left I could see the storm clouds gathering over the sea.

'I gathered up the goats as quickly as possible ... but you know what goats are like, father: when you don't want them, they're always hanging around, and when you need them, they run and scatter like lambs. Anyway, it was a while before I finally managed to gather the lot together, and by then the storm was closer. The sky was dark with heavy-looking clouds and, as I watched, one of the clouds flickered white and silver with lightning. A big boom of thunder came almost immediately and of course it scattered the goats.

'I shook my fist at the clouds and I swore, father, because I knew there was no way I'd be able to gather the goats together again before I was caught in the downpour.

'I got most of the herd together easily enough; they had gathered in the lee of a stone wall. I looked up into the heavens wondering how close the storm was ... and that's when I caught sight of the girl.'

'What girl?' the priest asked.

'I don't know, father. One moment I was alone on the

mountain and then suddenly there was a girl running towards me.'

'Did you know this girl?'

'I've never seen her before in my life, father, and I thought I knew everyone in all the villages hereabouts.'

'Can you describe her?'

'She was older than me, maybe one and twenty, or two and twenty, slender, with thick red hair that fell to her waist. Two braids had been woven into her hair on either side of her head.'

The young girl didn't see the priest's expression.

'She was very beautiful,' she continued, 'her face was small, with high, pronounced cheekbones, and her skin was flawless. I wasn't close enough to see the colour of her eyes. She was wearing an iron-coloured gown with puffed sleeves, and she was barefoot. I remember thinking that that was peculiar, because the ground is very rough on the mountain ...' The girl's voice trailed off into silence.

'What happened then?' the old priest asked, his voice sounding hoarse. He coughed and repeated the question. 'What happened then?'

'The woman ran past me. I could see the look on her face and she was terrified. But what frightened me, father, was that she ran without making a sound. Nor did the dogs which followed her.'

'What dogs?' the priest asked sharply.

'Two huge black wolfhounds, with massive spiked collars. And though they were running as hard as they could, they didn't seem to be gaining on her.'

The priest crossed himself.

'Thunder rumbled again, and this time it was a harsh, bitter sound, like breaking glass, and jagged lightning forked to the ground in a dozen places. I turned to look ... and this I swear to you, father, before God, His Holy Mother and all the Saints, I swear that this is no word of a lie: a black coach drawn by four black horses was coming down from the clouds.'

A hundred thoughts tumbled through the priest's confused brain: this might be a trick or a hoax, or the young woman might simply be mad or drunk. But somehow he didn't think so.

'It was the sort of coach the gentry used to drive in the olden times, but completely black. It was drawn by four jet-black horses, each one wearing black plumes, like a funeral carriage. There was a crest on the door, and it was blood-red against the blackness of the coach, and though there was a design on it, I couldn't make out the details, but I'm not sure I wanted to make out the details anyway.'

'Who was driving the coach?' the priest whispered.

'No one, father. No one at all. I thought that I was dreaming, but everything else was so real. I could smell the rain on the wind, the sweat off the horses and the peculiar bitter-sweet odour that came off the coach. I could feel the rain spattering against my face, feel the wind tugging at the clothes and hair. It had to be real.'

'Did the coach stop?'

'It stopped before me, and my heart nearly stopped with it when the door swung open.'

The priest had moved closer to the grill, and his voice had fallen to little more than a whisper. He was trembling. Though he could call up a dozen explanations for what the girl was describing – hysteria, alcohol, simple nightmare, lack of food – he never even doubted that she was telling the truth. 'Was there anyone inside?'

'It was dark as the blackest night inside the coach, but it wasn't empty. I couldn't see anyone or anything, and for that too I'm grateful, but I could sense a presence there, smell the odour of sour spices and rotting herbs. There was a sound, a crackling, spitting, coughing sound, and then that sound turned into a voice, a harsh terrifying man's voice.

'"Child," he hissed, "have you seen the hounds and the woman who flees before them?"

'"I have," I answered, turning to point up the hill.

'"Child, would you care to ride with me awhile?" the invisible speaker asked next.

'I shook my head. "I would not, sir," I said.

'There was a long pause then, and I thought the horses were about to gallop off, so I asked, "Who is that woman, sir?"

'There was another long pause, and just when I was beginning to think that the invisible man wouldn't answer, he spoke. And there was such anger, such venom in his voice. "She cheated me. We had a bargain and she cheated me, and now she must pay."

'"Who is she?" I asked again.

'"She once loved a man who was forbidden to her, and she loved him with such a passion that she sold her soul to me in return for making him love her. But he was a priest and, though she succeeded in tempting him from his vows and they lived as man and wife, she did not fully separate him from the church, which was my wish. He eventually rejected her and returned to his church, who forgave him his sins and sent him away. They could not forgive the woman though and, in the community where they had both lived, she was ostracized and shunned. She had promised herself to me, promised me her soul, but she cheated me by making an act of contrition before the high altar of her church and then she lay down on the stone steps and died. It was not suicide; she simply willed herself to die. But her act of contrition wasn't enough to save her, though it did save her from immediate damnation. Now she flees the Hounds of Hell, but we will catch her. Sooner or later, we will catch her."

'"Can nothing save her?" I asked, remembering the look of terror on the young woman's face.

'"Only the Virgin, Mother of God, can intercede for her now. But first the Virgin has to hear her call ... and my hounds ensure that her lone voice is forever drowned out."

'Then the door to the black carriage closed of its own accord and it moved away, following the woman and dogs up the hill. And though the heavens opened and I was soaked through to the skin, I remained standing where I was, watching for any sign of that poor lost woman.'

'She had sold her soul to the Devil to tempt a priest,' Father Martin reminded her.

'She loved a man,' the young woman said very softly. 'She loved him with enough passion to make her disregard the future.'

The priest nodded tiredly. 'Pray for her,' he whispered. 'For your penance say a decade of the Rosary to Our Blessed Virgin so that she might hear the cries of that poor lost soul. Now I will absolve you of your sins ...'

The woman bent her head and heard the priest's whispered absolution. When he was finished, she lifted her head and looked through the grill at the dim shape. 'Is there anything you can do for her, father?'

'I too will pray for her soul. I will beseech the Virgin to hear her prayers.'

'Are we too late, father?'

'No, my child, you're not too late. But I'm fifty years too late.'

CHAPTER THIRTY
Dullahan

In the heart of the forest a twig cracked, the sound like a gunshot across the still night. Jack O'Brien froze and then slowly sank down behind the cover of the bushes, sharp eyes darting through the undergrowth, squinting against the evening gloom, watching for any signs of movement, ears tuned for any unusual noises. He slowly counted to one hundred and then, satisfied that it had been one of the many natural forest noises, he straightened up again, pressing his hands into the small of his back.

Jack O'Brien was a small stout man who would be sixty next birthday, and looked older. A lifetime of working out of doors, in the fields, in the bogs, on the fishing boats – doing anything he could to earn a living – had tanned and deeply lined his face. A hard life had made him a hard, often unforgiving man. His uneven temper, coupled with his fondness for drink, ensured that he had few friends.

Jack followed the barely perceptible track through the heart of the forest, his eyes taking in the markers he had fixed to the trees and bushes, the twigs which had been bent and twisted, showing him where he had hidden the snares.

There!

He stooped and parted a canopy of leaves ... and swore softly. The thin wire snare had caught the hare high on its hind leg, and while the leg remained, bloodied, covered with flies, the crazed animal had chewed off its own leg and crawled away into the bushes to die. Thick smears of dark dried blood disappeared into the heart of the bushes.

'Bad cess to ye,' he muttered. He had neither the energy nor the inclination to follow the animal's trail into the bushes, even though experience had taught him that it would not have got far. Anyway, from the condition of the ragged strip of flesh that remained, he guessed that the hare must have stumbled into the track shortly after he had laid it last night. It would have been long dead by now and some of the other forest scavengers and the flies would have feasted off it. He patted the heavy bag strapped to his back. Well, no matter; it had been a good night in any case. All of the snares he'd set up had taken something, and he'd three hares and a brace of rabbits. He'd two more snares to check before he circled around to the lake to check the lines he'd set.

Jack O'Brien was a poacher. Circumstances and necessity had dictated that this was the only way he could earn his living and keep some food on the table ... even though nowadays he was only putting food on the table for himself. The children had gone first, moving out at the earliest opportunity, running away from a father who was far too fond of the bottle, and then too quick with his hands – though he didn't have to be drunk to use his hands. His wife Mary had been the last to go; it was almost as if she'd been waiting for the children to leave so she could go with a clear conscience. He remembered the details of the last day vividly. She had gone up to Dublin for a day's shopping ... and had simply never come back. She'd been planning the trip for weeks, even promised to buy him something. She'd get the early train up to Dublin, spend the day there and get the six o'clock train home, so she'd be back by nine. Jack had been out drinking on the Friday night, so it had been late Saturday afternoon by the time he'd staggered from the pub and found the note on the kitchen table. The note had been neatly printed in pencil on a page torn from a school jotter. It was unsigned.

'I do not love you anymore, Jack. I won't be back.'

He'd once thought about going up to Dublin to look for her – she had family up there and he had a fairly good idea where he'd find her – but his own pride prevented him from following her. That had been three years ago. Since then he had fended for himself.

Mary had worked in a local factory and he had come to rely on her wage, so his first priority had been to find a job to pay the rent on a small house and meet the bills. But he suddenly found that he was virtually unemployable. He was close to sixty with no real skills, and all of the locals knew of his drinking and his temper and simply weren't prepared to employ him.

So Jack O'Brien had returned to the poaching tricks he had learned from his father, who had learned them in turn from his, and he abruptly discovered that he had an almost natural skill for tracking and trapping, fishing and hunting.

He started small, taking only a few animals during the course of fishing, hunting and trapping to feed himself. But the Kerry hills were rich in game, the rivers teeming with fish, and he soon learned that he could sell his surplus to the local butchers and fishmongers. Some of the smaller restaurants – especially those which catered to the tourists with promises of fresh local produce – also bought from him. They all knew he was a poacher, but they turned a blind eye to it, and for the first time in his life, Jack O'Brien discovered he was doing something he liked, something he enjoyed ... and something he was good at.

Wood snapped.

The small stout man stopped, heart beginning to beat

loudly now. He had had several close calls with the local gamekeepers and farmers whose territories and boundaries he ignored, and he knew that the police were suspicious of him. But it wasn't as if he was doing anything wrong, was it? After all who was going to miss a few rabbits and fish? And those conservation people who claimed he was decimating the local wildlife population were just talking so much nonsense. How could one man with a couple of traps do that much damage?

There was movement in the woods ahead and to his right.

He knew how the forest could change sounds, altering them, changing their timbre and tone, distorting them until they became almost unrecognizable. He remembered once hearing an owl hoot directly above his head and jumping – literally jumping – when he imagined he had heard someone murmuring a soft question in his ear.

Shrugging his bag off his shoulder, he knelt on the soft damp ground, watching, waiting. Jack O'Brien had infinite patience; if there was someone waiting for him up ahead, he'd easily be able to outwait them. He supposed it was almost inevitable that the police would attempt to catch him; better the police than the local gamekeeper or one of the local farmers, who'd more than likely set their dogs on him, or let him have a barrel of buckshot in the seat of his trousers.

The small man shivered in his thick coat. He drew the collar up around his ears and slouched down into the heavy wool's warmth. He was dressed as usual in deep brown and black, with a battered cap on his head and a scarf wrapped around his throat. He'd discovered that rheumatism and pneumonia were the two real threats to a poacher's continued existence, not police and gamekeepers.

He tried to position himself in relation to the town. He had come north, along the old mining route, and then cut up into the hills, entering the forest on the eastern side. He varied his route every time and, though his traps lay along fixed animal runs, he had made a conscious attempt to approach them from a different direction and in a different order every day. He counted slowly to two hundred and was just coming to his feet when he heard the sound again. This time it came from behind him. He whirled around, his heart beginning to trip madly. It sounded like wood snapping, or a distant gunshot, or a spark leaping off a length of wood.

Badgers, maybe, a fox ... though the night creatures rarely left that much evidence of their passage. And it took a deal of weight to break a branch. Only man was that clumsy. Taking a deep breath to calm his nerves, he sank back to the ground again, prepared to outwait them. And he would outwait them: patience was a prerequisite for a poacher.

What a way to spend an evening. A man should be at home before a fire, in front of the box, or maybe down at the local with a pint or two inside him, not crouched in the middle of a forest, soaked through and freezing.

It wasn't right, it wasn't fair ... but then he didn't think life had ever treated him fairly. A man of his age who had reared four children and looked after a wife, given her everything she'd asked for, a man like that shouldn't have to be doing this for a living. Wasn't right. He reached into his inside pocket for the curved hip-flask, and then reluctantly withdrew his hand. On the cold night air the sharp bitter odour of whiskey could carry for quite a distance.

No, a man who had brought up his children should be able to relax now, to be able to take it easy. He should be looking after his grandchildren ... he stopped suddenly. Had he grandchildren? He didn't know; he had no contact with his children ... didn't even know where they were, didn't know whether they were dead or alive. They were probably in Dublin or London now, rich, successful, but with no thought for their father scratching a living in an Irish village.

They were probably ashamed of him. Well, they always took after their mother's side of the family. And how had she turned out? Bitch had taken everything he had and then left him. He didn't know where she was and he didn't want to know either.

When he had counted to five hundred, he straightened slowly, turning his head from side to side listening, watching, waiting. Finally, satisfied that what he had heard was simply the natural forest sounds, he moved away from the concealment of the bushes and continued on down the track. He could feel the fire in his belly, the cramping agony that occurred now whenever he thought of his family and how they had treated him.

Oh, he knew they told a different story, but then they would, wouldn't they? They told how he had terrorized them, on more than one occasion beating their mother so badly that she wouldn't venture outside the door until the bruises had faded. On one occasion they said he had broken little Mikey's arm, though they all knew the boy had fallen.

Well, he was better off without them. He'd given them everything, and they'd taken it without so much as a thank you, and then they'd upped and left. But things were beginning to work out now; he was beginning to get his life in order. He had some good money coming in and, come the tourist season, there'd be even more money; maybe he'd even think about taking on lads and training them, teaching them his tricks.

Jack O'Brien stopped suddenly, realizing that he'd passed the spot on the track where he'd concealed a snare. Shaking his head in disgust, he turned and retraced his steps. He knew the dangers of venturing off the paths at night. Even during the day, it was easy to become lost and disorientated in the woods and, at night, if you wandered off the path, you could be seriously injured or even killed wandering amongst the trees. Without daylight to give the trees shape and definition, they took on a curiously flat, two-dimensional, surreal aspect. He knew of one lad who'd become lost in the forest at night and run smack into an old oak – impaling himself through the throat on a branch. On another occasion, a local man had caught his neck in a V-shaped branch and been strangled when he left the path. Then there'd been that tourist last year who'd wandered away from his camp, got his foot caught in an exposed root and snapped his ankle clean in half. You could hear his screams clear down into the town. Jack O'Brien smiled wolfishly. He'd been in the local that night, and he remembered the looks of horror that had passed across people's faces when the first of the screams had echoed down the empty streets, coming from the direction of the forest.

Dearest God, but this was the late twentieth century ... and what had been the first word spoken in the bar? Banshee. That's what they'd whispered. Banshee.

Then they'd all filed out into the street to listen to the howling. And suddenly everyone became an expert on the banshee and was full of opinions. One person claimed that the sound was wrong, another that the screaming wasn't musical, while a third was of the opinion that it was a man's scream they were hearing, and not a woman's, and, besides, a banshee's wail was only audible to members of a parti-cular family.

That's when they began to talk about the Dullahan. The Headless Horseman ... who rode through the forest from the old mine, on a pale white headless horse, *that* appari-tion was also accompanied by an unearthly screaming.

Several of the people present crossed themselves, including Jack, though he wasn't a religious man. Nor did he believe in the story of a headless horseman or a wailing woman, but he did believe the evidence of his own ears and what he was hearing was certainly an unearthly screaming. Nor had he been amongst the small party of men who had accompanied the local constable when they'd gone up into the woods to investigate. He'd been there though when they carried in the poor Frenchman; he'd screamed himself hoarse and could only mewl piteously, but it had taught Jack a valuable lesson: it had taught him to respect the forest.

He was bending down to search for the missing snare when he caught the flash of red. It only lasted a moment, but it was enough to set his heart tripping madly. His hand went to the short-bladed knife on his belt as he melted back into the trees.

There *was* someone out there.

He tried to work out where he was and position himself in relation to the old mine and town. It only took him a few seconds before he realized that the light was coming from the abandoned mine.

All right. All right. All right.

He breathed deeply, feeling the icy air sear into his lungs. He'd leave the snares and traps and the lines he'd set on the lake. Right now he was getting out of the forest. Better safe than sorry. He'd head home to his bed and in the morning he'd have a good laugh at those who'd spent the night in the forest. A few more nights like those and they'd soon give up. He had a few bob saved; maybe he should take a few nights off.

Jack O'Brien was actually moving stealthily down the path when a sudden thought struck him and he stopped, a greedy smile twisting his lips. He'd just thought of another reason why the light should be coming from the direction of the old mine. He must be getting old – else why hadn't he thought of it before. The mine had been abandoned for years, the last of the coal long since worked out. But he remembered a story his father had told him about nuggets of gold that had been dug out of the mine. Jack O'Brien stopped suddenly; he abruptly recalled when his father had told him the story, the memory as bright and clear as if it had only happened yesterday, though it must have been nigh on fifty years gone: they had been wandering through this very wood doing a little poaching. Now, if that wasn't an omen, he didn't know what was!

Maybe someone had discovered one of the mine's secrets; maybe there was still a little gold in the old seams. And maybe he'd have a little look and find out.

He stood at the edge of the path for a moment, and drank deeply from the hip-flask while he considered his options. The quickest way to the mine was through the woods ... but he also knew the dangers of leaving the track. He drank again and made a decision, his greed overriding his caution. He stepped off the path and wove his way through the forest. And though he knew these woods, had grown up in them, played in them as a child, used them for his courting when he was a young man, he suddenly found himself in a strange, almost alien world, where the trees seemed to twist and shift and move, just on the very edge of his vision. He trod these paths every night, he knew their twists and turns and, drunk or sober, he could find his own way home. Now, though he was less than a dozen steps from the same path, he doubted if he could find it again. All he could do now was to press on; provided he travelled in a straight line, he should reach the old mine and he could find his way home from there. He stopped to drink again from the hip-flask.

And maybe there would be something worth investigating at the mine.

Maybe not. What was he going to do if he found nothing at the mine?

But there had to be something; hadn't he seen the red light? And what was that but a torch?

When was the last time he'd seen a red torch?

But if it wasn't a torch, then what was it?

He stopped in the midst of the trees and turned around slowly, looking for the lights. He stopped when he spotted the red light ... or rather two red lights. Two glowing red lights, set about an inch apart ... coming from behind ... and looking at him.

The eyes moved.

And Jack O'Brien suddenly knew what it was. The empty flask fell from nerveless fingers. He turned and ran.

It was the Dullahan of the woods. The Dullahan: a headless horseman on a headless horse.

The terrifying creature came crashing through the trees. A frock-coated soldier of another age, his uniform bloodied and shredded. One hand was clamped tightly around the reins of a bone-white headless steed, the other clutching the long ragged hair of its own dangling head.

He could hear it in the forest behind him. The Dullahan were rarely seen now, but they were savage and deadly. To look upon their terrible form was to invite an agonizing death. And even if they had not marked the watcher for death, they would douse the passer-by in foul-smelling blood that carried disease and madness.

Jack O'Brien ran, blundering through the undergrowth, stumbling into bushes, the branches tearing at him, the thorns ripping his flesh. He fell to the ground, sinking into soft oozing mud, but when he glanced behind him he could still see the creature's glowing red eyes. It was still coming towards him.

His imagination did the rest.

The dangling severed head was changing, altering even as he looked at it. Now it was his children ... one by one their faces appeared briefly, all of them bearing the cuts and bruises he had given them. And then it was his wife. His own Mary, but dead now, dead and lost to him forever. The flesh

*was green-slimed and bloated, the lifeless eyes were closed,
but the lips still moved, dark liquid trickling down the chin.
The lips moved, moved and moved again, as if they were
attempting to form a word.*

He remembered then. Remembered the truth. He had
lived the lie for so long now that even he believed it. He
believed his wife had left him and gone to Dublin. But she
hadn't. Only he knew she hadn't, but he hadn't admitted it
to himself for a long time now. A long, long time. There had
been a chance blow, an awkward fall, her head snapping
against the grate, and the blood – dearest God, the blood –
so much blood. He had carried her into the woods, these
woods, and buried her in a pool deep in the heart of them,
the sack he'd wrapped her in weighted down with stones.

*The Dullahan galloped right up to him, every detail distinct
and vivid. And then the head that bore his wife's features
turned to him. And the eyes opened. And the mouthing lips
formed a name. His name.*

'Jack … Jack … Jack. I've come for you. I've come back for you.'

His heart was tripping, pounding, hammering in his chest
… and then the pain took him.

Jack O'Brien opened his mouth and screamed.

Two miles away, three workman loading sand into the
back of a lorry, their faces washed red in the glow of the
brake lights, turned and looked up into the woods. Each of
them crossed themselves.

'Probably a badger,' one said.

'A fox,' the second added.

'An owl,' the third said with a shaky nervous grin.

But none of them believed it; they all knew they had
heard a human cry out in mortal terror. The three men
looked nervously up into the dark woods: they *were*
supposed to be haunted.

CHAPTER THIRTY-ONE

The Clock of Hell

'Listen,' the old man said suddenly, the firelight running crimson and gold on his face. 'Listen.'

The small group gathered around the fire raised their heads and listened attentively. The night air was chill, the north wind sighing through the trees, leaves rustling gently, branches rasping.

'What are we listening for?' one of the men, a big raw-boned northerner, asked.

'What do you hear?' the old man asked.

The men looked at one another. Matt O'Donoghue was an old man now; he'd been travelling the roads of Ireland for more than three quarters of a century and, while the other Travellers respected his knowledge and experience, they knew that his mind and memory were not as they had once been.

'I hear the wind, old man,' the northerner said.

'Nothing else?'

The six men shook their heads one by one. 'The wind ... the leaves ... branches ... the usual night sounds.'

'The fire crackling?' the youngest man present suggested.

Matt shook his head. He sucked on an empty clay pipe and looked into the shadowy faces around the fire. 'Do you not hear the ticking of a clock?'

One of the men produced a pocket watch and held it up by its chain. 'There's nothing wrong with your ears, old man,' he said with a gap-toothed smile. 'It's this you're hearing.'

Matt spat into the fire. 'Do you take me for a fool? It's no watch I hear. Can you not hear the tick-tick-ticking of a clock?'

'What clock, grandfather?' Miley, the youngest man, asked. 'There's no clock ticking.'

'It's there.' the old man turned to look at him, his eyes copper coins in the firelight. 'When you get to my age, you'll hear it.'

'Aaagh, it's the drink talking,' the northerner said. 'I'm for bed.' He rose to his feet, bones cracking as he stretched and ambled off into the night, heading for one of the caravans parked by the side of the road. One by one the other men followed him, until only Miley and his grandfather were left. They sat in silence for a while, watching the logs spark, glowing embers spiralling heavenwards.

'Tell me about the clock, grandfather,' Miley said eventually. He ran his fingers through his long curling hair, brushing it back off his face. The firelight threw his eyes into deep shadow, emphasizing the bones on his face, darkening the stubble on his cheeks to a beard.

'You shouldn't listen to an old man's ramblings,' Matt said gruffly.

'Please.'

Matt looked off into the night for a moment. His own caravan was parked by the side of the road, close to the hedgerow, but not beneath the trees. Experience had taught him that moisture dripping from the trees either kept him awake long into the night or would awaken him far too early in the morning. He still used the old horse-drawn Tinker's barrel-shaped caravan, though some of the younger people were starting to use cars to tow their ugly metal caravans. He had lived most of his life in that caravan; he was not going to change now.

'Put another log on the fire,' he said suddenly, and filled his pipe while Miley scrambled off to find some wood. Matt watched him: he was a good lad, and he still respected some of the traditional Tinker ways ... or what was it they were calling them nowadays? Itinerants. Travelling people. He was old enough to remember when they'd been called Gypsies. But those days were gone now – the war with Germany had changed all that. He had heard stories of Gypsies and Travelling People being sent to the ovens. A whole way of life had been wiped out, generations of lore and legends lost forever. The future lay with young people like Miley ... though Matt guessed that their life on the roads of Ireland would be radically different from his. The young man returned and dropped a bundle of sticks on to the fire, sending sparks fountaining up into the night sky. The bitter odour of burning wood permeated the air.

Matt poked the fire with a sliver of wood, coaxing it to a flame, and then used the burning stick to relight his pipe.

'Will you tell me about the clock, grandfather?' Miley asked.

The old man puffed reflectively for a moment, pungent smoke gathering briefly about his head before drifting away on the breeze.

'Do you believe in God, Miley?' he asked suddenly.

'Yes ... yes, of course, grandfather,' the young man said quickly, surprised by the question.

'And the Devil?'

This time there was a longer hesitation before he replied, but he eventually said, 'Well yes, I suppose so.'

'What do you mean, you suppose so?' Matt asked. 'If there's a God, then there must be a devil. If there's good, there's evil. We know evil because we judge it by good.'

Miley nodded slowly. He could understand that.

Matt's few remaining teeth flashed in a quick grin. 'You look so serious, boy. These are not profound truths, these are simple facts. And anyway, good and evil, black and white, right and wrong are not fixed and absolute, they slip and slide and shade into one another. Sometimes good men can make a bad decision for the right reasons.'

Miley shook his head; this wasn't making sense. Maybe Matt had had too much to drink.

'The Clock of Hell is an ancient Gypsy and Traveller story. When we are born into this world, the devil winds up a clock in hell for us, which has been set to our allotted number of days on this earth. And if you've committed an evil deed in your lifetime, then when your life is drawing to a close, you will hear the Clock of Hell that bears your name slowly ticking the time away, tick ... tick ... tick.' Matt turned to look at the younger man and his eyes were glassy. 'That's the last sound you will hear in this world, the ticking of the Clock of Hell.'

The young man shivered. In normal circumstances he would have been able to shrug it off, but now, in the middle of the night, sitting before a sparking fire on a lonely road in the heart of Ireland, the story took on a different feeling. He could feel the beer he'd drunk earlier turn sour in his stomach.

'Do you know what destroyed the Tinker way of life?' Matt asked suddenly.

'Plastic and aluminium,' Miley answered with a smile. At least here he was back on safer ground.

'Plastic and aluminium,' Matt continued, as if he hadn't heard him. He was sitting upright now, his legs drawn up to his bony chest, the point of his chin resting on his knees. Though he was staring into the fire, he was looking into a different time, a lost age. 'Tinkers were respected once. When most cooking pots were made of tin, people looked forward to the arrival of the Tinker to repair the broken pots and pans, and then the Tinker would also sharpen the knives, and they'd work in the fields at harvest or sowing times.

'And then the war came and changed everything. A way of life died with the war, attitudes changed. People were no longer working the fields the way their fathers had; sons were no longer following their fathers on to the land. There were new machines which meant there were less jobs for people like me; goods became cheaper and disposable. People like me were no longer needed to sharpen the knives and hone the scythes. Our jobs were taken by students who picked the potatoes and apples, helped with taking in the harvest, all for a few bob spending money or pocket money. People like me had families to feed and keep: we were more deserving of the jobs. We needed them to survive.

'And then of course there were plastic and aluminium. Between them they destroyed the Tinker's way of life. Many families were scattered or were forced to emigrate because of these new goods.'

'It's called progress,' Miley said very softly.

'An' what use is it if it destroys a way of life that's a thousand years old?' Matt demanded.

'The world moves on,' the younger man murmured, knowing Matt O'Donoghue wasn't listening to him. 'The world moves on and we must move with it ... if we don't, we won't survive.'

Only the crackling of the fire broke the long silence that followed. Finally, just when Miley's eyes were beginning to close, the old man spoke, 'We're Christians now ... but we weren't always so. Once we worshipped older, wilder gods.

It's fashionable to study the Tinker and Traveller way of life. I've sat around a camp fire and listened to a young chit of a girl tell me that the mythology of the Travellers is grounded in the ancient religion of the Egyptians.' His voice had turned sarcastic and bitter. 'But the gods my people worshipped are older, wiser than that.'

'It's getting late,' Miley said gently, realizing that the old man was rambling, the drink having made him maudlin.

'So I called down one of the dark gods,' Matt said suddenly.

The younger man had been rising to his feet. He sank down on to the ground again. 'You did what?' he whispered.

Matt turned to look at him, his wrinkled skin turned to old parchment at the firelight. 'After the war, we were in desperate straits. I had to support a large family, six sons, three daughters, all of them young. But I had no livelihood and no money. What was I to do? How was I to support them?' The anguish was clearly audible in the old man's voice, even after so much time.

'So, I called the Clockman, the keeper of the Clock of Hell. He sets the time of a man's life on the clock ...' His hand tightened into a claw on Miley's arm. 'He came to me in the flames of a camp fire. One moment it was nothing but burning wood – and the next there was a cowled figure looking out of the dancing flames at me. We spoke together, his voice like the crack and snap of burning wood, and did our deal. When I looked into the fire I saw Hell. I saw the clocks, row after row of them, line after line. I saw my clock. It was enormous, the biggest thing I've ever seen, like a grandfather clock, but its face was inscribed with demons and devils,' he added in a hoarse whisper.

'It was a dream,' Miley said quickly.

Matt O'Donoghue shook his head. 'No, it was no dream, not even a nightmare. I spoke to the Clockman and we did a deal together.'

'What sort of deal?'

The old man turned to look at him, the shadows racing across his face, turning it into a grotesque mask. 'What do you deal in when you're trading with the Devil?' He looked away quickly, his head tilted to one side, listening. 'Listen ... can you hear it? Its ticking ... ticking ... ticking ... the Clock of Hell.'

'There's nothing there,' Miley said firmly. 'Come on, bed for you.'

'I sold him some years,' Matt continued quickly. He turned to stare into the east where the first glimmerings of the dawn had paled the sky. 'In return for some good luck, I sold the Clockman some years of my life.'

'And ...?' Miley asked, fascinated.

'And in return he told me the day my own clock would run down.' He smiled humourlessly. 'And now that time is up. He said I'd hear the ticking of the clock, he said it would be the last sound I'd hear in this world.'

'Was it worth it?' Miley asked, almost unthinkingly.

'I think so. Our luck changed for the better the morning after meeting the Clockman. We were in the heart of Kerry at the time: we fell in with a farmer who needed some casual labour, but he wasn't interested in students, he wanted experienced people. He had a spot of land he wasn't using, where there was an old ruined cottage. He said if we would repair the cottage in our own time, he would let us stay on the land and we could do whatever work came up around the farm or the buildings. We did that and, though we travelled through the country during the summer months, we always returned to that spot in the autumn and wintered there. It was the best of both worlds,' he added simply.

'But it seems so little to have traded a part of your life away for,' Miley said, humouring him, determined now to get his grandfather to bed.

'The Devil is like God,' Matt O'Donoghue said simply, 'he'll only give you what you can appreciate.'

'And what did you trade for this ... this trusting farmer and winter halting site?' Miley asked, unable to keep the sarcasm from his voice.

'Ten years of my life.'

'Ten years ... and was it worth it?'

'Every day,' Matt said sincerely. 'I've known to the very hour the day I was going to die,' he continued, taking out a comb and running it through the thinning strands on his head. 'Now, some men might have found that frightening, but not me. I sometimes think it gave my life a purpose ... I was heading towards a particular spot at a particular time.' He nodded decisively. 'It gave me a purpose.'

Miley laid his hand gently on the old man's shoulder. 'It's only superstition.'

Matt turned to look at him, a smile on his lips, his eyes amber in the firelight. 'It is no superstition. And remember, Miley, if you are ever in real trouble, serious trouble, then as a Traveller, you have the right to call upon the Clockman. He will answer your prayers, but remember, he takes his payment in time from the allotted span of your years. And when your time comes, then you too will hear the ticking of the Clock of Hell ...'

Miley shook his head despairingly. 'Time for bed, old man.'

'Too late. Too late. Listen, listen, can you not hear it? I can hear it now. Tick. Tick. Tick ... ti ...'